ACHILLES'S WIFE

TROJAN THREADS

JUDITH STARKSTON

BRONZE AGE BOOKS

Copyright © 2026 by Judith Starkston

All rights reserved.

No part of this book may be reproduced in any form or by any electronic or mechanical means, including information storage and retrieval systems, without written permission from the author, except for the use of brief quotations in a book review.

This is a work of fiction. All rights reserved. Names, characters, places, and incidents are either the product of the author's imagination or are used fictitiously, and any resemblance to actual persons, living or dead, business establishments, events, or locales is entirely coincidental.

ISBN 979-8-9902499-1-2 (pbk.)

ISBN 979-8-9902499-2-9 (ebk.)

BISAC Subject Headings:

FIC009030   FICTION / Fantasy / Historical

FIC010000   FICTION / Fairy Tales, Folk Tales, Legends & Mythology

FIC014010   FICTION / Historical / Ancient

ACHILLES'S WIFE

PROLOGUE

Achilles bit back a scream. What had his mother done now? Where was he?

He stood between white sand and crystal sea, on one end of a long crescent of beach. Jagged rocks jutted into the water on both ends of the arc of sand. Familiar salty wind whipped at his hair and tunic, but he did not recognize this beach or the cliff and mountain that loomed behind him.

He sucked in another breath to control his reaction. He must never object, even after being yanked from his life and brought to who knew where in the blink of an eye. The last thing he remembered, he'd been racing through the woods with his tutor Chiron, learning to hunt and trying to keep up with the centaur.

A wave crashed near his feet, and he jumped back to avoid getting soaked. Having a divine mother meant watching out for himself. Thetis made no allowances for mere mortals, not even her son.

A few strides away, his mother floated dry and untouched amid the breaking waves—of course. She'd created a dress intended to dazzle some mortal, no matter how powerful and wealthy. His mother had an artist's sensibility when it suited her purpose. He'd gotten that from her. She'd thrown alluring elements from her watery realm into the gown's design. Its diaphanous layers fluttered, delicate as sea foam glinting with light. Whoever the man was, he'd have no chance against whatever scheme his mother was launching.

But what was she up to? Wherever his mother had brought him, this wasn't a friendly visit, no matter how pleasing she'd made her costume. Thetis was never friendly to mortals. She used one word to describe humans, including his father: worms.

She stepped out of the curling waves, surrounded by a blinding glow. Was it the morning sun rising behind his mother or inner fury lit by her relentless pursuit to outwit his fate—his foretold early death? Her single fixation. He exhaled in frustration. She neglected everything else about motherhood.

Approaching him, she extended one of her long arms to tousle his red-gold waves of hair. He leaned into her touch, although he tried to hide how much he yearned for it.

"Come with me," Thetis commanded. Her flinty tone hadn't changed in his fifteen years. He'd wondered if it might as he grew up, but what was time to her? She pointed and glided across the sand toward the forbidding mountain that rose so high he had to tip back his head to see its top.

Stormy seas had crashed against the mountain's base, eating it away, so that a sheer cliff of tan dirt and stones hemmed in the white sand. Above that seemingly impossible climb, rose a steep slope covered in windswept shrubs and dead grasses and, forming the summit, a massive block of granite looked as if a giant had pushed it upwards from the mountain's core. On that rocky top, two areas of dwellings clung like stony beetles. A narrow, level patch of ground held some close-packed buildings that might form a palace. A small climb above those, a citadel's stone wall encircled the highest point.

Along these heights that his mother had ordered him to ascend, he saw several goats grazing on thorny plants. The beasts must have made hidden trails. He glanced about. If he went farther down the curving beach where the shore was edged by a fertile plain with a river trickling through, it'd be far easier to make his way inland, but his mother's imperious gesture indicated the buildings on the peak directly above, where some king had sought to build out of the range of pirates and marauding armies.

A divine snarl snapped his attention back to his mother.

He risked a question. "Why have we come here?"

Her eyes narrowed, and her lips became a pale red slit. "For your well-being."

"I was doing well with Chiron, learning many things, even healing. I had Patroclus for company. I was happy and safe. Isn't that what you want?"

"You have no understanding of what matters in your life."

"Does Father know you're bringing me here? Does he agree with you?"

"Your father?" The scorn in her voice cut Achilles. His father was a good man. Achilles loved him. His mother continued, "I told him if he interfered with what I am doing, I would kill him. Nothing can stop me from protecting you. Terrible things will happen to mortals if they are careless of my wishes." If she'd been a person, he would have thought this was an exaggeration and there was some grim humor behind her words, but her bloodthirsty look reminded him that his goddess mother had no sense of humor. And only one limit on her power—the length of his life.

He opened his mouth to answer, but her fingers twitched, about to act, and he stopped.

When he was a small boy, his father had whispered Thetis's story to him, both in admiration and warning. Once, long ago, the other gods bound Zeus and would have overthrown the king of gods, but Thetis undid his chains with a flick of her hand. To put an end to the uprising, she'd summoned a hundred-handed giant to lurk for a time as Zeus's bodyguard. Achilles wished he'd seen that giant. He never doubted his mother had such a monster at her beck and call.

"I have brought you to Skyros, a dismal island, but its isolation suits my purposes." He'd heard the name of Skyros, but nothing more about this island. "You will hide who and what you are." Her mouth moved when she spoke, but never quite as human mouths did.

"Yes, Mother." Hide who and *what*? This was puzzling. *Only half immortal? Not immortal enough to escape death?* That wasn't the *what* she meant. Her purpose would become clear. Never ask unnecessary questions. No one challenged this sea goddess for long. Even the king of gods kept on her good side. At least she'd taken a form she considered maternal, which showed she might not be out for blood on this journey.

Her idea of maternal would make him laugh if it weren't so intimidating—a mortal woman's form, but taller and imposing in a way no mortal could achieve. *Nobody* wanted a mother who looked like this, although she must think this female shape was comforting. On several occasions, she'd flopped out of the sea shaped like a seal. He'd liked that form of his mother best but could never tell her that.

"This concealment will protect you."

Anxiety buzzed inside him like a swarm of bees. *Protect him?* That could not be good. She would go too far. His feet shifted on the unstable sand, his arms clamped across the muscles of his chest.

Up and down his body, she ran a gaze so sharp it seemed to cut him. Her towering form loomed even higher, and her hands spun in glowing circles, flashing so brightly it hurt his eyes. Bolts of pain shot through his body. The skin across his chest felt ripped open. Some force seemed to twist his arms and legs, ringing out the bone and flesh as if his limbs were rags, flinging him to the ground. His torso and groin felt as if warriors threw spears into him as the target on a practice field. The blinding light from his mother's hands dimmed.

He crawled onto all fours and got his feet underneath him. Weakness around his mother was never safe. He blinked, nearly sightless from the echoes of her sparking power floating across his vision. Hazy shapes of the beach around him came slowly back. As his eyes recovered, the pale sand and restless sea reappeared. Keeping upright with difficulty, he dragged in a shaky breath. *What had Mother done?*

He glanced down. The beating of his heart stopped in shock. She had changed him. He jerked his arms away from his chest. Why was it soft? Panic knifed through him like an errant sword blow during practice, unintentionally lethal. A roaring in his head drowned out everything else. He tried to breathe but couldn't draw in air. Tightening through his chest closed in until a desperate gasp broke through and a sip of sea coolness bathed his lungs.

He ran his hands over the strange curves of his body. When his hand reached an emptiness at his crotch, blackness overtook his vision. *No!* Wooziness dropped him to his knees. This was a different *what* than all the previous days of his life. A different who, though not inside. That much should be reassuring, but the discord already pressed him hard. *How could she?*

"Forever?" he asked, trying to hide the terror shooting upwards through his torso.

"Of course not." The goddess's voice was laced with the special hate she reserved for female humans. "And I would never take away your strength, even in this form."

He drew in another broken breath. His mother didn't hold womanhood in high honor. Even as a goddess, being female had been an unacceptable weakness, had led to her one humiliation, forced into the marriage bed of a mortal. She meant this as a temporary mask.

A particularly good disguise. Understanding bloomed in his imagination. His mother's scheme. A nightmare she called protecting. Did she really have so little sense of who he was?

Then it occurred to him. She *couldn't* understand how a body mattered. She was a goddess who could take any form she liked. What her body felt and looked like had nothing to do with who she was. Did any particular form offer her the comfort of its rightness? He doubted it.

He touched his soft chest and ran his hand over the flatness between his legs. This wasn't who he was. His goddess mother could not understand, but he feared this concealment by transformation might destroy him. *I can't endure this for long.*

PART I

1

"You must come to the throne room, Princess Deidamia," her father's chief advisor said. "To receive visitors."

"Only me?" Mia frowned.

"Yes, Princess." Her father's advisor made the throat clearing sound that meant he was agitated. Too bad for him. He could cope with royal troubles without involving her. Her father was always cross about something.

She wrapped her arms around her waist. "Wouldn't my father prefer one of my younger sisters to attend on the visitors?" What he'd prefer was a son, but anyone except Mia would do.

"King Lycomedes sent me to bring you." The man's jowls jiggled when he spoke. The belt around his chiton had slid on top of his bulging belly so that he looked pregnant.

Her sisters, seated nearby, as well as their attendants and servants, had fallen silent, drawn to listen in on her small confrontation. A summons from the king should be a common occurrence, but she was resigned to her father's wish to avoid her. You had to love your child to want to see her often.

It annoyed Mia to draw the attention of everyone gathered in her reception hall—her mother's hall, actually, except her mother had been missing for three years. Because Mia was the oldest of her many sisters, everyone referred to the room now as hers. She hated that ownership and the willingness to forget it implied—no one else expected their mother to return. Everything about this room, especially its bright frescoes of dolphins leaping through turquoise waves, caused Mia to feel her mother's influence even in her absence. Everyone else pretended that her mother had never existed.

"Who are these visitors?" Mia glanced at Dione, the one servant she could trust, but the girl shook her head. No helpful gossip from that source.

"You are to hurry, not ask questions." The wagging flesh under the chief advisor's chin would have made her laugh if her stomach hadn't tightened into a knot.

Her father was the one who received visitors, not her. He beguiled envoys from more powerful kingdoms into cooperation. Other times, he wooed traders through whose hands valuable goods passed, the lifeblood of his rocky island realm. She never interacted with these travelers beyond being decoration at her father's feast table when he forgot how sullen she would be and required her presence. Afterwards he would remind her what a failure she was as a dutiful princess, and she would not attend his feasts for another long stretch of time.

Lady Harmonia, the stout older noblewoman who was her chief attendant, rushed toward her with a gold-trimmed veil and a bronze pin to hold it in place. "A summons from the king. You must be properly attired."

Mia yelped when the long pin jammed into her scalp, but Lady Harmonia adjusted it quickly enough that Mia couldn't accuse her of stabbing her on purpose. Given how many times she'd found ways to escape Harmonia's supervision, she couldn't blame her for a poke of revenge.

She hated the throne room. The memory of what had happened there slithered through her mind like a venomous serpent.

She rose, straightened her back, and pretended to cast her veiled gaze modestly at the floor.

A narrow passageway without windows connected the women's quarters to the main palace. Whatever oil lamps the servants remembered to light cast an indifferent illumination, and this walk always seemed like passing through night. Sometimes she used that darkness as cover to escape a world made up only of women, but today she felt trapped in it, dragged to the throne room.

She followed the chief advisor's heavy tread. Eventually he took her through another hallway to the small door at the side of the throne room, shielded, once they entered, by a decorative screen. With the flat of his palm, he signaled her to stay behind this screen while he stepped out from behind it. He would stand there, visible to her father, as a cue that Mia waited behind it. The king would beckon for her when he chose.

Fortunately, she had once used a hair pin to poke a hole in the screen at her eye level. If anyone had noticed it, they had left it untouched. Maybe others found it useful. The leather screen's painted image of hunters bringing down deer added enough concealment that the hole was not visible from the front.

She edged close to the hole and peered through. Oddly enough, her father stood to one side below the dais rather than sitting on his throne, a bulky, high-backed seat meant to be imposing, but to her eye, ugly. Its dark wood was carved with the bared jaws and piercing glare of a lion on the upper panel and the beast's heavy paws stomping at the base of each of the chair's legs.

Mia scanned the large, shadowy room. Light fell from narrow window openings, but the low ceiling and dark colors of its frescoes absorbed much of the daylight. The room represented her father's power. The upper half of the walls were blood red with mustard yellow below. Separating the two colors was a band of black spirals that left Mia dizzy if she looked at them too long. None of the customary clusters of men were gathered in the room. Her father must have ordered his audience hall emptied of all but his chief advisor, his visitors—and Mia.

A woman and girl, both shockingly tall, stood alone upon the dais, raised above her father. They were finely dressed, as nobles would be. But why did they stand atop the dais? Where were their men? And what noble women traveled without a bevy of female attendants? Mia was practiced in escaping her own attending ladies, but she'd thought that misbehavior was singular. Lady Harmonia claimed as much.

The woman wore an extraordinary double-layered gown. Mia knew of no one who could spin thread as translucent and glistening as the upper film that floated around the woman, reminding Mia of the curling movement of waves. The room's air was still, and yet this delicate foam swirled of its own accord. The narrow inner sheath, shimmering like golden sunlight on water, draped closely over the woman's breasts and hips. Could it be spun of pure gold?

This woman exuded power. None of the noblewomen who attended on Mia would dress like this. The slight tip up of the woman's chin, the veil over her dark hair so transparent it scoffed at the need for modesty, and the relaxed drop of her bare arms, a pose of ease in this surprising situation—all spoke of dominance that should outrage her father, and yet his posture was respectfully humble.

The girl, around Mia's age, was almost as tall as the woman and yet less impressive, although her gown was richly trimmed with embroidery in a gorgeous blue the shade of lapis lazuli. Mia had never worn a gown as costly as that one. A cascade of red-gold hair glistened through her sheer veil. But there was something tentative about her posture as if she was unsure how to hold her shoulders, and twice she shifted the stance of her legs. "Fidgeter!" Lady Harmonia would declare while looking down her nose. But no matter how the girl arranged herself, she still looked as if she was preparing to lift something heavy, not present herself to court.

The unusual woman towered over Mia's father. The king cast his gaze downward, while the woman spoke to him in an attitude of command. Mia tried to catch her words, but strangely, though their sound filled the big room, Mia couldn't make out their meaning. Foreigners came here speaking various languages, but these words were those of her own tongue, and yet somehow they didn't make sense. Her father didn't look pleased about what the woman said, but he seemed to understand the conversation. Was there a way to shield one's meaning from all but one person? Was this a court trick she had never heard of?

Who were these women and why had they come to the island of Skyros?

Her father must have noticed his advisor because he lifted his head and looked toward the screen with a nod. Mia stepped back from the peephole, straightened her back, and dropped her shoulders. She checked that her veil was properly arranged.

The chief advisor brought her out and walked her halfway toward her father and the two strangers. Then, to Mia's surprise, he turned and left the throne room.

"This is my eldest daughter, Deidamia," her father said to the elegant woman. Mia felt his disapproval even in these simple words. The woman's chilly glare seemed to understand Mia's secret thoughts and find her below further consideration.

The king turned to his daughter, his hand outstretched to indicate the younger visitor. "Bring this girl to the women's quarters. She will be living with you from now on—until such time as her father deems it appropriate for her to return home."

As Mia stepped forward, she noticed the tall woman's eyes narrow in a flash of annoyance at the last of her father's statements. The girl herself looked apprehensive, her full lips pinched in, her rather thick neck held stiffly. A girl like this would usually travel with her mother, and perhaps they were mother and daughter, but Mia didn't see a hint of motherliness in the way this domineering lady treated the awkward girl.

Her father hurriedly stepped near and took hold of Mia's arm to catch her full attention. "As is proper for my womenfolk, keep this girl hidden within the quarters away from men outside our household. This lady is one who deserves the greatest respect and deference from us, and she particularly warns of this. No outside men must see or speak to this maiden. Do you understand?"

Mia did. Her chest felt heavy. This girl would trap Mia, undoing each of her slowly devised strategies for making life pleasurable. She hadn't asked for much up to now, brief, unsupervised excursions to enjoy the nearby shore and hills with their offerings that beckoned to her senses. She heard what her father meant in "proper for my womenfolk." This obsession had begun with her mother's departure. Now it fell upon Mia like a boulder.

"As my eldest child," the king went on, laying emphasis on each word, "this is your duty for the good of the kingdom."

Another voice saying those same words rang inside Mia. She'd been instructed about her duty to their small island realm once before, and she had failed disastrously. Her mother had paid the price.

What lies and secrets did her father hide behind these words? Mia still didn't understand what her mother had concealed when *she* had used them.

Her mother lost forever, and it was Mia's fault. Mia's duty *for the good of the kingdom*. Was losing her mother part of that good?

A wave of dizziness caused Mia to wobble and grab her father's arm. For a moment he looked at her, his eyes widening in concern. "Daughter?"

She pulled in a shaky breath. "Yes, Father?"

She was responding to the sympathy in his voice. She didn't mean to say yes to what he asked of her, but he nodded, taking her question as a statement. "Do not disappoint me. This is a favor that must be honored in every detail. Without fail."

This girl was a trap. Mia wasn't good at traps. She'd failed to save her mother. The finality of her father's tone sank in. It was as if the heaviness inside dragged her underwater, squeezing out her last gasp of air. Her father pushed her toward the strange girl.

If the girl had not reached out and taken Mia's arm, Mia would have collapsed, but the arm she leaned on now was surprisingly strong and somehow pleasing.

Mia shook her head. There was nothing pleasing about this situation. For whom were they doing this dreadfully important favor? Some king her father couldn't refuse. There were so many of those.

Her father's kingdom had so little power that he was forever borrowing it from others and then paying the demanded price. How this woman, lording over a king, could be entrusted with such authority puzzled Mia. It also intrigued her.

Together, the tall girl and Mia stumbled toward the screen and then out the small door. The chief advisor stood watch in the hallway. Without comment, he turned and led them toward the back of the palace and the women's quarters.

She glanced up at the newcomer's face with features too heavy to be considered pretty, despite an underlying grace. No one had even bothered to tell her this girl's name. "What are you called?"

There was a long pause. Was the girl too simple to say her name?

"Pyrrha. My name's Pyrrha."

Redhead, a nickname? It occurred to Mia that the girl had been ordered to hide who she was. She'd had to learn a different name, and it didn't come naturally, or else she'd just now made it up. Mia felt a flutter of sympathy. "Everyone except my father calls me Mia."

"Thank you, Mia. I didn't choose this. So you know."

"What would you choose?"

"Anything but this."

"We agree on that much." Whatever trouble this Pyrrha had gotten herself into, Mia wished she hadn't let her punishment get dumped on Mia at least as much as herself. Infuriating girl.

Then Pyrrha squeezed Mia's hand and flashed a perfect, white-toothed smile that seemed for a moment to lighten the weight pressing on Mia. Maybe not always infuriating.

2

The next morning in her reception hall, Mia tucked her head to feign that her whirling drop spindle held her attention. In fact, she didn't think at all of her spinning as she fed out fluffs of wool tugged from the bundle of fleece lying over the back of her left hand. The fire in the large circular hearth sizzled and spat when a few drops of rain found their way through the smoke hole. The wild wind drove the rain sideways past the clay shield on the roof. Mia scooted her stool closer to the fire's warmth. She was stewing in a sour mood—no point pretending otherwise to herself. Pyrrha sat nearby, and Mia only felt worse watching the girl with her father's warnings echoing in her mind.

At the sound of one of Lady Harmonia's emphatic sniffs, Mia glanced at her attendant sitting next to her and caught a questioning raised eyebrow. "Are you as unhappy as you appear, Princess Mia?"

"Well, I—"

"Straighten up and compose your face to reflect the way you wish to feel." Harmonia stabbed her needle through the linen veil she was embroidering and gave Mia a stern look which said that was all it took to feel cheerful. But Harmonia's horselike face was permanently marked by frown lines. In fairness, it wasn't Harmonia's fault that Mia did not want motherly advice from someone who wasn't her mother.

Mia scanned the room, but her eye fell once again on the offending Pyrrha. The way the girl sat on her stool was almost humorous with her knees splayed in an ungainly way. Mia glanced at Harmonia to see if her attendant was itching to correct this unseemly posture. Harmonia held her head tipped down, away from Pyrrha, but her eyes kept flicking at their guest. During a lengthy summons by the king yesterday, Harmonia must have received detailed instructions about this guest. Apparently, the noble girl's status was shielding her from comment for now. *That* wouldn't last long. Could she talk her sister Idomene into a wager on how long before Harmonia gave up restraining herself?

The girl's behavior *was* provoking. Like Mia, Pyrrha was supposed to be spinning, but the new guest grasped her combed wool far too tightly as she pulled it from the soft bundle flopped over her other hand. With that ridiculous grip, she would never be able to draw out the fibers into thread. If she caused her feeder thread to break one more time, Mia was going to grab that useless spindle and hit her with it. Spinning was boring, but it wasn't hard, by all the gods.

Maybe Pyrrha was trying to get out of having to spin by pretending this incompetence. Mia sat up and watched her more carefully. This time Pyrrha's movements struck her not as ungainly so much as confident. She sat with both feet braced squarely on the ground.

Harmonia launched another sniff and then rose with ladylike poise despite her formidable size. "Excuse me, I have something to attend to." She took herself speedily to the other side of the room away from the sight of Pyrrha.

Mia held down a giggle. The old lady couldn't bear not to correct Pyrrha, but Mia found herself intrigued and unwillingly drawn to the girl. Pyrrha claimed wherever she sat in a way that Mia hadn't seen women do, not even her mother as queen.

Pyrrha's gaze, restless and assessing, darted to Mia's sisters seated around the hearth. Her movements shifted in imitation of the girls.

Pyrrha studied Mia's sister Idomene and then slid her own right foot forward, straightening that leg, while tucking the other foot under her stool. Mia sat the same way. A much prettier pose. Now that Mia thought about it, it was the best way to sit so that the spindle had room to drop in front for the twisting. It was habit for her, but not, apparently, for Pyrrha.

A flicker of movement at the doorway drew Mia's attention. Dione, her maidservant, had returned from washing clothes, a task that required she go outside. Both the front of her shapeless tunic and her thick arms were soaked from the work. Goose bumps marked her rough skin. Where was the warm cloak Mia had given her? The servant caught Mia's eye and tipped her head slightly as she passed from the reception hall to the corridor leading to Mia's sleeping chamber, the first room off the big hall.

Mia caught her spindle and stuck it in the basket at her feet. She rose and walked slowly enough not to look eager. In the shadowy corridor she caught up with Dione, leaning close to whisper, "Tell me what you found out."

Dione lifted a lit oil lamp from one of the brackets lining the corridor and followed Mia through the door curtain of the sleeping chamber. Around the white plastered walls, wooden chests held Mia's possessions. Her small bed sat in the middle with a three-legged stool next to it that served as table or chair. Dione was close in age to Mia, but far ahead of her in experience—mostly from hard work. The maid set the lamp on a wall bracket to cast a flickering light around the room. The windows were tightly shuttered against the wet, cold day. Mia sat on the bed piled with soft fleeces and wool blankets, and Dione huddled close enough for whispering.

Mia rubbed Dione's cold arm. "Why didn't you wear your cloak?"

"And get it all wet?" She reached under Mia's bed, drew out the woolen garment, and then wrapped it around her shoulders.

Mia laughed. Of course. Dione was better at thinking ahead than she was.

Her maid shook her head. "You won't like what I got to say. It's what you feared."

"My father's made it worse, hasn't he? All his safeguarding for that Pyrrha."

"There's a guard now at both ends of the hallway into the rest of the palace."

"Two?"

Dione nodded.

"It'll be impossible to distract both long enough to slip by without making it obvious what I'm up to. I'll have to figure out some other way. Curses on my father and his walls."

Before her mother disappeared, the women's quarters had been separated from the rest of the palace for the women's privacy, but not to confine them. Hallways and open courtyards had connected the brightly painted rooms to the rest of the royal home and its nearby citadel.

Then life had changed, and workmen had laid bricks and pounded timbers into place, isolating the women's quarters.

"Careful now," her maid whispered. "The other maids say guards are keepin' watch outside these quarters. You'll get outside with your sisters and Lady Harmonia."

Mia made a disgusted sound in her throat. "Lady Harmonia's outings are as bad as staying inside." After her father's ugly alterations to the women's quarters, Mia had still found ways to slip out. Escaping her attendants and serving women was an adventure. Or it had been until now. Now it might be an impossibility. What was he so afraid of now? Pyrrha didn't look like any great prize. Why the need for such protection?

But, she admitted, there was something else about the girl. Not beauty, but watching Pyrrha move around the women's hall sparked something inside Mia.

She shook that away and asked Dione, "Did anyone hear who the tall lady is who brought Pyrrha? You'd think she'd be Pyrrha's mother, but she didn't act like that. She would have checked on her or something, but she didn't even come into the women's quarters."

"Not a word."

"Where is she? She's not staying here—which is peculiar no matter who she is."

"The serving women wondered about that. I asked around. Someone said she left in a hurry. Must a had her ship moored somewhere secret because not one fisherman saw it at the harbor."

"Really?" Mia tapped her foot impatiently against the floor. "Someone wanted to prevent any gossip between the crew and our people. But it's not safe to moor a ship outside the harbor, I thought. Look at the weather we've been having."

"Not safe for sailing," Dione said, "but everyone says that must be what they done."

"They could still be hiding."

"On Skyros? Some of the fishermen's boys didn't have nothing better to do than run to every nearby cove. No ship." Dione shook her head. "Like she weren't worried about danger. Like a god."

"Pshah," Mia answered. "No god or goddess would bother with us—especially here. Gods visiting mortals—those are just stories to make us fear them. Have you ever heard of anybody seeing one?"

"Course not. But strange how she left in a hurry. Who knows why."

"She keeps a deep secret." Mia stood up with a shrug, heading back to the reception hall before anyone came to look for her.

From the darker hallway, Mia scanned the activity going on around the big hearth. Pyrrha still sat close to where Mia stood in the corridor outside her room. The girl's intent gaze focused in Mia's direction, and Mia fell back a step at the unfamiliar twinge that arose in response to that attention. Then Pyrrha lowered her eyes as if Mia hadn't caught her looking.

Mia's two youngest sisters, five and seven years old, squabbled over a ball Mia had made from hard-packed wool wrapped tightly with yarn to hold its round shape. Mother used to make balls like that for her, and she'd wanted her sisters to have one. She'd wanted to tell them their mother taught her to make a ball that could bounce against the stone floor, but the word "mother" had stuck in her throat, refusing to come out.

She caught the stool she'd abandoned with the tip of her foot and dragged it closer to the fire's warmth, away from Pyrrha, then sat down, still separate from her sisters. She couldn't stand pretending to be happy surrounded by them. They could go on as if nothing was different, but not her, not when she'd caused her mother to disappear.

She picked up her spindle and soft, combed wool she was turning into yarn. The clump left an oily, sheepy smell on her fingers that she secretly liked. She wound and dropped her spindle with its clay weight at the bottom, setting it whirling. Looking up, she caught Pyrrha watching her again. Mia wrinkled her nose and looked away, ignoring a flutter in her belly.

Pyrrha didn't look any happier than Mia felt—thrown into a household where she knew no one and put to work at the most boring task anyone ever thought up—but Mia had done what she could for her. She'd given the girl the most pleasant room set aside for visiting women. She wasn't the one locking them away like one of those unfortunates in the stories Mia had heard. There was the juicy tale about a monstrous man-eating half-bull, half-man trapped in a dark maze. She preferred that story to the one about a daughter imprisoned in a stone tower because someone said it would be her fate to bear a child who would kill her father.

She could be happy, alone, walking along the shore or exploring the creatures in the tide pools with the briny smell of seaweed filling her nose. She enjoyed climbing the rocky hills as fast as she could so that her breath came hard and it felt good to rest in the shelter of the low pines that clung to the wind-swept hillsides. The world outside could turn her sourness to a fleeting sweetness. Even the smallest pleasures could lift her spirits, like crushing the feathery leaves of rock fennel between her fingers and releasing their spicy odor, touching them to her tongue for the pleasing burn.

She wasn't going to let her father wall her in. Not because of a girl who wasn't even part of their family. Even if she was a lonely girl.

Pyrrha's brows were drawn together, making her heavy face even less refined. To Mia's annoyance, Pyrrha stood up and came over, squatting beside her like her sisters had done when they were very young, although there was something decidedly grownup in the fluid grace of the motion. Hadn't anyone told this girl how to move like a lady?

From across the room where Harmonia had taken herself came an outraged humph, and the old lady pursed her lips as if to stop anything more from escaping.

Mia shrugged at Pyrrha, who'd clearly noticed Harmonia's reaction. "You could sit on a stool."

Pyrrha frowned and stretched out one of her long arms to grab a cedar stool. She plopped onto it. "Better?"

Mia couldn't hold in a smile. "It's just—"

"That I don't behave properly? I thought you didn't care about that."

Now it was Mia's turn to frown. She'd never told Pyrrha anything important like that. She responded with an imperious silence, Lady Harmonia's favorite fallback.

Pyrrha waved one hand, as if brushing aside some objection that Mia hadn't said. "Thank you for taking me in. I like the room you gave me. The wall paintings are especially beautiful."

Surprise flustered Mia. "My m—" She couldn't go on. "I'm glad you like it." That room had a scene of men and women harvesting saffron in bloom. Paintings in a bedroom was quite a luxury. The flowers were pretty, but the men and women, their limbs hard at work, appealed most to Mia.

Pyrrha leaned closer, and a whiff of sea breeze floated around Mia. Pyrrha's voice dropped to a husky murmur. "I heard what your maid told you. People like to gossip." Mia drew back, a flash of anger breaking the spell. How had this girl overheard them? She'd been sitting closest to Mia's room, but Mia hadn't thought their whispers would carry that far. "Tell her not to ask questions about the lady who brought me here. It will anger her."

"Anger her? She'll never know what my maid asks or doesn't ask."

Pyrrha pressed her lips together for a moment. "You'd think not, but still, don't ask about her. You don't want to anger her. It never ends well."

3

The next day started as monotonously as the one before, with Mia seated in the women's hall as usual during stormy weather—until Mia felt a tap on her shoulder. She whipped her head around to see who it was. There was Pyrrha, so tall it made no sense she could sneak up on Mia like that. She was hardly dainty.

Mia shook off her startled feeling and the strangely pleasing twinge that Pyrrha's closeness set off. "Yes?" Then she cleared her throat to cover the harshness she'd put into her question.

Pyrrha's lips turned up slightly and then, with a barely noticeable twitch of muscles, she restrained her mouth into polite blandness. Mia blushed. Was this girl laughing at her?

"I would like to ask you for a favor," Pyrrha said, looking down at Mia. "Not that you owe me one. Quite the reverse."

Mia indicated a nearby stool.

Pyrrha drew the stool closer and sat. "I would like to speak to your father. Will you request permission for an audience? I have something I need to discuss with him today. It shouldn't be put off."

"Discuss with him? What is it?" Mia remembered Pyrrha's strange warning. "About the lady who brought you?"

"Not directly. You may stay and hear what I have to say."

"Isn't everything about you a big dark secret?" Mia couldn't help but ask.

Pyrrha sighed. "I hate secrets. I didn't choose any of this. But I should speak to your father. It's for your advantage as well."

That was an interesting idea, and she wouldn't have to say anything much to her father. That would be up to Pyrrha. Besides, dark half-moons of sunken skin lurked below Pyrrha's eyes. She was suffering. Talking to the king wasn't likely to bring comfort, but she'd asked and, apparently, it mattered to her.

"I'll send word. If he hasn't gone off somewhere—which he does a lot—you may speak to him. He's not so important like your father must be."

"My father? But you don't—"

"Don't worry. I don't know who your father is, but I know he's someone powerful enough that my father can't refuse him. I have lost count of the times my father has told me that Skyros is a small island off the trade routes, dependent on others with greater power and wealth. He tells me this right before I'm meant to charm some king at a feast, so that the king will not choose to overthrow my father and add Skyros to his realm." Mia found these encounters with "important" men humiliating.

"Is there such a constant fear of that? Doesn't your father have warriors to call up when he needs them?" Mia couldn't tell if she heard surprise or disdain in Pyrrha's voice.

"I suppose he has warriors, but I think the real reason no one has taken this island for their own is that any king would gain so little for his effort." Mia hesitated, restraining her laughter, but this girl would be as amused as she by her favorite ruse. "When I'm required to attend the feasts, instead of complimenting the ugly old men, I plant hints about how infertile our fields are, how barren our vineyards, how off the usual paths of trade and power the island of Skyros is."

Pyrrha laughed loudly. For a moment every head in the room turned to stare at her. Women did not laugh like that. Pyrrha bowed her head and muttered an apology for causing a disturbance. Then she leaned in close to Mia. "I'm guessing your father doesn't like that at all, but it's clever, very clever."

Mia's heart felt light, and the unfamiliar thrill Pyrrha caused tingled below her belly. "I'll send Dione now."

KING LYCOMEDES HAD NOT GONE off hunting or to any other outside activity. Lightning bolts lit the sky in rapid succession, and thunder crashed so loudly Mia felt the walls shake. Even her father, who sought any excuse to escape his household, had the good sense to stay inside. In a flash of satisfaction, she imagined the new guards out in this weather. It was a mean impulse, but she savored it while she went with Pyrrha to her father's private quarters. His personal manservant led the way, not his advisor. She whispered to Pyrrha that this was a good sign. Her father would be more relaxed and willing to listen.

Mia's curiosity about what she'd hear drew her forward like the smell of bread fresh from the oven.

The servant tapped on the doorframe and then slipped through the curtain. After a murmur from her father, the man pulled aside the curtain and beckoned them into the large square hall. Mia did a quick curtsy and bow of her head. At the edge of her vision, she glimpsed Pyrrha copying her movements while observing her. Protocol would differ from one court to another. The girl did have the good sense to drop into an especially low curtsy. Her movement forward and down reminded Mia of the curling flow of waves. Pyrrha held the lowest part of the gesture longer than usual, and for an instant she looked crouched like the hunters Mia had surreptitiously watched, ready to spring in attack. Mia blinked, and the illusion vanished. She shuddered and turned her attention to her father.

He gave Mia a questioning look followed by a scowl. He hadn't expected this visit and must assume it meant trouble—caused by Mia somehow, presumably. The servants had brightened the king's private rooms by lighting an abundance of oil lamps in the wall brackets and a crackling fire in the center.

"I hope you have settled in comfortably?" the king asked Pyrrha.

Pyrrha bowed her head. "Yes, your majesty. Your daughter has given me a lovely room. I have no complaint at all."

"And yet here you are," Lycomedes said. A smile hovered around his lips, softening the annoyance in his voice.

Mia took in the familiar room. She'd always loved it. Its walls were painted with animals of the hunt—but the painter had left out the hunters. The design felt like a purposeful joke, one her father must have permitted. Instead of pursued, frightened animals of the more common hunt scenes, her father lived surrounded by a peaceful cluster of grazing deer on one wall, on another, a jaunty pair of boar climbing among some rocks, one rooting its snout in the dirt for some tasty morsel that Mia had never been able to identify, and across from the door, a leopard, perched high on a painted slope with some branches as a backdrop. The room's furnishings were straightforward, armchairs and tables around the fire, simple ones without much carving or other adornment. Unlike the showy mosaic floor of the throne room, here, brown stone pavers formed a plain surface that seemed right for its painted animal inhabitants.

"Your majesty," Pyrrha said. "I know . . ." She glanced at Mia and paused. Choosing her words? "The, er, lady who brought me stressed the need to preserve the greatest secrecy about, um, my presence here. I have become aware that in response, you placed a new rotation of guards around the quarters where I am living." *Goodness*, this wasn't what Mia had guessed she'd hear. "I can well understand this precaution, but I must warn you that this action is a misunderstanding of the lady's wishes. As you will realize, I am more familiar with her thinking than you can be, so I implore you to attend to what I say."

Mia shot a glance between her father and this unusual girl. His mood had shifted and not for the good.

Lycomedes interrupted, "You're a high-born maiden and due respect—which I grant you—but do not presume to give me advice about the placement of my household guards. It's hardly something you know anything about."

"I do not need to in this case," Pyrrha responded with heat in her voice. "On the one hand, these guards are unnecessary because no one will actively seek me out, not here. Not if you maintain the secret the lady bound you to. So, there is no need to protect against intruders. However, the newly placed guards draw attention. They create questions. Placing guards will most likely lead to the undoing of the very secrecy you are attempting to preserve. You will draw the lady's wrath. Don't you see—er, your majesty, sir?"

Mia held very still so as not to draw any attention. It was an excellent argument, although it implied there was no need to keep Pyrrha in against her will, and Mia was not certain about that.

Lycomedes waved his hand dismissively. "I understood the . . . lady's wishes. She wants outside men kept away and you kept in. Your father is a man I will not offend by ignoring his directive, by whomever it might be delivered."

Pyrrha drew in a long breath. She looked ready to answer back.

Mia almost reached out to warn her. Instead, Pyrrha made an unladylike grunt of agreement and then said, "My father intends that I will be happy here, despite the change of circumstances." Pyrrha cast her eyes around the king's personal reception hall with a tinge of disparagement. It was lightly done, but implied that she was accustomed to greater luxury. Her look implied she'd accommodate life below her standards but would expect something from the king in return. "You would like a treaty of mutual protection from my father, would you not?"

The king's face sparked with surprise. "That would be an opportunity I would pursue if it were offered. I was not aware it had been."

"Offered? No. But I could raise the idea with him." Pyrrha cast a slow look at Mia. "He usually listens to my advice."

Lycomedes gave a short bark of laughter. He didn't believe Pyrrha. It was in the lines around his eyes as well as the dismissive sound. "By all means raise the idea. My scribes will happily record a letter for you, and I can hide it within other correspondence so that it does not reveal your location."

Her father looked at Mia. She couldn't guess what he was thinking. "I was in negotiations for just such a treaty—with another kingdom—three years ago. Things went awry, although not for any fault of what Skyros offered. Your father will find me a worthy partner in such an agreement, and I would be glad to enter discussions with him—a far more powerful partner than the treacherous king of Peparethos. You can warn your father never to negotiate with *him*. It will inevitably lead to betrayal."

Mia shuddered. How would her mother describe the king of Peparethos?

4

A life of quiet, proper sameness—Harmonia's goal for Mia and her sisters—was going to kill Mia. Pyrrha's presence had closed off Mia's previous route to flee daily suffocation, and that morning, she had reached a point at which she no longer cared about the dangers posed by the only other means of escape she could access.

Mia's sleeping chamber opened onto a courtyard. Like the women's hall, this small terrace and garden was now referred to as hers, but it was her mother's. The other door onto this courtyard, the one from her mother's now abandoned suite of rooms, had remained closed for three years. The servants who tended the garden had placed a large potted fig tree in front of the door, but that only made Mia see the door more sharply each time she stepped outside.

The chairs and table on the stone-paved terrace formed a pleasant seating area and a fresh alternative to the smoky air of the woman's hall. She frequently brought her sisters there when the weather allowed. But what Mia most loved about her mother's walled garden were the narrow beds of herbs and flowers, a profusion of color packed into the tiny mountaintop space. Her mother had taught her which plants flowered in each season, and she directed the gardener to be sure some plant was in bloom almost all the time. The spiky leaves of rosemary and thyme gave off a heady scent no matter the season.

In one corner, next to the wood pile that supplied the hearths of the women's quarters, a gnarled old pine tree fought the wind and rocky soil to grow tall and provide a splash of vivid green needles. Mia thought the tree would be much happier growing along with its fellow pine trees on the forested slopes that covered the northern part of the island, but she appreciated the shade it offered her.

The walls of the women's quarters surrounded the courtyard on three sides. The remaining side looked out—or used to look out—across the plain of barley and wheat fields and the mountain slopes beyond and, with a slight shift of Mia's gaze, across the limitless, shimmering sea. Originally, a hip-high wall along that open side had protected anyone from falling down the dizzying drop of mountainside that edged most of the garden there.

In the corner of the garden where the pine grew, instead of a sheer drop on the other side of the wall, there was a crumbling ledge about two or three strides in depth and, in Mia's memory, a gate that opened onto it. From that perch, rough stone steps and a hint of a track led downward and over until joining one of the main trails where the mountain was far less precipitous. Her father had always dismissed this exit as no better than a goat path. He didn't like that his wife slipped out that way, often holding her oldest daughter's chubby toddler hand in hers. He feared they'd fall, but her mother told Mia that if she was to rule over an island of goat herders, she must learn to be as surefooted as a goat.

Now the gate was gone and the wall transformed.

After her mother's disappearance, her father ripped out the gate and ordered the wall built up, taller than a man's height. He doubled the thickness. Sharp shards of pottery had been fixed into the top of the wall like thorns to gash anyone attempting to go over it.

The tree and flower beds remained, although they didn't thrive as they once had because the rebuilt wall limited their sunlight. Mia's courtyard had taken on a hostile feel. She'd softened that with honeysuckle and grape vines that climbed the ugly wall, and she'd spread the seeds of tall hollyhocks whose pink and red blooms in springtime cheered her up if she ignored the wall behind them.

But her courtyard, cut off from the goat path, remained a barely concealed prison. And then Pyrrha came, and Mia's old tricks for slipping out of the palace by other routes became impossible.

Pyrrha had lived among them for five days that felt like five seasons or five years or five—whatever measure was more than a year. Mia didn't have the patience for another afternoon in the women's hall, spinning and weaving. There would never be an end to the boredom. She had to escape into the countryside as she had before. Somehow.

In the quiet after the midday meal, while Harmonia and the others rested, Mia dragged one of her outdoor chairs across the pavers and to the corner where the pine tree stood. A light drizzle gradually soaked her hair and gown. She'd left behind her cloak because it would get in the way. Dione would have to help her change clothes and rearrange her hair before she returned to the women's hall, or she'd have to think of a good excuse for being out in the rain. Maybe she'd claim a bird with a hurt wing had needed her help. That would be believable.

She placed the chair under a branch of the pine tree that might hold her weight. She jumped to catch hold, but her fingers missed, and she tried again, jumping higher. Her fingers scraped against rough bark, but she couldn't grasp the branch and instead, toppled off the chair, smacking her knees and elbows against the muddy ground.

She eyed the stacked firewood. Gritting her teeth against the pain of torn skin on her palms, she pried out a log with one flat cut end that she hoped would stand upright when she put it on the chair. Jumping had been a rash choice.

Balancing with both feet on the log was tricky, but she grabbed hold of a wobbly grape vine and lodged her left foot higher up where a winding branch grew from the main stalk. With that support, she made an awkward hop and push until she placed a hand on the upper side of the tree branch. Getting both hands there took a sharp shove against the vine with her foot. The log tipped off the chair when her foot rose from it. No going back.

She pulled upward, imagining her body lifting to the branch so she could swing her leg over it. But her imagination and her body did not work together. Her arms were getting weaker and the cuts in her hands deeper, but letting go of the rough branch without ripping her palms even more wasn't going to be easy either. Her gaze darted around.

She swung her legs up, kicking the folds of her peplos gown so that her legs were exposed. She felt suddenly naked, despite the coating of mud. Pray to all the gods no one caught sight of her right now. The leather of her closed-toe sandals stuck to the wall sufficiently that she could push against it and work her lower body upwards in an even more awkward position, but she got her shoulder and then her side onto the branch. The wool of her peplos snagged and ripped, but she swung a leg up and finally straddled the branch. The wall rose above her head still, but she reached for a branch above her, pulled, and then peeked over the wall.

She looked to one side through the swirls of damp mist where a steep spur of the mountain provided the main access up to the palace. Scanning its slope, she saw none of the extra guards Dione had warned her about. Maybe her father had taken Pyrrha's warning to heart, even if he hadn't been willing to admit it to the girl.

Then Mia looked directly down.

The long drop to the ledge made her dizzy, and the sheer plummet off that small area was worse. It was one thing to step onto the ledge through a gate. It was another to jump and land on it from this height.

Plops of rain fell on her from higher in the pine tree. She shivered and looked up at the low hanging clouds that closed around her, then studied her situation.

One pine branch angled over the ledge. She'd have to edge along the wall to reach the outward facing branch. The wall was thick enough to sit on if it weren't bristling with shards. She slid out the small dagger she tied to her belt whenever she went on her explorations. She'd long ago stolen it from the dinner table and made a linen holder for it. She slid the blade against the base of a shard and with a closed fist pounded on the hilt. To her surprised satisfaction, the shard broke free. Gradually, she popped away shards from a big enough patch. Her hands were bloody and aching, but she could place herself next to the branch.

She untied the leather strap that crisscrossed twice around her waist and under her breasts to hold the overfolds of her peplos in place and tied one end to the branch. She let the strap hang free. It would bring her feet closer to the ledge. But she might not have the strength to pull herself back to the branch.

The wisest course now would be to untie the strap and use it instead to lower herself safely back onto the chair in her courtyard. That would be challenging enough. She wrinkled her nose and considered.

She scooted out on the branch over the small, wet rectangle of rock, keeping her eyes from the plunge off its edge, then turned herself so her belly braced against the tree limb and slowly lowered more of her body down. Gingerly, she grasped the leather with one sore hand and looped it around that arm. What if she couldn't hold her weight or her bloody hands slipped? Would she lose her balance and go off the ledge? She glanced down and her stomach swooped.

Movement caught her eye. A deer? A goat? A guard? It hadn't seemed to come from as far over as the spur where the guards would be, but maybe her father had ordered them onto this nearly inaccessible portion and the fog had concealed them. She scanned the area but couldn't find whatever had drawn her attention. She drew in a shaky breath. A flash came to her of standing shamefaced in front of her father covered in mud and torn clothes. Of facing his fury that she'd so directly ignored his orders. Was an afternoon of freedom worth that? She smiled, and with a yelp at the pain in her hands, dropped her weight onto the strap.

At that moment, a form darted up the impossible slope from a scrap of bushes below, calling, "Let go. I'll catch you." Someone grabbed her legs.

Mia didn't have a choice about letting go. She couldn't hold onto her belt. Her body fell heavily against... "Pyrrha?"

"You couldn't stand another day trapped in there either, huh?" Pyrrha said while gently placing Mia on her feet. With a big grin, Pyrrha looked her up and down. "You look terrible. I think you need a better way to get out of the women's quarters." Pyrrha looked at the wall, the tree, and the ledge they shared. "You could have killed yourself. Brave though."

Mia tried to straighten out her unfolded peplos which was dragging on the ground, but she couldn't do much because her belt was still tied to the tree. How had this girl sprinted up the cliff face? And how could she be so strong? Even hardworking Dione would have struggled to catch her like that, and Pyrrha's arms were far more shapely and graceful than Dione's. "I didn't have to climb over the wall until you came. Because of you, it's impossible to get out. You ruined everything."

Pyrrha's face fell. "In fairness, it's your father who shut you in, not me." With no warning, she sprang up and grabbed the pine branch with one arm and untied the strap with the other, then dropped effortlessly to the ledge and handed the belt to Mia. "Will this help?"

"I was going to use that to get back up."

Pyrrha shrugged. "If that's how you want to go, I'll put it back later."

Mia quickly wrapped her belt around herself and arranged the overfold. Pyrrha wore a short brown chiton, narrow enough in the chest that her breasts strained against the wool, and the lower edge came only to her knees. She'd wrapped pieces of wool around her legs with leather straps like a man would. Much better clothes for wall climbing, but how did her family allow her to own such clothes? Mia hadn't worn a short tunic like that since she was a small girl.

Pyrrha paused with her head to one side and then grabbed Mia's arm, leading her down several of the stairs and tugging her to sit inside the dripping foliage of a mastic shrub that grew in a hollow carved into the hillside. "We must hide now. There's one guard who climbs on this track. His rotation is bringing him by." She smiled. "He curses a lot about this trail and goats."

Small, leathery leaves provided a soft shield around the two girls, although they didn't block the rain that fell in a sudden flurry. On this rocky slope, the mastic didn't have a chance to grow into a tree, but its shiny, low greenery, still dotted with a few blackened berries the birds hadn't eaten, formed enough of a hideaway to conceal them on this misty day. Pyrrha put her finger to her lips and drew Mia close, wrapping her legs and arms around her, covering her brightly colored peplos with the dullness of her clothes. Mia curled comfortably against the cushion of Pyrrha's breasts and melted into the strong arms. From Pyrrha's skin wafted the scent of fresh sea air, beckoning with an alluring hint of saltiness. This closeness brought on a pleasing tingling sensation that spread upwards, disorienting Mia and making her want more.

From the trail came the guard's heavy footfalls. Mia snuggled closer against Pyrrha's warmth. How did Pyrrha know about the guard's rotation?

When the footsteps passed, Mia twisted her neck and shoulders to look at Pyrrha. "How did *you* escape the women's quarters?"

"I . . ." Pyrrha lifted Mia's hips abruptly, shifting her in that tight space so they were face to face.

Mia found herself staring into the depths of Pyrrha's sea green eyes. The air around her felt suddenly hot even in damp clothes. Pyrrha hadn't moved her hands from Mia's hips, and the warmth as they pressed against her rose through her body like the updraft from a blazing fire.

5

Seated on the ground in their precarious hideaway below the walls of the women's quarters, Mia held Pyrrha's gaze until Pyrrha made a strangled noise and drew her hands from Mia's hips.

"Is something wrong?"

"No, I'm glad you're my friend." Pyrrha shifted and rose. "We should get away before a guard returns. Let's get down the exposed part of the slope quickly."

Crawling out of the bush, Mia followed her friend—that was something new, a friend who wasn't a sister. Pyrrha scrambled rapidly down the irregular stone stairs and muddy track, which had washed out in places since Mia had last come this way. It had been more than three years, and her feet no longer remembered the path's uneven rhythm. She concentrated to keep up with her swift friend.

Through the rain, they traversed the steep mountain face and worked their way down to one of the established trails on the near-side of the spur. Then Pyrrha put on even more speed, and Mia struggled to run fast enough, but racing along felt good so she ignored the burn in her legs. The gusts of rain stopped, but the air she sucked in with her panting was heavy with moisture.

Finally, completely out of breath, she gasped out, "Slow down!"

"Sorry." Pyrrha flashed a smile of apology. "I'm used to—" Pyrrha cut herself off.

"What are you used to?" Mia asked in between panting.

"Someone who runs fast. Anyway, I should have asked you where we can go. I suppose we have to get back before our absence is obvious?"

Mia looked at the rips in her peplos and the cuts, scrapes, and smears of mud along her arms and legs. "It may be too late for me to keep it secret, at least from Harmonia. How did you get out?"

"Over the wall, like you." Pyrrha's room, designed for the highest status of women guests, also had a courtyard, but it had never had a gate or a track outside it.

Pyrrha's long limbs did have a couple dirty streaks, but Mia suspected she got them from Mia's own hands, and there weren't any visible scrapes. "But . . . not like me." Mia chewed on her lip a moment. "I don't think I can climb back over the wall. I used a chair and a log on my side, and even so, I could barely reach a high enough branch."

Pyrrha laughed, but not unkindly. "I saw you struggling. Pretty good for a— I'll boost you up onto the wall and catch you on the other side, so you don't get hurt. Don't worry."

How Pyrrha could do all that was a mystery, but Mia nodded and thanked her. "One of my favorite places is that way." She pointed along one of the forking trails. "Down this side of the spur and then along the river before it drops onto the plain. We can head into that patch of forest between those two mountains. You see that green area?"

Pyrrha nodded and launched like a deer.

Mia pushed her legs as fast as she could and called out again, "Slow down." Pyrrha slowed a little.

They wound down through the bristly, grayish mounds of thorny burnet and thyme that dotted the spur's slope. Mia held her skirt to keep it from catching on them. Here and there, taller mastic bushes softened the rocky hillside with loose greenery. They'd soon reach the riverbed that cut along the high valley before it dropped down to feed the wide plain.

Mia glanced over her shoulder and up at the citadel walls high above. The guards watched for a threat from the sea, and she always hoped they wouldn't notice a harmless girl outside the palace. They had never told on her, so she didn't worry too much. But now she was with Pyrrha.

They raced along, passing through a grove of olive trees and then some apricot, pomegranate, and fig trees planted where their roots could reach out to the river. Even now in the wet season, the river itself wasn't more than two or three strides wide, but it was fed by many springs.

Gradually the lushness around the riverbed surrounded them, oleanders, water reeds, blackberry brambles, and wild fig trees. Mia touched Pyrrha's arm to signal her. The track they were following would soon join the well-trod path to the main spring where the village women and palace servants collected water and washed clothes. They should avoid it. "Let's leave this path and go up to the forested area this way." She pointed and tugged on Pyrrha's arm. It felt good to take the lead. It was *her* island.

They passed under the bare branches of plane trees and navigated around evergreen oaks, low to the ground and prickly, and then climbed along one of the mountain slopes that rose gently on either side of the river, entering the deeper green of pine trees.

"Most of the forest on the island lies well north of here," Mia said. "I love this small patch of forest. It's like a secret palace of my own." She glanced shyly at Pyrrha. Would she make fun of her for that?

Pyrrha's eyes shone. They were multiple shades of green, layer upon shifting layer like the sea. With a dreamy look in her eyes, Pyrrha whispered, "a palace of trees," and smiled at Mia.

They walked quietly together. It was no longer raining, but Mia shivered in her damp clothes without a cloak. Pyrrha didn't look chilled, and there wasn't anything to do about the cold, so Mia crossed her arms tight against her body and kept up with Pyrrha's long legs.

Pyrrha asked, "Does your father use this forest for hunting?"

"No. The best prey live on the northwest part of the island where there's a much larger forest. We won't run into him. It doesn't matter if one of the farmers sees us. They sometimes cut wood in this patch of woods. This part of the island is otherwise so rocky, here is the only firewood they can gather close to the village. They're not supposed to, though, because it's royal land, but I never tell on them. In return when they see me, they wave and treat me respectfully."

"You are the king's daughter. They would give you respect no matter what." Pyrrha's smile widened. "But they wouldn't wave. That means they like you. They see your generosity in sharing the firewood."

That her silence would be understood as a kindness surprised her.

Pyrrha continued, "If everywhere else nearby is rocky, no wonder they steal wood from this forest. It would be difficult to drag all their firewood from a distant forest."

Mia hadn't considered what would drive the farmers to risk the king's anger by stealing his trees. They usually took the fallen ones, so she didn't see what harm they did, but Pyrrha's view went beyond that. It was far to lug the wood down from the northern mountain slopes. The palace slaves loaded it on a special boat and brought it around from the western side of the island that way, but the farmers wouldn't have such a luxury or the time away from their farms and herds.

"Do you ever go to the villages or farms?" Pyrrha asked.

"Someone might bring word to my father. I stay away from people as much as I can."

"That must be lonely."

"Not usually. I have so many sisters that when I can, I like to be alone."

Pyrrha shrugged. "I guess so." A bird's trill came from the branches above, answered by another. "You might get into trouble with villagers if you visited them. I shouldn't have asked that."

"You understood that the villagers need this forest more than my father does."

"A king must provide for his people. And protect them. Sometimes for those duties, he must give up something dear."

Mia's eyebrows rose. "I've never heard a king's duties described that way. My father always talks of protecting himself. He is a wily negotiator—that's what he does as king."

"He may not have a choice."

"My father can choose whatever he wants. Unlike me. He's the keeper of choices."

"He can go where he pleases, that's true. I've only lived with you for a few days, and I enjoy the company of your sisters. They laugh a lot. But staying inside every day is . . . not what I would choose. You don't seem to like it either."

Mia shook her head. Her teeth chattered with cold. She clamped them shut.

Pyrrha asked, "Should I build a fire?" A mischievous twinkle flashed in her eyes. "We'd be stealing royal wood, but you are a member of the royal family, so it won't count."

"A fire?" Mia looked about. Everything was wet, and they had no hot embers to put to the kindling even if they had some. She gave her new friend a doubtful look.

"Help me gather some wood."

Mia picked up some small fallen branches. She shook the water from the dead pine needles and gathered more. Pyrrha stomped on an old fallen tree, weathered gray, and ripped it apart. Mia laughed at this action. Harmonia would have fits at such indelicate shows of strength. But the trunk split into several pieces that were a good size for a fire if they could ever light them. Pyrrha scraped back the wet leaves and pine needles from one open area and piled the wood in a pattern Mia had seen the servants make. Clever of Pyrrha to have watched them enough to be able to do it herself. Mia hadn't thought of that. Then Pyrrha went to a place where the pine needles were especially deep and dug her hand underneath, drawing out dry needles to use as kindling. She took Mia's small branches and poked them here and there among the rest. Then from a pouch at her belt, she took out two stones, one flat and larger than the other. Crouching next to the dry kindling, she hit the smaller one against the flat stone, causing sparks to fly. She repeated it until tiny twirls of smoke rose from the needles and then flames started licking at the piled wood. In the palace, servants relit fires by bringing embers from elsewhere. Mia had heard of fire stones, but she'd never seen them used. She envied Pyrrha's strange skills. Waves of heat rose, and Mia held out her cold fingers to the warmth.

Pyrrha dragged over a piece of the old tree trunk she hadn't broken up. She lowered herself onto it as a seat, bouncing a little, apparently to test whether it would hold. Then she patted the spot next to her. Mia sat. It did feel good to rest.

Mia wasn't sure how to put what she wanted to ask. "How do you . . ." She trailed off with a vague wave of her hands.

"Making a fire isn't hard if someone teaches you." Pyrrha spoke as if this remarkable skill was an ordinary thing for a girl.

Mia stretched her hands to the fire again. "Where you lived did you ask a villager or farmer to show you? Maybe I shouldn't avoid them. This fire is nice." She smiled at Pyrrha.

"My teacher was a . . . woodsman—and other things. Not a villager. My father knew him."

"Did your father know he was teaching you things a woodsman does? That can't be."

Pyrrha looked embarrassed at this question, so Mia said, "You are better at getting outside than I am." She held up her bloodied hands.

Pyrrha took hold of her wrists and drew her hands close to examine them. "The river flows nearby. Over there." She waved one hand to the right.

"Yes," Mia said, puzzled by the change of subject. She looked at the folds of hills and the abundance of greenery. "How did you guess that?"

Pyrrha looked up, her brow wrinkled in confusion that then melted away. "I can hear it. Come with me to wash the mud from your cuts."

Mia couldn't catch the sound of water from where they sat. Pyrrha's hearing was sharp.

Pyrrha kept hold of Mia's wrist, pulling her quickly through the screening bushes and trees to where the river burbled around rocks.

Mia tried to follow Pyrrha's orders to dip her hands into the flow of water. The folds of her peplos fell forward and would have gotten soaked but Pyrrha grabbed them. She grunted in annoyance, then gathered the fabric tightly in one hand, and steadied Mia with an arm around her waist. Mia felt an odd mixture of exposure and safety. The cold water soothed her scrapes, and eventually she got brave enough to rub them together, working the dirt away.

"That's good," Pyrrha said and hefted Mia from the river's edge.

They sat on a boulder and Pyrrha hunched over Mia's hands, which were bleeding freely again. She drew a strip of clean linen from the pouch at her waist. Folded into the linen were some dried leaves, black in color. Pyrrha pressed one of the leaves on the deepest cut. To Mia's surprise the leaf didn't crumble but molded to her hand almost like a piece of fabric. Immediately the pain and bleeding stopped.

"Did the woodsman teach you this as well?"

"He did. His skill as a healer was even more prodigious than his hunting and tracking skills." Pyrrha finished treating the cuts and wrapped each hand with linen strips.

"Your father has a very different idea than mine of teachers for his daughter. I'd like to know how to do that." With her chin she pointed at her hands.

"It's useful."

"Lady Harmonia knows some healing," Mia said. "I asked her to teach me. She helped my mother when my youngest sister was born. I watched, but now she won't discuss childbearing with me."

"*That* I know nothing about. Sorry."

"What do you call the leaves you used? I've never seen them before."

Pyrrha looked shamefaced. "You wouldn't have." She hesitated. "Only certain kinds of people can use them."

"Could I?"

Shaking her head, Pyrrha looked away.

What certain kind of person did she have to be? Something else she wasn't allowed to do. "Let's go back to the fire. I'm cold." She heard the peeved tone in her voice but didn't apologize.

They sat on the log by the fire. A little sunshine burned through the gray, but Mia shivered with goosebumps along her arms. She scooted closer to her friend and leaned against her sturdy body.

They sat in silence. After a while Mia looked up into Pyrrha's face and asked, "It sounds much more interesting wherever you grew up. Why did you have to come to Skyros?"

"Remember when I told you not to ask questions about the lady I came with?"

"Yes, you said it never ends well. I can't ask about you?"

"It's much the same." Pyrrha shrugged. "Sorry."

"If you'll help me escape another day without—" She held up her bandaged hands. "Then I won't ask about you."

"I like that."

"I like you." Mia looked up into her friend's face. Their gazes locked again, and heat wafted deliciously through Mia's body. Pyrrha's hand dropped to Mia's thigh.

Somehow their lips came together. Pyrrha's were soft and yet firm. They teased and then pressed. Mia's surprise melted into an intoxicating pleasure, even better than the feel of being oiled after bathing. Pyrrha nibbled ever so lightly on her lower lip, each nip releasing sensation within Mia and making her want more. Mia responded with a tentative kiss, then another, then, as she sensed Pyrrha's eagerness, a tiny nibble of her own, which seemed to send shivers through Pyrrha, so she tried a slightly harder bite. Pyrrha groaned in approval. Pyrrha's tongue explored hesitantly until Mia let it slide around her mouth and slowly deeper and back in a rhythm that caused Mia's back to arch and called up a low moan she'd never heard from herself. She wrapped her arms around Pyrrha and let waves of pleasure overrun her as Pyrrha's tongue grew more insistent and daring, doing things that should be disgusting, but Mia didn't want them to stop. To encourage her friend, she mimicked with her own tongue the sliding plunges that caused her such pleasure. The urgent tingling from between Mia's legs grew more insistent.

Then Pyrrha pulled away from the kisses and undid the pin that held the right shoulder of Mia's peplos closed, letting the double fold of fabric fall. Mia drew back for a moment in surprise. The air was cool against her bare breast. What was happening?

Pyrrha looked her directly in the eye. "May I?"

Mia didn't know what she was asking, but she nodded.

Pyrrha leaned down and the warmth of her mouth closed around Mia's breast, sucking and rubbing. *Oh!* Mia braced one hand against the log, fleetingly surprised that didn't hurt, and her head lolled back. Waves of sensation overwhelmed her, and she pushed her breast harder against Pyrrha's mouth. Pyrrha made a growling sound muffled by a mouth full of Mia's rounded flesh. She slid a hand under the covered side, squeezing and kneading the previously neglected breast. Mia couldn't stop her moans that came louder and louder and then a shriek as something like a lightning bolt shot through her. She would have collapsed backward, but Pyrrha caught her and drew her tight against her chest.

When Mia's heart slowed a little and she could breathe without gasping, she giggled softly. *This was a game for two.* She undid one of the pins on Pyrrha's shoulders, exposing a small, lusciously rounded breast that called to her mouth like a ripe fig or a cake drenched in honey. She ran her tongue around the hardened nipple in the center and sucked as Pyrrha had, listening for the moans her friend had drawn out of her. Instead, Pyrrha groaned as if in pain and drew back. Pyrrha's hand scrambled from her chest to her belly and between her legs.

Pyrrha buckled forward, her head in her hands. "I'm sorry."

"What's wrong?" Mia rubbed Pyrrha's back.

Suddenly Pyrrha jumped up, leaving Mia to catch herself so she didn't go tumbling off the log. Pyrrha yanked up the shoulder of her chiton and closed the pin. She breathed in ragged gasps.

"Are you hurt?" Mia asked. She'd only done the pleasing things Pyrrha had done to her. Did Pyrrha have some unseen injury?

"Yes, but not by you."

"I thought I was doing what you wanted," Mia said. "I'm sorry I did something wrong."

"Wrong? Everything's wrong. I can't bear it." Pyrrha stomped off and disappeared into the forest.

Mia sank onto the log, tears brimming up. What happened? Why did Pyrrha suddenly hate her?

Mia hunted for her shoulder pin, clipped her gown into place, and put herself together as best she could. So much for having a friend or help climbing back over the wall. Could she pile some rocks on the ledge to reach the branch she'd swung down on? She looked at her bandaged hands. If she marched up to the front gates of the palace, they'd let her in, and she'd be safe, at least in one sense of the word. She would never be allowed outside again. That would be the first of many unpleasant consequences. Maybe she could think of a good story that would buy her father's forgiveness. Could she blame Pyrrha?

6

"I didn't think you'd want trouble with that lady, Father," Mia said in a carefully remorseful voice.

She stood in front of him in his private quarters, usually a less hostile location, but his dark eyes flashed with anger, and the furrows on his brow were so deep they looked more like rolls of dough than flesh.

"That lady? What nonsense are you talking about?"

Mia pinched a fold of her gown to keep calm. His dismissive tone made misleading him less painful. She had to defend her ability to escape. Her filthy, bruised appearance supported the explanation she'd chosen to tell, so she didn't hide how sore and tired she was. She'd removed the bandages that didn't fit the story.

She kept her voice soft. "The lady who brought Pyrrha. She did not want the girl to go outside. So when I saw Pyrrha jump over one of the courtyard walls, I went after her. I thought I could bring her back so quickly that no rumor of what she'd done would reach the lady." It would be a mistake to openly remind her father how cowed he'd been by their mysterious visitor. The idea of rumor making its way to the lady was ridiculous, but Pyrrha herself had suggested it.

Mia had decided on this plan after walking along the goat track and seeing no way to lift herself high enough to sneak back into the palace. It was Pyrrha's fault she was stuck, and Pyrrha obviously didn't want to be a friend, whatever she'd said at first. While her father would savor punishing Mia and find some new way to make life unbearable, Pyrrha would get no more than a polite reprimand. He might even ignore her escape. Pyrrha had suggested she could assist him. Let her take the blame. Pyrrha and that lady had some power over her father she didn't understand, but she'd use it.

Her father sighed. "But you did not bring her back." Her father's peevish tone made Mia cringe, although it seemed he believed her lie.

"I couldn't find her. I did not dare venture out very far. You wouldn't want me to, I'm sure."

"I don't want you anywhere outside the palace without your attendants, but that's never stopped you before."

Mia pressed her lips together. Had Lady Harmonia told on her more than she'd said?

"Don't take it out on poor Harmonia," her father said, apparently guessing her thought in that alarming way of his. "You don't really think news of your wandering never reaches me? Until now, such childish misbehavior didn't matter much. I will keep you safe and always attended when noblemen come to my court. I won't make *that* mistake again. But the ignorant villagers you might chance upon offer no danger. They know it will cost them their life to interfere with you."

Interfere with her? Mia had a sense of what her father meant. Would her father kill a villager if one went somewhere with her? That's what her mother had done. Gone away with a visiting king. Had she become mother to other children? Mia had guessed that much from whispers of servants' gossip she'd overheard.

It had started when her mother made her give the welcoming speech for a visiting king instead of doing it herself as usual. Her father was negotiating a treaty with him, the king of Peparethos. This wasn't the first time he'd visited. On each previous visit, her mother had been eager to greet this king.

This time, her mother said it would be good practice for Mia to do the greeting alone. Mia had to learn to be a queen so that when her father selected a princely husband for her, she'd be ready. But her mother stressed how important this visit was. The treaty was essential to the kingdom's safety, and Mia must make the king feel welcome and honored. It was Mia's duty for the good of the kingdom. At ten, Mia had been terrified to take on this duty, but her mother gave her no choice. It wouldn't have been so frightening except she sensed her mother was lying. About what, she didn't know, although as her mother left the room, she'd heard her mutter under her breath, "I cannot be near him ever again. It's over."

The only thing Mia knew for certain was that she'd been the one who had said the wrong thing, had revealed what she never should have. What happened was her fault, and no one had let her fix it. They wouldn't talk about it. She'd said the things her mother practiced with her, but the king of Peparethos sat stiff and uncomfortable, so she'd added a little more. Reminded him of his previous visit when, in the women's quarters, she'd inadvertently witnessed a friendly meeting between him and her mother. Her mother had been warm and effusive, smiling, even laying her hand on his arm. And he had returned her cordiality with an embrace.

At these words, her father's anger had exploded with screaming at the visiting king, "The women's quarters? You stole in and took my wife's virtue?" He sent guards to drag her mother from her quarters and throw her out of the palace. "I will not have a whore for a wife."

The king of Peparethos had rushed out of the throne room, surrounded by his own guards with their swords drawn.

That was the disaster she caused when she was doing her duty *for the good of the kingdom*. She never saw her mother again. The king of Peparethos sailed away and took her mother with him.

And her father had grown distant and mean. Clearly, he knew who to blame.

Mia shook off these painful memories. She straightened up and glared at her father.

He rubbed his jaw with one hand. "Did Pyrrha really go out on her own? Don't lie to me."

"All on her own." Mia looked straight into her father's stern gaze.

"It doesn't look like you enjoyed yourself. Falling from the wall might kill you. You won't ever do that again, will you?"

"No more falling, Father."

There was a knock at the doorframe.

The king's chief advisor stepped through the curtain. After a bow, the advisor said, "I sent men to find her. They haven't returned, but she appeared in the women's hall saying she'd had a long nap."

"A nap?"

"When I suggested that I'd sent a serving woman to look for her in her rooms and she had not been there, she smiled and said perhaps that was while she was out for a walk." The man's saggy frown deepened. "I told her of Princess Deidamia's return in a deplorable state. She said she hoped the princess was enjoying a soothing bath to repair herself into a more suitable state."

Mia had to force herself not to smile. Pyrrha had been clever.

"Is Pyrrha as scraped and cut as my daughter is?"

"No, no sign of that. I did tell her that she was not permitted to walk outside of the palace. She nodded. I did not feel it was my place to press her further."

Her father gave a wave of dismissal, and his advisor left.

Her father studied her. "You are responsible as an example for your sisters." He gestured at her. "This is hardly what a princess should be."

Mia pictured the scenes of her escape, especially the royal forest and its forbidden firewood. Did her father understand what a king should be?

She took a deep breath before answering. "I'm sorry. I didn't know I would end up looking like this." She wanted to scream what she was really sorry for, for causing her mother to disappear, and let him rail at her and blame her. To hear her guilt admitted and recognized. Maybe he'd forgive her then.

He shook his head. "Finding you a husband is already hard enough. People fear like mother like daughter."

She jerked back at that. Her mother had been a good queen, beautiful, kind, and gentle. Mia wanted to be like her. People were stupid.

Her father grimaced. "Whoever you marry will have to be my successor as king. That means he must agree to live here, not take you to his home. If Skyros weren't so—" He stopped himself and looked away. "I don't want to hand my throne to a minor princeling, fourth son of a powerless kingdom, nor do I want Skyros to be absorbed like some conquered city, forced to pay tribute and follow orders." He narrowed his eyes. "You must stop this childish behavior. Do at least that much for me."

Pyrrha's voice floated in her mind, *If everywhere else nearby is rocky, no wonder they steal wood from this forest.* She didn't think time spent outside the palace would be childish. It might be necessary to learn how to be a good queen. It might be worth falsely blaming Pyrrha if that lie meant avoiding some new restriction that would stop her from escaping again. Instead of wandering to entertain herself, she'd get to know the needs of her kingdom.

"I will not behave like a child. I promise." She paused and plunged ahead. "I remember the example my mother set as queen." Her father shot to his feet. She fell back a step. "I know you hate her and me, but you didn't always. Before that, she showed me how to be a good queen, and I will grow up to be like that."

Silence choked the room. Her father's blank expression gave her no clues.

"I'm sorry," she mumbled.

The silence stretched on. Mia whispered, "I need a bath." She turned and left her father standing as still as a statue.

7

The days that followed her confrontation with her father weren't pleasant. Mia felt like a rabbit with a hawk circling overhead. Lady Harmonia noticed everything she did. Pyrrha kept to herself. Sometimes she played with Mia's youngest sister, tossing her in the air so she laughed and begged for more, but Harmonia would glare and Pyrrha would suddenly tell her she was too tired, which was a lie since Pyrrha lifted little Bura effortlessly over her head.

Most of the time Pyrrha shifted restlessly on a stool making a mess of good carded wool while attempting to spin it into yarn. At one point, when Pyrrha looked ready to jump out of herself, Mia offered to help her set up warp threads for a new tapestry. There was room for another loom against the same wall that supported the tall posts and crossbeam of hers. It took two women to measure out the lengths of yarn, tie them at the top to the beam onto which finished fabric would be rolled, and then guide every other strand through the heddle to form alternating sheds and, finally, wind them evenly around the hanging ceramic weights at the bottom. Setting up a warp was tedious, but weaving a story was far more entertaining than the endless spinning Mia and all the palace women had to do.

Her own current project showed a stormy sea with a ship of

raiders struggling as they headed toward a peaceful fishing village on the shore. Mia liked the contrast between the dark ship and the villagers going about their chores in the rain, unaware of the threat, the looming fate of slaughter and slavery. Her maid Dione had told Mia about her childhood in such a place and the way pirates killed her father and rounded up her mother and sisters. Mia had woven in a sea monster poking up its scaly head beside the ship. No one in this village would suffer Dione's fate.

Pyrrha had given Mia a panicked look when she offered help setting up a loom, so Mia left her on her own. What did Mia care if Pyrrha disliked her so much she wouldn't do any activity with her? She'd tried to cheer Pyrrha up, but like a tapestry that hadn't been properly tied off, she seemed to be unraveling. Let her annoy Harmonia with her endless fidgeting.

Standing before her upright loom, Mia worked in a thread of brown wool for the ship's mast against the dark blue of the sea. It was tricky to make the streak of mast stand out against the blue. If the sailors knew their business, they'd have taken down the sails before the storm took over, but it'd be dramatic to have the pale canvas of a sail gusting loose. They might not be skilled enough to have drawn down their sail in time. Maybe one of the sea gods brought up the storm very suddenly. The sea was a dangerous place, and the gods often took offense at mortals.

Behind her, Harmonia's chair scraped across the stone floor. She must have risen in a rush. Not Harmonia's usual manner. Mia peeked over her shoulder. Her attendant wasn't headed toward her, thank the gods. She was plowing toward Pyrrha like a fury from the Underworld. Her arms flailed, and her face reddened.

What was Pyrrha doing on the floor like that? She was on her back like a dead bug. Bura straddled her and pounded her tiny fists against Pyrrha's chest. Her sister giggled wildly. She was even more entertained when Pyrrha grabbed her in an imitation of a wrestling hold and pretended to pin her to the floor. The white moons of Pyrrha's buttocks were revealed for all to see, and Bura's baby-sized chiton was hitched up around her waist.

Mia recognized the wrestling maneuvers. She had snuck up on men practicing, watching from a hiding place. It was fascinating, oiled naked bodies writhing like that. But to see a girl doing it. Pyrrha had gone too far.

Harmonia was boiling over. She snatched up Bura, smoothing down her tunic and handing her off to Mia's dutiful sister Idomene. "Take the child to her room for a nap."

Bura wailed, but Idomene disappeared down the hall with her.

Pyrrha had scrambled up and smoothed her own peplos, adjusting her belt under the overfold and hitching the pinned shoulders into place. "I was just playing with her."

"Your behavior," Lady Harmonia announced, "is appalling. I do not know where you grew up." She raised a hand palm out. "Nor do I want you to tell me who you are. That's a secret I have no business hearing. The king made that clear. But while you live here, you will behave like a noblewoman."

Mia wished her sister Idomene hadn't been sent out. She would be mad that she missed Harmonia's breaking point when she could no long hold back her criticism of Pyrrha, king's orders or not.

Harmonia's hand wavered in the air. "That . . . that rough play will not take place in this hall. Did no one teach you to work wool like a proper lady?"

Pyrrha pressed her lips together. Then she shrugged as if giving up. "No, no one did. I would be honored, Lady Harmonia, if you would teach me how to spin wool. That would be better than ruining the work of others who carded it."

Harmonia opened her mouth and shut it again. Pyrrha had a clever way of soothing people.

Harmonia fell for this tactic. "I would be happy to teach you, child. How could your mother have been so remiss?" Harmonia's face clouded over. A hand flew to her mouth. "Poor child, your mother died when you were a babe, didn't she? That must be it. Don't tell me your story. I'm under strict orders not to ask. Please accept my apology. I will mend the errors of your sad childhood."

Mia couldn't tell if Pyrrha was holding back laughter or about to cry. Maybe it was both. They took seats by the hearth.

Mia peeked as Harmonia instructed Pyrrha. "With your left hand, child, hold the fleece loosely with your thumb and forefinger. Let the bulk of the fleece rest on the back of that hand."

Mia found it interesting that Harmonia had concluded that Pyrrha grew up motherless. If that was Harmonia's guess, whatever the king had told Harmonia about Pyrrha, it hadn't included hinting that the forceful lady who brought the girl was her mother.

Harmonia made a little clucking sound. "Like this. Use your right hand to guide and tug the feeder out while keeping the spindle whirling. Let the weight at the bottom of the stick do the work of keeping it twirling."

The commanding lady Mia had watched in the throne room certainly hadn't done anything motherly, but then, who could she be otherwise? Why entrust Pyrrha to her? Pyrrha's menfolk would be more appropriate if she had no mother.

Pyrrha watched Harmonia's fingers intently. "When I get to that point and tug out the bit you call the feeder, the wool breaks."

"A light touch, that's what's needed," Harmonia said. "Try again." She handed over the fleece and spindle.

Pyrrha set up as she'd been shown.

Harmonia shook her head. "Lighter."

Pyrrha tried several times more, but the feeder broke each time. She stomped her foot and handed the wool to Harmonia. "I don't think I can do this. It's too... small."

Small? What did that mean? The other day, in one leap Pyrrha had caught a branch, swung up, and untied Mia's belt. That must be the sort of thing that was big enough.

Harmonia wasn't pleased. Her mothering wasn't going as planned.

Mia slipped closer to them, picturing Pyrrha in the woods, relaxed, far more at home than she was here. "Imagine stretching out a spider's web without breaking it."

Pyrrha's face lit in a smile. "Spider webs are excellent for wounds. You're right, they have some give, but only so much."

Harmonia gave Pyrrha a puzzled look down her nose.

Mia took the spindle and wool from Harmonia and handed them to Pyrrha.

Rubbing the spindle shaft against her leg to set the twist, Pyrrha delicately held the wool with her left hand, and then dropped the weighted spindle and guided the feeder into thread with her right. This time nothing broke. Nor did it when she'd wound that bit of thread onto the shaft and set it whirling again. "I've got it! Thanks to both of you."

Harmonia gave a small nod and returned to her usual seat on the other side of the hearth. Mia felt a pang for her. She was never going to understand Pyrrha.

But then, Mia didn't either. She wasn't sure what had made her think of spider webs.

Pyrrha's gaze focused intently on her fingers as fluffs of wool passed gently through them and spun into thread. Mia remembered those hands lighting the fire, which also required precise and delicate actions.

Mia turned back to her loom and lost herself in her own work for a long stretch until she heard Pyrrha drop her spindle and shift on her stool, the legs scraping with the force of her movement. Mia stole a glance. Pyrrha stared at her hands and the clump of unspun wool lying across her lap as if someone were forcing her to eat a foreign, unknown food that looked poisonous.

She pinched her face tight, holding in some emotion threatening to burst from her. The strange girl ran her hands over her chest and thighs, shuddering at what she touched. Her hands fell into her lap, open palmed. Her gaze moved from one hand to the other and then, with a strangled sound from her throat, locked on the fallen spindle. She drew back, a hand to her mouth.

Mia glanced at Harmonia. The noble woman's head was studiously tucked down to avoid catching Pyrrha's attention. She'd had enough of the troubled girl. Mia scanned her sisters' reactions to this disturbance. Each of them was looking away, trying to pretend they did not notice. To them this was a matter of embarrassment that they didn't understand.

Suddenly Pyrrha shot off her stool and raced out of the women's hall, going down the corridor toward her rooms.

MIA LISTENED to Pyrrha's angry footsteps retreating down the hallway toward the guest suite. It didn't seem like a spinning lesson caused her to run out of the women's hall. But what did?

Mia glanced at Lady Harmonia. Her attendant was still pretending not to notice Pyrrha. She wore a collected look of disinterest. A life of calm disinterest? That was what Mia was supposed to reach for? Pyrrha never would. She was sure of that much.

Pyrrha's rooms were farther down the hallway than Mia's, but, still, the complete silence from that direction was concerning. Pyrrha seemed too restless to lie down, and yet Mia caught no sound of movement. She must have gone into her outside courtyard. The idea of Pyrrha alone outside the palace in her current state worried Mia. She needed to catch her before she escaped and at least go with her.

Mia faked a yawn and rubbed her neck. Then she rose languidly and wandered toward her rooms. She turned into her sleeping chamber long enough to open a shutter so that light spilled in, showing under the drawn door curtain so it would look like she was occupied in her own suite. Then she slipped back into the hall and down toward Pyrrha.

She didn't linger outside Pyrrha's rooms where she might be seen but went through the curtain without knocking. She gasped in surprise at what she saw in the far corner of the room.

Pyrrha was curled into a ball on the floor. Mia rushed over and knelt.

"Make the noise stop. Make it stop," Pyrrha whispered, but not to Mia.

What noise? Mia rubbed Pyrrha's back. "What is it?" She brushed strands of red-gold hair back from Pyrrha's cheek. Pyrrha's skin was red, and her breathing uneven.

Pyrrha buried her head in her arms. "Make it stop."

"Make what stop? What noise do you hear? Are you in pain?"

"I'm not in pain. Go away."

"How can I make it stop if I go away?"

"You can't do anything. Go away."

Slapping Pyrrha—what she wanted to do—probably wasn't going to help. Should she leave this impossible girl alone? A girl who had already proven her untrustworthiness?

"Go away. You can't help."

Mia preferred to be alone when she was miserable.

Pyrrha uncurled enough to drag herself out of Mia's reach, but whatever bad feeling plagued her didn't stop. Pyrrha kept hitting the side of her head with the heel of her palm and moaning, "Make it stop. Make it stop."

"Hitting your head won't help," Mia offered. It sounded stupid as soon as she said it. She understood being haunted by thoughts she wanted to knock out of her head.

"Leave me alone. I don't know what to do with my feelings. They're killing me."

Mia crouched and watched, unwilling to abandon Pyrrha but also unwilling to intrude where she was scorned.

Pyrrha's state didn't improve. Now her breath was growing more ragged. Each inward gasp jerked her chest. She hadn't stopped hitting her head, either.

Mia rose and found a pitcher of water and cup on a table beside the bed. She filled the cup and knelt beside Pyrrha without touching her. "Try to sip some water. You are red in the face, and it will soothe your throat."

"Water?"

"Yes, cool water. Would you prefer wine? I can fetch some."

"No. Give me water. It will feel right."

Feel right? Mia handed her the cup.

Pyrrha gulped it down.

Mia brought the pitcher and poured in more each time Pyrrha held out the cup. She sat cross-legged, watching Pyrrha's face grow less red, but the strange girl's distress didn't soften.

"Maybe," Mia tried, "if you talk to me, you'll feel better. It works for my sisters when they're sad. I know you have secrets you can't tell. But—"

"Even if I could tell you my secrets, I couldn't explain. There isn't any way for me to feel less overwhelmed. I'm wrong. Everything about me is wrong now. I'm not who I am. It feels like there's a loud noise in my head that keeps getting louder and louder and won't stop. Only there isn't a noise. That's just the only way I can explain what I feel. I need it to stop, but it won't. There's nothing you can do."

"I'm sorry," Mia whispered.

"I shouldn't complain about feeling this way. It'll cause trouble with . . . It's another of those secrets I'm forced to keep. I hate this."

"And sitting by the women's hearth all day isn't helping. When you were wrestling with my baby sister you forgot the noise for a moment, didn't you?"

A weak smile lifted Pyrrha's mouth, although the despair in her eyes seemed like looking into a endless pit. "You are lucky to have your sisters. I'm the only one in my . . . family."

Mia thought for a moment. "The only *child*. You have your father and—" Harmonia assumed Pyrrha's mother was dead, but while that didn't seem quite right, Pyrrha lacked mothering. "You're welcome to my sisters whenever you like. I'll share."

The smile grew slightly. "Thank you." Pyrrha sighed. "I can't go on this way, but I don't have a choice except to go on, and yet I can't." She squeezed her hands into fists. "What am I going to do?"

"I understand. At least a little. An unbearable life. I always used to run free outside to relieve the misery."

"I love to run." Pyrrha's voice came out in a wail, but then she shook her head. "I wish I could tell you what's wrong. I'm not who you think I am."

8

Mia held firmly onto Pyrrha's hand, drawing her down the corridor and into her own room. She'd brought Pyrrha's cloak, and she grabbed her own. Jarring shudders tortured the girl's body, and beads of sweat ran down her face. Soothing her friend with drinks of water and shared confidences hadn't calmed her. Pyrrha's desperate voice crying out, "I love to run," echoed in Mia's head. *Please don't let my father discover I've taken Pyrrha out of the palace. Please, by all the gods. He'll lock me in a room and never let me out.*

On the small terrace, the weak winter sun fell on Mia's shoulders. It caught the gold in Pyrrha's disheveled hair. Mia tied her mantle around her waist and then tied Pyrrha's around her friend. No more freezing cold walks.

Mia glanced at the wall and the pine tree. "Can you help me get over this wall? Onto the ledge where you caught me?" She pointed.

Pyrrha gave her a bleary look, her eyes gray like a sea fog, but she nodded. Mia drew Pyrrha forward toward the portion of wall where she'd popped away the shards.

A spark of life flashed in Pyrrha's eyes. "Stand there, and when I lift you, grasp the wall." Pyrrha pointed, and Mia stood where ordered.

The hands that grasped Mia's hips still shook, but up Mia went, feeling for a moment like a bird in flight. She braced herself by grabbing the top of the wall. With a soft grunt, Pyrrha maneuvered Mia's feet onto her shoulders and then held Mia's legs and gave her another even higher lift. Mia had no trouble swinging one leg over and straddling the wall. She sat there a little breathless, as much from the alarming distance to the small ledge as from effort.

"I don't want to fall."

"You won't." Pyrrha stepped back several paces. From Mia's elevated view, it seemed the juddering of Pyrrha's torso had softened.

Mia wondered how her friend would get up without someone to lift her. Then Pyrrha ran, flying into a leap that ended with her hands gripping the wall's top and her feet braced against its stones and mortar lower down. Pyrrha swung herself up so that she sat beside Mia.

Mia gulped and looked down. Still, was she going to regret trusting Pyrrha? She hadn't figured out why she'd been abandoned before or what so devastated her friend. "You won't leave me on the other side, no matter what?"

"I promise." Pyrrha's face had a ravaged look that undercut that surety, and when she pulled her wild hair out of her eyes and twisted it into a knot, Mia noticed her hands hadn't stopped trembling.

But the sun shone brightly enough to keep the bite out of the crisp air, and the sky arched over them in an achingly deep blue. A good day for a walk and freedom. Maybe this outing would mend her friend and be worth the risk.

Pyrrha pushed off the wall and landed directly below on the rock ledge.

Mia followed Pyrrha's commands and with a sucking-in of breath, launched herself carefully into the air. She felt heavy and awkward landing in Pyrrha's arms, clamped tight against the girl's soft breasts by those long, supple arms, but Pyrrha didn't seem to notice. She held Mia like cradling a child, although Mia didn't feel like one.

"How are you so strong?" she asked Pyrrha.

"That's who I am." Pyrrha lowered her feet to the ground.

That didn't make sense, but Mia untied her mantle and drew it around her shoulders. She gestured to Pyrrha to do the same, but Pyrrha ignored her. She headed down the stairs and goat track.

They reached an actual trail, and Pyrrha turned back. "Maybe the noise in my head will stop if I run at my fastest until I can't go anymore. I've never reached that limit."

"Don't hurt yourself." Mia hadn't intended that hard a run.

But Pyrrha took off. Mia ran after her, but the gap between them increased fast.

Running might be what Pyrrha needed, but she'd chosen the worst possible path, the main one running between the palace and, eventually, the shore far below. Soon she'd run by the area where the slope had been terraced for an olive grove, and the king's men used the leveled ground there to practice with bows, swords, and javelins amid the trees. On a clear day like this, it would be full of her father's men.

Mia called out "Stop! Not that way!" but Pyrrha didn't respond.

"I hope you're enjoying your running," Mia muttered under her breath. "It's going to cost us our freedom."

Ahead, the trail wound around a rocky outcrop, disappeared from view as it dropped sharply, and became a long set of steps, after which lay the practice field. The soldiers couldn't miss Pyrrha flying by.

Mia shouted, "Get off the main trail."

Pyrrha sped on, her feet a blur of motion, but she veered off the trail and soared over a low shrub that lay in her way, cutting down the slope without the benefit of a trail. Mia sucked in a gasp, more worried now that Pyrrha would fall and kill herself. Further down the steep drop, two goats watched as they yanked up mouthfuls of thyme.

Pyrrha waved one hand toward the outcrop. A breeze carried her words, "Wait for me there."

Mia watched Pyrrha's pathless progress, her body so beautiful in motion that Mia forgave her. Mia climbed to a nook she'd discovered long ago that would hide her from anyone passing on the trail below. She found Pyrrha's movement and kept track of where her friend headed. If the stubborn girl ran until she couldn't anymore, Mia might have to find her.

Mia leaned against the bumpy perch, her legs folded. It had been too long since she'd scanned the landscape from this spot, the mountain slope around her, crisscrossed by narrow trails, the white shoreline arcing below, and the translucent sea, all surmounted by an azure sky. Behind her, the palace and citadel clung to the bare rock of the mountain's topmost layer. She could feel the presence of those stone walls keeping watch above the landscape.

Pyrrha disappeared when she reached where the trail dropped below the cliff's edge to the shoreline, but Mia watched the distant sand and after a while she saw what she first took to be a bird skimming along the shore, but realized that the flying speck must be Pyrrha, and then, even that speck grew too small to see.

Mia wrapped her cloak around her and looked out over the sea. Islets poked up, hardly more than piles of rocks not far off the shore. She'd seen them up close when her mother had taken the girls sailing in the small royal boat her father used to visit other parts of the island. Skilled servants had handled the craft, men who'd grown up the sons of fishermen. The trips were for fresh air, her mother had claimed, but Mia felt the call of the openness on the water, and she'd seen the happiness in her mother's face each time she turned it into the wind.

Now she tried to imagine another island, bigger than Skyros she supposed—however the island of Peparethos might look—and she sought what her mother's life was like there. But she couldn't bring herself to picture the people who now surrounded her mother and whether they laughed or cried. A tear rolled down her face. She dashed it away with an angry brush of her fingers.

Mia wanted to do more than sit and wait, but remarkably soon, Mia caught glimpses of Pyrrha's movement through the shrubs and rocks as she climbed the spur's seaside slope and neared the outcrop where Mia sat.

Mia thought she'd fool Pyrrha for a moment by staying hidden up in the nook and only calling out to her friend when she looked for her, but Pyrrha climbed straight for the nook and crouched down in front of her, drawing in great gulps of air, but looking relaxed. "This outdoor palace is smaller than the forest one." She stood and looked out.

"You remembered." Mia pushed up to stand beside her friend. "This one has a good view."

Pyrrha's arms hung calmly at her sides, no shaking. Her cheeks were rosy with fresh air.

"You feel better, don't you?" Mia asked. "Have you run yourself to exhaustion?"

Pyrrha took one more deep breath and rolled her shoulders. "It wouldn't be fair to you if I ran that long, but I do feel better. Let's walk that way." Pyrrha pointed to where the main path beckoned.

"No! That leads to the soldiers' practice area." In the past Mia had snuck close to the practice terraces and watched her father's men. It was very entertaining, especially the naked wrestling. She assumed they hadn't seen her or didn't care. Back then it hadn't mattered much. "We can't go there now. I promised my father I'd stay inside the palace."

"Soldiers practicing?" Pyrrha smiled. "Trust me. They won't see us. It's been so—" She took off, but she did reach out a hand to Mia.

"This is a bad idea." Mia hurried to keep up.

"Do your father's men practice with spears?"

"Sometimes, I think. Mostly swords."

"So you've watched them before."

"Well, yes, but—"

"I can move through the undergrowth without startling a deer. They won't notice us."

Mia was so taken aback at this assertion that she fell silent.

Pyrrha pulled her off the path. "I'll show you. Crouch lower." They moved slowly behind a screen of thorny burnet, mastic bushes, and rocks. Mia had to clutch the folds of her skirt in one hand, exposing her legs. Harmonia would be horrified.

Mia studied what lay ahead, trying to guess where Pyrrha would draw her next as they gradually followed a circuitous downward route toward the olive terraces. As best she could, she imitated her friend's light, soundless movements, imagining herself as a breeze fluttering around the rocks and through the leaves. Then Pyrrha drew Mia next to her and opened her mouth to speak but then shut it.

"Yes?" Mia whispered.

"Err . . . I—" Pyrrha stopped.

Mia crouched uncomfortably, waiting. Finally she whispered, "Say whatever it is you're trying to get out."

Pyrrha rolled her shoulders. "It's hard to say."

"Will it be hard for me to hear?"

Pyrrha shook her head. "I need to apologize for leaving you the other day."

"You do."

Pyrrha laughed softly.

Mia liked the sound of it. "I'm glad you can laugh now."

"The running. Thank you. How did you know?"

"I didn't."

"Anyway. I'm sorry. About leaving you."

"I'm not really angry anymore." Mia paused. "A little hurt."

"I would have felt hurt," Pyrrha said. "I didn't mean to run off and leave you. I want to be friends. You're the only person here who's any fun. And you were the only one who cared when I . . ." Pyrrha shrugged.

Mia brushed aside the last part with a smile and wave of one hand.

Just then, heavy footsteps pounded toward them. They weren't far from the trail, screened from it only by some patchy oak branches and tall dead stalks of grass. Pyrrha drew Mia even farther down, but the man who jogged by turned his gaze to their hiding place. Mia caught a frown forming on his face. She recognized him as one of her father's messengers. *Gods, why now on this trail?* Her heart pounded so hard he might hear it.

The royal messenger's steps slowed for a moment, but then he raced on.

Once he'd gone, Mia whispered, "Thank the gods, he must not have seen us."

Pyrrha's lips puckered. "I think he pretended he didn't see you."

"Why? None of my father's men would ignore his orders like that."

"For you?" Pyrrha shrugged. "They know he locks you in, and it didn't used to be that way. I'm guessing they sympathize." She drew them farther away where they could stand upright to talk without being seen. "By the way, I really mean it. I'm sorry. I shouldn't have run off. I'm miserable here, but none of that is your fault. You are the one good thing about being stuck here."

"Thank you, I guess." Were those kisses part of what Pyrrha liked? It had seemed so, and then Pyrrha broke away suddenly, and it hadn't.

"You're pretty and I like you. A lot. But . . ."

Now she'd say it. All the reasons to dislike Mia. Would she have even more reasons than Mia's father?

"But what?" Mia asked.

"But no more kisses or . . . It isn't you. It's me. I don't know how to explain."

"Like the noise that isn't a noise? I never did anything like kisses before. My only friends were my sisters. I didn't even know about . . . things like that. You started it. You knew all about that kind of kisses and what you did when you unpinned my peplos. So, if you don't want to do things like that, don't. But don't start and then run away. No one loves me, but I try to forget that sometimes. It hurts less."

"No one—wait, of course your family loves you. You are the favorite among your sisters."

"No, I'm not. No one can forgive what I did to my mother."

Pyrrha stopped as if she'd bumped into a wall. She stared straight ahead. Mia held her breath. She hadn't meant to say that. She would never talk about her mother with anyone. Why had those terrible words come out?

Pyrrha drew in a slow breath. Her gaze remained disconnected. "You know what it's like to have a mother who's absent."

That wasn't at all what she'd expected Pyrrha to say. She felt guilty at the relief that poured through her. Pyrrha crouched low again, and they approached the far side of one of the terraces.

Ahead of them, men's shouts and the clanking of practice weapons rang out. Pyrrha tugged Mia into the cover of a cluster of junipers and oak that edged the olive grove.

She and Pyrrha lay on their stomachs under one of the oaks that was more shrub than tree even with a gnarled trunk. The spiky leaves prickled Mia's neck as they watched two men sword fighting.

"You're sure they won't notice us here?" Mia asked.

Pyrrha waved a hand dismissively. Mia didn't like that, but the scene before her grabbed her attention.

Both men wore short chiton tunics pinned on the left only, with the right shoulder exposed, leaving their sword arms unimpeded. Despite the cool day, they both glistened with sweat as they darted forward and back, landing blows with stout wooden swords.

One was a head taller than the other and broader in the shoulders. His legs had the look of tree trunks—if trees had bulging muscles that rippled and shifted in the sunlight. The smaller man, who couldn't be much older than Mia, had the advantage of greater agility and speed. So far he'd dodged any big blows. Mia liked the look of him, even with his brown curls plastered by sweat around his face. His hair would be more appealing fluttering dry through her fingers. His smooth chest contrasted with the hairiness of the big man, whose mat of fur and barrel chest made him look part bear.

When she'd watched soldiers secretly before, she'd been excited by their brawn and vigor. As that sensation arose now, it seemed confusedly similar to the draw of Pyrrha's embraces against soft breasts and tender lips. Doubly so with Pyrrha lying in the dried grasses beside her.

Mia stole a peek at Pyrrha, whose eyes followed the men's movements, saying, "The smaller man is more fun to watch. He's not as swollen with big muscles, but he moves like a dancer, feet and arms in harmony. He's no good at hitting a big man with a sword as far as I can tell, but I'm guessing his arms would feel good around me."

"I agree." Pyrrha's tongue flicked over her lips. "The leaner man has plenty of muscle for me. Look at his calf. Like intertwined ropes." She glanced at Mia. "I liked kissing you the other day. Breasts are—" Pyrrha held her breath for a moment and then sighed in a way that sounded like pleasure. "But men's bodies are even better."

Mia looked at the young man she found so appealing. "They're supposed to be, aren't they?" Was this the answer to Pyrrha's abrupt breaking off from their kisses? "I'm not the first girl you've kissed, though, am I?" There'd been a sureness to Pyrrha's kisses, a familiarity she certainly couldn't have gotten with a man. They'd have husbands soon enough, but not yet. What they'd done was fun. She'd like to do more of it. She was sure Pyrrha had also enjoyed it, despite whatever distressed her. "You like it, don't you?"

Pyrrha was silent, her attention seemingly on the two sword fighters.

Mia touched Pyrrha's arm and raised an eyebrow in question. Pyrrha blushed and dropped her gaze, her long lashes veiling the green intensity of her eyes. "I like *you*, very much."

That wasn't quite what she'd asked. "Watching men's bodies is a little like drinking too much wine." Mia poked Pyrrha in the arm.

Pyrrha's mouth twitched in a smile. "I do like wine." She pointed. "Watch when his chiton flips up. I can almost feel my fingers running over *those* muscles."

Mia swallowed. Did Pyrrha mean his thigh and that delightfully sculpted butt? She couldn't have experience with . . . "Something to look forward to when our fathers choose husbands for us — providing they're not built like that bear."

A puzzled look passed across Pyrrha's face for a moment. "Ah yes, husbands." She turned to Mia. "Will your father force you to marry some ugly old man?"

"Not old—or not very old. He needs a prince who can succeed him on Skyros's throne. So young and probably smart, or able to trick my father into thinking he's smart, but I don't think my father will care what the man looks like."

"These men are terrible fighters. Will you show me some of the farms?" Pyrrha asked.

"Farms?" That was a surprise.

"I know it will bring us closer to people and maybe trouble, but I'm curious."

"About what?"

Pyrrha looked at her with astonishment. Apparently, the fascination of farms was supposed to be obvious to her.

"There are some at the base of the mountain, aren't there?" Pyrrha wriggled backwards and then crouched low as she moved away from the practice field.

Mia had to follow. "By the plain there's a cluster of farms and their village called Seaview. The farms won't be impressive. My whole life I've heard my father gripe about the lazy farmers who don't produce enough to keep the island fed."

Pyrrha's green eyes darkened like the sea at dusk. "It doesn't seem likely that every farmer is lazy, does it?"

Mia stopped short. She ran through the words she'd said. *Her father's words.* She thought of her servants and how varied they were. How different her *sisters* were. Of course it wasn't likely that every farmer was negligent. She ran a few steps to catch up. Now *she* was curious. "Let's go look." After a few more steps, she asked, "Do you know what a good farm or a lazy farm looks like?"

Pyrrha laughed. "We'll have to see, won't we?"

"But let's avoid the village, right?"

Pyrrha ignored her request.

They followed a narrow footpath protected by the arching branches of plane trees down through the river valley toward the broad triangle of plain the stretched to the shore. The shielding hillsides broke the cold wind that had batted at them on the heights.

Winter sun warmed Mia's shoulders. "Did the woodsman you mentioned also teach you about farms?" She wanted to know why Pyrrha thought about farms at all.

"No. My father did. Farmers are important to kingdoms. He travels around talking to them."

"And he brought you?"

"Of course." Then Pyrrha's lips pressed together. She sighed. "My father treats me differently than yours does."

Mia tried to imagine visiting farmers with her father. She couldn't even imagine her father going alone.

Even without visiting, her father knew how much or little the farmers grew by what he stored each year. The palace steward oversaw each seasonal intaking. She'd watched the bustling entertainment as farmers delivered their portion of the crops through the citadel gates, sometimes loaded on donkeys, sometimes on their own backs. She'd learned early on princesses did not ask questions about such things, but she figured out what was going on.

Her father stored much of the grains, olive oil, and other food stuffs the farmers produced to keep them safe within the citadel's fortification walls. That way, no pirates or raiders could strip Skyros of its food without a major invasion. She'd heard a lot about pirates and raiders from listening to her father's conversations at feasts, so protecting the food made sense to her. If the villagers needed more food than what they kept for their families, the palace would have some to distribute from the storerooms.

Mia asked, "Does your father worry about raiders and pirates? Mine keeps his stores of crops inside the citadel walls."

Pyrrha nodded. "Any king keeps his wealth inside his walls, but it would be a foolish raider who attacked my father's lands. My father is still a formidable warrior."

They came to the top of a small rise and below them lay a field of winter wheat, pale and small now as the plants waited for the warm spring days to burst into growth. Other fields held only dirt and a few weeds, plowed in rows ready for seed. Off to their right further on, the village called Seaview lay behind a scraggly wood that protected the huts from the wind and sun. Smoke from cooking fires rose above the stunted trees.

"The village for these fields is over there?" Pyrrha pointed.

Mia nodded, but hoped examining farms didn't mean they'd go to the village. When the tall girl loped along the edge of a field, away from Seaview, Mia followed with relief.

On the far side of the field, the land rose gently up along one of the foothills framing the plain. The gray leaves and pale trunks of an olive grove covered this hilly part. Pruning had formed each tree into a similar height, low enough for harvesting the olives. The trees had been spaced so that the branches nearly touched, using the hillside to the fullest.

She scanned the orchard and surrounding fields. "I don't think a lazy farmer works here." She flashed a smile and shrug of apology. "My father should probably visit his farmers."

A sawing sound wafted across the orchard. Someone was pruning. She was about to suggest they move away when a great crack rang out, a panicked shout, and a scream of pain.

Pyrrha set off toward the scream at a fast pace.

"We shouldn't be seen here," Mia called out, but Pyrrha didn't slow.

Mia fell way behind. Pyrrha flew over clods of dirt, gliding around olive trees. Mia stumbled. Her chest hurt from trying to breathe. Finally, farther up in the olive grove, she saw Pyrrha crouched next to a man lying entangled in a fallen branch.

Mia slowed, wanting nothing to do with this peasant and his accident. He would do whatever was usually done without interference from Pyrrha or her. She wanted to draw Pyrrha away before the man saw her, the princess, out in the fields, a bit of gossip that could make her life miserable.

Pyrrha looked up. "Come here. I need your help."

Mia sighed and approached. "We shouldn't be here." Then she looked down. To her horror the man's side was soaked red with blood. Her gaze skidded away and landed on his face and his eyes wide with fear. His jaw clamped tight with pain.

"Lucky we were near," Pyrrha answered. "His saw must have slipped when the branch gave way. He landed on it." The man groaned. "A deep wound." She pulled off her mantle and folded a corner of it into a thickness of layers.

The man's eyes darted between the two girls. Did he guess who Mia was, or could he even think through the pain? Entrusting his life to two girls wouldn't be reassuring no matter who he thought she was.

Mia knelt. So much blood made her head swim. Pyrrha took a small piece of linen from the pouch at her belt. Was the girl applying her healing skills, the ones she acquired from the mysterious woodsman her father let her visit?

Mia said, "I can't help with this. I don't know how."

"You must." Pyrrha packed the linen into the wound and then pressed the ragged edges of skin together with her palms. The wounded man bellowed in pain.

Mia's vision dimmed and spun.

"I'll show you what to do," Pyrrha insisted. "Just while I run for help."

"Don't leave me alone with—" Her head was still swimming. She couldn't be alone with the blood and a strange man.

"We need others to carry him to the village. Much faster if I go, and I know what to bring back. Take my mantle. Keep the corner folded like I have it. Press it over the wound. I'll slide my hands out as you do. Press hard or he'll bleed to death."

"I—"

"Don't argue. It's a man's life. You owe care to your people."

Mia's hands shook as she brought the cloak down on the man's torn flesh. Pyrrha moved her hands away gradually.

Pyrrha quickly wiped her hands on an unused part of the cloak and then braced her hands over Mia's, showing her how hard to press and explaining that any letting up would kill him.

"Do you understand what to do?"

Mia nodded shakily.

Then Pyrrha rose and seemed to launch into flight like a bird. Her feet skimmed the ground as she sped in the direction of the village.

With her departure, the man closed his eyes, gasping in each painful breath. With the wound covered, this task wasn't so horrifying. She was grateful Pyrrha had told her to lean forward and use her own weight to press down so her arms wouldn't give out. How did Pyrrha know these things?

Mia had wanted to argue that she should go—she knew the way to Seaview best—but that would have been foolish. Like Pyrrha's absurd strength, her speed far surpassed any running Mia had seen. Dione's words "like a god," describing the lady who brought Pyrrha, came back to her. Were Pyrrha's abilities beyond mortal? Then she remembered the silliness of Pyrrha's bare bottom sticking up in the air as she play-wrestled with Bura. Pyrrha had an enticingly extraordinary body, but she was just a girl, more or less like Mia. Gods and mortals only mixed in stories. Mia told herself to stay sensible.

She shifted her weight slightly, and the man groaned. She straightened back to the exact way Pyrrha had shown her. Her arms felt shaky.

It wouldn't be long. Not too long. Bossy Pyrrha would yell out what was needed the moment she reached Seaview and confused villagers would follow her orders. They should. Pyrrha knew what to do, that much was clear. Mia's lips twitched in a fleeting smile. Giving orders from knowledge was a good way for a woman to take command and make people listen.

Mia needed to learn how to do a lot more things than she had so far been taught. Pyrrha might be a good teacher.

The man groaned again, but she hadn't moved at all. She closed her eyes in panic but forced herself to look down at her hands pressing Pyrrha's cloak. Bright red seeped through the folds and a sticky wetness began to coat her fingers. Another groan gurgled from the man. Her gaze leapt to his face and its ashen pallor with staring eyes that saw nothing.

Was he dead? The panic she'd been holding down flooded through her, making her lightheaded. *No!* She forced herself to draw in a shaky breath and focused on the man's chest where a weak rise and fall still showed. She felt small and unskilled, but she pressed hard.

"Please come back, Pyrrha. Now. This man needs you."

9

Sticky blood covered Mia's hands, but she shifted her weight experimentally against the folds of Pyrrha's cloak, and gradually the bright red seeping around her fingers slowed. Her arms burned with exhaustion, but pressing was the only help she could offer him. *Please come soon, Pyrrha. He's dying.*

She glanced through the close-packed olive trees. Patches of sunlight mottled the rough ground underneath the gray branches, but nobody came running. An ominous silence cloaked the orchard, broken only by the man's irregular, fading breaths.

It was easier not to look at his face, but she made herself check on him. His blank gaze focused when her eyes met his. She offered a slow nod to reassure him. But that gesture was a lie.

Whenever she couldn't bear the burn in her arms, she focused on the blood covering her hands and pictured the wound below. *Please do not die. Hold on until help comes.* His eyes had closed and relieved her of returning his gaze.

Finally, a loud group of men and women hurried toward her with Pyrrha in the lead. They brought a litter. Pyrrha knelt by Mia and to her relief released her from the job of pressing on the wound. Mia stood up and stepped outside the clustered villagers, wiping her bloody fingers on her handkerchief. She felt shy among these farmers, although the presence of women reassured her. She wanted to catch Pyrrha's attention and slip away, but two men lifted the injured man from the ground, and Pyrrha wrapped a length of linen tightly around his middle over the wound.

When four men picked up the litter and set out, Pyrrha went with them without looking back for Mia. Mia hurried to her side, whispering, "Shouldn't we leave? He'll be cared for now."

Pyrrha's brows drew together as if the idea hadn't occurred to her. "There's much more to do. I can't leave him now."

"Won't the villagers do those things?"

"Not what I can do. You go if you wish, but I am staying for now."

Mia frowned. This was another abandonment. She couldn't get over the wall by herself. "I can't go without you, *if* you remember."

"Oh." Pyrrha took Mia's hand. "Sorry. Of course. I think we can persuade the villagers to keep quiet about seeing us, and we'll get back before we're missed at the evening meal." She looked down into Mia's eyes. "It's a man's life. To live or die."

Mia felt uncomfortable. She hadn't meant to be selfish. If Pyrrha could save him and these farmers could not, then they'd stay.

Pyrrha rejoined the men carrying the litter, her gaze intent on the wounded man. It stung to have no role here, but Mia understood. Instead, she looked around, feeling guilty at how intrigued she was to walk into the village. As they passed one of the huts, winter sunlight fell through its open door, and she glimpsed a single room with fleece pallets rolled against a wall, a small hearth, and a few stools, baskets, and pots as its sparse furnishings. Such a small collection of belongings would fit in one of her clothing chests.

Pyrrha followed the litter into another hut—the man's home, Mia assumed—and immediately a woman's wails filled the air. Pyrrha didn't call for Mia, and the small hut looked overcrowded, so Mia stayed outside—the only helpful thing she could do.

In previous walks, Mia had spied the clustered mud-brick huts from a distance, their low roofs of mud, reeds, and branches blending into the landscape. Now she noticed an open area of hardened dirt in the middle of Seaview with three cooking hearths and a mounded communal oven at one side. The smells of wood smoke and stewed barley mingled in the air.

Several spindly-limbed children stared with frightened eyes at the activity of adults fetching water and whatever else treating such a wound required. Mia crouched down near them. *I can comfort children.* She smiled at a toddler dressed in a rag of a chiton. She peered more closely—a clean and patched rag. No warm cloak or wool wrap despite the chilly day. Bare feet. At her smile, the little boy—he seemed to be a boy child—reached for the hand of the taller child next to him.

A woman came near and put a protective hand on the boy's head. He hid in her skirts.

Mia rose. "Your child has a sweet face."

"Thank you, my lady," answered the woman, bowing her head. "I'm Kissa. You come from the palace?"

Mia groaned inwardly. "Yes, we were taking a walk, but we aren't supposed to be out in the countryside like that alone. Perhaps—"

"Good thing you were," Kissa said. "The other lady you were walking with knows about keepin' a wounded man alive. This and that she ordered us to get ready. Like a healer. Do you noble girls get taught such things?"

"I haven't. It isn't usual, I think, but families differ."

"She's not family, a sister? Pardon me, you're the princess, aren't you? An honor." Kissa bowed again.

Mia nodded. No point in lying. But both Pyrrha's secret presence and Mia's future freedom were at risk. "I'm glad my friend has been able to help, but word of our . . . er . . . visit will cause trouble."

A smile broke out on the woman's face. "Ah, I see. You won't remember me, but you and your mother the queen come upon my daughter crying over a broken water jug. You had your servant run to the spring and bring one of the palace's. I still have it. Things like that keep along among people. There are other little stories. People love you. I'll keep quiet for you."

Mia nodded again. "Thank you. My father the king didn't give permission for our walk."

"It's not just me. No one from Seaview will tell. We see you walkin' about in the woods and there by the sea often enough. But for our men to be near you—that's danger. Our king is careful of his princess—as a good father must be." The last was added hastily.

"I hadn't considered it like that," Mia said. "I didn't mean to cause trouble for you. He is just as protective of my friend. Such things are hard to keep out of gossip." Mia waved a hand toward the hut where Pyrrha was doing unusual healing for a noblewoman.

Kissa nodded. "We'd never want to offend the king."

"His temper is easily roused," Mia said, only meaning to say something sympathetic, but it came out wrong.

The woman's eyebrows lifted. "He is the king."

Mia almost choked. What a lot was implied in that simple statement. She smiled. "I understand." They needed to get away from this difficult subject. Mia peered into a clay pot resting on a tripod over coals in the nearest fire. "What are you cooking?"

"You're hungry?" the woman asked.

"No. That wasn't what I meant." Mia felt an embarrassed flush rise on her face. She looked at the scrawny children scattered around them, who had shifted their focus onto her. "I wouldn't want to take your children's dinner."

"You wouldn't like it anyway," Kissa said with bitterness in her voice.

"Why is that? Aren't there good cooks among you? Surely there are." Mia tried to put a touch of humor into her tone.

"You need enough for good cookin'. It's winter."

That stopped Mia. Obviously, winter limited the available foods, but these villagers should have enough of the foods they'd put aside. "Didn't you store up for winter?"

Kissa gave her a sour look. "Put away all we could."

"Isn't that enough?" Mia said. "The palace protects the food the villagers bring there for storage."

"Plenty for you. Best go back now. Your friend's comin'."

Pyrrha, accompanied by two men, walked toward them.

Mia said, "We will go to keep trouble from you and your menfolk, but first tell me." She swept a hand over the gathered children. "The palace distributes food when needed in the winter, doesn't it? Do the farmers not grow enough? The children look thin, much thinner than my sisters."

Pyrrha hurried to Mia's side.

Kissa greeted the tall girl with a bow of her head and then said to Mia, "We work hard as we can. You see what you see. Scrawny young'uns. That'll answer you."

Mia peered more closely into the nearby pot. A watery barley stew with some bits of onion and what looked like parsnip. None of the other fires had pots going. This one pot would be meager if it was intended for all the villagers. She was intruding and should drop these questions, but instead she asked, "Did you prepare this stew for both your family and the other families? Or yours alone?"

Pyrrha gave her a puzzled look. Was it really such a strange question?

"All that food?" the woman asked. "It's winter, Princess. You go along, you and your friend. Thank you for the healing." Her head tipped toward the hut where the injured man lay.

Pyrrha took Mia's hand. "We should go. I've spoken to the men. No word will come to the palace."

"Yes, I had a similar conversation here." Mia tucked her head respectfully to the woman. "Thank you for talking with me. There are many things I need to learn."

A surprised look flitted over Kissa's face. "You're the princess."

Mia knew what she meant, but she corrected that idea. "A princess can learn from her people."

"We are late returning," Pyrrha murmured. "I'm sorry. It's my fault, but let's hurry." She drew Mia into a walk on the verge of a run.

Mia watched the rough ground so she wouldn't stumble despite their pace.

"Why were you talking about how much food she was preparing?" Pyrrha asked.

"I didn't intend to. At first, to make polite conversation, I asked what she was cooking."

"An idle enough question."

"Not to that woman. I don't think they have enough food—which doesn't make sense to me. They put aside part of their harvest for winter, and another part comes to the citadel for safe storage so there's never a shortage no matter what happens."

"This may be a hard winter after an especially poor harvest," Pyrrha said, "something that can't be helped for now."

Mia thought about that. "No. During the ingathering, I heard both the steward and my father say this year was a good harvest. My father was especially pleased by the abundance of grain. He said his plans were going well. Something about new storage pits. If there's not enough this winter, it's a deeper problem than this year's harvest."

"Perhaps your father is right. Even if the farmers aren't lazy, they should grow more. If he added new storage pits, perhaps he's encouraging them to, but they haven't yet."

"That woman didn't think it was the farmers' fault." Mia scanned the rocky path ahead of them. "But she wouldn't be likely to, would she?"

"There's only so much a group of villagers like that can grow."

Tripping on a loose stone on the path, Mia nearly lost her footing but managed to catch herself by grabbing Pyrrha's elbow. Her mind was back with the starving children. "Seems like parents, some of them at least, would do whatever they could for their children. I would. This isn't something they can solve easily."

Pyrrha took Mia's arm and tucked it against her own. "You hint to visitors how barren Skyros is."

Mia let out a sour laugh at that reminder. "I do tell them that." She leaned against Pyrrha, letting her friend draw her forward. "It's only repeating what I've heard my father grumble about."

"Well, maybe this island can't always feed its people."

"Maybe." They were climbing out of the river valley onto the spur. Mia glanced at the citadel walls high above. The guards visible on the tower were dark, unrecognizable silhouettes to her eye. Were she and Pyrrha equally indistinct to them?

"Kings acquire food from other kingdoms when there are shortages," Pyrrha said. "But they have to trade for it with something, the promise of soldiers, woven goods, copper or silver—that sort of thing."

Mia looked up in surprise at what Pyrrha understood about her father's rule. "My father welcomes trade as much as he can, but I only hear him complaining about how little he has." She had avoided her father's court, but not entirely. She'd heard him trying to wring a lot from others and offer the meager things Skyros produced in exchange. Boring and annoying, she'd thought, but not to Pyrrha, it seemed.

"A kingdom's crops and trade require balance," Pyrrha said. "Too small a harvest one year, raids, the loss of a source of trade, or too little produced by the royal workshops, anything can tip the kingdom into trouble. If something like that happened here, then neither the farmers nor your father may be able to right it. Children go hungry."

"Like a ship under full sail that founders in too much wind," Mia said. "Or is becalmed by no wind at all."

"Deadly either way." Pyrrha shrugged.

Mia imagined the island of Skyros as a ship, sails filled with winds of crops, amphoras of oil and wine, the farmers' labor, the products of the palace looms and metal workshops, and the success or failure of her father's negotiations with traders and other kingdoms. A complicated balance. These were familiar parts of her daily life, but she'd never considered them together, nor questioned how they worked—or seen herself with a purpose in their midst.

She wrinkled her nose. The tapestry she'd nearly finished floated in her mind with its image of a ship. That was a pirates' ship, but now that she'd pictured her island kingdom as a ship, she shivered at the monster she'd woven, rising to destroy the ship.

10

The sun was low on the horizon as Mia scrambled up the trail along the spur a few steps behind Pyrrha. She struggled to keep up with the tall girl—and not just with her fast-paced walking. Her friend understood so much more than she did about kingdoms. Envy was an ugly thing to give in to, but she had to admit to the feeling, at least to herself.

"Do you talk with your father about crops and trade and such things?" Mia felt timid asking Pyrrha. "Did he teach you about them?"

Her friend's lips pressed together, losing their lush bow shape. Her gaze went far away to another place. The land of her secrets. Mia muttered an apology.

Pyrrha shook her head. "It's not that. I just don't . . . It's different for me, but I do talk with my father in ways you haven't."

"I wish I could ask my father to explain why there isn't food for those children." She stepped around a protruding thorny burnet. Its branches formed a spiked maze of needles that would draw blood at the lightest touch. "I'd like to understand it as he does, but at best he'd tell me to be a proper princess and attend to what Lady Harmonia teaches me."

"At worst?"

"He'd have one more thing to be angry at me about. I am never the person he wants me to be."

Pyrrha frowned. "He doesn't know who you are."

That confused Mia. Her father knew her *too* well.

Mia panted from the speedy climb upwards. The angled light cast long shadows that darkened the trail and distorted the shapes of the bushes on either side. Mia's skirt caught on something sharp, pitching her toward the ground. Pyrrha twisted backwards in a leap and caught Mia before she hit and tumbled. "Hurt?"

"No." Mia looked down the steep slope. "Thanks to you."

They'd reached the crest of the spur and the well-trodden trail, where they were most visible. Mia's chest tightened. She tipped back her head to see the citadel walls and the guards keeping watch on them at the top of the mountain. She didn't want to be caught and stopped from slipping outside again. There was too much to learn.

"How clearly do you think those guards can see us?" she asked.

With a grunt, Pyrrha ducked under a holm oak branch and guided them parallel to the trail under the cover of bushes and low trees.

Pyrrha looked like she wanted to say something but was holding back. It didn't seem like friends should be so hesitant to be honest with each other, but then Mia considered how many things about her mother she never spoke of with her sisters. "What do you want to say to me?"

Surprise flickered across Pyrrha's face. "Just an idea. Your palace steward probably knows as much as your father about food and the villages. Ask him about it. Why shouldn't you understand this?" She held out her hand to help Mia up a gravelly, steep part. It wasn't easy climbing off the trail.

"I suppose."

She'd known Galene, the steward, her whole life. He was polite to her and didn't mind when she and her maid watched the bringing in of the harvest, although he was so busy he paid her little attention, and he'd avoided the few questions she'd asked.

"I could speak to our steward, but Galene's not much for talking to me, and I think it will sound like I'm finding fault with my father—asking about his starving people." She looked up into Pyrrha's eyes and wrinkled her nose. "He'd likely tell my father what I asked." She shrugged. "If Galene would answer me fully, making my father angry might not be so bad, but I don't think he will. He won't think it's his place, not at the risk of angering the king."

Some cautious steps got her up the next steep stretch. Her eyes flicked to the dark palace walls above them.

Pyrrha's gaze also focused on the palace walls. "Maybe it's best to leave it. I suppose it doesn't matter whether you know."

"Maybe not." But it should. She'd seen Pyrrha use knowledge. Her father didn't want his people to go hungry, but he hadn't prevented it. However complicated the problem was, he blamed it on laziness and ignored it. Or maybe that was only what he said in front of her. There were the new storage pits and plans he'd mentioned. Maybe he did not know how desperate the villagers were. If he did, he would provide more food. He wouldn't like her interference, though. "I wish I had a way to convince Galene he shouldn't report our conversation to my father. I suspect that's what it would take for him to speak openly. For today, we'll be lucky if no one brought the king word we are missing. We stayed out way too long."

They reached the place to turn upwards on the barely visible goat path that cut upwards toward her courtyard wall, the hardest part of the climb.

"At least the citadel watch can't see us here," Mia muttered through her panting.

Pyrrha made a low murmur of agreement and added, "Yes, but there's probably still a guard stationed to watch this trail. I wish I knew where he is in his rotation. We'll have to be quick." Pyrrha grabbed Mia's waist and propelled her upwards on the trail at an alarming speed. Mia didn't look at the unbroken drop below them.

They continued their climb, and in the growing dusk, Mia could see not too far above, the blocks of stone of her courtyard. Then she heard a scrabbling sound nearby, too large and awkward to be a goat or deer. Her heart sped up. She dared a glance down. A guard moved toward them. "We've been caught."

Pyrrha nodded. "Yes, I thought we might outrun him, but we didn't. Let me talk to him."

The guard caught up to them, standing just behind on the narrow track. "Princess. Please let me help you."

Shame overwhelmed Mia, the humiliation of being brought again before her father, dirty and bedraggled and hated.

Pyrrha turned to face the man. Mia sighed and carefully edged herself around.

The guard bowed. "Princess. Lady. It's my duty to escort you back safely. This is not the trail to the palace entrance. Please come with me."

"We are glad for your assistance," Pyrrha said. "Tell me, did you notice us during your rotation on this track or were you sent by orders from within the palace or citadel?"

"I was taking my turn patrolling this part of the mountain and spotted the princess and you. Since the other day, our orders are to keep good watch on you here."

"So you haven't sent word to the king as yet?"

The guard looked suspicious about these questions, but he shook his head. Mia brushed off a twig that clung to her skirt and considered what Pyrrha was up to.

Pyrrha continued, "You're supposed to keep a good watch on the princess and me? Those were the orders?"

"Yes, my lady. But—"

"Then the princess and I will help you hide your failure to follow orders." She paused. "We'll keep you from being punished as the guards on watch were the other day." *That* surprised Mia. Punishment for the *guards*? For her misbehavior? And how did Pyrrha know about this unfairness by her father? "That's what happened, isn't it?"

"They didn't keep watch well enough." The guard's sullen tone undermined his defense of her father's action. "The princess must be kept safe."

She *was* safe around the island. Her father had admitted as much to her. He only cared about keeping Pyrrha hidden.

Pyrrha nodded. "A respectful answer. But consider this. Those guards escorted the princess in through the main gate where everyone could see. They must have thought they were following orders."

"Lady? I am following orders."

"You have found us as we *return*. You did not notice and stop us from going *out* as you were ordered to. Bring us in the main gate and you will be punished, both you and the others on watch this afternoon. Instead, I have a better idea of where to safely escort us. You will truly be doing your duty."

"I don't—"

Pyrrha pointed to the courtyard wall above us. "Escort us to the princess's garden wall where we will reenter the palace safely without the king knowing we ever slipped past your good watch. We will be safe, which is what your orders were meant to accomplish. No trouble for you."

"If the king hears, it'll be worse trouble."

"The king won't hear."

Mia stepped up to Pyrrha's side.

It was time to add her own voice. "Lady Pyrrha's idea of escorting us to my garden wall is wise. Think of the king's anger if you bring us before him as the guards did the other day. I did not realize he'd punished those men. The fault was mine, not theirs. You fear he will do the same to you. I must help you so that doesn't happen. Take us where we ask." Mia pointed upwards. The guard gave the track a skeptical look. "It's not as hard to climb as it looks. More importantly, if, by some unlikely chance, the king learns of our outing, I will ensure that he does not make you or the other men on watch pay. I am the cause of his anger and fear. I will be sure he remembers to aim it at me, not his hardworking guards." Doubt still haunted the man's face. "I am your princess. Will you trust me? I rely on you and your fellow guardsmen to fight for me, to fend off danger when it comes. In return for that loyalty, it's my duty to defend you against unfairness."

The man's eyes softened. "Me and the other guards—we don't never want to bring trouble to you, Princess. If you think this is best. We've watched you grow up from a sweet little baby with never a cross word. You're ours, and we'll keep you safe no matter what." He took a deep breath and grabbed hold of a bush to pull himself past them on the track. "Please follow me."

Pyrrha watched the man climb and then gave her an appraising look.

Mia waited for the guard to move ahead. Then she whispered, "What punishment did the guards receive? Ridiculous of my father. His men will resent him."

"They certainly don't resent you. I don't know what the king ordered. I didn't actually know he *had* punished them. I was just making a good guess because it was all I could think of. If the king wants us kept in, he must be able to rely on his guard, but you and I showed him he couldn't. Most commanders would mete out a warning punishment to tighten the watch." Pyrrha tipped her chin toward the guard. "It worked with him. I'm guessing before this, that man has seen you escape and never said a word."

Mia glanced at the guard trying not to fall off the steep goat path ahead of them. "What would you have done if you guessed wrong and there had been no punishment? And how do you know what most commanders would do?" Knowing the way soldiers thought turned out to be useful. Mia envied the way Pyrrha's father had trained her.

"It worked," Pyrrha said, as if that were an answer. "But I realize now we could have persuaded that man without the threat of punishment. You are well loved—and honored. I'd only seen hints of that before."

Mia studied the broad shoulders and gray hair of the man. She recognized this old soldier. *Loved and honored?* Why?

The guard glanced back and beckoned to them. Mia and Pyrrha continued climbing.

As they neared the wall, the guard wore a worried look. "Princess, there's no gate anymore."

"No, the king prefers tall walls. Don't worry." Mia turned toward Pyrrha.

Pyrrha put her hands around Mia's waist. "Ready?"

"Yes." Mia reached for the wall as she was hoisted upwards. With the support of her hands on the wall's top, she steadied herself as Pyrrha shifted her feet one by one onto Pyrrha's shoulders to push Mia high enough to lean her torso on the wall and swing over a leg to sit on the top of the wall.

The guard gasped.

It was quite unladylike behavior. "You won't tell the others?"

"Not a word, my princess."

Pyrrha stepped back as far as the ledge allowed and made a flying leap at the wall. The guard yelped. Mia looked down at him. "She's good at jumping, isn't she?"

"I . . . I . . . Yes, Princess."

"Good-bye and thank you. Send me word through my servant Dione if any trouble comes to you because of this. I will take care of it. You understand?"

"Yes, Princess." He bowed low. "Thank you. You can get down safely?"

"Yes. Don't worry."

Pyrrha jumped down into the garden and waited, her arms outstretched. Mia waved to the guard and pushed off toward Pyrrha's arms.

Mia caught her breath, expecting to see Harmonia's angry face staring at them from the courtyard door, but there was no sign of her.

Dione hurried out. She must have been watching for them. "I laid out a clean peplos. Also one of Lady Pyrrha's, so I can help her and the others won't know. It's late for the meal, but I told Lady Harmonia you're napping."

Pyrrha laughed. "Lady Harmonia wants to believe everything is as it should be."

They went into Mia's sleeping chamber. Mia tugged off her dirty mantle and gown and let Dione rub dirt and blood from her arms with a cloth dipped in a basin of water.

Pyrrha yanked off her clothes and quickly pulled on the clean peplos Dione had brought her. The manner of her dressing reminded Mia of Pyrrha's abruptness in the woods when Mia had unpinned her friend's gown. Pyrrha did not like her own form. And yet her body was beautiful.

Pyrrha was making a mess of tying her belt, and the folds didn't fall gracefully. Dione tsked softly, and so Mia took the wet cloth from her maid, pushing her toward Pyrrha. After placing the belt exactly so, Dione tied it firmly and arranged the dress in a seemly way.

A scan of her own bare arms and legs showed they were clean enough, and Mia ducked so Dione could slip a gown over her head and tie her belt. Then the maid took an ivory comb to Mia's hair, pulling hard on the tangles, a painful process Mia kept silent for. The snarls were her own fault.

Pyrrha untied a leather strip that held back her red-gold hair, ran her fingers through the strands, gathered it together with a twisted knot, and held it in that arrangement with the tie. The guard who'd let them jump the wall back into her courtyard had had his hair tied back like that. Maybe Pyrrha had noticed and thought she'd give the hairdo a try. It was remarkably attractive on her, despite being a man's style.

Done with her hair, Pyrrha sat on the bed watching the longer process of Dione's work on Mia. "I've been thinking," Pyrrha said. "You're respected and liked. There's a way you could persuade the steward to talk to you and not feel he should tell your father. If you still want the answers to your questions."

Mia shrugged as she adjusted the folds over her belt and pulled them even and neat. "He likes me, but that won't be enough. His loyalty is to my father, not a young princess."

"Draw part of that loyalty to you. Remind him of the future."

"What do you mean?" Mia asked.

When Pyrrha explained, Mia wanted to stuff the words back into her friend as if she'd never said them, and at the same time, the power her friend described gleamed like a bolt of lightning in the dimness of her life.

11

At the sight of her father's steward, Galene, in the doorway of the women's hall, Mia jumped to her feet, a mixture of apprehension and eagerness warring inside. His narrow shoulders and great height made him look sticklike, but that was deceiving. She'd witnessed his wiry strength in action. Gray speckled his brown hair and beard. He wore a bland expression that gave her no hints of how to start the conversation she wished to have with him.

When she'd told Dione to bring Galene her message, the maidservant had frowned and dropped her gaze. Mia had started to ask what was wrong, but Dione rushed off with a quick "Yes, Princess Mia."

What bothered her maid? Probably not the message itself—that was only a request that Mia accompany Galene to observe his duties and in this way learn the palace's workings. But Dione was Mia's closest confidante and knew the larger purpose Mia intended for this time with the steward. Mia wished she'd gotten Dione to explain because the maid knew the servants better than Mia did, even one like the steward who, as overseer of the palace and citadel storage, had influence enough to consider himself above the others.

Stepping into the women's hall, Galene bowed to her. "Princess? I'm afraid you'll find what I do very dull."

It seemed the man didn't want her company. Mia ignored that. "Not at all, Galene." She took her cloak from Dione, who'd slipped in before the steward and collected it.

Maybe Galene was worried about her father, but she'd thought of that. If the king found fault with this activity, she would tell him she was learning her future duties and containing her boredom so she could stay well-behaved even while confined to the palace. Galene had long been a reliable chaperone, provided she was also accompanied by a maidservant. Pyrrha was staying behind in the women's quarters, as commanded.

Galene cleared his throat. "Today's work is important to your father, but you'll only see stones and mud bricks. Nothing interesting to a princess."

Stones and mud bricks? "You would be surprised at what I find interesting. Will you have time to speak with me while overseeing something so important?"

"Of course, Princess. I always have time for you."

That wasn't yet true, but she liked that he said it.

Harmonia looked up, saw the steward, and nodded to Mia. On the surface, there was nothing unseemly about this adventure. Only the true contents of her intended conversation made Mia's hands clammy with sweat. She surreptitiously wiped her palms under the folds of her peplos and pulled her cloak around her shoulders. Perhaps she could learn enough simply by following Galene around as she'd said she would, without pursuing Pyrrha's strategy for gaining Galene's loyalty.

No, that would be cowardly. But she flinched when she imagined asking how it was that a village of children was starving when she had seen a good harvest stored inside the citadel. First, the steward must see his future tied to her at least as much as to her father. Pyrrha had shown her such a future. She was building an alliance, one that would extend beyond the question of her island's food.

Mia led the way, stepping past the guard at the door of the

women's quarters and starting along the dim, narrow corridor that connected the quarters to the rest of the palace. Scuffling sounds came from behind her, but when she turned to see what caused the noise, the steward fell into step with her, and Dione came along a short distance behind, adjusting her cloak. They passed the guard at the far end and continued across the royal residence by entering another, larger hallway.

She glanced at the steward, took a deep breath, and said in a quiet voice, "One of my father's greatest responsibilities as king is the safe storage of the harvests. A king must prevent famine. You are the one who oversees the intake and careful maintenance of the storage. It's a weighty responsibility, isn't it?"

Galene glanced at her with a small frown. "Yes. An honor."

"It must have taken you a long time to learn everything you needed to know to serve so well as my father's steward."

"In the beginning I made mistakes, but I learned my job quick enough for the king."

Mia smiled at him. "Father can be demanding. But now you know Skyros's villages and how much each should contribute. When need arises, you also oversee distribution of those stores. The king gives the overall orders, and you follow them with independence earned by skill and experience. I know my father trusts you greatly and with good reason."

Galene's brows drew together. "I work hard and follow the king's orders."

Perhaps she'd overdone her flattery. "Of course, but by now you must not need him to give detailed orders. You know what to do in each season—without bothering the king."

"You needn't worry. I know what to do. A princess doesn't have to understand such things." He waved one hand in a dismissive way that made Mia want to scream.

She glanced back at Dione, who lagged several steps behind, catching her maid's eye for sympathy. Dione shrugged in a way that seemed to ask, *What did you expect?*

Mia tried again. "I'm *not* worried. That isn't what I meant. I was noting your skill and how little indeed either my father or I need to worry because you have worked out how to do your many duties smoothly. Understanding how you do them is *not* too complex for me. I consider gaining such understanding as *my* duty—not that I'd interfere in what you do. I simply want to learn."

Deep furrows across Galene's brow showed wariness, the opposite of what she was trying to build with him. He murmured indistinctly. The word "princess" was the only one she could make out.

She wanted to shift his way of seeing her, not as the child he felt familiar with, but as the future queen. But also as the solid, commanding queen she'd begun to imagine, not the vague, self-effacing notion her father and Harmonia offered her, that her own mother had presented to her childish understanding.

Walls of dark cut stone surrounded them. In her legs, Mia began to feel the climb upward to the citadel. Sometimes the corridor rose along ramps, other times by stairs deep enough to strain her short legs. Deep window slits threw them into alternating pockets of shadow and dawn.

"You are very good at remembering what the king requires of you in each season. But what if someone suddenly gave very different orders?" Mia said. "Ones which you in your wisdom knew would be dangerous for the well-being of the palace and people of Skyros?"

The steward's eyes squinted in confusion. "Why would such a thing happen? Is this one of your fanciful stories?"

Mia forced a smile. "You know me well, but I'm afraid not. You're aware that soon my father will find a prince to be my husband, and that man will eventually take my father's throne?"

A small nod.

"This prince will not know Skyros's ways, but he may think he knows better ways. Such mistaken thoughts might cause him to give orders that harm my kingdom. If you help me understand how you oversee that care, then when it is time, I will guide my husband's view and give the familiar orders that have worked so well. Do you understand?"

Another small nod. Galene moved ahead of her as if to assist her farther on, but his burst of speed also broke off their conversation.

In her mind, Mia heard her own alarmed reaction to Pyrrha's devious suggestion. *Go behind my husband's back before I am even married?*

Pyrrha had laughed. "Yes, even before your father selects this husband. Take control before this unknown prince does."

"Take control?"

"Why would you let him rule *your* island without your strong influence? What if your father makes a bad choice? You called your father the keeper of choices. Why should he be the only one?"

Why indeed?

Watching Galene's back, she thought the steward might prefer to follow a prince's orders no matter how stupid. But maybe he was considering what she'd said and wouldn't be too pigheaded.

The darkness increased as they approached the end of the tunnel-like corridor that connected the palace to the citadel. Two soldiers with spears held upright in their hands stood guard, chests bound in leather armor. Behind them, the wooden postern door was distinguishable from the stone wall around it. On the other side of this small, barred door stretched an even narrower tunnel that exited underneath a watch tower within the citadel. Any enemy using the postern to break into the citadel would have to do so one man at a time from the tunnel's trap.

One of the two guards nodded to the steward and thumped the butt of his spear against the door in a rhythmic pattern that echoed against the stones like a giant's footsteps.

After a wait, from the other side, the sound of a heavy bronze-reinforced bar scraped across the door, and it swung open. The steward beckoned Mia through, and she stepped over the stone threshold, forced by the tunnel's blackness to make her way by memory more than sight. Galene called to Dione to hurry along. Dione's footsteps rang in the tunnel, and from her startled squawk she must have bumped into the steward, but Galene just laughed at this and hurried toward Mia. They neared the exit, and morning light blinded Mia as she stepped into the muddy, open courtyard of the citadel keep. When her eyes cleared, she glanced at the two guards stationed above, bows in hand. As Mia had heard many times, a single Skyran guard with a bow and quiver full of arrows could defend this diminutive doorway in the massive citadel wall.

The citadel served as the final defense for Mia's family. The first generation of kings had split the fortress from the palace to fit the necessary buildings on the forbidding lump of rock that shot sheerly up from the earth to provide an impressive natural defense. The citadel's thick fortification walls could not surround the royal residence and its throne room that perched lower on the mountain's side like an eagle ruling from its aerie. Past kings of Skyros could manage such an expenditure of stone and labor only around the citadel, enough to protect their stored wealth and to provide a place of secure refuge if the island was invaded. Mia couldn't imagine how the royal household and the island's people could all huddle inside the cramped citadel walls during an attack, but this problem had not been put to the test during her lifetime.

Standing at her side, Galene blinked in the brightness. He turned to Dione when she also exited, but the girl slipped past his offered hand and came to Mia's other side. Dione was scowling, and Mia gave her hand a squeeze, wishing again that she'd learned Dione's thoughts about the steward before she found herself here, trying to persuade him to trust her.

Mia scanned the citadel, an impressive part of the royal mountaintop that she rarely visited. Soldiers stood on duty along the top of the walls, which were made from blocks of orange-brown limestone. Each cut stone stretched wider than the span of her arms. A single gate led into the citadel, standing, like the walls, as tall as the height of four men and barred with an ancient tree trunk wrapped in bronze that required several men to move it into place.

With a grimace, Galene turned to Mia. "You have been thinking about this—your need to understand what I do."

Mia nodded. She felt a little spark. Maybe she'd won him over.

"Teach me so that I can protect what you do." She sighed. "It will be better for now not to bother my father with these details."

"I do what your father the king orders me to, but I won't make a point of telling the king you came along today. That's for Lady Harmonia."

"Thank you, but he won't mind that I came along, not much anyway." Once again Galene was ignoring the real point of what she said to him. She was pretty sure he hadn't missed any of it, but he refused to treat her as anything but the familiar little girl with no meaningful role in the palace. "But if you also keep silent about what I *said* to you today, I'll know we can trust each other, which will be useful in the future. Don't you think?"

Without answering, he walked toward a group of workmen bent over tasks in the center of the open space of the citadel.

That expanse of yard was large enough for soldiers to assemble or for farmers and artisans to unload their goods from nimble donkeys who climbed the royal mountain. The main trail was considerably more accessible than the goat track leading from Mia's garden, but it was still narrow and steep. Wooden doors securing deep storerooms lined three sides of the yard, with the fourth holding stables and herd pens.

Weak winter sun lit the roughly circular space lying before Mia. She took Dione's hand, and they stepped nearer to the workers. Men mixed muddy clay and straw in a shallow pit, and others dumped buckets of this mud into wooden forms. They were making bricks. Rows of drying bricks filled one side of the open area. Mia glanced at the sky and shared a doubtful look with her maidservant. More rain would undo the labor. She wondered if the men had a way to cover the bricks.

"This work here," Galene waved at the brick making and beyond toward the other side of the yard, "must be done exactly as your father instructed me or the grain rots—a terrible loss if someone foolishly let that happen. I see how teaching you the way the ingathering and storage ought to be done might be useful sometime later. Especially about the storage pits."

"Thank you. Please show me." Brick-making seemed a long way from feeding starving children, but this mattered to Galene and had something to do with grain, so she followed him into one of the empty goat pens on the far side of the yard. Dione hung back by the enclosure's open gate.

The pen they stood in was no longer suitable for sheep or goats. One half had been dug up. Close beside that hole was a low mound covered in the kind of layered timbers, reeds, and mud that usually formed a roof.

"What is that?" Mia asked, pointing to the mound and stepping closer. "Why did you build a roof on the ground?"

"Underneath is a sealed pit that can keep the grain from spoiling, even if it isn't used for two or three years. This way your father can save his kingdom's wealth over time."

"His wealth?" The citadel and the village did not seem to exist in the same world together. Why would her father keep so much to store for years at a time when villagers were hungry? "Isn't grain food for the people?" She turned to Galene in surprise.

"Of course," he said. The steward had stopped closer to the gate and was giving Dione an unguarded look he surely did not intend for Mia to notice, a hungry look and not for food. Mia suddenly felt foolish at what she'd misunderstood. She tried to catch Dione's eye, but her maid was studying the ground.

Galene quickly wiped his face blank and looked directly at Mia, but he didn't return to her side as would be respectful even when he went on, "Much of the grain is kept by the farmers or distributed in payment to others for their labor. And there's the seed grain we store in the citadel that gets used and replaced each year. But along with oil and wine, the stored grain Skyros grows increases your father's power."

He pointed to the dug area and suggested she look into it so she could understand how the pits were made. "We are building a second pit for next year's harvest. The men have partially lined the bottom with stone, but we haven't started the mud-brick walls." Mia stepped closer and peered into the muddy hole with its tightly fitted stone foundation as he continued, "The rains slowed us down. Winter is a bad time for this work, but it's the season when the men can be pulled from work in the fields and orchards."

"Why is this a good way to store grain?" She studied the pit, but from the corner of her eye she saw the steward edge toward Dione and press against her.

Mia ground her teeth. Maidservants had little choice when men stationed above them wanted to touch them. Mia had noticed that even before she'd understood what more the men wanted. She wasn't sure whether she was angrier about Galene bothering Dione or about what his barely concealed actions said about his assumption of her girlish inability to notice them. No wonder he couldn't imagine her as a queen worthy of respect.

He had turned his face toward Mia as if doing nothing untoward and answered her, "It doesn't look like a safe storage place now, does it?"

"Come here and explain it to me." Mia tried to keep the anger from her voice.

He had a startled look as he hurried over. "Yes, Princess."

Dione shook her head slightly. That signal could mean either that whatever Mia said here might make his behavior worse later when she wasn't nearby, or it meant that Dione was willing to put up with Galene's unwanted touching to help Mia win the steward's trust. Whichever Dione meant, Mia agreed it was not strategic to reprimand him now, but she wasn't going to leave Dione to deal with him.

Galene cleared his throat. "I . . . take this work very seriously. Don't misunderstand. It's safer to store grain in these big pits than our old way, but if I failed to build the pit the way your father ordered and so much grain rotted—" He shook his head.

Her father would punish him with death. That's what he couldn't say. *Good.* She had his full attention.

Galene drew her away from the hole. "How can I explain how it works? You probably haven't seen the way the farmers keep their grain stores—the same as we've always done here in the storerooms before these pits."

She shook her head, but then she pictured her earlier experiences watching the gathering of the harvest when she'd peeked into the storerooms as the farmers brought in grain. "You put it in clay pots buried in the storeroom floor."

"That's right, but it's hard to keep the mice and pests out, or worse, water or any moisture that'll rot the grain, even though we seal the pots with clay. At least if a storage pot leaks, it's small and separate from the others. The farmers do that same thing in the floor of their huts. The pit your father ordered is far larger and works even better, so we're adding another. I was doubtful at first. He learned of it from a noble visitor. Every step must be done thoroughly. The first year we tried it I worried we'd remove the roof as you call it and the clay seal to find rotted mess. We didn't have any to spare that year. I had sleepless nights. But your father is a good king, and he was right to try such a change."

Mia offered, "I would have been checking it every day."

"You can't do that." Galene shook his head.

To Mia's surprise, Dione came close enough to Galene to look into the pit. Mia pulled her to her side and listened to the steward's explanation, "The visitor told us that once you open one of these sealed pits, you must take out the grain immediately and use it for seed or eating. Left in the pit, even with a new cover, it will rot quickly. And the pit must be full to the top when you seal it."

"I can see why you worried," Mia said.

"Everything must be just so," the steward said, "And you must leave it alone. This could be important to guide the future prince in thinking about, as you say. I wouldn't want him to interfere out of a lack of understanding."

"I see that. I'm glad you're telling me about this." Strangely enough, these pits were helping her win Galene over. A young prince might be even more likely than her father to blame the steward and punish him with death if such a costly mistake happened. But she didn't see a way to turn this so that the villagers got more food. "You say you can keep these pits for three years or so? What will my father do with these pits of grain—eventually."

"I don't know. I am happy to do my part."

"He is lucky to have you as his steward," Mia said. "I have a difficult question. Please don't be offended. Did gathering so much grain in that pit mean that the farmers have less grain to keep for feeding their families? Could there be hunger among them because of this storage? I know neither you nor my father would want that, but perhaps that happened?"

"Why are you asking about farmers?"

"A queen must be like a mother to her people. I am not yet queen, and I hope that day is far, far off, but isn't that how I should think even now?"

Galene caught a twist of his beard between his fingers. "The farmers are not helpless children. At the start of the planting season, your father offered more seed grain than before. He warned the farmers that he would take a greater amount of grain from each of them, but he gave them the means to grow more even though it would cost him in seed."

Two voices rang out in Mia's head. A mother's, *We work hard as we can.* And then Pyrrha's, *There's only so much a group of villagers like that can grow.*

Galene let go of the strands of his beard and turned both his hands palms up. "They could have prevented hunger."

Possibly. "So you are aware of hunger among them?"

He wagged his head in a guarded way. "There's been some complaining. Winter is always a time of want. They will plant more next season."

"Not if they are weak from hunger." Mia's voice rose more than she intended. "Not if their children die and do not grow up to be strong farmers."

Galene's eyes widened in surprise. "I heard you had been outside the palace. Your father must be furious. The villagers told you tales. I don't blame you for a kind heart, but—"

Mia gasped in fury.

Dione stepped toward Galene, her head lifted, her eyes flashing. "It doesn't matter how Princess Deidamia learned the children are hungry. I wash the princess's laundry at the same spring the women from Seaview use, and I talk with 'em. Their children are starving. They don't bother making up stories for a slave girl like me, and they don't weep lying tears. The cold season makes the scrawny babes sick. It's killing 'em. I don't understand what you're doing here." She waved at the muddy hole. "Not my place to. But when Princess Deidamia tells you of starving children, she is right."

Mia feared for Dione. She held her breath and watched Galene's reaction.

He pulled on his beard and shook his head. "You are a brave girl and kindhearted like your mistress." He shrugged. "But I believe you. Calm yourself—and the princess. When spring comes, the fishermen will go out in their boats, the women will gather wild greens and berries, their gardens will grow food. The island will provide and all will be well. The king must look beyond any one season."

Dione released a soft huff of disgust.

Mia had no interest in allowing herself to be calmed out of caring. "My father must prevent the unnecessary deaths of children."

"Must I?"

Mia whipped around at the sound of her father's voice.

12

"Your Highness," the steward said in a tight rasp.

Mia stared at her father, wondering how much he had overheard.

The citadel's stone fortification wall rose behind her, casting its shadow over both her and Galene. Her father stood outside the fence that surrounded the grain pits, within the open yard and the brightness of winter sunlight. She saw his bodyguards left behind at the main gate. From where he stood, he could have concealed himself behind the wooden wall of a nearby horse stall, although such intentional eavesdropping wouldn't have been kingly. But not so unlikely.

"Father," Mia said. "I'm glad you are here." Despite her anger at the steward, she would protect him. In the long run, maintaining whatever small trust she'd built today would serve her best. "I have questions for you that your steward cannot answer." *That* she realized was true. "I thought I could speak to him and not bother you, but you'll have to forgive him. He could not help me."

Mia touched Dione's arm and sent her off. She was with her father—no need for a chaperone. She turned to Galene. "I am sorry to have taken up your time to no effect. I'll let you return to whatever it is you are overseeing in this mud pile." She hurried out of the sheep pen before the steward could react.

She drew her father away, peeking sideways at him to judge how upset he was.

"Do you imagine," her father asked in a voice strained by anger or hurt, "that I would avoid doing what I could to prevent the unnecessary deaths of children?" He took hold of her arm and pulled her in front of him, looking straight into her eyes. "Do you hold such a low opinion of your father and king?"

How dare he claim hurt feelings. "How can I know what you would or would not do? You never want to talk to me. You hate me and spend as little time as possible with me."

"You accused me of hating you the other day. I was so taken aback I couldn't say anything." He sighed and gently tucked her arm next to his. Her first reaction was to pull away, but suddenly she was fighting tears and gave in to walking with their arms linked. He enfolded her hand inside his large one. "You are my daughter. I love you. Someday you will have children, and you will understand how completely love for your children overtakes you. It's not a feeling anyone can let go of."

She blinked away the blurring tears. "I don't believe you. You want nothing to do with me." She pulled her arm from his.

"That isn't true. You're being obstinate."

"Me? No, Father. You're the one insisting on living a lie, sticking to it *obstinately*."

"How dare you! I told you I love you, as I love each of my daughters. It is forbidden to speak to your king like this."

"At least we are speaking. I prefer arguing to being ignored—like I'm nothing more than a chair."

"A chair? Mia. What makes you say such things?" His lips pressed together and then he blew out a sharp gust of air. "I guess we haven't spoken much together since . . ." He couldn't speak of her mother, either.

Her mother had become a splinter under the skin. The painful swelling would never end until they pulled it out.

"We haven't spoken since I caused Mother to abandon us. You hate me for being the cause of that so much you can't even talk to me." She glared at him, daring him to ignore the truth yet again.

"Is that what you think?" Her father stumbled, and she found herself grabbing his arm to support him. "That isn't . . . Let's sit. To talk."

He glanced around the rough courtyard and pointed to an area partially concealed by a low dividing wall. She nodded, and in silence they went to the bench set on the inside of that wall, where they had privacy from the eyes of his guards and Galene's workmen.

Once they'd seated themselves side by side, he said in a soft voice, "You think I hate you because I have said nothing to you about that awful day?"

She nodded, but the immovable logic of this truth seemed to waver, and she couldn't understand why.

"You are my daughter. A wife's betrayal . . . How could I ever talk about this with you?"

"She betrayed me as well. You said a parent can't let go of love for a child. But she did."

Her father sat very still. She thought he'd refuse to speak as he had the other day, and she would not forgive him. The shadow cast by the citadel wall crept toward them. The mud-brick bench underneath her seat was cold and hard.

She watched her father's face. His eyes looked toward a horizon much farther away than the fortification wall. His hands fisted and opened and fisted again. He shook his head as if disagreeing with some silent argument he had with himself. The color had drained from his face.

Then her father buried his face in his hands. "Do you know what your mother did?" His words came as a barely intelligible murmur. "What actually caused trouble? It had nothing to do with you."

"She told me to give the welcoming speech to the king of Peparethos. She told me how important the treaty was and how much it mattered that he feel welcome. So, when he still looked uncomfortable after I said everything Mother told me to, I went on. I reminded him of how cordial he'd been with Mother. You reacted in fury, and suddenly everyone else was angry as well, and Mother must have left with that king."

Her father lifted his head slowly, but his eyes avoided hers. "Yes, she left with that rat of a king. She had lain with him as a wife lies with a husband." Mia struggled to hear her father's words, breathed out as if the strain of saying them was too much to bear. "She wished to be his wife."

Mia jerked back at that. "No, she didn't. She made me give the speech so she could avoid seeing him. I heard her whisper under her breath 'It's over,' and she didn't want to be near him ever again."

Her father groaned. "When my anger finally let me out of its clutches, I guessed as much. I spoke to her servants, and they hinted at your mother's regret. I had ordered your mother dragged from her quarters like a peasant caught thieving. She deserved that. She stole our marriage bond. I still can't forgive her for what she did. But she didn't leave you. I forced her to go. She had broken my heart, and in revenge, I broke hers even more by separating her forever from her children. I'm the one who betrayed you, Mia. Not your mother."

Mia's vision blurred with welling tears. "Do you think she still misses me? As much as I miss her?" The pools overflowed down her cheeks, but the lump this conversation had created in her throat was washing away.

Tears glistened on her father's eyelashes. He wiped a stray tear from his jawline with the heel of his hand. "I have been cruel to you, leaving you with such doubts. I didn't realize you would think these things. Of course a mother never stops loving and missing her daughters." He pressed his fingers into his forehead, working them in small circles.

"May I see her someday?" Her chest felt as if something sharp had lodged in it.

"No." Her father's voice boomed, abruptly loud.

The sharpness in her chest carved in deeper. It was never going to be soothed. And the familiar ache of responsibility for all that had happened had not waned. "Would you have made her leave if I hadn't given the welcoming speech?"

Her father touched her cheek and then his hand dropped. "It was your mother's fault not yours. She did something so wrong that your well-meaning words easily uncovered it." He paused, his gaze on the hard-packed ground and his fists repeatedly closing and loosening as if they were separate beings from him. He still didn't look at her when he continued in a rasping voice, "Even so, if I had not burst out in anger, but in that one, essential moment pretended that I had been at the meeting you described or gave some other way to preserve your mother's reputation, it could have been 'over' and forgotten, as you say she wished. But I don't think I could have found such restraint, even if I had known. It was your mother's wrongdoing. Don't blame yourself."

"But *you* blame me."

He sighed. "No, at least not anymore. I couldn't think about any of it. You look so much like her. And I felt guilty. Whenever you were near, I felt guilty."

"But you say it was my mother's wrongdoing."

"A man cannot ignore the insult when his wife lies with another. No man should—even less a king. That is true. I did what I had to. But..."

Mia understood. Part of him wished he had found a way to ignore what she'd done and lived on with his wife who had lain with another. As he'd confessed, he had choices that day. As he always did. He could have covered up what he'd learned from his daughter's "well-meaning words." Her mother had already chosen to stay. She would have helped him live with the unspoken deception. It would have been hard. Mia's mother had explained to her about the making of children, the binding of bodies in marriage. For that to have happened with someone other than her father was unthinkable to Mia, but he could have chosen for his beloved wife to stay. That was why he felt so guilty.

Her father whispered, "Will you forgive me?"

"I will never stop wanting my mother, however great her sin, but I understand what you faced was unbearable." She couldn't say forgive. "I still need her."

"I know. I tried with Lady Harmonia."

"Pfff." Mia shook her head. Then she turned and looked at her father directly, touching his arm to make him look at her. "Will you teach me how to rule wisely as future queen?"

Her father let out a startled sound. "Since your mother cannot? Is that what you mean?"

"I must learn to care for our people as my mother did."

Her father rubbed both hands over his face and sighed. "Is that why you were discussing with my steward how I starve children?"

"He's my steward, too. Have you visited your villagers and seen how hungry their children are? It is your responsibility to provide food."

"They must grow enough of it. They've played on your sympathy, which is another reason why you shouldn't have gone to any of the villages."

She flinched, but she was the one who'd confessed she'd seen their children. Too late now. "No, they didn't try to influence me. They wouldn't even admit their need for food, not directly, for fear of upsetting me—or more likely you. I saw the dangerously skinny children myself. If your daughters looked like that, you'd be terrified. Their parents love them as you say you love me."

"A few neglected children and you're sure everyone's starving. How about this? I'll let Harmonia take you to some of the villages. It's just as well you become familiar to them as their future queen. Be gracious and show you care. You're good at that. You'll tell me if you find all the children are starving. I'll also ask Harmonia. No stories, Mia."

"May I inspect their food stores? To make sure they have enough?"

Her father frowned. "How would you know what enough is?"

"I can speak to them and learn. You know I'm clever. Like my mother." It was his turn to flinch, but she didn't look away.

"Fine. Look at the children and the food stores. You are not going to find anything of great interest. No bringing our guest Pyrrha with you. *That* I absolutely forbid."

Mia scowled, but she knew a lost argument. "You have a lot of grain stored in a pit, taken from the farmers. If I discover some of the children are starving, will you give it back?"

"We'll do something for the children, if need be, but I'm not removing grain from the pit."

She started to argue, but he held up his hand and looked at her with a raised eyebrow. "That grain is for you. You and the independence of my kingdom. Your kingdom. I need a dowry for you full of the things Skyros produces, full of promise of future wealth, and large enough that it persuades a king that his son will do well as the king of this island. That grain is your future."

13

It was early morning, and her sisters still slept, but Mia's mind ran about too busy to stay abed. She got up and sent Dione to the kitchen for some bread and cheese.

They ate their breakfast together sitting cross-legged on the bed in her sleeping chamber. Harmonia would not approve, but that made it more fun. If they'd gone into the women's hall, Dione would have had to stand as her serving maid, and besides, they might have woken one or more of her sisters, or even worse, Harmonia herself.

Between bites, Mia brought up Galene's mistreatment of Dione. "What do you want me to do? He shouldn't. I won't let him."

Dione rested her head on Mia's shoulder. "That's how men do with us serving girls. At least Galene only goes for me with his hands, and he's not mean. He could'a yelled at what I said about the children starving."

"He called you brave, but that doesn't mean he gets to grab at you. Should I tell him to stop?"

"He'd only stop when you're near." Dione grimaced for a time in silence, then turned to Mia. "Tell him, if he likes me so much, he should claim me in marriage."

"What?" Mia dropped the piece of bread she was bringing to her mouth. "But . . . he grabs at you."

"Men do that. To likes of me, anyway."

"And . . . and he's so old."

Dione shook her head. "To you. But he's hearty and handsome enough. If I'm known as his wife, him being the steward and all, the others won't bother me no more. And his children won't go hungry."

Mia struggled to accept all that was implied in this about Dione's life. She'd known and she hadn't known. Guilt seeped through her like the mucky water of a stagnant pond. "How can—"

"Make sure he wants me for wife. Leave him to it one way or other. Not forced 'cause you're the princess and you say."

"Him not forced, but you've been—"

"It's a long time, being a wife. Only if he *wants* me for wife. That's my choice as much as his."

Mia looked in astonishment at her maid. "I don't know how to bring this all up. It seems excruciating, but I'll do it. I promise. And only if he chooses you as his wife, so it's a choice for both of you."

She gave Dione a hug, and they finished the bread and cheese.

Dione slipped out to do her morning duties.

Mia had too much to think about. The women's quarters were still silent with sleep, so she went out to her courtyard garden where her thoughts would have enough room. She scanned the plants and knelt next to a cluster of acanthus plants along the terrace. They died back in winter, and she hated the grim, messy look of it, so she wanted to cut away the dry leaves with a small sickle she'd borrowed from the gardener. He claimed it was better to let them be until the weather warmed, but the tough old things weren't going to suffer from a cleanup. They'd more likely take over the whole side of her garden if she didn't keep after them.

Her mother taught her to love digging in the soil, so she had always ignored Harmonia's promptings that garden chores weren't appropriate for princesses. She could still hear her mother's soft voice say, "You must learn to make the land flower—and the land is made of both soil and its people."

She crawled between the browned foliage and dead flower stalks, cutting and throwing the trimmings into a pile behind her. It was good work to do as she considered the duty her father had proposed she take on, inspecting the villages and their food stores. Harmonia was to accompany her. *Fine.* But Mia would plan each journey herself. She would not let Harmonia turn this duty into a series of suitable, meaningless outings. Mia would bring back to her father the information he'd challenged her to gather. Whether he did anything with it was something else.

He probably wouldn't. But he'd *talked* with her in earnest for the first time since her mother left. That warmth glowed in her heart. And he felt as guilty as Mia did. By his word, *was* guilty. She'd been angry and hurt for so long, these new feelings seemed to belong to someone else.

At the sound of footsteps coming from her chambers, she craned her neck to see who it was, expecting Dione. Instead Pyrrha lurched forward, her limbs jerky and not at all like her usual graceful movements. Pyrrha looked like she had the other day when she'd curled up and complained of noises in her head. *Not again.*

"I'm here," Mia said, rising from the acanthus and brushing off the dirt and crushed leaves from the worn tunic she'd pulled on. "Are you sick?" Sweat ran down Pyrrha's face and arms. "Were you running again?" If so, it hadn't had the beneficial effect of Pyrrha's mad run to the shore and back two days ago.

Pyrrha looked at her with a blank expression as if she couldn't understand what Mia asked. Then she shook her head. "You didn't tell me how your conversation with the steward went."

Mia frowned at the reproach in Pyrrha's voice. "I looked for you, but when I couldn't find you, I stopped because I didn't want to draw Harmonia's notice if you'd left the palace, especially when you did not join us for dinner. I told her you weren't hungry. Why she believes us when we give such sorry excuses, I don't know, but she did."

"Lady Harmonia believes what she wants to be true. It's easier." Pyrrha paced back and forth on the small terrace with an uneven gait, like a badger in a trap. "How did it go?"

"Can you sit down?" Mia pulled two chairs close together and sat in one of them.

Pyrrha studied the other chair, a confused glaze over her eyes.

"Sit down, and I'll tell you about my conversation."

When Pyrrha slumped into the chair, Mia studied her friend. Beads of sweat ringed her brow, and her breaths came fast and shallow. "Have you been out already this morning?" Then another idea flicked up. "Did you stay outside all night?" If that was so, as Pyrrha's friend, she should have known, should have done something.

Pyrrha shook her head. "I couldn't sleep."

Mia wasn't sure that meant she had been in the palace, but she gave up on that question. "My father talked with me. Really talked."

That seemed to rouse Pyrrha. Her gaze focused on Mia, and her lips formed a hint of smile.

Mia explained about the steward and the grain pits. She described how her father had overheard them and the conversation that followed.

"He told *you* to find out how widespread hunger is among the children and villagers?"

"I'm to bring Harmonia, but it's my job. I'm pretty sure he doesn't intend to do anything. He won't touch the grain he has stored in the pit." Mia touched Pyrrha's shoulder. "You're trembling. Are you cold? Let's go inside."

"I'm not cold. I'm happy for you."

"My father said I can't bring you with me. He forbids it. I'm sorry. As far as he is concerned you may not leave the women's quarters for any reason." Mia ran her fingers across Pyrrha's forehead, wiping away trickles of sweat before they ran into her eyes. "I won't tell on you when you slip over the wall, of course. I don't know how long that means of escape will last."

"Longer than I can last like this."

Mia frowned in confusion. What did *that* mean? "If you hadn't come to live with us, I wouldn't have . . . I wouldn't have seen the children or talked with my father. I know being locked inside my father's palace is terrible for you, but I'm glad you're my friend. How can I help you?"

"Only my mother can help me. And she won't."

"Your mother?" They both had absent mothers. Pyrrha had said that. "Why won't she help you?"

Pyrrha shook her head. "She's protecting me. That's what she calls this."

"Locking you in our women's quarters? What is she protecting you from?" Mia pictured the tall, intimidating woman who had brought Pyrrha. Other than similar height, Pyrrha didn't look much like that lady, and the woman hadn't treated Pyrrha like her daughter, but they shared some hard-to-define quality. Her growing suspicion seemed confirmed. "The lady who brought you here is your mother, isn't she? She's ... a very powerful woman."

Pyrrha sucked in a sudden, hissing breath. "You can't say that. Don't think about her. It will cost you your life if you do." Urgency in her tone made these strange words persuasive. Mia shivered.

She remembered her father using that expression of the villagers, the *ignorant* villagers. *It will cost them their lives to interfere with you.* It hadn't settled into her until now that her father meant *he* would order a villager killed. And now Pyrrha believed her mother would kill Mia for even less. For saying or thinking the wrong thing. An unusually powerful woman. In the stories, the gods struck mortals at whim.

Were the stories of gods only stories or did they sometimes visit mortals and threaten them?

Pyrrha's mother didn't seem to think much of Skyros's royal family. Yet she chose this palace as protection for her child, a child who was not doing well. Pyrrha trembled and drops of moisture poured down her face and neck. Mia put her hand on her friend's damp forehead and touched her cheeks and neck. Clammy and cold, not hot. She didn't seem to have a fever. If Pyrrha were one of her sisters, she'd get her into a soothing, warm bath.

"I am dirty and cold from gardening so early in the morning," Mia said. "I need a bath." From the first, Pyrrha had avoided bathing with Mia or her sisters. She washed alone as if it was a private sort of thing.

Puzzling, but maybe that was how it was in the household she grew up in. Her mother didn't sound very nice as company for ordinary activities. "You aren't dirty like me, but I think you'll feel better with a hot soak. Will you come with me?"

Pyrrha slouched lower in her chair.

"Come with me."

Pyrrha sighed. "Okay."

"Good. We'll both feel better."

Mia took Pyrrha's hand and hoisted her out of the chair. She looked Pyrrha up and down. Defeated and miserable. Helping her friend might take more than a bath.

14

Mia brought Pyrrha to the bathing room in the women's quarters and gave the two serving women who worked as bathing attendants orders to heat water, fill the tubs, and set out cleaning sponges, oil, and linen towels. She sent Dione to bring some food so they could eat while she and Pyrrha waited for the hot water. Maybe a meal would help.

Pyrrha looked even worse than she had in the garden. Her skin glistened with sweat, and her limbs shook hard enough to be noticeable. Afraid her friend would collapse, Mia guided Pyrrha to the squat wooden bench that served as both a table and seat in the small room with plain whitewashed walls.

The bench they sat on rested between two stone tubs that took up the center of the room. From the floor beside a corner hearth, the attendants lifted water jugs they'd filled earlier at the well and poured them into two bronze cauldrons resting on tripods over hot coals. One of the women took down a long-handled pitcher from a shelf to the side of the hearth, ready to scoop hot water from the cauldrons into the tubs.

Mia loved the swirling mosaic floor formed from smooth gray and white stones gathered on the island's beaches. When she was little, she'd pretend she was washing at the seashore. She kicked off her dirty sandals and rubbed her toes over the gentle bumps of the floor.

Wrapping her arm around Pyrrha's shoulders, she asked, "Are you sure you're not sick? I can call for the healer."

"I don't need a healer," Pyrrha said. "I need something you cannot provide. It isn't your fault. I'll be fine."

She didn't look fine. Pyrrha had shown amazing strength over and over, but today she was frail, emotionally frail. Something was tearing her apart, like an eagle with a broken wing who tumbles to the ground and can no longer fend off destruction.

"Dione will bring us some food. Maybe you're too hungry. You missed dinner and breakfast, didn't you?"

Pyrrha's muscles worked as she clamped her jaw. She balled her hands into fists and crossed her arms over her chest. Mia glanced around for some way to distract her friend enough so that when food arrived, she might eat.

"Come over here." She pulled Pyrrha from the bench, leading her toward two stools underneath the big window used to air out the bathing room.

Heavy shutters covered the window opening. Most shutters were plain and uninteresting. Not these. Mia thought of the time they'd spent in the woods. Pyrrha would enjoy the shutters' delicate carvings as much as she did.

Mia rubbed her finger over the raised outline of a rabbit. "When you bathed here by yourself, you probably noticed the animals carved into the shutters."

Pyrrha nodded.

Of course the whimsical creatures had caught her friend's attention, but the unpainted carvings were subtle. The creatures emerged from the wood, and, at the same time, they blended back into it. Looked at closely, they were delightful. Mia had observed that few of the palace's female guests showed the imagination to have any interest in them—a good reason to ignore such women.

Pyrrha reached her hand to touch a salamander wrapped around the paw of a polecat. "I don't think the wood carver knew how animals behave," she said with a slight brightening of her eyes.

"Maybe not," Mia said with a giggle, "but the animals look so much like living ones, the carver must have known their forms well." She admired a pair of deer sniffing the air while beetles balanced on their backs. "I sometimes think there's a secret message in the way the animals play together."

"A secret message?"

"They aren't running away or eating each other, are they?" Mia saw this distraction was calming her friend.

Pyrrha shrugged. "No fleet hooves or bared teeth."

"Perhaps that's the message. Play together."

"Then a child must have done the work."

"You know that can't be. Such carving takes skill no child has."

Dione slipped in and set a tray on the bench between the tubs. Mia answered Dione's questioning look with a shake of her head. Dione had work to do, and she wasn't needed here. Dione nodded, checked with the attendants about fetching anything for the ladies' baths, and then left.

Mia tugged Pyrrha back to the low bench. A linen napkin covered the tray, under which Mia found dried figs and apricots, boiled quail eggs, and flat bread warm from the oven. She handed bites to Pyrrha as if she were one of her younger sisters. Pyrrha rolled her eyes and plucked each bite from Mia with her lips in an exaggerated imitation of a small child, but she ate steadily. They were sitting next to each other on the bench with Pyrrha's thigh snug against Mia's. Through that contact Mia could still feel Pyrrha trembling, but not as much as before.

The attendants scooped boiling water from the big pots into each tub, following with enough cold to make a pleasant bath. Mia stood and pulled off her old tunic. The hearth-heated air was warm against her bare skin. "Do you want rose oil in your bath? I always have that."

She glanced over at Pyrrha, who had hunched down. Her head looked too heavy for her neck.

"May I help you get in?" Mia hurried over to Pyrrha and wrapped an arm around her, pressing her to stand.

She untied Pyrrha's belt. "Raise your arms." For a moment, she thought Pyrrha would refuse, but eventually her friend raised her lithe, powerful arms enough to let Mia pull Pyrrha's peplos over her head, revealing her naked breasts and the soft curves of her belly and hips. Pyrrha's eyes squeezed shut.

Mia dropped the gown onto the bench and reached out a hand to guide the forlorn girl into a tub full of soothing warm water. But Pyrrha groaned, sagged back onto the bench, and slid from there to the floor where she drew her knees tight against her breasts, her eyes closed. "This is not who I am."

Mia crouched beside her on the floor. "What do you mean? I like who you are."

"This is not who I am." Her eyes stayed closed.

Mia glanced at the two attendants, who kept their gazes lowered. She rose and said to them, "The Lady Pyrrha prefers privacy. Please see that we are not disturbed."

They left with murmurs of "Yes, Princess."

Mia knelt against the gray and white stones of the floor, wrapping her arms again around her naked friend, but Pyrrha didn't respond except that her breathing grew shallower and more strained.

"Shouldn't I send for the healer?" Mia stroked Pyrrha's bright copper hair.

Pyrrha slammed her fist against the floor. "No!"

Mia brushed her hand in steady, light circles over Pyrrha's back. She stayed that way for a long time without speaking, but the shaking that racked Pyrrha's body grew more violent.

Mia bent down to peek into Pyrrha's face, so close the irregular bursts of Pyrrha's breaths brushed her face, and she touched her sweat-streaked cheek. Was her friend dying?

Pyrrha opened her eyes, looking directly into Mia's. Mia searched those moody eyes, whose green color shifted even as she stared into them, from the grayish tone of sage to the deep forest of pine needles after rain. Mia smiled in response, her fingers curling against Pyrrha's pale cheek.

Tipping up her face, Pyrrha met Mia's lips. They pressed their mouths together, opening into a slow, exploratory kiss, smooth and sweet. Mia reveled in it, lost for some unmeasured time.

But when her hands caressed Pyrrha's neck, slid down her silky, naked back, she felt Pyrrha draw away, her muscles tightening as if ready to bolt. *From her?* Not if she believed the even more insistent embrace of Pyrrha's lips against hers, the joining of tongues radiating desire through Mia so overpowering that she had to brace her hands against the floor, dig her nails into the stones in order to pull her mouth away. It didn't matter what Pyrrha was running from. However sweet, these kisses would only make everything worse for her friend. Whatever was happening to Pyrrha, kisses were a deceptive poison for her, food she longed for but could not hold down.

Mia drew back, smoothed a strand of red-gold hair from Pyrrha's face, and whispered, "This won't help you, will it?"

Pyrrha dropped her head so low Mia couldn't see her face. "No. I want you. By all the gods, I want to taste your kisses and—" Pyrrha groaned. Her whole body shook. "I can't. Not as I am. This—" Pyrrha's head shot up, and she grabbed one of her breasts in her hand and shrieked, "This is torment. Mother! I beg you. Mother!"

Mother? Mia looked around the room. They were alone. She didn't know what was happening to Pyrrha. She reached for the frantic girl but withdrew her hand when she saw Pyrrha's eyes wide with horror.

Pyrrha crawled away from her, dragging herself across the pebbled floor. Her breaths came in harsh gasps, and she curled on her side into a tight ball in the open space before the hearth, her head buried under one arm. She pounded a fist over and over against the stone floor, so hard Mia feared she'd smash her hand into a bloody wound.

Pyrrha's scream broke the horrible drumming of the fist. "Mother! Now. *This* will kill me. Mother!" The shout reverberated like the pounding of a waterfall beating against rocks. Mia shivered, alone on her knees across the room from her friend.

Dread of what would become of Pyrrha if her mother didn't answer her pleas—whatever those pleas meant—warred with Mia's alarm for herself. Her friend was both dangerously broken, beyond what Mia could understand or mend, and terrifyingly capable of calling on a mother who, she'd warned, would not forgive Mia for the audacity of wondering what was happening to her friend. Not an ordinary mother.

"Mother!" This repeated cry had a carrying resonance beyond its natural flow, calling out to the heavens. The sound left a trail of terror as it echoed through Mia.

As Mia knelt, fearful and unsure of what to do, a sea mist rolled like a veil between her and the curled-up form of Pyrrha. Gray swirls billowed and massed until they blocked sight of her friend. The fog blocked sound also as an unnatural silence fell around her, cutting off not only Pyrrha's cries, but also any small noises of the living.

Mia tried to rise, but her body no longer responded, as if her limbs were carved of stone. Panic, sharp and biting, rampaged inside the enforced stillness of her body. Was this death?

Threads of muffling fog reached toward Mia, wrapping around her naked limbs, neck, and chest with icy fingers that wormed through her skin and bone and cradled around her heart in warning —*We can crush or shield. Whatever is needed. We serve at the goddess's command.*

Goddess? Ringing in Mia's head were Pyrrha's words, *It will cost you your life if you do.*

Mia stayed in forced stillness for a terrifying, boundless time, kneeling in the blind silence, her hard-beating heart the only sign that she might still live. The veil of gray mist remained unchanged, what happened behind it a divine mystery that Mia forced herself not to imagine. Burned into her was Pyrrha's warning that to question was a fatal offense against her mother—an immortal mother. But Mia could not slow the ever-faster thrashing of her heart. That pace seemed impossible to keep up without breaking her heart into pieces and ending her life.

She knelt, trapped in a state beyond what flesh and blood could endure that carried on and on. Until finally, a golden light infused the grim mist. The glow didn't let Mia see through the mist, even as it grew ever brighter. It did not offer a nurturing warmth, but for a moment, it seemed to hold a promise.

For Mia, that promise shriveled with the roaring of an implacable voice, "You, stupid girl, will share my child's agony. You failed me. If I must undo this shield, I will make you suffer the same pain."

Behind the veil, a searing brightness sliced through the air like a jag of lethal lightning. No sound reached Mia, no sign of Pyrrha, but when dagger cuts of pain radiated through Mia's body, she knew Pyrrha's pain tore through her. The time of torment stretched on and on until Mia crumpled to the ground, released at last from the slashing agony.

Had that bolt of burning light torn Pyrrha to shreds?

15

Under Mia's cheek lay the smooth stones of the bathing room floor. She drew in a full breath. The overwhelming pain was receding, although not the dread. Glancing around without lifting her head, she saw the mist had dispersed. Instead, she saw two pairs of feet. One pair was large and bare—Pyrrha's? The other feet were encased in impossibly brilliant golden sandals.

"Get up, mortal."

The harsh voice of command reignited Mia's terror. She scrambled to her feet, fighting her fear-stiffened muscles and keeping her head bowed in obeisance, her eyes locked on the shining sandals.

"You did not follow the orders I gave your father, mortal." The divinity's words rang more like a clanging cymbal than a voice. "Nor did you bring sufficient comfort to my son."

Mia quivered. *Her son?*

"You did not prevent this inconvenience as you should have." Each word hit hard and cold.

Inconvenience? With her head tipped low, Mia stole a sideways peek at Pyrrha. She gasped, seeing a young man, his naked body powerfully muscled and broad chested, his male parts hanging conspicuously. Her face flushed hot, and she flashed through the many times she'd secretly watched naked soldiers wrestling.

This embarrassingly and beautifully naked man had Pyrrha's red-gold hair and echoes of her face in his masculine one, but otherwise, he was distinctly not the same Pyrrha, the girl she'd come to love. Suddenly Mia's own nakedness felt exposed. She swallowed around the suffocating lump in her throat and kept silent.

"Because of your failure," the goddess continued, "I have granted his plea and restored him to his proper form. His strength did not belong in a woman's body, but it was a perfect concealment." *Being a girl had been a trick? Who* was *her friend? Pyrrha had deceived her all this time?*

The man—Pyrrha?—stepped forward. "Mother, none of this is Mia's fault." The man's voice was deep and resonant but nonetheless held reassuring similarity to her friend's. "You went too far. I could not endure what you did to me. Giving me back my body is not a mere inconvenience."

"Isn't it? Do you have a better plan?" the goddess intoned. "I will not allow my son to be dragged toward death by crawling mortals who seek his strength for their greedy, small purposes. They would use you for the brief, foretold time and then cast you aside when death demands payment."

"If my life is to be brief, then allow me to live it fully. What do you accomplish by leaving me on Skyros?"

"Your life will *not* be brief. I will not allow death to take you—not yet. The time is near, but I will defeat them. I have taken charge of your fate."

The son shook his head. "You have pushed me too far. Is this the same prophecy of my death that warped your motherhood into cold and furious hardness? You denied yourself the closeness that we both yearned for."

The goddess expanded in size, and the brightness surged, forcing Mia to shade her eyes from the pain. "Warped?" The divine voice echoed off the stone walls. "Be cautious what you say, child. You are too limited in understanding—even you, my dear son. A mortal son cannot sufficiently imagine eternal sorrow. Once I lose you, my grief will never end. I gave you the motherhood I had to."

"Perhaps, but you did not give me the motherhood I needed."

Mia gasped. *Take care!*

"I am the one to judge your need. And besides, I have listened to you and worked this transformation. What you begged for and swore you *needed*." Was it disdain or hurt that laced that last word? The brilliance in the room was like staring into the midday sun. The goddess's voice rose like a war horn. "But there must be a new plan." She turned her burning gaze to Mia.

Mia bowed her head lower.

"You know too much."

Mia felt searing heat as the goddess's immortal light centered on her. She whispered, "I don't know anything, Goddess." Her heart's pounding rose from her throat so hard it choked her. She scraped out any words she could think of, "I don't know who you are, or your son. Nothing."

"Nonetheless you will reveal my son's presence. You have already jeopardized him." The goddess raised one hand.

"No!" her son screamed and dove toward his mother, seizing her hand. The goddess let out a bellow of rage that shook the walls, but he did not let go. With a quiet voice, he said, "You will not harm Mia. Killing her will not make me safer. *I* chose escape. I will choose it again if you force me to live inside this cage—even in my right form."

Gratitude for her friend filled Mia. He defended her against the attack of a goddess—like the girl who had refused to let an injured man die. But the betrayal of his lying disguise as a girl still stung.

The goddess peeled away his fingers from her hand, one by one. "She knows what you are. Humans fail to keep secrets. Only death closes their mouths."

"Mother, these are the same riddles as always, of my early death and men who would bring me toward it. Why must I stay concealed? You have the power to drive off any mortal men who threaten to harm me."

"They must not find you. That is your only safety. I know the prophecy. Do not question me. You will stay hidden here in the women's quarters on Skyros."

"How is that going to work? Soon enough everyone will know that I am not a woman. Mia's awareness isn't the problem." The tall man reached back to the bench and lowered himself onto it. "I'm exhausted. What you did to me was terrible."

Mia studied him. The familiar lines of strain still haunted his face, although his movements were more natural, his posture relaxed in a way he had never been as Pyrrha. He appeared more comfortable in this form. At home.

The mother spoke, "I will not allow you to leave Skyros. As long as you stay hidden here, you will not be drawn into . . . that which will bring an early death. We will find a way."

"Drawn into what? You are hiding some part you don't trust me to know. What will bring this early death? What are you keeping from me, Mother?"

"Do not question me." The goddess's command slashed like a dagger stab.

Mia willed her friend to stop asking provoking questions. Pyrrha, or whatever her friend's name was, would have to remain hidden on Skyros. But how could that be arranged? The goddess's hand had been stayed for now, but without a solution to this *inconvenience*, Mia doubted the son could restrain the divine anger when it rose up again, and Mia feared it might extend to her father and sisters. None of this was their fault. None of them had forced this misery on Pyrrha, but laying the blame on his goddess mother would be deadly. Mia bowed her head in silence.

"So what are you going to do this time, Mother?" The son leaned back along the bench, propped on both elbows. The maleness and beauty of that body drew Mia's gaze as she remembered kisses on her lips and breasts.

Then a sad thought filtered in. She'd lost the brave, commanding girl who had been her friend. She felt drawn to this man, but her Pyrrha was lost forever.

But none of that mattered in this moment. She must appease a goddess by hiding the son.

How could that be done?

16

The king stood at one side of Mia. The shadows of the throne room crept around them, the dark red and mustard walls feeling too close. The goddess sat on King Lycomedes's throne, her hands gripping its ebony-carved arms as if she had to work to restrain herself from blasting both father and daughter out of the room with a flick of her hand.

On a stool below the throne's dais, clothed now in a man's chiton, sat the person whom Mia knew as Pyrrha, but whom his mother called Achilles. His father was King Peleus, who ruled over an enviably powerful mainland kingdom called Phthia. No wonder when Pyrrha had talked to Lycomedes, her father had been eager to form a treaty with him.

Mia's thoughts raced.

Here was the smart young prince her father had been seeking. A treaty by marriage ought to please him, as long as he didn't feel threatened by the imbalance of power.

But why would the goddess give her half-immortal son to a princess of Skyros? Mia grasped at any idea that would persuade this threatening presence seated in her father's place.

Mia had heard stories about Achilles. Even as a child his preeminence as a warrior had caused tales to be sung by the bards. And Mia now guessed the identity of the "woodsman" teacher her friend had mentioned, the master fighter, tracker, and preparer of young hunter-warriors. The bards sang about Achilles's tutor, the centaur Chiron, whose skills as a healer far surpassed those of any human. It seemed so unlikely that Achilles would have died if he had remained in Chiron's protection. Why had his mother—Thetis, that was the goddess's name—decided this small, weak island kingdom and the company of an ignorant princess would be safer?

When Mia had heard the bard's song about Achilles, she had assumed the part about Chiron being half man and half horse was a made-up embellishment, but she didn't now. The stories of divinities and otherworldly creatures had appeared around her. They had entered her life, and if she didn't want them to turn deadly, she had only a few moments to weave them into a story that both Thetis and her father would agree to.

She wished she had been able to talk privately to Pyrrha—Achilles—but that wasn't permitted.

Fury flushed her father's face. He'd been tricked. As far as he could understand, his daughter had lived in the intimate, unchaperoned company of this man. He would never allow a man to stay in the women's quarters—unless that man was husband to one of his daughters. Fortunately, the shock of a goddess claiming his throne and the terror inspired by her divinely enraged presence had so far held his anger in check.

Now he bowed in preparation to speak. Mia put a warning hand on his arm.

"Goddess," she said before he could, gulping down the panic that scrambled up her throat and pitched her voice high and squeaky. "You wish, above all else, to keep your son hidden in the women's quarters on our small, unworthy island." She deepened her bow. "Is this what you command us to do?"

Mia heard the outraged rumble from her father and sensed him begin to rise. She grabbed his hand, holding him in his respectful obeisance, and whispered, "Can you trust me?"

He shifted his head, locking his bowed gaze on hers. Fear chased anger in his eyes.

Mia felt the goddess's attention fix on her like the searing heat of a bonfire.

"That *is* what I wish to command," Thetis's voice boomed, "but you have failed utterly at my previous commands." Hatred flooded through the goddess's words despite their strange, flat intonation. "You and your father served only as impediments."

Mia straightened slowly, respectfully. She stepped forward and drew her shoulders back. "Your son's inability to endure the disguise you chose for him did create a significant impediment. I apologize for our failure to sustain him. But I see a way to follow your command—the true core of it. You want us to provide an impenetrable concealment for your son."

"Mortals always fail."

Achilles rose from his stool. "Mother, you cannot take me to your palace under the sea, nor any other place of divine shelter. I am mortal. If you wish to hide me among mortals, listen to this girl."

The piercing light from the goddess flashed like lightning, and a growl of thunder shook the room. Even the goddess's son should not dare to give orders to his mother. The terrified thumps of Mia's heart climbed her throat.

"Well, girl? Speak." The goddess's scorn was biting and unfair. Infuriatingly unfair.

Mia's indignation gave her strength. She willed her heart back into her chest and her breath to flow. "I suspect you chose Skyros's humble court because we are obscure and unnoticed by travelers and bards."

A wave of the goddess's hand assented to this while communicating her impatience.

But hurrying would be a mistake, so Mia considered each word as she made her plan and ignored the painful flutter of her heart. "If our meager court were to offer its throne to the son of a goddess that would be an insult. I understand this. But I see a secure means of concealment for him if you can countenance such a lowly offering. I do not suggest, of course, that this small island throne would be your son's only source of power. He also has the promise of his father's throne to come, but our court would be an allied power joined with his greater, paternal kingdom."

The painful immortal light flared in fury again. "You are a grasping bitch in heat. Do you think I would give my son to the likes of you?"

Mia gasped and fell back a step. *What a deluded fool I am.* She forced herself not to look at her father. She couldn't bear to see his disgust.

From the side, Achilles turned to confront his mother. "Princess Deidamia is more than worthy to be my wife." Mia's heart sank. She loved her friend for defending her, but he would only enrage his goddess mother further. Pyrrha's voice floated in her mind, *It will cost you your life.*

Then she jumped in surprise when her father gently took her hand and drew them both closer to the foot of the dais. He looked directly at Thetis. His wide-eyed gaze, hiding nothing, followed by a slow, deep bow, gave the goddess proper respect and humility, but the press of his lips hinted at determination.

"Lady Goddess. I agree with you that children should not be the ones to decide whom they will marry." At her father's words, a mollified flicker passed across the divine brow.

The king continued, "When you concealed your son's identity and required my daughter to receive him as her guest, you put them close together and a friendship has grown, a worthy fruit despite its deceptive roots." Fury pulled at the divine lips, and Mia's throat locked in fear even as her father dropped her hand and took a step closer to the divinity occupying his throne. "They reach now for each other because of that bond—which perhaps we should not completely ignore since you want your son's happiness as I want my daughter's. But that is a small side detail."

A dismissive release of air came from the divine mouth. *Was her son's happiness really so insignificant to her?*

Lycomedes held out his hands, palms up. Mia could not judge

whether it was a call for mercy or a gesture of conciliation. "Let us not be distracted from what is most important—your son's continued safety and how we can best aid you in accomplishing that. You chose the women's quarters of my court. It struck your divine wisdom as the best location, and I do not challenge that in any way. I continue to welcome your offspring in that shelter, but as a young man, he can hide there only as my daughter's husband. Otherwise, the outrage of the household at his presence would threaten your secrecy. The servants and family must view everything as ordinary and proper."

"There is nothing ordinary about marriage to my son." Thetis's eyes narrowed, but Mia thought she read in them a concession to her father's point.

A subtle squaring of his shoulders suggested Lycomedes felt a measure of confidence. Mia sighed. It would not be the first time he'd overreached, but they shared a common purpose, so she listened intently. "This marriage has value. As my daughter's dowry, I will make your son heir to the throne of this sea-girt kingdom, a fine balance to your husband Peleus's inland realm. These independent kingdoms offer strengths to each other, and being king of two increases your son's prestige."

Her father put his arm around Mia's shoulder. "My daughter's blood is as royal as your mortal husband's. Her appearance is lovely. Her wit lively. Her kindness ever present." Mia glanced toward her father in surprise at this praise. Was it a negotiating trick or his true feeling? "Unless you intend to choose an immortal goddess for your son's bride, my daughter is as honorable a choice as you may find. And in approving this betrothal for Achilles, you ensure him a safe haven from the threat you foresee through prophecy."

Her father bowed low, bringing Mia with him. The hand that clasped her shoulder held on with reassuring strength. And yet, more heat emanated from the goddess. Crackling thunder rolled across the wide room in answer.

To Mia's alarm, Thetis rose from the black throne and lifted her arms. "What fool thinks his household would not gossip far and wide about a marriage like this? You can give him a false name and background, but his mere presence is so extraordinary that suspicious rumor of a prince far too fine for such a meager kingdom will destroy his safety. If this marriage is the only device you can offer to mend your failure, you waste my time." The goddess turned her palms outward, fingers splayed.

What spell of destruction the goddess readied, Mia dared not guess. Instead, she shouted, "We will shut them up with a terrifying tale of Medea." She fell back several steps, frightened by the sound of her own voice and the silence that followed.

Thetis's arms dropped. A flash of confusion marred her face for a moment. Then that burning gaze aimed at Mia. "Why do you speak of my cousin, the sorceress Medea?"

Cousin? Uh-oh. Mia had anticipated Thetis's justified distrust about gossip. A casual description of Achilles to a stranger would give him away. His physical appearance—his size and strength, his speed and grace, his red-gold hair—was legendary. The bards sang of it. Anyone focused on secrecy would feel as the goddess did. Hiding him would take more than a deceptive change of name and origins. Earlier, as her father brought her through the palace toward the throne room, she'd sifted among every story in her memory, searching for some figure whom she could use as a threat to guarantee the household's silence.

She'd chosen Medea, the witch so bent on vengeance in every situation of her life that she had struck at kings and sons of kings, a young bride, a brother, and even her own children. She wouldn't hesitate to slaughter an entire royal household or an island's people —if they had sheltered her enemy. She'd disappeared into the east in a chariot drawn by flying serpents, but that offered little surety she would not return.

Everyone knew this story. When the bard sang Medea's tale, no one could resist listening with horror and shivers down their spines. Everyone feared that such violence might somehow be real and enter their lives. Mia now recognized how thin lay the veil between the human and divine worlds, the normal and magical, and she could convince her island that a single unwise word of gossip about their oversized prince could unleash this murderous witch upon them all.

In Mia's mind, the threat of Medea had bloomed into a sure way to keep her household and island silent about this distinctive new prince.

But Mia had not known there was a connection between Medea and Thetis. She struggled to decipher what that meant. She'd blurted out the name Medea. No way back from that.

"Medea is your cousin?" Her voice croaked out like stone against gravel. She lifted her gaze to the goddess and saw arms crossed in annoyance or perhaps impatience—not as bad as arms ready to strike.

Thetis deigned to answer. "My grandsire Oceanus, eldest of the Titans, is also her grandfather, though I claim him through the powerful sea-god Nereus, and she traces her descent through the weak Oceanid nymph Idyia."

Mia couldn't follow that complicated lineage, except to sense Thetis's confidence in her own superiority. Then it occurred to her that Thetis would not take offense at using her cousin's reputation to terrify humans into silence. The goddess would revel in paralyzing mortals with Medea's hate-filled notoriety.

So Mia explained how, if she became Achilles's wife, she would ensure with a vividly told tale of Medea that no word of his presence would slip outside the boundary of Skyros's shores—or even word of some mysteriously grand prince that might draw the wrong eyes.

She explained how she'd see that her people contained within the island's shores the true appearance, strength, and fighting skills of this extraordinary prince. She would convince her household and island that this prince, whatever they would call him, was a man at whom Medea aimed her revenge.

Medea had lived and done evil in several places—none of them associated with Achilles's true life. He could be from any of the places from Medea's past, such a confusing trail, yet another innocent target of the witch's poisonous hate. This tale would achieve two things. It would hide Achilles's true identity. But, of equal importance, it would inspire fear that would keep the island from talking to visitors who might carry suspicious details to these men, whoever they were, that the goddess commanded must never learn of Achilles's hiding place. Mia would see to it that her island was reminded that sorceresses can hear gossip whispered to them by the winds. A single word could bring death upon them.

Mia would stop rumor with terror.

A cruel smile curled on the goddess's face. "You have a knack for ruthlessness. Perhaps you will not make such a disgraceful wife for my son." Thetis took her seat on the throne again. "But do not fail this time. I have been far too patient with this court and its blunders. I will not be again."

17

No stranger stealing a glance inside the throne room would suspect that the goddess, stiff and regal on the throne, was *not* the rightful ruler of this kingdom. Nor, Mia suspected, would an outsider guess that the two frightened mortals huddled below the throne dais were the true king and princess of the realm. The echoing room was stripped bare of its usual servants and courtiers.

"So, my child," the goddess said to Achilles, who stood beside her temporary throne, "you will stay hidden here in the women's quarters, away from men who might come to this island. Let King Lycomedes meet with any outsiders." Mia's father made a sound of agreement, but a shadow fell on Achilles's face, showing in the downturn of his lips and narrowing of his eyes.

The goddess pointed a finger at her son in warning. "You like this mortal girl who will be your wife. Good. Let that guide your behavior. No sight or word of your presence must slip from these shores, or I will return with death in my fingertips for these untrustworthy mortals—all of them. If I must suffer your loss, *they* will pay to the full."

Achilles stumbled back at this threat, and Mia trembled. She saw he believed his mother and took her at her word. There could be no mistakes. None. Skyros must hide the most renowned and promising warrior of his generation. She and her people would allow no word that would reveal his identity to slip past their sandy beaches.

Her mind jumped between the various challenges involved in constructing a story that would not fail. They must first bridge between Pyrrha as guest and the startling news of a prince for the island, a husband for its princess. Mia looked up at Achilles. "You don't have a sister, do you?"

Puzzled, he shook his head, stepping down from the dais and reaching out to take her hand, but then his arm fell to his side. They were no longer two girls together. They must marry before they could fall into the easy touch of dear ones.

Thetis's upper lip twisted into a sneer. "*Another* child with my mortal husband? Never."

Mia bobbed her head toward the goddess, trying to placate her with humility. "Then it will further hide Achilles's true identity, if we say to this court and my people that the Pyrrha they knew is sister to this prince and has gone to a marriage or returned home, safe there now, while her brother is not. It will also win the new prince goodwill since Pyrrha took care for my people." She dared a direct look at Thetis. "What should we call your son?"

"Pyrrhus will do. Mortal girls often receive a version of the names their fathers and brothers hold. When you have a son, you will use this same name until he comes of age and shows his immortal strength and receives a more appropriate name."

When she has a son? Mia bit her lip to keep from asking the goddess if she saw this in a prophetic vision. More likely, it was her imperious presumption that *her* son would immediately sire a son. Mia had trouble enough edging around the idea that she would be wife to this towering man.

Her father cleared his throat. "I am honored that you, Lady Goddess, accept my daughter as bride for your son. Perhaps we should formalize this immediately, while you are here. These two young people have already spent too much time close together. We can forgo the pomp and elaborate preparations. Shall I summon the priests and priestesses for a marriage rite?"

"I did not enjoy my own hateful marriage ceremony. I care little for this form. Do as you wish so long as it brings my son safety."

Lycomedes left the throne room.

Achilles stepped back up onto the dais, approaching his mother. "My marriage to Princess Deidamia will allow me to hide within this court. I will stay away from any visitors to this island. They will neither see me nor hear anything of my presence that would hint that I am Achilles, son of Thetis and Peleus. We have settled on that."

Mia tried to guess what Achilles would ask for.

Thetis crossed her arms and raised one eyebrow.

"I cannot intermix closely with the warriors of Lycomedes's citadel," Achilles offered, "not as close companions. That would be unwise given my need for concealment. They will be held to silence, but that is easier if they know little."

"I would not approve of your intermixing closely with them. That is true."

Mia watched this interaction between mother and son. It was familiar to both, the mortal son negotiating the form of his daily life from his controlling mother. The goddess aware that she would concede something to him. The tightness in Mia's chest loosened.

Achilles continued, "My marriage, which I welcome, frees me from the pretense of womanhood while I stay within this court, but it does not provide me with an appropriate male companion. I must return to my daily training as a warrior, a future king. I must have at least one attendant who matches sufficiently my skill and yet someone whom I can trust without question, one who will never reveal my identity. There is only one such person. Allow Patroclus to come to Skyros. A squire to the new prince on Skyros will draw no attention. Patroclus has no renown of his own." Achilles paused, chewing on his lip. Then he added, "He must be in despair, wondering whether I live or die."

Thetis leaned forward from her seat. "He does despair, but not because he fears you are dead. I ordered his silence and made sure he did not go in search for you."

Achilles fisted his hands and then released them. "So you understand both that if you had silenced him by killing him, you would have caused my never-ending despair, *and* that you can trust him sufficiently to honor my heart in this. Our separation has no purpose but cruelty. Bring an end to it, for my sake."

Never-ending despair? An extreme state over an ordinary companion in arms. Mia's gaze darted to Achilles's face. Who was this Patroclus over whom her almost-husband would despair forever if he lost him?

From the hallway came the sound of footsteps and voices. The door opened, and her father led in a group of priests, priestesses, and servants. One priest carried the silver pitcher of cedar oil to consecrate the marriage, another the portable altar for the occasion. A servant carried a saffron-dyed veil and headed toward Mia. The brilliant yellow linen, finely woven enough to be translucent, bore the creases of long storage. It must have been her mother's veil.

Like her parents' marriage, would her own suffer from the presence of another?

18

In her small sleeping chamber, Mia stood alone with Achilles—Pyrrhus, she must remember to call him, even in her thoughts. She pushed the saffron-colored veil away from her face. The familiar feel of the room clashed with her discomfort in his presence. The extraordinary height that had intrigued her in Pyrrha, now made her feel small and vulnerable.

Pyrrhus stood at the doorway as if unwilling to enter. To his mother, he'd said he welcomed the marriage, but his mother would have killed Mia and her family if they hadn't settled on it, so he might have agreed only to save her life. That was a kindness she valued, but she thought with longing of the trust and closeness she'd felt with Pyrrha, the way their friendship had inspired her to be someone new to herself. This man behaved like a different person.

She'd helped Pyrrha without understanding what was destroying Pyrrha's well-being. That help had built a bond, but it didn't seem like a connection that this huge warrior would want to honor. He might view her with shame and dislike. His hesitance confirmed that.

Mia stood in silence. Each breath caught in her chest like goat fur on thorns.

Pyrrhus sighed. Mia's eyes darted toward him, trying to interpret his meaning.

He took another step inside the room. "I'm sorry." He reached for the veil.

"Sorry?" Her voice came out as a croak. *Was he going to do something awful now?*

He frowned and shook his head. "You're my friend."

Mia's knees gave out, and she reached for her bed to support herself. "Oh. Can we be friends? Still, I mean."

"You don't want to be?"

"I do, but—"

"Nobody has ever started a marriage in this way, have they?" Pyrrhus laughed and gently guided Mia into sitting on the bed.

"Nobody," she whispered.

"I meant sorry that the wedding ceremony was so—" He shrugged. "Girls dream about their weddings, don't they? This veil must have been pulled from some chest. It's shabby with age."

Mia touched the veil and nodded. Pyrrhus reached to her head and found her hairpins, tugging them out and lifting away the veil. Mia had to raise herself from the bed for a moment for him to free the bottom edge of it where she'd sat on it.

"My mother's veil . . ." A sob cut off the rest of what she tried to say.

Pyrrhus wrapped his arms around her and held her so tightly she expected her bones to creak. After a while, Pyrrhus began rubbing her back in slow circular movements, the same as Mia had done for Pyrrha when she'd been falling apart. This reminder of their friendship helped soften the strangeness of this man to her. Perhaps she had not lost all of what Pyrrha had meant to her. Mia buried her face into his strong chest, taking in the familiar salt-sea scent. Now that singular odor made sense to her, son of a sea goddess that he was.

His hands stopped circling her back and strayed into exploring. She was his wife. This was what they were meant to do, and she wanted it. She ached to run her hands over his muscled chest and thighs, to let him show her much more than their previous kissing.

He felt different to her, a little frightening, but a similar desire flushed through her, waves of warmth with the promise of pleasure.

He wanted her, her body and her friendship. She was lucky.

Sitting beside her, his eyes smoldered as he unpinned one side of her peplos.

She caught the fabric and held it covering her breast. "Before we ... I need to know something. I am your wife no matter your answer, but I will know what kind of wife I am to you. I would prefer to understand beforehand."

Pyrrhus drew back, frowning. "What is this? Has my mother terrified you too much?"

"She has, but that's not—" Mia closed her eyes so that she could not see the concern and kindness on his face. "You spoke of your heart and never-ending despair. Who is Patroclus to you?"

His breath flooded out as if she'd punched him. Her eyes flashed open. She saw the truth she'd dreaded.

"I love you, Mia, and now you are my wife. Leave this question. When Patroclus arrives, you'll see that he does not make you less to me."

At least her husband didn't pretend this mysterious man was nothing out of the ordinary to him, a fellow warrior to train with and nothing else. That lie would have broken her.

He hadn't lied, not quite. Going forward, the nearness or distance of Patroclus would not affect how little or much she meant to her husband because well before she met Pyrrhus, he must have already given his heart to Patroclus.

She studied the small lines her question had etched beside Pyrrhus's eyes. He wanted to love her as much as he loved Patroclus, might even tell himself he did, but she imagined him as unrestrained with that first gift of love as he was in his running, holding nothing back. That was his nature, part of what drew her to him. Could a person pour out all their love and still have as much left behind?

She didn't know the answer, but his mother had love only for her son and no one else. Immortals—and even half-immortals—might suffer a limitation in love.

"Let's ignore my question," Mia said. *For now.* She was his wife. That would have to be enough. She leaned against him, her hand still holding her gown in place.

The lines on Pyrrhus's face relaxed. He kissed her, parting her lips and caressing her tongue with his. This was Pyrrha's familiar, delicious kiss. She felt another veil of strangeness fall away from the touch of this godlike man. Her lips pressed against his, her tongue sliding against his. She opened wider, groaning when his tongue flicked down her throat and lit a line of heat from there to her groin.

He drew back. The sea depths of his eyes gleamed. His lips turned up in a wicked twitch, and he loosened the pin from her other shoulder.

Mia let her peplos fall open, sliding her hand downwards, stroking the muscles of his thigh, drawn to their barely contained power. Then her motions stole up under the chiton's edge, and she explored him with as much vigor as he was exploring her breasts with his mouth.

Her fingers traced upwards. She flinched at the size and hardness her hand discovered. Nothing in her play with Pyrrha had felt so alien. But its surface was silky, irresistible to her fingers, the muffled gasp from her husband even more alluring. She understood in an instant why in a girl's body, their play had always turned intolerable to him.

How disorienting he must have found the sensation radiating outwards from between her own legs. She let it fill her, opening her legs wider and falling back onto the bed.

"No more clothes," she said.

A low groan of need answered her. He stood.

She undid her belt's knot. Pyrrhus's hands dragged her peplos downward. She arched her hips as he tugged the loose gown to her knees. She kicked it off, leaning back on her forearms, her legs open.

He reached for the pin holding one shoulder of his chiton, flicking it open, and then the other. The short tunic fell to the ground.

She gazed at him. Eventually their eyes met. She held his

ravenous look and sat up so she could brush her fingers up and down this part of him she was getting to know. He stepped closer, standing directly before her, and shuddered in the best possible way, giving her courage to clasp him with her whole hand.

When he whispered, "kiss me," she knew what he meant.

How would this be?

She'd arched in pleasure under the thrusts of his tongue in her mouth. Now she saw that for what it was, an enticement to more.

She ran her tongue along the silky skin, then closed her eyes and tried more, discovering *more* lit the fiery line down to her groin, unbearably so. She wrapped one of her legs around his thigh trying to press against him.

He rested his hands on her head. "For now, stop. I . . . well, there will be plenty of time later for that. This time . . . lie back. I'll give you what you want. All of it."

19

By the next morning, Mia decided she liked marriage. She untangled her limbs from her husband's, stretched her arms, and pushed her tangled hair from her eyes, blinking sleepiness away. Her movement didn't stir Pyrrhus, who lay on his side facing her. The bed was small for the two of them, but she'd slept well. By the look of it, so had he.

But what now? Her life was so transformed in a single day that she couldn't sort it out. She watched the rise and fall of Pyrrhus's chest. The contours entranced her, and she couldn't resist running a finger over the firm outlines. His chest wasn't hairy like some men's.

His eyes opened. "Again?" he asked with laughter in his sleepy murmur.

She shook her head. "I'm . . ." She felt her cheeks flush and couldn't say she was sore. He'd been so concerned and gentle about that.

"I know." He reached for her and pulled her down against his chest.

"What now?" Mia asked from the embrace of his arms. It felt both strange and good not to be alone in figuring everything out. "Your secret—"

"And my mother."

"Mmm."

"My mother is gone at least. She reacted to my marriage far better than I would have guessed. I think she liked that I was tied to Skyros now. Even she must have realized her plan to lock me away in a women's quarters was not going to hold for long. She couldn't simply will me to stay. Now I have reasons to be here, you, most of all, and I owe your father allegiance to this kingdom's rule."

She snuggled closer against his body and hoped an honest question wouldn't break her heart. "Are you glad to be tied to me, to Skyros?"

"I'm glad you are my wife. I've always known I'd have a wife, but girls puzzled me. The ones I knew at my father's court existed in a world I didn't understand or care for. My father suggested betrothals. I always pretended he hadn't and left it at that."

"Patroclus was who you really wanted."

She felt him shrug. He avoided the subject of his preference for Patroclus as he had with his father, but he wouldn't deny what she'd forced herself to say.

"I liked you from the beginning," he said. "I watched you with your father when he ordered you to receive me as a guest. Our parents are not so different. Controlling our lives. But even when you did what he asked, you stood up for yourself, not openly, but . . . I'd never seen a girl like that. Then I learned your mother had abandoned you, as mine had, and I felt I could understand your sadness. That you could understand mine."

"You don't mind that I saw you in a girl's body? You're a warrior, a prince."

"That was my mother's cruelty. I don't want to think about it."

"I promised your mother I'd silence my father's court and household. The whole island. Nobody can describe your true appearance to an outsider. We can't fail in that, but—"

"What you said to her was brilliant." Pyrrhus pressed a kiss into her tangled hair. "Using fear to silence people—that's how my mother thinks about mortals. You persuaded her. You didn't have to have a real plan. Fortunately, you have a lot of practice telling wild stories to your sisters and that was enough."

Mia pulled free of his arms, sitting upright. Her plan hadn't started as much more than a rushed idea, but it was *real*.

"My mother trusts the power of fear overmuch. If people can escape from fear, they will, no matter how much harm they do to others. If we rely *only* on fear, that harm will come about. Fear, on its own, can be dangerous."

"That makes sense, but..."

He stroked her leg. "Don't worry, I'll figure out something workable. I owe you and your family protection. My being here brought the danger to your island. I'll keep you safe." His hand slid up her belly and cupped her breast.

She brushed away his hand and looked directly into his half-closed, languid eyes. "Something workable? Nothing that involves me or any of my wild stories, then."

Pyrrhus sat up, his eyes alert. "You're angry. I don't understand."

"Moments ago, you said you liked me from the first because I stood up for myself. Now you treat me as my father does, as someone to ignore, someone who can't do much besides spin wool."

"No, that's not fair—"

"Isn't it? You had no plan to talk to me about figuring out something workable as you put it, did you?"

He shrugged.

No, not this time. She wasn't going to let him avoid this with a shrug. "When I was Pyrrha's friend, for the first time I met a girl who didn't act like the docile girl everyone wants me to be. I admired her. She needed the freedom of the world outside the palace even more than I did. She talked about the threads that hold kingdoms together and my responsibility to my people as if these were things I had been considering all my life. She showed me choices I had to face and act upon. She saved a man's life and gave orders to men that they followed because she'd learned skills and knew best what should be done. You remember all this, don't you?"

Pyrrhus nodded. "I was—am—your friend, but I never felt like a girl. That's not who I am."

"No, but I saw a girl, and she changed me. That's what *you* did. Pyrrha and I talked together. We listened to each other, but maybe only I was listening. Maybe I mistook that because I saw a girl like me, and girls listen to each other."

"I thought I was listening. You helped me. When I wanted to die, you kept me alive."

"And you showed me a new way to be, one that felt right for the first time since my mother left. Because of you, or you as Pyrrha, I see how *I* want to be. But you're a man. That girl was a lie."

"Not a lie, but being a girl didn't feel right to me. I'm surprised I showed you this way to feel right, but I'm glad you have it. Everything you described—our conversations and what we did—that part seems so ordinary to me. I didn't mean to change you. The agony of looking at my body and seeing a girl was all I could think about. You gave me moments when I could escape that dread, and that was everything. I didn't know what those moments meant to you."

"You dislike the way your mother controls your life—gives orders and tells you nothing. Don't you remember how it felt to be a girl? Not the body you hated, but the way everyone treated and spoke to you? Toward girls, everyone acts like your mother."

Pyrrhus opened his mouth to speak and closed it. They sat silently looking at each other.

"So I should never treat you like a girl?"

Mia wrinkled her nose. "Can you treat me like you want to be treated?"

"You make it sound simple." His eyes sparkled like sunlight on wind-ruffled sea.

She clasped his hand in both of hers. "I don't suppose it will be. Could we start by figuring out a workable plan together? Rumors of what happened yesterday are no doubt already spreading throughout the royal household. How long before they slip out of the palace and make their way around the island? Keeping a court and an island silent about your unusual appearance will not be easy. Perhaps my wild storytelling can silence these rumors with fear of Medea. If your goddess mother thought it was clever, perhaps it is."

Pyrrhus pressed his lips together and wrinkled his brow. "It is clever, but I don't see how to make it work."

"Maybe I do."

20

Standing alone with her maidservant in the dim corridor outside her father's throne room, Mia grasped Dione's arm. "Did you persuade him?"

"Don't you worry," Dione answered Mia. "I led him on like you told me. He's sure he knows how to please you. All them details about the blood and killing you taught me. Lucky you always were one for a monstrous story. The silly man believed me. He's looking for a gift from the princess when he's done."

"It's lucky then that I've never much liked him and won't mind disappointing him."

Dione's eyes flashed in merriment that quickly faded. "I hope it all goes well."

Mia gave her maid a quick embrace. "Thank you. Everything depends on this."

"You'll think of something if this don't work."

Mia shook her head. "This is what I promised. You haven't met my husband's mother."

Dione shuddered. "I don't never want to."

"She'll kill my family and me if I fail, so I can't fail." The tightness in her chest might crush her if she let it.

Dione squeezed Mia against her for a moment. "You're not alone." She stepped back, looking Mia over. "Seeing you so lovely, no one will wonder why a lofty prince chose Skyros."

"That's the least of my worries."

Dione tugged slightly here and there at the folds of Mia's gown so that they draped closely around her breasts. Then she tucked in a loose strand of dark hair where it had come free of the twists of hair and gold beads framing Mia's face and adjusted the shimmery white veil cascading around Mia's shoulders. Among Dione's many tasks that afternoon had been polishing the veil with a smooth stone until it glowed as if lit from within.

Dione nodded in satisfaction. "Now, off with you. Everything's set just as you and that big husband of yours hatched up."

Mia turned to hurry inside where the sounds of the many guests already rang loud. She was late, and ordinarily that would annoy her father. Possibly not tonight, not over something so trivial. He was aware of the strands set in motion, had assisted with them, and knew the stakes.

As she approached the double doors into the throne room, servants pulled them open. The central hearth fire and oil lamps glowed against the dark red and mustard walls. She stopped at the doorway, scanning the unaccustomed fullness of the room.

Pyrrhus had argued for as few observers as possible at this wedding feast, but her father had feared offending men he depended on as warriors. At the door end of the room where Mia stood, furthest from the throne, servants had set up benches wide enough for sitting or reclining and stools scattered in front as tables. She saw familiar faces of the lesser noble families. Dominating the area closest to the throne dais, in an arc of carved armchairs paired with side tables for food sat the guests of greatest honor. Her place remained empty at the center between Pyrrhus and her father.

She realized with a start that the opening of the doors and her entrance had drawn attention. All eyes were turned to her, and the room fell silent. Everyone rose, including her father. She swallowed down the wooly choking sensation in her throat and strode down the aisle left open between the benches and chairs, grateful for Dione's final inspection so she could feel confident nothing was amiss.

She caught Pyrrhus's eye. He gave her a gratifying smile, but she saw the discomfort in those green depths. She didn't blame him for hating the part he had to play.

She stepped toward her father. He took her hand in both of his, laid a paternal kiss on her brow, and then guided her to stand in front of Pyrrhus, who reached out to her, open palmed.

Her father placed her hand into Pyrrhus's. When her new husband closed his fingers over hers, her hand disappeared inside his huge fist.

"Your marriage was sealed," Lycomedes said, "with sacred cedar oil. I entrust my daughter to your dominion."

"And I swear loyalty to your sovereignty." Pyrrhus bowed his head and raised it. The two men stared at each other in silence for what seemed a long time to Mia.

Then Pyrrhus gently tugged Mia close and pressed a kiss on her lips before sliding his hand against her lower back and ushering his bride to her chair.

Before anyone sat, her father signaled for his silver libation cup and made a wine offering to the king of the gods and his divine wife, the goddess and keeper of marriage bonds. Mia watched the deep red liquid splash into the silver wine bowl, looking like the blood that would soak the tale tonight if all went well. *Never the blood of my family, please the gods.*

After a servant carried away the bowl and libation cup, her father signaled that the meal should begin and took his seat, gesturing to everyone else to do likewise.

The servants laid out baskets of flatbread and poured wine for all the guests. They carried in trays loaded with rows of polished red-clay bowls. From them arose the steamy tang of soup made from fennel and dried fish. Mia took her bowl from a servant and breathed in the combination of aromatic sweetness and brine. She loved this soup, but fear of what would or would not happen later with their plan cramped her belly.

Pyrrhus raised his bowl to his lips and sipped politely. When he brought his bowl down, he turned to her and whispered, "I wish we could be done with the feast and reach the last part of the evening."

She nodded and then almost smiled at the meaning anyone overhearing him would assume he'd intended.

Servants cleared away the soup bowls and replaced them with fresh plates, and then maids dished out food from trays of cumin-rubbed goat grilled on spits, pots of mutton stewed with onions, beets, and coriander greens, bowls of boiled chickpeas and garlic, and piles of cheese soaked in mint and olive oil. Mia wished she had an appetite for all these delicacies. She'd make sure any leftovers went to the nearby village where she'd seen the hungry children.

Then, sooner than she felt ready for, the dirty plates were cleared, fresh wine poured into cups, and her father called for the bard. There was only one on the island. Many of the nursemaids and elders told better stories than this man, but he accompanied himself on a turtleshell lyre and knew how to sing the tales of heroes and gods. He played at the king's feasts and at any other nobleman's hearth if hired. Mia had known he'd sing tonight. Everyone would expect that.

He swaggered from his place at one side of the room. His dark hair was oiled to make it shine. He wore a full-length robe in the manner of a nobleman or priest, a sign of the honor due a bard. He held his lyre on one arm and stepped into the open space in front of the arc of chairs, stopping in front of Mia. That was a good sign that Dione's gossiping had done its work. Ordinarily, this obsequious hanger-on would have centered on the king. She gave him a false smile and a tip of her chin that he should begin.

He plucked the strings, letting the notes fill the air while he chose his first words. "Muse, sing through me a song of a mighty hero and the beauteous maiden who aided him when once she'd been struck with indomitable love for him."

Mia hoped she would prove to be the hidden muse of this song.

"I sing a tale of newfound love and heroic deeds, the meeting and marriage of Jason and Medea," the bard continued after another interlude of plucked strings, "to honor our King Lycomedes and the marriage of his daughter, Princess Deidamia to Prince Pyrrhus." He plucked again, his mouth puckered in concentration. "Not so long ago, a king set a challenge for a young prince so that the youth and his comrades could test their mettle."

That was one way of describing a threatened usurper sending the rightful heir to his intended death. Mia had to admire the way the bard skirted this awkward conflict between a king and an heir while performing in front of two such. She glanced at her father and then at Pyrrhus. Neither had missed the glossing over. More to the point, Pyrrhus had stiffened at the mention of Medea and grasped the arm of his chair with white knuckles.

"The heroes built a mighty ship, the Argo, with the help of Athena, the goddess of all crafts and warlike wisdom. The king of gods, Zeus, lent a prophetic beam from his sacred oak to speak out guidance to the fresh-fledged champions. So armed and outfitted, the brave company endured many terrors and battles—tales for another day—until they passed through the straits of Helle and came at last to the land of Colchis where lay the golden fleece they must retrieve to prove their strength and prowess."

Mia fingered the polished smoothness of her goblet. When she had been deemed old enough to sit at the royal feasts, she'd been given this cup. The delicately painted design of dolphins leaping among an octopus and fishes, her mother's choice, had always made sense to Mia, a combination of Mia's love of tide pools and her mother's of the wild freedom of dolphins. But now Mia wondered if the cup's design foresaw her unlikely marriage to the son of a sea goddess. How would all of this have differed if her mother had never left?

The bard was searching for words as he always did. She wanted to shout at him to sing what he'd been told—although he mustn't realize how much he'd been guided. It should be easy for once. But he was no doubt struggling with how to tell of Medea's aid to Jason without stressing the daughter's betrayal of her father and home. So many awkward parts of this story, but Mia didn't want him to smooth any of them out. She wanted a gruesome tale that would put fear into her people's hearts.

Eventually he worked his way through Medea's swooning love and decision to side with Jason over her own kin. Jason survived the yoking of fire-breathing bulls and fending off attacks of armed men born from dragon teeth sowed in the ground. But he succeeded only through the sorcery of Medea's potions and spells. When the treacherous king refused to hand over the promised golden fleece, Medea singlehandedly overcame the guardian dragon. She conquered the monstrous serpent with magical words wielded like an invisible spear and followed that up with a drug made by grinding roots sprouted from Prometheus's tortured blood. She'd compounded the drug in the dark of night under Hecate's shadows and the howls of monsters trapped in the bowels of Tartarus.

Mia smiled. He'd remembered the details.

Mia's husband grew increasingly uneasy. Most of the room must see his constant shifting and growing frowns. His hand crept to the dagger at his belt and then he withdrew it, then it crept back again.

The bard delayed the essential parts of the story with an unnecessary interlude about Medea's adoration of Jason and the hero's oaths of love sworn to her. Mia tapped a finger against the arm of her chair, hoping to prod the singer into the exciting parts that were, admittedly, singularly inappropriate for a wedding feast. Any true singer would never have allowed himself to be tricked into singing this tale tonight.

Finally, the bard reached Medea's ruthlessness during her escape from her father's kingdom in the company of Jason and his comrades.

The bard glanced at Mia, doubt on his brow, and she gave him an encouraging nod, putting on an air of excited listening.

It hadn't been easy to plant the seeds for including this bloody betrayal of family ties that should be held dear—a brother's murder. According to the tale, to prevent her father from catching her lover's ship, Medea tore her brother's flesh into small pieces and tossed them into the sea so that her father's progress was slowed as he gathered them for burial. Mia, not content with the innate horror of this deed, had Dione slip in a new version as she'd whispered all the princess's favorite bits to the bard. The slaughtered brother was no longer the grown warrior of the usual tale, killed in a battle with Jason and then cut up, but a little boy taken by Medea for this grim purpose and ripped to death by her own hands.

As the song turned ever darker, Pyrrhus groaned and covered his face in his hands.

This violence was heart wrenching enough, and Mia saw horror written on the listening faces all around her, but she knew the shift in the story to a small child would further remind those listening of one of the worst versions of Medea's story, a part they wouldn't hear this night, when Medea took revenge on her husband by killing her own children. Mia wanted everyone to picture that implacable, bloodthirsty sorceress who would stop at nothing for vengeance.

The bard paused, again looking toward the princess for encouragement, and then described the fraternal blood that covered Medea's hands and soaked her gown. Pyrrhus jumped from his chair with a shout of "Silence!" and leapt toward the bard with his dagger drawn.

The bard screamed, dropped his lyre, and backed into a bench of feasting men who shoved him away, so that he stumbled back toward Pyrrhus and fell on his knees.

"Why do you torment me with this tale of that sorceress Medea?" Pyrrhus yelled.

He grabbed the trembling man by the waist with one hand, lifting him off the ground while swinging the dagger at his chest with the other hand. "What have you heard? Who told you my fear?"

The bard dangled, his legs kicking uselessly until Pyrrhus dropped him in a heap and stomped out of the throne room.

21

The next morning, Mia led Pyrrhus along the palace corridors to the citadel, Dione following close behind. By the time they'd passed through the postern door and tunnel into the citadel's muddy open yard, the morning sun had crept high enough to be visible above the great stone walls.

As Pyrrha, her husband had never visited the citadel and seen the fortifications. As they exited the low tunnel and Pyrrhus straightened to his full height, his interest was palpable, and she felt a little forgotten. Without waiting for her, he crossed the open space to inspect the gate and the defensive tower rising beside it. Standing in front of the massive wooden gate, he looked all warrior, assessing the bronze-reinforced beams with his hand on the hilt of his sword. The citadel rang with loud men's voices and clanking bronze. Underneath those martial noises, the wind whistled against the stone walls, and a hawk screeched as it dove for prey against the blue sky.

With Dione at her side, she watched her husband, certain the reason they'd entered the citadel—the grain she'd been promised—had slipped his mind, and she would have to draw him back to it.

Falsely attacking the scrawny bard had put him in a foul mood. It was beneath him. Pyrrhus had made that clear. He hadn't even complimented her on how successfully she and Dione had tricked the bard into singing exactly the right tale. She watched the admiring guards who quickly gathered near this startling new warrior prince as he studied the citadel and hoped the distraction of defenses and guards would mend his mood.

Mia beckoned to a servant and explained what she and her husband had come for. The man stammered that he must bring Galene. Only the steward knew the proper way to remove grain without it spoiling. He hurried off.

Mia turned to Dione. "I've been so fearful and distracted, I haven't told you. Good news," she added quickly when she saw Dione's alarm. "Yesterday Galene came to see me about the preparations for the wedding feast. On his own, he apologized for being distracted and not giving me his full respectful attention when I questioned him by the pit. I told him it was you he had insulted and should give more respect to. To my surprise, he agreed. He said, 'She is only a slave but she defended the villagers as if she were powerful.' He made it easy to ask him if he would choose to marry you. He is eager for it." Dione's face was hard to interpret. "You may still say no. It is your choice as much as his. You've had more time to think."

"I have thought about it. This is best for me."

Mia squeezed her maid's arm. "I hope you will be happy." Why couldn't Dione find some happiness as Mia had? After all, there were compromises in her own royal marriage. She'd sought protection through it no less than Dione did through hers, and she doubted Galene had already given his heart to anyone else.

Dione nodded with determination in her eyes and set her attention on Pyrrhus, as if to remind Mia what the princess had come for, although the grain supplies weren't holding the warrior's attention.

Mia drew Dione closer to where guards stood around Pyrrhus. He was questioning them about the number of men stationed on the walls and elsewhere, their rotations, armor, and several other things, not all of which Mia understood. Pyrrhus stood more than a head taller than any of the others. They gave him rapt attention.

Pointing, she whispered to Dione, "Let's go over there while we wait."

They walked toward the empty herd pen where the storage pits were situated. The roofed-over pit that her father had told her was for her dowry lay undisturbed. Two men worked near the new pit cutting stone. They must be adding to its foundations. Mia glanced over her shoulder at the rows of mud bricks along one side of the citadel yard, still drying and hardening. The two stonecutters had their heads bent low over the work, and they were talking together.

Mia tugged on Dione's arm, slipping behind the wooden stable wall where they could overhear the men's conversation.

"You'd think this were a treasury for gold with all this stone." The stonecutter's voice was rough and louder than was wise for such complaining.

"Stop whining and get back at it. Pull your side of the saw."

The scraping sound of two men drawing a stone-saw back and forth silenced their talk. Mia exchanged a disappointed look with Dione. It was probably too much to expect that lowly men like this had already caught the gossip she and Pyrrhus had hoped to launch from last night's pretense.

She rested her shoulder against one of the posts holding up the lean-to roof of the stable. Across the citadel yard, Pyrrhus was climbing the ladder up to the gate tower platform, followed by the attentive guards. Dione raised an eyebrow with a sympathetic smile. Mia shook her head. A donkey noticed them, shuffled over, and stuck his nose over the wooden divider. Mia scratched the base of his ear and stroked his neck. The donkey was better company than her husband.

The sawing noise stopped again.

"Hand me the bucket of water," one of the men said. His gulping was so loud Mia wrinkled her nose in disgust.

"Did you hear the serving girls?" one man asked. Mia caught Dione's eye.

"The carrying on at the feast?"

Mia's heart sped up. They *had* heard the gossip.

"Screaming-like and cutting the singer's throat. All 'cause he'd sung a song the new prince hated."

"Look at him over there. I wouldn't want that warrior's sword at my throat, but the girls swear the foolish singer's unhurt."

"He won't sing about that witch Medea anymore."

"A witch who kills her kin and everybody else, near as I heard. Good riddance to that tale. I wouldn't say her name aloud if I was you. Why he ever sung it at a wedding feast?"

"That's a big man the king found for his daughter. A warrior like that stands apart. I guess his size got the bard thinking of that Jason. Forgot about the sorceress wife."

"Then just as well the singer got some sense scared into him. Our princess's not a bloodthirsty witch and no one should'a said so."

"That's so. She's always been kind to the likes of us, anyway. Sets aside wool for us servants so we're not wearing rags. That's her doing and you know it. And now there's a fine prince for her."

Dione smiled and nodded at Mia.

The screech of the saw scraping back and forth against stone picked up again. Mia and Dione left the shelter of the stable. Mia saw her father and Galene hurrying out of the tunnel from the palace. *Her father? Curses.* It was *her* dowry. She didn't need his permission. Galene veered off toward the storage pits at a worried run. Her father stood, expecting her to come to him. She peered at her father's face and realized he was ready for a fight.

Mia leaned to Dione's ear. "Go to Galene. Maybe he'll speak to you. Distracting him from his precious pit might be all to my good, anyway." Dione set off.

Alone, Mia hurried across the yard, lifting her skirts to avoid the mud. Talking to her father without Pyrrhus might help. She'd watched them together. They were both accustomed to being the highest. Pyrrhus was not yet a king, here or in his father's kingdom, but as semi-divine, he'd always been treated as greater than his father, and his prowess as a warrior exceeded all others. No wonder being a woman had been intolerable to him.

"Father, I didn't mean to disturb you."

"Then you should stay out of the citadel. You and the new prince. He quarreled with me about every nobleman I invited to the feast, insisting he has to stay hidden, but here he is displaying himself." He flung his hand up at the tower where Pyrrhus was prominently visible. "I've spent the morning in the unpleasant task of lying to my nobles, explaining Pyrrhus's rage and spreading the tale you made up that the sorceress Medea wants to kill the prince and his 'sister' who stayed with us for a time. I've warned my nobles that only silence about the distinctive appearance of the new prince will keep us safe. It's bad enough he's so huge, but did he have to have red-gold hair?"

"You can't blame him for the color of his hair, Father."

"No one has hair that color. But I've done your bidding. That should be enough for you."

"Thank you, Father. You and I are both bound by the goddess's wishes in this. I'm sorry you've had such a distasteful task. It *is* working. I overheard those two stonecutters over there gossiping about Medea. Now your task is most important, spreading word that because of the witch, no hint of our prince's presence can slip out from Skyros. The bard's tale of fear was only the first step. I need your help."

The glare in her father's eyes softened. "You did put the most gruesome details into the bard's mouth. He's more foolish than I thought, I guess, but you struck fear into everyone's heart. I can do my part after that."

The credit pleased Mia. "Dione has already been to the spring putting the tale out among the women from Seaview. No one will risk drawing Medea to the island. Soon it will be on everyone's tongue." From the corner of her eye, she noticed Pyrrhus descending the ladder.

She glanced across to the pit area. Dione stood near Galene, her head bowed. He was speaking.

"Rumor is a dangerous sword," her father said, "but at least we can assure the goddess we have done as she commanded. None of this will ensure—"

"I know, Father, but we can hope."

"Can we? You are young, aren't you? Persuade the prince to stay hidden and leave the grain pit to Galene." He turned to leave.

"Father, you gave me the grain as my dowry. To me, not your servant." Mia caught movement as Dione lifted her head and looked into Galene's smiling face. Dione's suitor lifted her hand to his lips for a kiss. One thing was going well.

Over his shoulder, Lycomedes said, "We can discuss your dowry another day. Take your husband inside."

"My wife does not take me anywhere I do not choose to go," Pyrrhus called out. "Your defenses are inadequate. I will train more men and see to the safety of you and the rest of the royal family."

Lycomedes turned slowly around and faced the prince. "Your mother poses the greatest danger to me and my family. If word of your presence on my island gets out, she will not be merciful. She ordered you to hide in the women's quarters. For Mia's sake, do that."

Pyrrhus stepped close to her father, towering over him. His stance was relaxed, his arms hanging loosely at his sides. She glanced at her father. That confidence was an insult, one her father did not miss. Pyrrhus looked down at Lycomedes and said, "I explained to my mother that I will not live as a woman anymore. I will not sit in the women's hall spinning wool. Nor will I ignore what my greater abilities as a warrior can offer to our realm. A small band of warriors would take this citadel without difficulty, and you do not realize that."

Mia moved to step in between, but Pyrrhus brushed her aside as if she were a feather on a breeze. She started to speak, "Fa—"

"My citadel," her father interrupted her in a strained voice, "has never been taken. The mountain is steep, the walls strong. Young warriors see battles and attacks everywhere because they wish to. I do not expect you to behave like a woman, but behave sensibly."

"Even if I stayed entirely inside the palace walls," Pyrrhus replied, "servants and others would see me. Already you chose to show me to all your nobles. I will be cautious, but my appearance is hardly a secret on this island. Either the people of this island keep silent to outsiders, or they don't. If they fail, whoever my mother wishes to keep away from me may attack. It is my duty to prepare for that. Kings often give such responsibilities to crown princes."

Lycomedes made a rude noise with his lips. "Crown princes are usually the sons by blood of those kings."

"You don't trust me? If I wanted a throne so much, I would seek my own father's. He would give it willingly."

"Your mother would prevent you from going to your father's realm. Isn't that the point?"

"Father," Mia interrupted. "Pyrrhus has no intention of taking your throne. *I* trust him, and I know him far better than you do. He will limit where he goes and who sees him as much as possible. We came to the citadel to begin another way of ensuring the people's silence. Please listen to what we planned instead of dismissing us. You shut me out long enough after Mother left. I thought we understood each other better now."

Her father shook his head. "What *you* planned? The protection of this citadel and its grain stores are my responsibility. You cannot come here and order the servants around without asking me first. Yet you dare to say that I shut *you* out." He sounded hurt as much as angry.

Perhaps she should have checked first with her father. Then she wouldn't have upset him, and maybe he'd agree with her. "When you said the grain was my dowry, you told me it was my future. I knew you loved me when you said that. I only thought . . ." She touched his arm. "I'm sorry Pyrrhus went off on his own with your citadel guards."

Pyrrhus stepped back from Lycomedes. "Your majesty, I was thinking of your well-being. I didn't mean to offend you." His posture had shifted into respectful attention. "Don't be angry at your daughter."

"My daughter should explain what she intends to do wasting grain I worked so hard to gather in."

Mia gasped. *He* worked so hard? "Wasn't the hardest work that of the farmers who labored to grow the grain? You gathered in a great deal of the harvest, perhaps without enough thought to their needs."

"It was for you. I knew full well there'd be suffering. I couldn't help that."

"I came to the citadel today because I wish to end that suffering," Mia said. "I do not want to be responsible for starving children, and Pyrrhus pointed out that—"

"Your majesty," Pyrrhus interrupted. "We should have discussed this with you. Forgive our eagerness that led us to act quickly without talking to you."

"Tell me." Her father crossed his arms over his chest.

Pyrrhus tipped his head in a sign of agreement and respect. "My mother uses only fear to force mortals to bend to her will. Mia understood that Medea's story would appeal to her. I don't think Mia would be alive if she hadn't suggested it. But the goddess relies on fear too much. Fearful people can only think of breaking free of what terrifies them, even if they destroy the safety of those around them. That is our nature as mortals. Don't you agree?"

Her father gave a grudging nod.

"But it is also our nature to protect those we love or admire." Pyrrhus took Mia's hand. "The islanders already love their princess. I have seen that. She hopes to expand that feeling to include me and thus win their cooperation and loyalty in keeping silent. Not only because they fear harm to themselves, but because they do not want harm to come to us. Mia wishes to distribute the grain during this season of hunger as a gift in honor of our wedding, from the new prince and their beloved princess. I will accompany her to the village called Seaview where I, or at least my pretend sister, appeared already. Did you hear of that?"

Lycomedes nodded. "Your sister's reputation as a healer spread more than you intended. You might as well use it."

Pyrrhus shrugged. "We will distribute grain in Seaview first, where it is easiest to win goodwill, initiated by the earlier healing. Then Mia will continue around the island's villages alone."

"I will bring Dione with me, and guards, of course." Mia was eager for her father to understand how well thought-out their plan was. "While I oversee the grain giving, Dione can visit with the village women and, seemingly by accident, spread the story of Medea's persecution of my husband and the great need to say nothing out of the ordinary about the new prince, nothing about his appearance, and to shut out any foreigners who come to the island. We can accomplish so much. It's not a waste of the grain. It's the best use."

Her father shook his head again, but he also smiled. "You have a good heart, my daughter. We'll see what we can do, although I am unwilling to open the great pit for this. It's far too much grain. I'll discuss it with Galene."

Mia burned with frustration. Somehow her good heart was once again an excuse to ignore her wishes. "Isn't the pit filled with the grain that in any other year would have stayed with the farmers?"

"You don't understand," her father answered. "While we took somewhat more this year, every year the palace keeps a large portion, wherever I store it. The new style of pit storage simply allows me greater freedom because I can keep it longer and accumulate a greater amount to bargain with. You know nothing about trade and the royal treasury."

"I want you to teach me. I should understand these things. I do know that feeding my people is important. You taught me that much." She started toward the storage pits at a fast pace where Galene and Dione stood at the open gate, out of hearing. As soon as Galene saw her heading toward him, he looked uncomfortable. The apologetic glance he gave Dione cued that he probably feared Mia was going to rob his grain pit.

Her father grunted in annoyance and followed her. Pyrrhus smoothly caught up, walking beside her.

Her father grabbed her arm. In an angry, hushed voice he said, "Galene knows nothing about the trickery we got up to at the feast or that this tale of Medea is a lie. He heard rumors that the woman who dropped Pyrrha off was an unusual visitor, but he has been wise enough not to ask about any of it. Leave him out of this. You confide in your servant Dione about too much, but stop with her. Servants should never be entrusted with secrets. Secrets are power."

"I have no intention of telling Galene anything, Father." Mia hurried forward. "You said you would discuss my request with him."

They gathered inside the pen, looking at the roofed-over pit.

Her father said to Galene, "The princess wishes to make a gift of grain to her people in honor of her wedding. There is merit in the goodwill such kindness will bring, if done in a small way. She wishes to go to Seaview. She mistakenly thought the grain kept in this pit would be best for her to use. I reminded her that that's not what this grain was set aside for."

Galene tugged his beard. "We can take grain from the storerooms for that. Break the seal on some storage amphoras. If the princess wishes to be seen as generous."

Mia tried to keep her face blank despite how annoying her father's and Galene's attitude toward her was. How could they treat her like this? She wanted to yank Galene's beard out by the roots, no matter how nice he was to Dione.

Pyrrhus placed a hand on her arm. "We'll start with this today," he whispered into her ear.

Then he straightened and looked first at her and then directly at the king with a challenge in his eyes, even as he pretended the words were addressed to her. "My dear wife, didn't your father ask you to visit the villages around the whole island and determine how widespread is the hunger you had observed at Seaview? We will support this one village today, and then you can go to the others. Once their need is clear, I'm sure the king will supply what is needed to his people. After all, he is a good king, and the care of one's people is the greatest responsibility of any ruler."

22

When Mia and Pyrrhus arrived at the village of Seaview, the donkeys carrying loads of grain were greeted with surprise and exclamations by the village women, and then by the men who were called in from their work.

Dione's spreading of the fearful tale of Medea showed in the villagers' reaction to Pyrrhus. They shied away from the prince, as if being near him would bring the sorceress's revenge directly on them. But then Pyrrhus began to unload the hemp sacks of grain himself, placing them into the farmers' arms, and they understood what his presence had brought them. Their taut faces relaxed, and they responded to him in a friendlier manner, even laughing with Pyrrhus when he made a small jab about the donkeys knowing the way to the village because they'd carried the grain both directions.

She caught Pyrrhus's attention and shook her head at that ribbing. Storing the grain safely in the citadel wasn't the problem, if it came back to villagers in times of hunger, and, worse, Pyrrhus shouldn't let his chafing at his interactions with the king show.

The unloaded grain won over the villagers as she had hoped. Mothers glanced with sighs of relief from their gaunt children to the piled sacks. They stood straighter, their shoulders less bowed with worry and defeat. Mia's gaze lingered on one mother's fingers stroking her child's soft, brown hair. She'd been right to push her father.

Some women brought out wooden cups and a jug of beer to make a simple tribute to the new prince and their princess. One of the women was Kissa, the woman Mia had spoken to while Pyrrha took care of the injured man. Kissa caught her eye.

Mia stepped close to her. "We brought this from the citadel storerooms since there is need. A return of some of your grain set aside for times like this."

The men handed Pyrrhus a cup, and they raised them with a cheer. This enthusiasm reminded her of the effect her husband had had so quickly on the citadel guards. Men loved him. They followed him gladly. It would be better if her father didn't observe this.

Mia gathered her courage. She must learn enough about the year's harvest and the village's winter food supply to persuade her father to do more to support their people. He'd given her only a small portion of what he'd promised her.

She turned to three farmers standing near Pyrrhus. "I'm glad the prince and I could bring this grain from the citadel storage. I want to ensure that all is well at Seaview. That is a princess's duty. How was this year's grain harvest for you? More or less than usual?"

The farmers hesitated, their brows hinting at the difficulty of answering such a simple question. One glanced at the others and then said, "Our fields grew well for once. We brought our share to the citadel."

"I know you did." She understood from his manner what he couldn't say directly to a member of the royal family. To these farmers, the share the king required was too great. She agreed. "When I visited before, I saw thin children and that raised my concern. Are the village's winter stores of grain very low?"

Surprise and hints of alarm followed her question. She guessed her father had never asked such obvious questions, and they feared their answer would offend her.

She pictured the citadel storerooms and their sealed amphoras filled with the grain. She knew the villagers had similar containers in their huts. Perhaps she could ask another way, one suitable enough for her to get an answer. "When the women need grain for bread, do they find empty jars in this season?" She held the gaze of the farmer who'd spoken to her.

His eyes widened. He nodded.

Off to the side, Mia noticed Kissa beckon to her. "Would the princess like to see?"

"Thank you." Mia followed Kissa toward one of the huts, ignoring the worried looks on the men's faces. They didn't trust her to accept true answers without angrily blaming them—not yet.

Mia stepped inside. On the floor against one wall, the upper lips of two deep amphoras stuck up from the hard-packed dirt. As in the citadel storage rooms, the jars were buried to protect the grain and save space.

Mia knelt and peered into the open mouths of both containers. They were no longer sealed, and when she reached her hand down as far as she could, she found no grain in one and very little in the other. "Is it this way throughout the village?"

"Most families have some barley left. Not much. No wheat."

Mia could describe this situation clearly when she spoke to her father.

She and Kissa returned to the gathering around Pyrrhus. Mia asked in the hearing of the others, "Your grain is almost gone. What other stored foods are left?"

The farmer who'd spoken to her said, "We are not complaining, Princess."

"I'm not angry at any of you. I've heard no complaining, but I do want to understand how things are. Perhaps I can help."

He studied her face and then said, "Root vegetables and nuts. A bit of dried fish."

Kissa said, "Many, many dried figs. The trees were heavy with them this year. But no one can live only on figs."

Pyrrhus shook his head. "They shouldn't have to."

"The grain you brought will help," said the farmer.

"It is the grain you harvested. I'm glad it was safely stored for you, as the seed grain is each year." Mia glanced around at the men. "The king is willing to give you more grain for seed. He wants you to plant more this growing season. Will you do that?"

The men looked at the ground.

"We plant what we can," one muttered. "There's only so many of us."

"You need laborers?" she asked.

They all nodded. One said, "Not all the time. Could the palace spare some servants at planting and harvest?"

Mia doubted that, certainly not if this same lack of workers were true of the island's many villages, as seemed likely. "How can you increase your fields without more laborers? What else can you do?"

They shrugged in answer.

Later, over many days, she traveled to other villages further out. Two guards and a servant who knew the trails and villages went with her, along with Dione and another, older serving woman in place of Harmonia. Fortunately, Harmonia no longer viewed it as essential that she go with the married princess. They walked or rode donkeys over the hilly tracks. Mia was especially glad for Dione's company. Now that Dione was also married, they could whisper together about the strangeness of living so closely with a man, and the process of gaining familiarity and ease with their husbands. Whether a prince or a steward didn't seem to make such a big difference in this respect. From each of these journeys, Mia returned cold and tired, but she loved going on them.

Each village had different amounts stored away for the winter. She learned a great deal and was braver each time with her questions and persistence. The farmers didn't like her prodding at first, but as she kept on and showed genuine care about their situation, she gained their respect. To understand the farming problems, she applied what her mother had taught her about growing things. Some villages had better farmland or other sources like more dried fish, but in all of them she saw hunger enough to know she would have to win over her father. Even if these people could survive without more grain, their need was great enough that the gift would bind the island to her and to the new prince. Love and admiration. Loyalty stronger than fear.

She'd visited enough villages with questions. Now she must return with food.

She wanted her dowry as her father had promised. To persuade him, she brought him on one of her trips and showed him what it would mean to his people. He'd been genuine in offering the grain as her dowry, but when it was no longer needed to buy a prince, he'd seen a way to go back on that, a way to increase his wealth by pretending he hadn't really promised. She tried not to hate him for this greed. He had a genuine need for some wealth. While Pyrrhus had innate power in his being and knew it, her father could only acquire power from outside himself.

While she journeyed around the island, Pyrrhus occupied himself with the kingdom's defenses. The uneasiness between her father and husband grew more pronounced, but Lycomedes didn't forbid Pyrrhus's efforts. Mia suspected that was because he knew Pyrrhus would ignore him and do what he chose anyway. The guards practiced far harder than before. The noble warriors her father depended on came to the practice field as never before. Pyrrhus pointed out that they'd all seen him attack the bard at the wedding feast, and there was nothing good to be gained by hiding from them now. Better to win their loyalty by training them. That their loyalty would be to Pyrrhus not the king was an unspoken tension like a drawn-back arrow on a taut bowstring.

In the quiet of their bed at night, Pyrrhus frequently confessed how boring these practices were for him. They posed no challenge. He didn't say it, but she heard the other part, that he longed for the male company of Patroclus. If that longing were only for a better sparring partner, she would have sympathized.

One night when she'd tried to lessen his tedium by drawing him out about his earlier life, he told her, "For my own training, I took on the best warriors in my father's court, crafty fighters who could outdo me now and then. When even those bouts grew tiresome, my father persuaded his old friend Chiron to take me on. I went to live with him."

This "old" friendship surprised her. "How did your father come to be friends with an immortal centaur? Did your mother have something to do with it?"

"My mother?" Pyrrhus sounded shocked at the idea. "No, she and Chiron have little to do with each other among the gods, although she saw the value in letting him mentor her son. It was one of the only things my parents agreed on. The friendship arose out of a dire moment when Chiron helped my father who'd been left without a weapon while under attack. My father is a good man, in a way that Chiron recognized immediately when he came across my beleaguered father on the slopes of Mount Pelion. Chiron is like that—he sees into each man, not the man's future like some gods, but the man's character."

"I would like to meet such an immortal," Mia said. "What did he teach you?"

"Everything." Pyrrhus laughed, making a sound of true joy that she'd rarely heard from him. "Try fighting someone with the power and speed of a horse, joined with greater dexterity and wisdom than any mortal man's. He worked me with every weapon a warrior should know, although he prefers a bow when he hunts."

"You told me a woodsman taught you the healing you know. That was really Chiron, wasn't it?"

He sought her body, wrapping his arms around her. "It was."

"Teach me that healing knowledge."

"There are some things I can show you, but he also taught me to pour my immortal power into the healing. Much of what I know, I cannot pass on to you."

"To a child of ours?"

"I hope so. That idea makes my heart leap." Pyrrhus's arms snuggled her more tightly against him. "Chiron said the immortality in me was far stronger than in the other young heroes he'd taught. It will be strong in my son."

"What if we have a daughter?"

"I don't think we will. A son. I can almost see him."

Mia shivered. *See him?* This child didn't feel so real to her yet.

"Every night in Chiron's cave, he sang the tales of heroes to me, infusing in me both the lessons of their lives and the inspiration of the music. I learned the stories and how to play the lyre in rhythm with the words."

"You can sing? You never told me that. Why do we listen to my father's terrible bard?"

Pyrrhus let loose a belly laugh. "He is more than terrible, but I think that's partly because he's still terrified of me. He's sure I'll run him through with my sword—which I might if he mangles another tale."

"He was bad before you landed on this island. You should sing and play."

"Not for your father's court. Your sisters, maybe." He sighed. "Warriors sing the deeds of heroes for their dear companions, as Chiron and Patroclus were to—" He stopped awkwardly.

Ah, another activity he longed to do with Patroclus. She'd learned to back away from such things. To push would widen the hole that would always lie in their daily path together. Whether Patroclus was near or far, he held an unshaken place in her husband's heart. Neither Pyrrhus or Mia knew whether Thetis had told Patroclus to make his way secretly to Skyros as she'd told her son she would. Mia pushed down her hidden hope that he'd never show up.

Pyrrhus slid his hands around her waist and lifted her so she knelt with her legs straddling his groin. A distraction, but she was ready enough to play along. Sometimes she'd come to their bed sure she was too tired, but he showed her otherwise with delightful ingenuity. The bedroom was one place where neither of them were bored.

Two cycles of the moon passed in this way. Winter squalls gave way to an unusually hot spring and with it, safer sailing weather. For the islanders that meant fresh fish for hungry bellies. But Mia wondered if sailing might also be useful for her restless husband.

One afternoon when Pyrrhus came in from his duties with the guards, he flung himself into the large wooden armchair that had been added to the furniture around the central hearth in the communal women's hall. Clearly, he wasn't happy. Mia left her loom and sat beside him. Like her, he wasn't locked in the women's quarters anymore, but he'd kept his word about being cautious. He lived constrained in a small area. None of the traders or other visitors to the island would have any chance to stumble across him, and he kept out of sight from all but his regular group of warriors and royal guards. Those men would die before mentioning to anyone the extraordinary prince who had honed their skills.

"Do you know how to sail?" she asked.

"Sail?" He looked at her in surprise.

If nothing else, she'd gotten those green eyes to brighten. She nodded. "Could you sail a small boat without anyone else—or if you taught me to help? My father's royal sailboat needs a crew, but there's a much smaller one the servants use. I don't know how to sail it, but could you? Or have you never sailed?" She enjoyed the outraged look she received. She was thinking of the sailing trips she'd taken with her mother and sisters and how free she'd felt, but she couldn't say that out loud. Pyrrhus wouldn't mind, but the rest of the palace looked jumpy and shocked any time she reminded them that her mother existed.

Pyrrhus leaned toward her, his eyes alight. "Show me."

"We could sail without harm to your secret, couldn't we? You wouldn't be seen if we avoided the harbor that the traders use. There's a strange place up the coast of ruined homes where no one ever goes, right on a bay with a sheltered lagoon. We could explore and enjoy ourselves outside away from everyone."

"Why is it abandoned?"

"I don't know. No one does. My . . ." She dropped her voice. "My mother took me there in the boat once. She said the islanders think it's haunted. That some god-sent giant wave washed a big part away, and the drowned could never be buried properly, so they wander the broken houses and temples."

"Does that frighten you?"

She shook her head. "No unhappy dead bothered us when I went with my mother. But it means no one will come near and see us. The angry god must have acted a long time ago and no longer cares. Now it's crumbling houses with collapsed roofs. There's the ruins of a fortification wall, what wasn't taken by the sea."

Pyrrhus smiled. "That sounds enticing. Take me to see this boat."

23

Mia ordered the small servants' boat to be prepared and beached for them in a nearby cove away from prying eyes. Over several days, Pyrrhus taught her how to sail and row until she felt confident in her skill and ready to leave the protected cove. She loved guiding the boat and playing with the winds, although rowing was less enthralling. He laughed when she made a mistake, not at her, but with her. He didn't care what happened. With him it was easy to be fearless.

"What if I capsize the boat?" she asked.

"I'll dive down if you sink. No matter how far. I'm—"

"Your mother's son. But I won't need your help. I know how to swim."

On the day they set out for the haunted city, they guided the little boat far enough offshore to avoid notice by any islanders working near the coastline. They had a steady breeze and a blue, cloudless sky. The clear, turquoise water sparkled around the boat. Leaning over the side, she saw clearly the rocks at the bottom and here and there the flash of fish.

Pyrrhus gave a cry of joy and pointed. "Look! A group of dolphins to keep us company."

Mia shifted cautiously to the other side of the boat and leaned out to see them better. In graceful arcs the shiny gray creatures leapt through the air and plunged into the water. Soon they surrounded the boat. They were bigger than she'd thought they'd be, sleek and powerful. She drew away from the boat's edge.

"Don't be concerned," Pyrrhus said. "The dolphins serve my mother. Often when I swim in the sea, they come close and glide alongside me. They protect and play. They have always been my companions, and they are a good sign."

Mia leaned out and let her hand trail through the water. Fast and true, a dolphin skimmed toward her fingers, gently bumping them with the smooth curve of its head. It passed by and lifted its head out of the water, making a cheerful, chattering sound with an open mouth.

"That one likes you," Pyrrhus said. "You have a friend for life."

She laughed. "I'll remember that should I find myself afloat and in need of help."

After they'd gone what she judged must be most of the distance up the coast, she kept her eye out for the bay and the point jutting out with the curious ruined fortifications on it. She scanned the shoreline.

"There it is." She pointed ahead.

Pyrrhus adjusted the sail. When they came into the bay and the breeze dropped, he took the oars and pulled them through the water, driving the little craft at a remarkable pace toward the sandy beach edging the bay. With that kind of rowing speed, she needn't worry if the winds didn't cooperate on the way home. When they'd drawn into the shallows, Pyrrhus swung off the boat, pulling it with one arm through the waves and up onto the sand.

He made a sweeping bow to her. "Enter your kingdom, Princess Deidamia, with dry feet."

She jumped over the side, placing her sandals onto the white sand and leaning back to grab the ones he'd removed before jumping in the water. She handed them to him and kissed his lips. "Let's explore my kingdom. Should we bring the food with us now?"

Pyrrhus put on his shoes and then took the basket and wineskin from the boat. His wet chiton clung to the small of his back and over the muscled curves of his butt. She cupped a hand around one of those curves and squeezed. He let the basket plop to the ground and mimicked her gesture, cupping one of her breasts and drawing her to his chest.

She laughed and shook her head. "Explore first." She walked through the sand, her feet sinking backward with each step, and he followed. Given her husband's appetite for coupling—and hers, if she was honest—it was no wonder she had noticed the various signs a baby was growing in her womb. She hadn't told anyone, but she hoped to find a chance to tell Pyrrhus while they were alone on this journey. It should be easy news to share, but being joyful about raising a child required believing you would live long enough, and that was the thing she had not persuaded Pyrrhus to trust.

They reached the red-brown dirt at the base of the low promontory and climbed up, stepping over loose stones and spiky grasses. Small hints of green showed the promise of spring, but most of the stalks and branches were brown and dead.

Pyrrhus slipped ahead of her, his lower half disappearing when he stepped over a broken wall near the edge of the promontory. She clambered up behind, sitting on the wall to swing her legs over, and found him crouched, studying the wall's thickness. Dirt and broken stone had accumulated, covering much of it.

"I think it was an outer fortification wall, a solid one, before it fell," he said.

Pyrrhus stepped onto the irregular top of what remained of the wall. It formed an uneven path around the ruined city, broken through in places. He turned back toward her with a reached-out arm. She was glad he didn't yet know she was with child and wasn't feeling overly cautious with her. She tucked her skirt into her belt and grasped his hand.

They walked along, balancing on the bumpy surface. It lifted them enough so that she could see crumbled buildings inside the wall laid out around her. They stopped when they reached one of the scalloped areas that bulged out in several places around the fallen fortification.

"Are these the remains of a tower?" she asked, studying the piled dirt and stones that filled a barely distinguishable, low crescent of stone foundations.

Pyrrhus walked the curving arc, crouching down several times, pushing away stones and debris, and peering below. "To support its height, a tower like the one at your citadel has a different foundation than the surrounding wall. This area matches the wall's foundation, which was very thick. I think it was a defensive bastion the same height as the wall." Pyrrhus stood up. He pointed to the other scallops that had studded the fortification wall. "They remind me of horses' hooves."

"They would be very large horses," she teased.

"But smart defenses. Warriors could fend off attackers in several directions at once, all along the wall. It's a good way to build a wall."

"I don't think you'll talk my father into adding any horse hooves to our citadel." She was teasing again, but she saw that it wasn't something he could be lighthearted about even here, away from the annoyances of the citadel and palace.

"I'd settle for more men. Your father says he can't arm or feed them, but if men come, eager to defend their king, what can he do? I sent out word to the villages, asking for strong young men to train as guards."

Mia grabbed his arm. "Why didn't you talk to me before you did that?"

Pyrrhus looked startled. "You? You're not a warrior."

"Thank the gods for that," she said. "Did you consider what will happen in the villages if you draw away their young men? They already have too few hands to grow the food my father demands of them."

Pyrrhus at least looked downcast.

She stomped away from him, as far as the moldering bastion gave her space. She turned toward him in frustration, her hands on her hips. "You'll leave them starving, you selfish mole. If you're going to steal their children, you might better include labor in the fields as part of their training." Her anger drove quick, unthinking words.

Pyrrhus smiled. "That's an excellent idea."

"It is? What did I say?"

"But a mole? Really?"

She waved away the silly insult with her hand. "Your men can provide crews for the farmers? You'd do that?"

"It's a smart plan. Will you tell me where to send the men and when they'll be most useful? I can't give them to you all the time. I do have to train them to be warriors." His eyes danced with a brilliant green. He glided to her, sliding his arms around her. "The men also matter as warriors, dear wife. I must protect you and your sisters—and the food stored in the citadel. If we lose the grain for seed, everyone will starve."

"I'll grant you that, but when you get these yearnings for more guardsmen to defend us, at least tell me in advance what you're thinking." She frowned. "Warn the king, as well. Provoking my father and expecting him to accept what you've done afterward is not the best way to work with him. You know that, but you ignore it."

"He's easily ignored." Pyrrhus turned away from her, moving fast along the top of the old wall, jumping over broken areas.

"That doesn't mean you should," she shouted, but she didn't want to defend her father. She wanted to enjoy herself, so she leapt over a gap that should have made her careful and ran to catch up to Pyrrhus.

He'd stopped and now faced the inside of the ruined city where she saw caved-in roofs and rows of rectangular rooms filled with debris.

"That must have been the central road," Pyrrhus said, pointing to a faint line opening across the ruins.

Several walls had fallen into the long space he indicated, but it did look like a road with smaller ones branching off between the surrounding piles of fragmented buildings.

"Let's go look at the building where the road ends." Pyrrhus gestured. "See, over there?"

"If you like. It's bigger than the others."

His eyes narrowed. "A palace or temple?" He shrugged. "Let's go see what they left behind."

He helped her climb down from the outer wall into the abandoned streets and houses. They navigated around collapsed remains and entered some of the small dwellings that were still standing. Mia felt the eerie presence of those who had once lived there. She didn't remember that sense from the visit with her mother, but she had been too young to understand the loss that lay around her, and they had spent most of their time at the pretty beach along the bay and had not entered this pile of rubble, observing it only from outside.

"It must have been an enormous wave that took such a big bite from this city," she said. "What do you think these people did to so anger a god?"

Pyrrhus sighed. "Perhaps not much. If it was the sea god Poseidon who sent the wave, he may have shaken the earth at the same time."

"Where do you think the survivors went? There must have been some." She peered into one dark house blocked by its own fallen roof. A broken pot poked out beside a roof beam. Like the other houses they'd entered, she didn't see much else, so perhaps the people who hadn't drowned took what they could and left.

Pyrrhus took her hand. "Are there any stories among your people about living in this place, besides the haunting?"

"Not that I know of." She studied her husband's serious face. "Are you thinking that some of my people came long ago from here?"

"It makes sense. Maybe they didn't teach their children the story because they feared the god's anger that had destroyed them once. And now no one remembers."

"That could be. I feel the sadness of this place. I would like to believe that they didn't all die but are part of Skyros now in their descendants."

Pyrrhus brushed his fingers through her hair. "This is a hollow place, and that would make it feel less so."

Following a narrow path, they came out on what was left of the main road through the town and made slow progress following it until they reached the larger building Pyrrhus had noticed from above. Setting down the basket and wineskin, he lifted away a fallen beam and kicked aside some stones and mud bricks that blocked the entryway into a walled courtyard. Mia entered and followed along the courtyard wall, running her hand over its squared stones. Such care only went into a building of importance. With the toe of her sandal, she rubbed away dirt and saw cut stone pavement beneath her feet, finer than her father's palace and citadel.

"This must have been the altar," Pyrrhus called out. He stood by a large flat stone at one end of the open-air space.

Mia joined him. A channel carved into the altar still showed a dark stain from the blood of animals sacrificed there. She pictured priests gathered around, this courtyard filled with the lowing of sheep and the smells of burnt offerings, and lives suddenly interrupted. She shivered. This wasn't a place to disturb. She'd been mistaken about coming here. "Let's find some spot where we aren't intruding on the dead."

Instead of answering her, Pyrrhus strode to the temple's wooden door and shoved it open far enough to slip inside. Mia looked around the shadowed courtyard and hurried after him. She found a large room that had a gaping hole in its roof and a pile of debris underneath. She touched the surface of a broken wooden pillar that she guessed had once been smooth and painted, proudly supporting the roof. Traces of dark red paint reminded her of her father's throne room.

Pyrrhus walked around the room, bending down to look closely along the edges. He stopped to inspect underneath some fallen wooden planks that might once have been shelves. "There are no divine statues here, and the residents did not leave behind any implements to serve the gods. I'm not sure our presence is an intrusion, but let's find a better spot than a fallen temple to eat and relax."

She crouched down next to him. "You don't feel out of place here? Not just this temple, the whole ruined city."

A gray sea mist over-layered the green of his eyes. "No, but I understand why you do. This is a place of death that came unexpected and too early. That is my fate, according to my mother. This lost city feels comforting to me. For once, I belong."

Mia let out a small cry of sorrow and wrapped her arms around him, falling forward onto her knees. "You belong among the living. You belong to me." She thought of the child she carried and shuddered.

Pyrrhus gently pulled away. "Not the way others belong. Unlike me, you can root into life, believing you will have time for those roots to grow deep and your branches to spread. My mother took that from me."

Mia sank back on her haunches. "But no one knows whether or not they will die on any given day."

"True, but you can hope and believe your life will be long, as you should. I *know* that my days will be short."

"Your mother is keeping you safe so you will have a long life. That is why you have to endure in secrecy for now."

"My mother is determined to outstrip my fate for me, but even the gods must yield to fate. Whatever the seers have prophesized that will bring my early death will come one way or another, no matter what she does. She talks of men who will drag me toward my death. I don't know who they are or why she hides their identity and what they want from me, but you have seen her. She wouldn't hesitate to kill these men to save my life. If overcoming fate were as simple as that, I would be free of this shadow she has cast over my life."

They sat for a long stretch in the dim half-light coming through the broken roof.

Pyrrha put one of his giant hands on her knee, a preemptive comforting. That meant he would say something even more hurtful. "I love you, but I yearn for the life of a true warrior, surrounded by men I respect. No warrior can beat me on the field of battle, but there are some who can stand at my side as worthy companions. When I lived with Chiron, fighting an immortal each day, the old centaur made me feel whole by teaching me the arts of healing and music. I was happy for the first time in my life. *That* life is what I love. If I have only a little time to live, why can't I live as I wish?"

Mia's vision blurred with tears that ran down her cheeks. She pushed up from the dusty, rubble-strewn ground and headed toward the sliver of light coming through the door Pyrrhus had forced open.

She'd known he felt constrained by his life on Skyros, but she had not realized how hopeless he felt it was for him to be happy in his life with her. What meaning did his love for her have if he could only imagine happiness somewhere else without her? She couldn't tell him he would be a father, another trap in this life he did not enjoy.

She stumbled into the courtyard and out to the fragmented road. Why had she ever thought this was a good place to spend the day with Pyrrhus?

"Mia, wait." In a moment Pyrrhus was beside her.

"Did you marry me only to stop your mother from killing me?" Her chest burned with humiliation.

"No, Mia, of course not. I told you. I've never met any other woman whom I felt so close to, so akin to. I don't think I would ever have married anyone else. I love *you*."

The searing in her chest wouldn't let her be. "But you would prefer a life without me, somewhere with Chiron or your true warrior companions?"

"I am glad that you are here with me."

"That isn't what I asked."

"I don't lie to you. I cannot help who I am. I am here, and I love you. If you believe my mother's hope, I will live a long life with you on Skyros."

A long life that would never be his ideal, that would leave him always wanting something more than she, their child, and her kingdom could be. "Or you will die an early death."

"Let's find a place to sit outside the city wall, somewhere a little sheltered and out of sight. We can enjoy the day together." He took her face in his hands and pressed his lips on hers, his tongue inviting her to open to him. When she did, she felt him pour his whole heart into their kiss. He could offer love in this moment, but having grown up under the pall of the prophecy that grieved his mother, he would never give her a promise of more.

24

Mia and Pyrrhus left the crumbling walls and climbed down to a small cove on the shore. Scrambling over a mass of rocks that jutted into the sea, they jumped down to a tiny arc of sand. Here, protected by the rocks and the promontory above, they were hidden from the eyes of any who might appear on the beach where they'd left their boat.

Mia sat down, brushing sand from her hands. "I'm hungry. What did Dione pack for us?"

She took the wineskin and undid the tie around its wooden plug, passing it to Pyrrhus to enjoy and then taking a sip when he handed it to her.

He pulled off the linen napkin covering the basket. She drew out a lidded ceramic bowl that held squares of briny white cheese and pickled grape leaves wrapped around leftover barley porridge. She also found flatbread, an onion, and a couple handfuls of dried figs.

"Will you slice this with your dagger?" She handed Pyrrhus the onion.

He pared off thin bites, balancing a piece of flatbread on his thigh as a plate to hold them.

Mia pinched an onion slice against a wrapped grape leaf and took a bite, savoring the contrast of the onion's sweet sharpness against the grape leaf preserved in sour wine and the earthy barley. She chewed and watched Pyrrhus make a similar tidbit that he popped in his mouth in a single bite.

When they'd eaten and finished the wine, the sun stood high overhead. There was still time before they'd need to sail back.

Pyrrhus leaned back on his elbows, his long legs bent, his bare toes digging into the sand. He'd unpinned the shoulders of his chiton and let the sun warm his bare chest. Mia brushed her lips over the sculpted contours, nipping at his flat dark nipples and hearing his responsive moan. She stood and spread out her cloak like a blanket on the smooth sand.

Pyrrhus sat up, grabbing her around the knees while she was still standing. He slid up her skirt, burying his face against her thighs, nudging her legs wider, and letting the folds of her peplos fall over his head, so that she could not see what he was doing. She didn't need to.

His fingers and tongue explored the tender places between her legs, igniting sensation that built and built until she couldn't stay upright, and he caught her in a slow collapse onto her cloak. The light flickering of his tongue started again and found an answering call in the pressing upwards of his fingers from inside of her. She lost herself in the peaking waves that he brought to her over and over again.

"You," she panted, arching her back and reaching for his shoulders.

He moaned and shifted up his body, her legs on either side of his hips. She let loose a high scream of pleasure as he pressed her knees up toward her shoulders so that his plunge into her went deeper and deeper, and she found new realms of sensation. She floated above the unbearable intensity, never wanting the feelings to end.

His need now drove the rhythm, faster and harder until he collapsed and rolled her on top of him, after-shivers pulsing through him. Her head rested against his chest, the impossibly fast beat of his heart a love song against her cheek and in her ear.

He loved her, and they had made a child together. She had to tell him.

"Lately I've felt sick in the mornings and—"

"You're carrying our son? Already?" Pyrrhus's voice was joyful and warm.

She pressed her face into his chest in gratitude, kissing his muscled chest. "Yes, although it could be a girl. I'm one of seven daughters."

Pyrrhus slid her softly onto the cloak on her back. He covered her belly with his hands. "Little warrior, grow strong." Then he leaned down, and his lips brushed kisses against her skin, light as glints of light across wind-ruffled sea.

They lay together on the cloak, Pyrrhus wrapped around her.

Mia intertwined the fingers of her right hand with his. "Why are you sure it's a boy?"

He pressed a kiss on her shoulder. "Sometimes immortal knowledge comes to me, but I don't know how."

"My father will be happy."

Pyrrhus gave a small snort.

A little warrior. How would she raise a warrior? She knew all about sisters.

"The sun is past the center of the sky," Pyrrhus said.

"Mmm." She stretched and sat up.

Pyrrhus also sat up and found his chiton, sliding it over his head and pinning the shoulders. Mia walked down to the water and squatted in the waves with her dress pulled out of the way, letting the salt water wash and cool her. She returned to the sand, cinched her belt, and adjusted the folds so that her gown draped over her breasts in the revealing way Dione had shown her.

They put the empty wineskin and the bowl and its wooden lid into the basket. Mia took it on her arm. "Do you think we can climb around the rocks on that side and get back to the boat?"

"I might have to lift you once or twice." Pyrrhus set off, leaping onto the rocks that were damp and darkened by the sea. He turned and looked down to her.

She passed the basket and climbed up where she could until he grasped her around her waist and swung her up the rest of the way. She liked that he did not treat her differently now that he knew she was with child. There would be a time when her movements would be limited, but not yet.

She picked her way carefully across the rough surface of the rocks, which were etched with tiny circles and partial rings as if made of burst sea foam. But the edges were sharp and hard through the leather of her sandals, nothing like the ephemeral gleam of bubbles.

"Careful," Pyrrhus said. "It's sharp and steep on this side. Let me jump down, and I'll catch you."

"Like our escapes from my walled garden," she said.

Did she miss the girl she'd befriended? Sometimes. There had been a comfort to being with Pyrrha, familiarity of being with another girl and thinking she understood that girl simply through that shared experience. But now she wondered if that had been an illusion. Pyrrhus had never felt comfortable in that form. Now he wrestled with his unfulfilled yearnings for a life with his warrior companions, but that longing was not as horrific as his frantic need to escape a woman's life.

Loving this person was never going to be simple. Maybe this baby would give Pyrrhus more happiness on Skyros. She thought of the failure of her parents' marriage. Could theirs have been simple if her mother had chosen differently? Or had some hurt sprouted and grown, as it was growing for Mia, who felt second to a warrior life and possibly second to a warrior named Patroclus? Did such a hurt push her mother inevitably toward another man?

"Jump," came Pyrrhus's command.

She looked at the dagger-like edges of the rocks immediately below her and ran a couple steps to build speed to send herself flying past them into Pyrrhus's arms.

He caught her and was bending his head down to give her a kiss when he started back and placed her quickly on her feet. "I sense something." He turned and scanned the sea and shore along the bay.

A breeze off the water caught Mia's hair, and she heard a strange, uncanny roar of rushing water. The smooth sea suddenly rippled and rose. The bay split into two mountainous waves, not facing the shore as they should, but each other, drawing back like two sides of a gate, leaving bare sea floor cutting a path between.

And stalking toward them on that path was Thetis.

Pyrrhus took Mia's hand and drew her quickly down to the place where his mother would step out onto the shore. The goddess stood several heads taller than her son this time. Her face, veil, and dress glowed so brightly Mia couldn't look directly at her without pain.

"Mother. What brings you here? All is well with me." His voice was calm, and the hand that held hers was cool and steady. She tried to believe they were safe. He added, "Everyone has followed your commands."

Mia bowed her head, trying to stop the quivers of fear that shook her body.

"You still wish to protect these mortals you find yourself trapped among, my son. Surprising, but just as well."

Mia understood the goddess's words, but she flinched because they sounded not like speaking but like the clanging of swords against bronze shields when soldiers want to terrify an opponent. She'd heard her father's soldiers make this noise at each other, practicing fearfulness. The goddess was not practicing.

"These mortals are part of my family now." Pyrrhus pulled Mia behind him, and he raised his arm, palm out. "I will fight to defend them."

"I bring you word that you will have help if such an occasion arises—as if you'd need it."

"Help?"

Mia heard the joyful hope in her husband's voice and felt a damp coldness flood her chest. They'd both guessed who the goddess meant.

"I have sent Patroclus to come to you as we agreed. He must take a roundabout route so as not to give away your location. Too many know you are companions. Your father sent him off on trade to various places, so the boy had a pretext to leave on a long journey. If he never returns, anyone will think he was shipwrecked. He will not be missed."

"Thank you, Mother, for sending him. I will look for his ship."

"I waited to tell you when you were at a distance from that ridiculous palace. I prefer this abandoned place, home to so many dead mortals. I have no wish to see this island's king nor will I creep in to see you, hiding my divinity. But now you know. I kept my word. Be sure these mortals keep theirs."

Mia could almost draw a breath as the purpose of Thetis's visit unfolded without violence.

"Girl!" The clanging sounded like a command, although Mia could not imagine what she was supposed to do. She raised her head enough to show the goddess she attended to her words. "The lies you spread with that pathetic bard's tale amused me. I visited Medea, and we both laughed."

There was a flash of lightning and a crash of thunder. The goddess was gone. The two sides of curled-back sea crashed in on each other, flooding up high onto the shore. Mia screamed and raced up the beach, the crushing waves drenching her before she dragged herself free.

The violent thrust of water caught their boat, drawn onto the sand, and washed it out into the churning sea.

Pyrrhus cried out. He rushed into the water, diving through the waves and propelling himself toward the foundering boat with huge pulls of his arms through the seething water. Reaching the craft, he grasped the rope, yanking it back toward the shore with great kicks of his legs. Would he reach for their love with the same strength and desire?

25

Morning light came in through the high windows of the women's hall. Servants cleared away the dishes from breakfast. Mia's youngest sister Bura trotted around the hall pretending to be a horse. Someone would need to take her outside to run and play. Mia put down the flatbread she'd been nibbling and handed her plate to Dione. Her stomach wanted nothing else in the morning. To Mia's annoyance, Harmonia had noticed how little she was eating and gave her a knowing look. She would prefer to be left in peace.

After a large breakfast, Pyrrhus had gone to fetch his cloak and sword. Returning now, he bent down to kiss Mia. "I'll be in the citadel all day. Send Dione if you need me."

"Why would I need you?" she asked, only slightly teasing.

Her husband frowned. He trusted her sense that she didn't need to limit what she did yet despite being with child, but he'd been uneasy since his mother's visit, especially over her strange comment about revealing to Medea how Mia had used the sorceress's story. After their return to the palace, Pyrrhus had paced their chamber, raging about how cruel his mother been to do that to them. He doubted the sorceress's amusement had been genuine, if she'd laughed at all.

Mia flinched, remembering the visit. Thetis had nearly drowned them without even noticing. Had she also drawn the vengeful ire of a powerful sorceress? Mia shook off this new worry. The flooding waves had been a goddess's carelessness. Seeking out vengeful Medea a more active choice. The goddess wouldn't draw harm to her son on purpose. Or would the harm be only to Mia, and Thetis didn't care? Mia wondered if Thetis would have acted differently if she'd known that Mia carried her son's child.

Mia reached up and drew Pyrrhus's face down for another kiss. "I'm fine. Go train your warriors." She thought of their quarrel in the haunted city about his call for young men from the villages. His recruiting had been far too successful, but his willingness to share their labor would soften that blow to the island's farmers. It did nothing to soften her father's reaction. He watched Pyrrhus's control over the island's warriors and their growing numbers with an increasingly jealous eye. Pyrrhus used the excuse of keeping out of sight of possible outsiders to avoid being in the same room with the king. Mia found their tussles exhausting.

Unfortunately for the relationship between her father and her husband, Pyrrhus saw the island's men as "his" guard. His duties with them absorbed him completely. Mia flinched at the echo of his mother she heard whenever he gave in to this tendency to burning single-mindedness.

Pyrrhus crouched down beside her chair, eye-level with her. "Should I take the guards out to the fields today? Did you make your plan?"

She nodded. "Can you? Seaview badly needs help preparing the soil and planting if they are going to add the new fields. You can go there with the recruits and get the work started, but the men will know the work better than you do, along with the villagers. You don't need to go with them after this first day. Nobody else has to see you. If you are willing to send out some men each day during this preparation and planting season, I'll send word to the other places where they're needed."

"I like that plan. You are beloved for good reason." He lifted her hand to his lips. "I should have asked you earlier. I forgot about our agreement. The men are eager to learn sword fighting."

"And you are eager to teach them. But when you disappoint them, remind them they'll have full bellies if the harvest is good, and their families will eat."

"We'll find time for sword training." He rose and left.

Bura let out an outraged scream. Mia turned to see Harmonia holding the ball Mia had made for her sister just out of Bura's reach.

"Noble ladies," Harmonia said in a stern voice, "do not chase balls and run around like wild animals. Go sit on a stool and tend to your spinning."

Mia hurried over and lifted Bura into her arms, comforting her with a hug before letting the wiggly girl slide back to the ground.

Harmonia said, "Princess Mia, you shouldn't—"

Mia glared at her. "I am not frail and will lift whatever I wish to. And you will please keep quiet for now until I choose otherwise."

"Yes, Princess."

"And allow Bura to run and play sometimes. You will turn her into a monster if you make her sit still and spin all day."

"Princess, I—"

"Please do as I ask." Mia took the ball from Harmonia and gave it to Bura. She knelt by her sister. "Try to be as well behaved as you can for Harmonia. Keep the ball for playing outside."

Mia enjoyed the leap in standing her marriage brought her. Commanding Harmonia rather than following the lady's dictates made life much more pleasant. It was silly that a night with a husband rendered her suddenly in charge. It wasn't as though she had grown noticeably wiser or more experienced, but she gave no voice to these truths.

A court servant appeared in the doorway to the women's hall. He signaled to Mia that he had a message for her.

Before dealing with that, she called out to her sister Idomene, "Will you take Bura and all your sisters to play in the courtyard? She needs fresh air and room to run. So do the rest of you, by the look of it. Then you might pay better attention to whatever Harmonia wishes to teach all of you later."

With smiles they ran out, even Idomene forgetting to keep a demure, ladylike pace. Mia was enjoying being a bad influence on them. All her sisters were gone, the servants had finished the tidying, and only Harmonia remained in the women's hall.

She beckoned the court servant.

He bowed. "Princess, there is a trader who wishes to speak to you. He finished his business with your father yesterday, but now says he has brought some jewelry that is best seen by the princess. Your father has permitted him to show you his wares in honor of your wedding, but . . . er . . . he reminds you of the state of the treasury." The servant bowed again.

Mia repressed a smile. Her father was ribbing her for all the questions she'd asked about the treasury and kingdom's wealth, but he also showed trust.

Receiving a trader in the communal hall of the women's quarters was almost unheard of, but it would be intriguing. She liked news from the world outside. Pyrrhus was safely out of the way, but she caught Dione's eye, and her smart maid nodded in understanding and left the room. She'd run up to the citadel and warn Pyrrhus of this trader's movements, so no chance meeting could occur.

"Harmonia, would you attend on me while I examine this trader's goods?" Harmonia looked mollified and took her stand beside Mia's chair. Mia glanced at the servant. "Please escort this trader to my hall."

When the tall man entered, he was not dressed like most traders who made their way to Skyros. His clothes were finer. The short cloak drawn around his shoulders was held in place with a silver pin of two dolphins jumping side by side. Her gaze flicked to the dolphins frescoed on the walls around her, and her thoughts leapt to her mother. She gave herself a small shake of the head and indicated a seat for him while taking her own.

The man glanced around the room with an assessing look, although what he checked for she couldn't tell. The room was quiet, with only Harmonia and her there. She heard the small shuffles of the guard positioned in the corridor.

"May I move this table so you can examine the jewels at ease?" The dark-haired man rested a hand on the table standing next to him, and at her nod, he slid it out and unrolled a linen bundle so that a necklace of gold and lapis lazuli beads, a gold pin, and two gold rings lay revealed. He adjusted them to be prettily displayed and then looked at her with a disconcertingly piercing gaze.

She studied the jewels for a moment and gasped. They were her mother's. She caught his gaze, and he nodded to her ever so slightly.

"May I tell you about these?" His eyes flicked at Harmonia.

Mia considered. News from her mother, she guessed. Would such information be safe in Harmonia's ears? That's what he asked her. She nodded. Otherwise, she'd never hear it. Some chaperone was required with this strange man.

Harmonia had noticed their interchange. More than likely she also recalled the jewels. She rested her hand on Mia's shoulder, but with a small squeeze of reassurance not warning.

"You recognize these?" the man asked.

Mia drew in a sudden breath. "Yes. Do you have news of her?"

"She is well—as well as can be. She wants you to know she misses her daughters."

"Really?"

"I am only a courtier, sent by my king at her request. Because you should not share with your father what I say, I presented myself as a trader. I do not know the queen closely, of course, and can only relay the message she sent, but also, I will tell you that when I see our new queen sitting on the throne, her expression is often downcast. I believe she's thinking of you."

"She is queen there? I never—"

"I accompanied the King of Peparethos on the journey here that ended so . . . precipitously. So, I understand your confusion. He had lost his wife some years before. We arrived home to Peparethos with the announcement that the king had married a new queen. Tales come and go. The king withstands the murmurs against his honor and his queen's with a firm hand. She understands her duty and would do nothing that would stir up such murmurs, so neither she nor the king has inquired about you, whether with traders or by messenger here. Please understand. This was a choice she had to make, not one she liked. I risk much for her by coming now. I am directed to bring news of you and your sisters and slip away with as little notice as possible."

"Does she have new children with this king?" Mia heard the pain in her voice and hoped it wouldn't silence this man.

"They have not been so blessed. He has two sons from before, fine young men. Tell me about yourself. That is the comfort I wish to bring to your mother."

"Tell her I miss her terribly every day, and I don't think I'll ever stop missing her, but Lady Harmonia looks after me and my sisters, instructing us in the things we should know." She patted Harmonia's arm to show this was the lady she meant. "My father found a fine young prince to be my husband, and I am happy with him." Mia decided that would be all she'd say on that.

"A very fine prince," Harmonia burst in. "He's taking responsibility for defending the kingdom, like a proper prince. Training the guards and such." Mia pinched Harmonia's arm in warning to stop, but she spilled out more. "Tall like a ship's mast and stronger and faster than any of the young nobles on the island. As fine a husband as a mother could hope for." Mia dug in her fingernails, and Harmonia gave a little squeal and settled back behind Mia's chair.

Mia sighed, but telling her mother these things would be safe. The new queen of Peparethos wouldn't spread her shame by sharing such news with anyone. Her mother's secret meant she wouldn't inadvertently endanger Pyrrhus's. How strange that both her mother's life and her own had become so tightly bound by threads of harmful rumor that must be kept hidden.

Mia hurried on with something safe to say to hide Harmonia's error. "My sisters are all healthy and growing into princesses my mother can be proud of. They thrive. May I tell them of this visit?"

"It is better not to. It is fortunate that only you and your attendant are hearing this." He glanced up to Harmonia. Mia followed his gaze and saw Harmonia nod.

He rose. "I am to leave these jewels as presents, although secret ones, I'm sorry to say. Your mother wishes you to remember her love for you. She says you must know it has never wavered."

"Will I hear from her again?" Mia stood, wanting to keep this man talking about her mother, but not knowing what further to ask.

"That is not the king's intent."

The king's? Did her mother's wishes not matter or was she willing to forget about her children? A question came unbidden. "Is she a good queen?"

The man's eyebrows rose. "Yes. She is worthy of our respect and admiration."

"Thank you." Mia turned to Harmonia. "Will you walk my guest to the outer palace?"

He bowed to her and followed the slow step of the bulky old woman.

Mia gripped the arms of her chair. She should be overjoyed to have news from her mother, but she felt lost in a dark cloud. She wouldn't make the kind of choice her mother had and suffer the fate of being separated forever from her children. She would never do that. So why did she feel this deep foreboding?

26

As a married woman, Mia joined her father regularly in his meetings with traders and other travelers coming off ships. Although her pregnancy tired her, she didn't lessen her activities, especially accompanying her father. She had business in the court that she refused to give up.

Partly, she was quietly learning how to conduct such negotiations so she could persuade her father to allow her a greater role. Meanwhile, she observed and stored away an understanding of which traders were fair, what her island could offer in exchange for the items her father needed from outside, and how to back the traders into better deals. In her head, she conducted these talks differently than her father did, but that was neither here nor there.

She had another task in these throne room meetings, seated on a small chair to one side, with Dione standing behind her, one she disliked but pretended she was glad to do. Since Thetis's drenching visit, Mia paid even closer attention to ship arrivals and the men who came off them. Pyrrhus insisted she do this and asked her eagerly about them each day. He couldn't show himself, so greeting Patroclus was up to her, whatever disguise the warrior traveled under. From Thetis, Patroclus would know about the marriage and the secrecy

Pyrrhus hid behind. Patroclus would make himself known to her if she made herself available, and then Pyrrhus and Patroclus would be reunited. Watching each new face and judging whether this was the man her husband so loved rubbed her raw. Every ugly old man who trudged in through the royal hall's double doors cheered her up.

But when Patroclus stepped through one afternoon, she didn't need him to reveal himself. He was young and handsome, dark curls framing a face with pronounced cheekbones and a straight, narrow nose above a generous mouth with lips that begged to be kissed. His wide, self-confident stance and muscled arms showed that he was trained as a warrior no matter what goods he made a show of offering to her father. But what told her without doubt that this man was Patroclus was the hungry look in his eyes, the look of having lost the center of his existence. She knew this look intimately, having studied it each time she caught Pyrrhus thinking about his missing companion.

Patroclus's attention locked on her. He was studying her as closely as she had him. He looked distracted by her presence, and the tale he told her father was coming out garbled, but he drew himself up and got his invented details straightened out. His name was Pandion. He'd traveled as passenger on another trader's ship and could not speak for that captain or the availability of his goods. He was the youngest son of five, sent off on a long journey with tapestries as trade goods. The women in his father's household worked them, and he was to bring back wealth and thus show himself useful. He had already parted with most of these weavings but had one left to show.

Mia touched Dione's arm, alerting her.

Her father laughed congenially and said he had no use for weavings. His own household provided excellent work and his was not a wealthy court to spend trade goods on such luxuries from afar, but he appreciated the young man's need to prove his worth to a father so overly blessed with sons.

Mia rose quietly, drawing Dione beside her as escort, and left the throne room. She heard her father dismissing the man, sending him back to the ship he'd arrived on, and she stopped down the corridor from the throne room doors where this so-called Pandion would pass by. Her hand rested on her growing belly for a moment, and then she let it drop.

Soon enough, one of the court servants came along with the young man, guiding him out of the palace. He stopped short when he saw her, too awkwardly, which told her she hadn't been imagining who he was. He looked tongue-tied. Not a person who could easily engage in these deceits.

She would help him. "I heard your story."

He bowed to her. "Your majesty."

"No, I'm not queen, only princess. You spoke to my father. My husband is busy in the citadel."

"Perhaps it is he I need to speak with."

Mia noticed the immediate discomfort on the accompanying servant's face and silently congratulated the man on being a good keeper of the royal secret, as she'd come to think of it. He wanted to keep this man away from the prince as he'd been told to. "Why would you think that?"

"I am tired of the pretense this journey has forced upon me, a nobleman's son, trained as a warrior, going about as a trader. The gods tell me to choose otherwise. My father will not value me anymore when I return than before I left. I wish to make a new life. Perhaps your husband could use a well-trained warrior to add to his royal guard. If I spoke with him, I am certain he would agree."

"The gods told you?"

"It is always best to follow divine commands, whatever a god—or goddess—requires of you."

"That is sound advice," she said, catching his eye and seeing there a hint of the terror he must have experienced in Thetis's presence. "My kingdom does not take in unknown warriors. As a rule that would be unsafe." She glanced at the servant who'd accompanied him and nodded in reassurance. "This one time and only this one time, I will make an exception. Perhaps you can persuade my husband to give you a place. We will see."

She told the servant to go ahead and check with the prince if he agreed to see this one willing warrior, a traveler driven by the gods. "I like the sound of that," she said. "Use those words and tell him the princess will bring him."

Soon the servant came running back. Pyrrhus must have told him to hurry. "The prince will speak with you."

PYRRHUS STOOD in the middle of the citadel yard, under the bright sun. Guards and servants moved around the area, doing their tasks. Mia left the tunnel's shadow first and stepped to one side so that she could watch her husband's face when he saw Pandion, as they would apparently call Patroclus.

She thought she was ready for witnessing this, but the spark that lit her husband's face in that instant struck her heart like a lightning bolt. She fell back, her knees giving way. Only Dione catching her kept her upright.

Pyrrhus came nearer. She could feel the strain in his limbs as he forced himself, under the curious glances of citadel guards, to act as if Pandion were a stranger. She could almost see the cords of passion pulling them towards each other, even as they stood an arm's length apart.

Mia had the sense to dismiss the servant and glance around the area. No one stood near enough to overhear. Pyrrhus had arranged this well.

"You disappeared," Pandion said. "Even Chiron had no idea what had happened at first."

"However long your journey here, trust me, you would prefer it to the way my mother brought me here. Not to mention the torment she submitted me to once I was here."

Pyrrhus told of his days as Pyrrha and the rest. The way they'd convinced Thetis not to take out her fury on Mia and her family. The marriage.

"Eventually, I knew of the marriage," Pandion said. "Your father also knows. I suppose Thetis told him. He's pleased for you. He sent with me the proper bride price he would have given to her father if this had been arranged between kings as it should have been."

"Bride price?" Mia asked. She hadn't expected one when her father desperately arranged her marriage with Thetis. Her life had been enough. Every noble or royal marriage was accompanied by such exchanges, both a dowry from the bride's family and a bride price from the groom's.

Pandion made a small bow to her. "I will give it to your father privately to protect secrecy." His eyes flicked toward Pyrrhus. "He intends it as a sign of honor to you. I believe its generosity arises from an old father's longing for his son. None of us can soothe that."

Not while all these intertwined lives were constrained by a goddess. She said, "His kindness warms my heart."

Pyrrhus started to reach for Pandion and then dropped his hand. Instead of touching his longed-for companion, he said, "My mother has always had cruel schemes that she calls protecting me, but this is the worst." Perhaps he saw the hurt in Mia's eyes, because he added, "Turning me into a woman, that was the worst. She was determined to disguise me in a way no one could uncover."

"No one has learned of you, so it worked," Pandion said. "If your mother had not told me, I would have thought you'd died. Of course, she almost killed me in the telling."

Pyrrhus stepped closer to his fellow true warrior, his beloved companion. "This time, when I refused to stay in the body of a woman and she had to try something else, she let slip that she's hiding me from men who would use me for their own purposes and then leave me to die early. I have no idea what she means. Why doesn't she simply kill these men? But that can't be a solution, or she'd do it. What is she hiding? I've been trapped on this remote island, but you have been in my father's court where news comes freely. Tell me what you know, what you guess. Who or what is she hiding me from?"

Pandion put his hand on Pyrrhus's shoulder. "I have nothing to offer, not even a guess." Mia watched. Pandion did not meet Pyrrhus's gaze. "But I am here now. We don't need to know what is in her divine mind. You will be happy and so will I."

Mia looked at Pyrrhus. He drank in the sight of his companion's face, and his eyes roved up and down over Pandion's body. This longed-for presence was enough, so he accepted Pandion's careful answer without more questions. Pandion had said he had nothing to offer, which would be true if Thetis had forbidden him from speaking of it. Surely Thetis would never have allowed him to come if she thought he might reveal the foreseen evil that only her enforced secrecy could prevent. Mia knew how effectively she could bind a mortal into silence. Say the wrong word and die.

Pandion had spoken truthfully about one thing. Her husband exuded happiness in his expression and in the way he stood. She struggled against the crushing sensation in her chest. She'd never caused such a transformation in Pyrrhus. The cramped boredom that marred his grace had lifted in a moment. She suspected it would return at times, but if she was forced to share her husband, at least that husband might be far more at ease in his life, happier with her. Her hand slid down, supporting her growing womb. A child and his companion. Would they be enough to build a good life with her on Skyros?

27

An unusually hot spring and summer passed, and then a dry fall with little renewing rain. The island's crops had suffered, but as winter progressed, rains would surely come. Mia grew ever larger. She no longer traveled around the island to check on the farms, but she'd return to her duties once the baby came.

Over the summer and fall, the guardsmen Pyrrhus sent out as workers dug channels reaching from the island's springs and rivers to feed the fields, or where that wasn't possible, they carried water in buckets, however temporarily that helped. These projects had increased the harvest and endeared the royal guard and its prince to the people. Without these teams of laborers and the planning that guided their work, the harvest would have failed. But it didn't. Mia's organization of the island's labor to counteract the drought had seen to a sufficient harvest. Even her father congratulated her on staving off the worst. He did not grant Pyrrhus any of the credit.

To her surprise, Pandion had become the essential peacemaker between her father and husband. He would make mild, sensible suggestions, so different from Pyrrhus's extremes, and Pyrrhus listened to him. The private ceremony in which he had placed the jewels of her bride price into Lycomedes's hands hinted at his role of bridge between the two men. He stressed Peleus's respect for Skyros's king, signified in the generous price he paid for the princess. This was a partnership between equal kings in Pandion's words, although they all knew it wasn't. Pandion finessed the gift into a gentle attempt to alleviate the power struggle between the king and her husband.

She'd tried to dislike Pandion, but he made it difficult. He kept away from her life with Pyrrhus in the women's quarters. Pandion lived in the barracks with the guards. When and where Pyrrhus and Pandion spent time privately together, she didn't know, although she knew they must because when they were both present, she often saw their need for each other in their faces and postures. That hurt more than she allowed herself to face. Pyrrhus showed her love and respect, even more as their child grew in her womb. Except for sharing his heart with another, he was a good husband. What more could she demand from him? If she required his whole heart for herself, he would not be able to give it to her.

A sequence of unseasonably warm days in the middle of winter had increased Mia's restlessness and sense of being trapped in the palace. Despite her giant belly, she'd persuaded Pyrrhus to climb down the mountain with her and stroll along the trail through the river valley. "I need to be outside, away from the palace. Just with you."

"We could sit on your terrace," he'd answered.

"You know perfectly well that isn't enough."

He'd smiled. "Let's go."

They'd made it down the mountain smoothly enough. In the river valley, the winds had stripped bare the plane trees, and the broad, dead leaves crunched under their feet. Pyrrhus held her arm and for once didn't forget to go slowly. Her walk was more of a waddle, and she felt ungainly, but her husband's eyes wore the soft green she recognized as love and happiness. He leaned down to kiss her, and the passion in his lips would have driven them into some hidden leafy bower if she weren't struggling to put one foot in front of the other.

He laughed in understanding. "Being alone together outside is enough. You were right to insist."

"If I can climb back up," she said with laughter in her voice. Of course she could climb the familiar trail to the palace.

The pleasant sound of water burbling in the riverbed filled the air. The river should have been full from fall rains, but it flowed at a midsummer trickle, fed only by the year-round springs. But the greenery that thrived around the river made their walk refreshing.

They took a side path to a small pool that sparkled where the sun found its way through the arching branches. She leaned on Pyrrhus's arm as the track followed the riverbank down. She neared the pool, and then, without warning, a stabbing pain grabbed her belly. Mia cried out. She would have fallen to her knees, but Pyrrhus held her. "What is it? Is the baby coming?"

Eventually the agony subsided. "It must be, but it shouldn't be so fast. I've watched my mother—" She collapsed against Pyrrhus and howled as another spasm seized her. She tried to breathe down the pain, but sharp daggers were all there was in her world, blocking out thought and control.

She shrieked as the spasm tightened into another one without letting up. *This isn't how it starts.*

Pyrrhus lifted her into his arms. "I'll carry you."

His arms held her pressed firmly against his chest. "Draw from me," he said, which she didn't understand except she could draw in a breath before the next pang twisted around her belly, forcing out another scream. She felt the rhythm of his running, smooth and fast, against the harsher measure of her birthing labor.

Dimly through her torment she heard Pyrrhus apologizing. "This is my fault. I feared this might happen. My son has too much immortality in him. He is forcing your body to bring him out as a goddess does. Hold on, Mia. I refuse to let our baby kill you."

She couldn't hold onto anything. Her body was no longer hers.

The pain tightened around her, and she writhed in Pyrrhus's arms. A convulsion stiffened her body like a transformation into fiery stone. The arms around her never lost hold.

Each ripping spasm drove screeches until her throat was raw, and she tried to hold them in. But submitting silently to the force that had taken over her body felt like giving up.

The swing and beat of Pyrrhus's running stayed as the undercurrent of her labor, always predictable and secure no matter how lost she became in the tortured convulsions. The mountainside passed by as her husband climbed to the palace. The voices of palace guards sounded at some point, and Pyrrhus gave orders in turn, but she ignored them, focusing on the power that carried her forward and held on for her.

They passed the palace gates and through the central hallway. Harmonia's voice, high and panicked, sounded in an argument with Pyrrhus. About outside and irresponsible behavior. Then Pyrrhus took her to her own chamber where the birthing stool and all the other preparations lay ready.

Harmonia's voice said, "Help her onto the stool. She must be far into labor. I don't know why you waited until now to bring her back. You selfish fool." Mia shivered. Harmonia must be terrified to speak so critically to Pyrrhus. Ordinarily she doted on Mia's princely husband.

"Put those pillows for her back," Pyrrhus said. "She's in agony."

Harmonia did as he said and then helped him as Pyrrhus placed her gently on the stool. Mia let her weight fall against the stool's high back, into the cushions. To one side stood Dione, pale and wide-eyed, even though she had helped others through childbirth. Mia drew in a breath before another wave hit her, and her hoarse screams reverberated through her small chamber.

"Leave us," Harmonia said. "This is women's work."

Mia weakly reached for Pyrrhus. "No. Need him."

"Princess—" Harmonia objected.

"I'll stay," Pyrrhus interrupted. "She's right."

Harmonia fell silent. She knew he had healing skills. Pyrrhus had been unable to resist attending to small injuries and illnesses among her sisters and the palace servants.

Harmonia kneeled before Mia and delicately moved aside her

gown. "Thank the gods. Your womb has started opening. It may be you're through the worst."

The overpowering swells continued, getting worse no matter what Harmonia wished to make true. Being seized repeatedly without mastery of her own body drained her beyond enduring the pain. She lay against the stool, unable to lift her limbs or scream in objection.

"Mia, child, be strong for a while longer," she heard Harmonia say. "Your womb is opening. I've never seen such labor pains, but the baby is coming. Help it come by pushing."

Help this force that had taken control of her? That fought her as if she were a foe to conquer? How could she push when it had drained away all her strength?

Dione said something softly, some encouragement, but she couldn't sort out the words.

Another excruciating surge rose, squeezing her, crushing her soul and immediately rushed into a greater one, knocking away what of herself she had held onto. Lurking at the edge of the emptiness, a relieving darkness lured her. She had no will to move toward it, but she felt herself drawn toward that place of shadow.

"No, Mia." Pyrrhus's deep voice broke through. "Draw from me. Hold on. You can be as strong as a goddess today. Through the connection of our son inside your womb, I can help you. Turn toward my voice."

The voice she loved called to her, easy to turn toward. Then the pain returned, but that was necessary, and when Harmonia told her to push, she had the necessary strength. She opened her eyes, found her husband's bright emerald gleam looking deep into her, and her whole body pressed downward, harnessing a squeezing surge into a powerful push. She gritted her teeth and held onto the downward thrust.

Harmonia made a shrill squeak of surprise. "A boy. It's a boy."

"Of course he is," Pyrrhus said.

Mia fell back against the stool. Her body was exhausted, but it was entirely hers.

. . .

Harmonia supported the squalling baby in a soft blanket while Dione deftly wiped him clean with a linen towel. Mia watched as they finished with a swaddling blanket of softest wool. "Show him to me."

"Of course," Harmonia said. "He is a loud one. Perhaps he needs to nurse." She laid the red-faced infant on Mia's lap, and Mia curled her arms around him. Pyrrhus leaned over, their heads touching as they both looked at their child. An overwhelming need to keep any harm from this small being flowed through Mia. She pressed him close, love for him so strong in her veins she felt woozy with it.

Harmonia knelt before Mia again. "I need to see that all's done and clean you up."

"May I hold him?" Pyrrhus asked, with awe in his voice.

Mia nodded. Pyrrhus cradled his son where Mia could still see him, rocking him in his arms and making the soothing sounds she'd heard Pyrrhus use to calm horses. Their small son stopped crying.

"My little warrior. You will grow up fast and strong, won't you?" Pyrrhus studied his son, gently tugging loose the blanket so he could touch his tiny fingers and rub a finger along his arm. "His skin is so soft. It is hard to imagine the man he will become."

Mia gave a weak laugh. "Why don't we let him grow up first? He has a long way to go before he's a man."

Pyrrhus frowned. "Not so long." He stroked the dark hair that covered the little head. "I think he's hungry. He's moving his mouth. Should you nurse him?"

Mia looked at Harmonia, who nodded reassuringly. "I'll show you if you need any help. Babies know what to do with a teat. Just brush it against his lips and he'll take hold."

Dione reached over and undid the pin holding Mia's shoulder closed. Pyrrhus laid the baby next to her bare breast, and she followed Harmonia's advice. Her son opened his mouth wide when he felt her nipple and clamped on. Mia gave a little scream at how much his nursing hurt.

"He's so strong," Pyrrhus said with pride.

"Hopefully he will learn to put less strength into his feeding," Mia said. "He's hurting me."

"It will get better," Harmonia said, but there was a shocked tone to her voice that didn't reassure Mia. "For such a newly born child, he is a powerful feeder. Just as well. He'll grow into a strong prince."

Pyrrhus sat cross-legged on the floor near her, watching with a look of joy. Gradually the discomfort in her breast lessened or she grew accustomed to it. She wasn't sure which.

Dione went to tell the king that Mia had come through the birth and he had a grandson. The baby objected when Harmonia suggested she shift him to the other side to nurse, but after another fierce latching on, he settled. Mia dozed and Harmonia finished her work, telling her to stay upright against the supporting stool for a while longer and tucking a warm blanket around Mia and the now sleeping baby.

Mia opened her eyes when she heard a soft knock.

"May I come in. May I see him?" Her father stood in the doorway.

Pyrrhus rose from the floor, standing on the alert by his child.

"Come in, Father. He's eaten and is sound asleep."

Lycomedes stepped close.

"You can hold him if you like," Mia said.

Lycomedes knelt by the stool. "He's beautiful. Our prince. At last." At her prompting, he lifted the swaddled baby into his arms. "Greetings, Pyrrhus." Her father looked up at Pyrrhus. "To avoid confusion may we call the baby by a nickname, maybe Pyraki?"

"Pyraki? That sounds good," her husband answered. "He is a very small Pyrrhus."

The baby made some snuffling noises in his sleep. The king cooed at him and snuggled him against his chest. "You're perfect. Everything I've ever wanted."

28

Winter had brought cold winds in between stretches of unexpected warm weather, but there had been few storms and almost none of the rain they needed. Mia stood outside the palace gate, looking out over the road that wound down the mountain. The wind had cleared away the low-lying fog clinging to the coastline and pushed aside every hint of cloud. The sea sparkled as clear blue as the sky it reflected, but the hilly land stretched out brittle and exhausted.

Guards stood on either side of the gate, and Dione perched on a nearby boulder working her spindle while Mia met with the elders from some of the villages. She'd set this public and proper location once her motherhood made traveling around to the villages more difficult for her, and she'd observed how awkward the farmers were in the throne room.

The elders spoke their concerns. Listening to the village leaders served a reassuring purpose and reinforced the trust they'd built together, even if it did not fill any bellies. So far, thanks to planning and the efforts of Pyrrhus's men during the growing season, the food stores had not run out.

But the anxious faces were justified. She could not make the rain fall. She pushed them for more ideas of how to grow foods that would survive without so much water, picking through their rambling explanations of what their fathers or grandfathers had done in the past. They agreed to work through these ideas with the other farmers and come up with plans for the fields before planting time arrived. They were unused to thinking outside of their one village, and it was hard to get them to trust that if they grew what did best in their own corner of the island, someone else would provide them with the foods they hadn't grown themselves.

She sighed and hoped it'd be enough.

Standing there trying to dismiss these elders without offense, Mia heard a baby's wailing carried on the wind. Immediately she felt the milk in her breasts drop, leaking into the folds of linen she'd tucked against them. It was past time to nurse her hungry baby Pyraki. The unbreakable cord that connected her to her son no matter where he happened to be yanked taut, drowning out her other thoughts with an overwhelming drive to take care of him. She wondered at times how her mother had survived the separation. Comforted as Mia had been by the concealed message from her mother, she doubted that her mother had ever felt as she did now. She was convinced she could never be torn from her child and still have the will to live.

She used the baby's cries to signal the end of the meeting and turned to Dione, who had already hopped up and nodded in understanding. The elders bowed and departed. She and Dione hurried down the side path toward the practice field and Pyraki's cries.

No matter how much she loved her son, she found raising him challenging in ways that caring for her sisters had never been. Pyraki was very demanding, screaming in fury when he was tired, hungry, or startled, but fighting the sleep, milk, and comfort that would have soothed these infant troubles.

Earlier that morning, as he often did, Pyrrhus had taken the baby with him to the practice field, slung across his chest, tied in place by a length of linen in such a way that the baby could look outward. Whenever Pyrrhus held their son, he talked to the baby about the skills of a warrior. And their baby stopped his screaming when he heard his father's voice—and almost never otherwise. The first time Pyrrhus took him to the practice field, she'd come also, distressed for the safety of their child. But slung against his father, his small, still-blurry eyes were entranced by the sword fighting and spear throwing going on under his father's commands. Only a man of Pyrrhus's size and strength could get away with such a womanly behavior to hold a baby in this way. No one thought to tease him. She wondered if his experience living as a woman contributed to his willingness, but she'd realized gradually that his intense desire to show his son how to be a warrior came from his belief that he would live a short life. If he was to die soon, he'd teach now. As his mother had warped his childhood with the knowledge of looming death, so he perpetuated that sadness.

Mia went along with this pattern to their life since her son only quieted his angry wails while sharing in his father's mania or when he nursed or slept in short snatches that took great efforts of soothing and walking to bring about.

The terraced area of olive trees that served as training field came into view down the path from Mia and Dione. Her son's cries had risen in volume and now Mia saw why. Coming toward them up the path was Pandion with the squalling baby.

Dione turned to Mia with a look of amusement. "He's gone like a log, again."

Mia nodded. Her angry son had recently discovered he could tighten his whole body with his legs and arms stretched out, still wailing, and make it almost impossible to carry him or provide comfort. It did feel like carrying a very loud block of wood. Pandion was doing his best not to drop him.

Mia hurried toward him, glancing to the side of the trail for a place to sit on a rock, and then she held out her arms for her child.

"My apologies, Princess," Pandion said. "I tried to bring him to you sooner, before he got so frustrated with hunger, but you know . . ." He trailed off. She did know. Pyrrhus would have been caught up in the training of his men, ignoring the warning whimpers.

"Never mind."

Pandion bowed and excused himself, turning back toward the practice field.

She loosened her shoulder pin and with difficulty maneuvered her baby's angry, stiffened body so that his lips touched her dripping nipple. She had to try several times before he suddenly latched on, sucking so hard as usual that it sent shocks of pain through her breast.

Pyraki fed with a driving determination for a long stretch, and then he pulled hard on her nipple. It was his way of complaining that the flow of milk had slowed, instead of contentedly loosening his grip and waiting to be shifted to the other side like the babies she'd observed. When she slid her finger between his lip and her skin to loosen his grip, he screamed in fury once again, and she switched him as fast as she could to the other breast.

Dione, who had sunk down beside her, balancing on an edge of the rock, took gentle hold of the tiny hand that flailed wildly in the air as he suckled. "Silly baby. If you yell less, you'll get what you want the sooner."

Mia sighed. "I don't think he'll ever wait patiently when he wants something."

29

Now that Pyraki had learned to walk, his rolling gait and tubby round belly reminded Mia of a small bear. She laughed as her one-year-old barreled around the women's hall. To stop himself, he inevitably chose to collide with something or someone. He'd taken naughty delight in sending her wine cup flying by knocking over her side table instead of landing in her outstretched arms. Sitting on stools around the hearth, Mia's sisters called out to him, each enticing him to choose her arms to crash into, but he veered off into the corridor to the palace and Mia heard a mock "oof" from the guard standing watch there. Leave it to her son to choose the one available warrior to "attack."

She stood up to retrieve him before he ended up in the throne room or some other trouble, not that her father would mind. He was even worse than Pyrrhus about encouraging whatever activity her wild son wanted, no matter how willful or destructive. The king had waited too long for this prince and was too pleased about having a grandson to be sensible.

She ran into the dim hallway and scooped up Pyraki, who yelled in childish fury. She squeezed him in a wriggly hug. "Hush. You can cry if you wish, but no one likes a warrior who can't behave politely toward others."

Pyraki's face grew redder and his yelling louder.

The guard at the doorway called out over his screams, "Your mother the princess is right, and none of us fighters yell loud like that unless it's a war cry. We won't know when real trouble comes with you screaming like that."

Pyraki stopped to listen to this big man, and now Mia plopped him on his own legs, herding him back into the women's hall. She saw Dione coming down the corridor from the palace.

"Princess," Dione called out. "You're wanted in the throne room." Dione grabbed hold of one of Pyraki's hands. "I've got him."

Mia reached up to be sure she'd remembered a veil and hurried off. Dione's excellent mothering skills with Pyraki made Mia feel sad that Dione and Galene had not yet had a child. There seemed to be genuine warmth in their marriage, more than Mia would have assumed possible from her first conversation with Dione about Galene, but beyond anything, they wanted a child of their own. Mia hoped the delay did not drain Galene's goodwill toward Dione.

She slipped through the side door of the throne room and moved past the screen, taking her seat on one side of the lower level of the throne dais. Her father sat on his large black throne.

From the area below the dais, a burly man with a weather-beaten face spoke to her father. A ship captain, by the look of him, and to Mia's surprise, they were discussing grain, an important topic for her father and her. Hunger had been widespread this past winter, the second dry one. Spring had brought fishing, greens, and other foods, despite the continuing lack of rain, but without rain, the grain crop would fail again, and they'd used up the island's stored grain.

After listening for a while, she gathered this trader didn't have grain in his hull on this trip, but he was continuing to Egypt where he would trade the copper ingots he had for grain. Egypt was legendary for the bounty of its crops, so this caught her attention.

Her father turned to her and gave her a questioning look. She nodded, although not certain whether he asked if she'd heard this man's business or if she wanted to buy his grain. The gods had offered them this chance to save the island. They *must* buy it.

"I could stop at this island on my return," the trader said, "but I'd have to know what you'll pay. Grain will be like gold by the time I journey back."

Her father's eyes narrowed at this. "An exaggeration, I'd think."

"Hardly," the trader insisted. Then he seemed to gain some insight from her father's face. "You haven't heard, have you? I'll get plenty for my shipload of grain. The rains have failed across the islands, just when there will be a big army hungry for any surplus."

Leaning forward from his throne, Lycomedes asked, "Army? This news hasn't reached here."

The trader shrugged. "Some foreign prince was foolish enough to steal the wife of one of the mainland kings, Menelaus of Sparta, and now he and his more powerful brother Agamemnon are gathering men to fight—all the great warriors, they claim. With promises of looting and riches in return."

A chill fell over Mia. Was this war what Thetis had feared? The goddess's words echoed in her memory like daggers to her heart, "I will not allow my son to be dragged toward death by crawling mortals who seek his strength for their greedy, small purposes." The kings this trader spoke of would not imagine that anyone, even an immortal, would describe them as crawling, greedy, and small, but to Mia's ear Thetis's description matched far too well.

The trader added, "I suppose King Agamemnon hasn't sent anyone here persuading you to outfit a ship with fighters."

Her father made a dismissive gesture with his hand. "He wouldn't bother. This isn't an island of warriors. My citadel is well guarded, but I've got none to send off to some other king's quarrel or empty promises of loot." He glanced at Mia with a furrowed brow. He would share her worry about this news and Pyrrhus, but she also wondered how it must sound to him that a king brought an army to regain a stolen wife.

"I suppose not," the trader said. "You're wise to keep your warriors here. When food gets scarce for armies, the raiding begins."

Exactly the sort of danger that Pyrrhus had trained the guards to confront, but much as her husband valued protecting his son, wife, and kingdom, she suspected that wouldn't be enough to resist the temptation to join these warriors in their fight if he heard of it. *All the great warriors.* Not all of them if Pyrrhus stayed on Skyros. It was fortunate Pyrrhus was forced to keep away from outsiders, and no one would come to Skyros to build an army, so she wouldn't need to worry about a delegation from these brother kings.

Her father brought the trader back to his planned shipload of grain. In payment, Lycomedes promised the usual assortment of trade goods produced in the palace workshops and looms, some wine, and purple dye made from sea snails. That last surprised her. He rarely offered what little of that they produced, leaving it for the palace textiles. Then he described two gold cups and a silver bowl from his treasury, their sizes and artistry. He would send his steward to bring them out for viewing if the trader wished.

Mia sat up on her throne, her gaze flicking from one man to the other. Her father's offer would not drain the treasury, but it was significant.

The trader shook his head. "That isn't enough. Although I'd rather deliver grain to you than this rumored army. Armed kings could just as easily seize it without payment. But trade is always risky, and this is a chance that won't likely come again. You'll have to offer a lot more."

Lycomedes shook his head. "Good luck with those kings and warriors. You may find counting on unpredictable war is unwise. My offer is generous and as high as I'll go."

There was silence. Her father was good at waiting out others, but the trader broke the silence only to bow and ask permission to be dismissed.

Her father nodded and signaled a servant to escort the trader out.

Mia cleared her throat, feeling attention fall on her. "One moment. My father has made a generous offer. It is surely close to the amount you require, but under these circumstances I am willing to add a small portion."

"In times of lesser need, perhaps a small portion more would be enough." The trader turned toward the doorway.

The jewels of her bride price had been as generous as Pandion had said, and for grain, she would give up a lot, but this man was being greedy. "Listen to my offer before you blind yourself with greed. Remember, when you sail into our harbor with a shipload of grain, you will have no fear that we will slaughter you and steal it. No ship would ever come to our port again if such rumors flew. But an army of ravenous warriors? Don't fool yourself. Listen to what I will add to my father's abundant offer."

Her father glared at her. She wondered if he guessed yet what she would use for payment. Her bride price wasn't actually hers, but she would claim it in this self-sacrificing way that her father would be ashamed to stop.

She described the three golden necklaces with matching earrings and a diadem meant for a queen, filling her words with her desire for them so that she would persuade him of their immense value. Her father started to interrupt her, but she apologized softly to him and went on. The pieces were exquisite, and she'd looked forward to wearing them, but she would feed her people. There'd be enough surplus grain to put those storage pits into proper use and tide her people through drought.

The trader's eyes grew wide. "You would give your personal jewels—your crown—for something like grain?"

She kept her face blank. This trader had assumed exactly what she wanted him to about the jewels, but men didn't think much of women, did they? "I prefer to feed my people. If you are not interested, my father and I will speak to other traders now that we know this news you've told us. Many ships come to our harbor. They know this is an island of fair dealing and honor."

The trader tipped his head in agreement. "I came here because of that reputation. I did not know the princess was so skilled at such dealings. I will bring my shipload here for the combined payment your father and you have described."

"Good. We will remember the terms. I will order the royal scribe to record them for sealing."

"I will add my seal before I sail, Princess. I will return after the Egyptian harvest season." He bowed again and left with the servant.

The moment the door thumped closed, her father said, "Those jewels are yours to wear, not to offer in payment. You forced my hand in this humiliating way. Get out of my sight before I say something worse that I will regret."

She looked directly at her father. "Instead of saving our kingdom, shall I wear that diadem while the smoke rises around the island from countless funeral pyres?"

His gaze dropped.

She stalked out, letting out a sigh of relief. She hadn't realized how widespread the problem with rainfall was. If they had failed to bring this trader's Egyptian shipload to their island, they wouldn't have found any nearer sources of grain, and the drought seemed likely to last even longer than she'd feared.

But the other news from this trader struck even closer to her heart. His report of a gathering army that she must keep secret from Pyrrhus. Could she do that?

She remembered Thetis sitting on her father's ebony throne and threatening death if Mia and her father failed to keep the goddess's son concealed from the world. Whatever the upcoming months might bring, she would not reveal to her husband that he alone of the "true warrior" princes and kings was excluded from fighting in the coming war.

30

The drought had continued through the summer and fall, but the olive trees, hardy even in the driest times, came in with a rich harvest when the early months of winter came around. Across the island, especially in the northwest part where the lower slopes below the pine forests suited extensive olive groves, families picked the small fruits and gathered them for pressing. Soon much of the precious oil in large ceramic jars would be carried into the citadel on the backs of donkeys for safe storage. One small victory against the ongoing problem of feeding her people. She watched for the trader's return with his shipload of grain. His delay weighed on her mind. So many disasters or differing choices could have occurred.

Then came a day when Mia and her father were interrupted in the throne room by the panicked cries of a citadel guard calling for them. They raced to see what was happening.

Through the citadel gates flooded fleeing farmers and their families, terrified and exhausted, from the western side of the island. The men described raiders, who drove them with swords from their pressing stones and groves and then carried away the ceramic jars of oil.

Mia listened to these frantic accounts. "Are there wounded or . . .

dead?" she asked tear-streaked women, most of whom gave her silent, blank stares.

"Not that I saw," said one woman with a toddler tied in her cloak to her back. "But I wouldn't put it past 'em."

Mia turned to her father. "They knew exactly when to come for our oil, didn't they?" This was a dangerously well-thought-out raid.

Pyrrhus hurried up beside her. She'd seen him across the yard sending his guards to the battlements and massing them by the open doors of the citadel gate through which frightened people were still arriving. Pandion remained at the gate, fully armed and calling out orders.

Her father asked one of the farmers, "How many raiders? Did you see their ship?" The man hunched his shoulders with a beaten, haunted look in his eyes and shook his head. He shifted closer to a woman whose face was smeared with dirt and tears. A small boy hid in the folds of her skirt, and the man lifted him into his arms.

Pyrrhus beckoned over a pair of men, younger, unattached to families. "Tell the king what you told me. What you saw."

They described two ships drawn up on shore in the most sheltered bay on the western side. They'd seen more than forty or so fighters from each go ashore and move out from there, but then they'd been discovered by some of the raiders' scouts that had come around behind them. The armed scouts told them to run and stay away if they wished to live. Mia shook her head. More signs these raiders were organized. They'd strip her island. At least they hadn't turned to killing first. They didn't seem concerned with news of their presence spreading. They must be so confident in their large numbers and fighting skills that they didn't fear the island's defenders.

"Are they burning the villages?" she asked.

The two young men shook their heads. One said, "Not yet, Princess. Going after the new oil fast as they can, seems."

"Perhaps they'll leave as fast as they arrived and attacked," she said.

Pyrrhus asked, "Have any of the farmers fought back?"

These two shrugged, but another man overheard and said, "Some of us." He showed his arm, tied with a bloody rag. "But before I could think, the man had his sword at my neck. Told me go away or die. This were enough." He pointed at his arm.

"How were they armed?" Pyrrhus asked.

"Swords, spears, shields slung on their backs if they need 'em. All of 'em I seen, anyway."

"Then you did the right thing to come here instead of fighting," Pyrrhus said. "Warriors, not rough bandits," he said under his breath. He turned to her and her father. "You gather in the villagers as they come. Get them settled and provided for. The danger is on the other side of the island. We must stop it there. I'm going to gather my warriors and drive these raiders off before they do more harm. And take back our oil."

He didn't wait for their response, instead shouting orders to his guards to prepare for a fast march and fight.

Mia didn't doubt he'd clear the island, but she closed her eyes for a moment and weighed everything she'd heard. The pieces fit together into an alarming picture. Silently she repeated that trader's words, *two mainland kings gathering men to fight—all the great warriors.* Pyrrhus had no knowledge of that assembling of warriors. She didn't dare tell him now, but this raid might seek more than oil. She hesitated. That couldn't be it. No one knew to come to Skyros. Either way, though, she knew what she had to do.

"Pyrrhus," she called out, running to him where his warriors were forming up around him. "You are right that our warriors must drive these raiders off, but you should stay here."

"No—"

She grabbed his arm. "Trust your men. You have trained them well. And they know the island better than you do, so they can pursue these men as effectively as can be." He shook off her hand, but she flattened her palm against his chest. "Listen. A little apart from your men. You must."

He drew in an angry breath but nodded and stepped away, leaning down so she could speak to him without others hearing.

"If you go with your men, you will be seen, unmistakably seen as the pre-eminent warrior of half-immortal size that you are. It's exactly what your mother warned against. The rumors will go everywhere. Your mother will demand my life in exchange for your exposure. Instead, trust your men. Put Pandion in command. He's as skilled as you are. You can say to your men that you must stay to protect the king, your wife, and son."

She saw her dear husband sag in misery. She added, "Listen to me. You will never forgive yourself."

"No. I wouldn't." He let out a sharp cry of frustration. "I'll stay in the citadel, and I'll keep a small fighting force here." He started to turn away, but he grabbed her arm and glared into her eyes. "Pandion is skilled, but not invincible like I am. If these raiders slaughter any of my men, I won't forgive myself for that, either. It doesn't matter what I do."

The remaining guards barred the citadel gates. Mia went around to the families packed into the yard. They sat on the ground, filling the open space, even though only the families from the western side of the island had known to seek refuge. She'd ordered Galene to pull food and blankets or other coverings from the palace stores, which she handed out as she organized some centralized cooking fires, putting women in charge who didn't look at her with empty, frightened stares.

Her father had sent out orders to drive into the citadel as many flocks of goats and sheep as possible to protect them from the raiders. They'd crammed the animals into the citadel pens and stables. The herds would provide food if the worst happened and the raiding continued for more days. Her father insisted that these thieves would depart quickly with the oil they'd taken in their first forays. They'd come with so many men and two ships for a fast raid. Why else would they be so unconcerned with hiding their actions? The guards under Pandion's command would find nothing but retreating sails on the horizon. Mia shook her head at her father's words, but whatever these raiders aimed at, what she needed to do wouldn't change.

Her sisters and noble attendants occupied one of the citadel storerooms that had been nearly empty. The palace servants had carried stools and pallets for them. The treasury with most of the king's valuables was safely stored in the citadel already, but Galene had gone through the palace with large leather sacks removing silver and gold and other precious objects and sending all the servants from the palace into the citadel before the postern door was barred and the tunnel blocked with timbers that had been prepared for this purpose. Her father had a plan for his palace wealth, apparently, but not for feeding and accommodating the island's people inside his citadel. Messengers had gone out to warn the other villages of what was happening. They'd have to hide on their own.

Her father must have read her worry for the villagers they abandoned to the raiders. "They know how to hide in the mountains and sea caves. Leave them to it."

She turned away and went to find Dione, who was holding Pyraki on her hip while trying to reassure those huddled on the ground around her. Mia overheard her saying, "Prince Pyrrhus won't let any harm come to his little son, so you'll be safe here."

Pyrrhus stood on the defense tower, looking out across the sea and landscape below. She watched his restless movements. He always thought as a warrior and wasn't blind to the grim possibilities two ships of well-armed raiders could choose to inflict—enough men to attack the citadel.

31

A hint of gray light marked the coming of dawn. Mia looked down from the tower battlements where she stood near her husband. When she had snuggled Pyraki against her on one of the pallets inside the "royal" storeroom to settle him for the night, she'd slept briefly, but Dione had soon taken her place, and she'd gone back out to her frightened people. Her son would be safe with Dione, who would not let the two-year-old prince out of her sight for even a moment. They both knew how drawn to the guards and fighting the toddler was.

She'd asked her father to keep away from Pyrrhus and let the warrior do what he was best at. Because of the time in intense training Pyrrhus had spent with the guard, many by habit referred to the guard as Pyrrhus's men. To her surprise, instead of acting jealously, her father had had the good sense to hand off the command of the citadel guard officially to Crown Prince Pyrrhus and announced he was ready to fight beside his son-in-law. The king wore armor and his sword belt, but he stayed among the guard below while Pyrrhus ranged like a lion on the defensive tower that rose above the gates.

Pyrrhus scanned the land around the citadel, turning in a slow circle. "I wish," he said, "that this citadel had the scalloped bastions like the ruined city. Why did the kings of this island forget something so valuable? From this one tower and its battlements, I can't launch an effective defense against attackers on all sides of the citadel. I've positioned bowmen on ladders where I can, but . . ." He shook his head.

"The mountain is too steep for anyone to launch much of an attack on the other sides," Mia answered, echoing what her father had said many times. "This citadel has never been taken."

"I could take it with two ships of men."

"But Pandion will drive them away. They won't come here."

"Probably not. The oil harvest was an easy target. But the greatest wealth is always in a king's citadel. These men came armed as warriors, not petty thieves. Two ships of them."

"If they aimed at the citadel, they'd draw up their ships at the main harbor, most likely." Mia stood on her tiptoes leaning out over the low stone wall that topped the tower, even though the nearby harbor wasn't visible from here.

"I sent a scout to watch there," Pyrrhus said. "He's brought no news. So either they haven't landed, or they killed my scout."

Mia leaned against him, tucking herself between his chest and arm, in hopes of an embrace that would remind him that protecting her and his son was worth everything.

He held her for a moment and then turned back to the parapet. "They could draw up on the beach where we could see them right away." He pointed the opposite direction from the unseen harbor to where the fertile river plain rolled smoothly to the wide, sandy shore.

She watched his face. "Only if the sea isn't too rough. There's no protection on that beach. We'd see them, but you wouldn't launch an attack outside the walls, would you?"

He shook his head. "Your father claims warriors like me seek battles everywhere, but with the numbers of men I have here—" His full lips turned down in a bitter frown. "I wouldn't give up the advantage of these citadel walls, even with only one tower. Besides . . ."

"You must stay hidden."

"I hate this, Mia. My mother is still forcing me to live trapped in a cage, like a useless songbird. I can't stay like this much longer."

A cry went up from a bowman on one of the ladders. Pyrrhus leapt forward and took the tower ladder down in three springing jumps, racing to where the bowman stood on a ladder, pointing with his arm extended. Mia followed as fast as she could.

"Warriors below," the man shouted.

Pyrrhus waved him down from the ladder and sprang up the moment the bowman got out of his way. Mia reached the foot of the ladder, looking up at her husband. His distinctive hair was hidden under a bronze and leather helmet, and the wall partially concealed his height and huge size, but she cringed as he gazed out over the wall.

"I count twenty men picking their way up the goat tracks," he called down. "Armed warriors. So much for my scout at the harbor."

He climbed down, turning to the bowman. "Get back up your ladder. Shoot as soon as they come in range, but wait until then. Aim here." Pyrrhus pointed to the gap between shoulder and neck where his armor joined. "They are wearing full armor. Your arrows must find the vulnerable places as I taught you. These are not bandits who will run away quickly." The last was said to Lycomedes who'd run over.

Pyrrhus turned to servants hurrying toward him carrying supplies of arrows. They'd known what to do and were ready, Mia noted. "Good," Pyrrhus said. "Go to your stations at each ladder. Don't let any bowmen run short."

He looked at Lycomedes and said, "Take command of the tower."

A look of surprise shifted to understanding on her father's face. "You'll stay out of sight?"

"I have no choice."

Another shouted warning came from a guard on the tower. "Armed men running fast on the main trail to the citadel. They're just now coming into view."

"They've come from the harbor," Mia said. "We wouldn't see them until they were already on the mountain."

Pyrrhus said to her father, "An attack on all sides of your citadel, as I warned. Take what spearmen we have onto the tower, along with the bowmen already there. Keep these warriors away from the gate. Make them pay with lives for this assault. That's our best hope at driving them off."

Her father ran to the tower, shouting orders to the spearmen as he went.

Pyrrhus exchanged a look with Mia. "Go inside the storage room with my son."

"No. Dione will watch him. I'll stay with my people."

"Stray arrows—"

"I'll stay safe. I'm no more a songbird than you are."

"Then watch that the ladders and tower stay well supplied with arrows and spears. As long as your father's limited armory lasts." He pulled her into a kiss and then drew back, his eyes as sharply green as an emerald. She clasped his arms, feeling their power, and then released him.

He ran to another of the ladders to instruct that bowman and asked for a report of what the man saw. Her husband must have decided the approaching warriors were close enough to make standing at the wall's top a foolish risk. *Good.*

From outside the walls came deafening war cries and the sound of stomping feet and swords pounding against shields. An army of noise overran the citadel. Panic surged in Mia's chest. Screams rose from the villagers huddled in the exposed center of the citadel. Arrows arced over the walls, making Mia duck under the stable's lean-to roof.

No! Take hold of yourself. The raiders' warlike noises were intended to intimidate, and their arrows were being fired from too far away. They all fell harmlessly. She drew herself up and moved out through the crowded yard.

The terrified men and women who'd looked to this citadel for protection needed a purpose and a sense that her family was doing their best for them. Mia looked for Pyrrhus and went to him. "Can the farmers help in the defense? Can we place the women with small children somewhere less exposed?"

Pyrrhus pressed his lips together and glanced across the crowded yard. His lips softened, and he nodded to her. "Many brought what weapons they could from their farm implements. Station them on the ground before the gate. I had to move almost all the guard left onto the tower. And ask for any skilled in the bow." His eyes flicked up to the ladders and across to the tower. "We will soon lose bowmen, and they can stand ready to replace them."

"I'll give those directions."

"It's a good idea to move the children and their mothers, but . . ." His frown showed he didn't know where they'd go.

She didn't either. "I'll figure something out." She touched his arm in a quick good-bye and walked toward the center of the yard, gesturing to several farmers to follow her as she went.

She relayed Pyrrhus's suggestions to those gathered around her and when she saw understanding and enthusiasm light up certain men's faces, she counted off groups of ten and gave those men the job of leading a group. Her father's guard were arranged in similarly sized units, so she copied that. This process drew more men near enough to hear her. Several men stepped forward with the assertion they could wield a bow. Some even had their own with them. She distributed these men to the ladders and tower.

Her throat hurt from shouting these orders over the sounds of fighting, but the screams of women had mostly quieted. Her organizing had shifted most of the men into purposeful positions. She glanced at the staring women. A smaller crowd, but still a lot. There was a small amount of space left inside the storeroom where her sisters and their attendants had gathered. She'd been ignoring her own family.

"Sitting or standing here exposed in the middle of this yard under attack," she said in a carrying voice to the village women, "could terrify the bravest warrior. You are safer than it feels. You'll have seen that the arrows from far outside the walls have lost their force by the time they fall within. These raiders will have to risk their own lives far more against our bows and spears if they wish to send anything more dangerous against us. The din these bandits make is loud and terrifying, but it is only noise like the shouts and shrieks your children make when they play, harmless no matter how often your heart leaps, thinking a dangerous injury causes the high-spirited screams. Remind yourself of that and take courage."

Mia paused to catch her breath. "Some of the children can no longer bear what these raiders have forced upon us. They need some time in a quieter, sheltered place. There is a small space within the storeroom where the king sent the royal family. My sisters, the young princesses, would gladly comfort such children and their mothers. You may need to take turns escaping from the awfulness of this place." She waved her arm at the open yard. "I will take some of you now."

She looked across the huddled women. Some women helped others to their feet and pushed them forward. A few stood in postures that cried out to Mia, and she went over and drew them into her cluster of women and children.

"Come with me," she said, taking the hand of the nearest to draw them all with her.

She opened the wooden door to the storeroom. All eyes within looked at her, wide with fear. When her sisters and their attendants saw it was Mia, the taut terror released a little. Pyraki jumped up from Dione's lap and ran to her. She lifted him onto her hip and then drew the small cluster of women and their children inside. She hushed Pyraki's demanding cries and spoke softly to Harmonia and her sister Idomene. Both brightened at this job and immediately welcomed the women.

"Harmonia, there are more women outside who would benefit from comfort. Do your best to fit as many in here as you can and encourage a rotation of the women and children by going in and out with them. Can you do that? It will help bring calm outside and assist our fighters. The royal family is needed at this time of crisis."

"Yes, Princess Deidamia. We'll do all we can," Harmonia said.

"I'll stay with those outside," Mia said. To her son, who had buried his face against her chest, she whispered, "I'm sure you are being brave as a good warrior should and helping Dione by showing everyone how courageous and quiet you can be." She didn't want to let go of his warm body, cuddled into her as if a part of her own. The tight hug she pressed around him only heightened the ache at letting him go.

She tried to place him on the ground, but he clung to her. "Back to Dione, little one. A warrior does not cling to his mother in the middle of a battle. I'll check on you whenever I can."

"No!" he shrieked, making several of the women around her jump.

"Pyraki, this is naughty. Everyone is frightened, and you may not add to that with loud shouting. Play here with the other children. Dione is with you."

Next to her, there was a small boy also buried in his mother's arms. Mia gestured to him. "Show this boy the horse your papa carved for you. I bet he knows what sound a horse makes. Build a stable with the sticks we broke from the tree together. I see them on the floor over there." She pointed, drawing Pyraki's gaze.

Dione came over and pried Pyraki from Mia's arms, shushing his cries.

"Neigh, neigh," Dione said in a cheerful voice, "Your horse says to come play with him and bring your new friend." Dione smiled at the woman and beckoned her over to the corner where Pyraki and she had been seated on a blanket.

Mia dashed a tear from her eye and hurried out before Pyraki started up again.

She scanned the yard but didn't immediately find Pyrrhus. The volume from the raiders had increased. A glance at the tower showed her father and many guards engaged with spears, which was a bad sign that the attackers had drawn close enough to be in throw range. Bowmen sent arrows out over the line of spearmen onto the attackers below. The defense of the gate from the tower had drawn almost every guard. The farmers stood on the ground below, massed before the barred gates. If the gates gave way, they'd meet the full force of these attacking warriors. What had she done?

Her gaze shifted to the ladders, going from one to the other. There bowmen fired in quick succession. Servants climbed up with full quivers as planned. But what—

Her heart jammed into her throat as one of the ladders tumbled backward. The people below screamed and scrambled to get out of the way. The bowman on top clung to the ladder for a moment before flying from it with a grotesque thud followed by the clatter of the ladder.

A helmeted head appeared from the other side of the wall. Then another next to him, and a bow rose menacingly into view.

How could that be?

A roar of fury tore through the citadel, her husband's. Her head whipped toward the sound. Pyrrhus flew toward the fallen ladder. He held a spear larger than any she'd ever seen. He'd kept that a secret from her.

At his bellowed commands, men leapt into action to lift the ladder back onto the wall and braced its base against another push from the men above.

"No!" she shouted as she realized what Pyrrhus intended. But no one heard her over the battle, or no one wanted to stop the prince.

Pyrrhus snatched a shield from a guard who'd raced over and thrust it above his head as he climbed the ladder fast despite his full hands. How was that even possible? One raider above him notched an arrow into place, drew back the sinew, and aimed. The other lifted a spear high, directly above her husband.

Guardsmen below called out to bring more ladders over, but they'd never get there in time.

Pyrrhus jabbed with his spear as he approached the top, fending off both warriors enough to continue his climb.

Then a war trumpet sounded from outside the wall in three loud blasts, creating a shocked silence immediately after.

"Achilles, son of Peleus and Thetis." The shouted words rang over the whole citadel. Mia's insides went cold. "We seek you as our companion in arms. We wish no harm to this island kingdom, but we will not leave without you."

The speaker shifted aside his shield and faced her husband across the wall. Pyrrhus—or Achilles as he truly was—still aimed his monstrous spear at the man's chest, and he towered over the invader. He held still as if turned to stone, but no one watching would doubt that he was a half-divine warrior, greatest of the age.

32

"So the seer Calchas caused all this trouble? He is the one the Greek kings most rely on—even my old father at times." Achilles sat back in the largest of the carved armchairs, rubbing his thumb over his silver wine cup. "My goddess mother always feared my death. But even for her, hiding me as she did on Skyros was extreme. I didn't know what vision drove her."

The two leaders of the raiders sat in the throne room beside her father and husband. Mia had placed herself off to one side.

The raiding warrior said, "The war was not yet brewing, and yet the seer foretold that, without Thetis's son, the Greek kings would fail in a coming clash." It was the one called Odysseus who spoke, a man of short stature and bandied legs, but a broad chest and rich voice that gave him a kingly enough presence. He'd been the one facing Achilles's spear across the citadel wall, and that had taken courage stronger than bronze. "So now that the war has come, we have orders to find you."

Mia studied the two kings who'd led this pretense of a raid. The other who said little was called Diomedes. She still didn't understand how they'd known to come to Skyros. They couldn't be launching such careful raids on every city and island in search of Achilles. That was a preposterous idea, but what had given away her husband's hiding place? And would the goddess forgive her family for this failing?

Servants carried in abundant food and wine, but this meal was too fraught to be called a feast. Achilles could refer casually to his mother, but each mention of the goddess ripped Mia's insides apart. Dione stood behind Mia's chair, and the white knuckles clasping the carved back showed her maid shared this fear. Besides, the king Diomedes looked as twitchy as she felt whenever Thetis was mentioned.

Odysseus took a long drink of wine and leaned back, as relaxed in appearance as her husband. "You'll come with us?" His tone was only partially a question. Beneath was a command, softened enough that a strong-willed warrior wouldn't feel shamed. The man was clever with both words and raids.

Mia interrupted before her husband could commit himself. "How did you know to come to Skyros? We took many precautions to conceal Achilles and follow the goddess's commands."

Odysseus acknowledged her with a small bow of his head. "I'd nearly given up—although King Agamemnon, the leader of this attack on Troy, would not have accepted that. Then quite by chance, I uncovered a hint.

"Agamemnon and his brother sent me many places to recruit. I went to the island of Peparethos seeking a ship or two of warriors under their king's leadership."

Mia clutched the arms of her chair. She didn't dare catch her father's eye. *Peparethos?* What had her mother done?

Odysseus's eyes landed on her with a question in them that she didn't like. He'd noticed her reaction, but she hoped he didn't understand its source. He continued, "I also rule a small island and understood why he would put me off. He was cunning. After he insisted he had no men to spare, he dropped in a suggestion of where I might make up my count. He said he'd heard of a new young prince on Skyros, stronger and faster than any other. How did he put it, 'tall like a ship's mast' and now taking charge of the island's defense. This prince would be eager to lead warriors in a grand war." Mia heard Harmonia's words. Her mother must have shared them with her new husband, the king of Peparethos. A deadly chill settled in her core. The garrulous lady had undone a goddess with lethal gossip. She dared a glance at her father. He'd gone red in the face.

Odysseus gave a respectful nod to her father. "If you'll excuse my bluntness, Skyros is not known for such warriors. It got me thinking. We planned the raid to draw out this tall prince. We wanted no one to come to harm and figured we'd surround the responding men in an ambush tight enough to stop the fight. But I sent out scouts, good ones, and they raced to me with word that no distinctive warrior like Achilles showed himself among the warriors approaching us. You'd outsmarted me and stayed hidden in the citadel." Odysseus nodded to Achilles. "I left sufficient warriors behind to keep the coming guards busy and distracted but sailed around with the rest." He shrugged. They all knew what he'd done.

Mia frowned. It hadn't been Achilles who'd outsmarted this man, but her caution had gained them nothing in the end, only cost a bowman his life. "You terrified my people," she said with genuine anger, although she also wanted to distract her father from Odysseus's revelations of Peparethos. She and her father would deal with the subject of her mother later. "And you killed at least one of my men. Your raid was shameful."

Odysseus gave her a respectful tip of his head. "Agamemnon and his brother prepare for war against a mighty city with many allies. It does not count as shame when warriors arm themselves however they can for bloodthirsty war. I apologize for what we caused, but I feel no shame."

"Pay blood guilt to the families of anyone you killed," Mia answered. "And return every amphora of oil you stole. My people will starve without the richness of their olive oil. Drought has stripped my island."

Her father leaned forward. He seemed to have himself under control in this moment of crisis. "My daughter is right. And I have no more spare warriors for this bloodthirsty war than the cursed king of Peparethos does. Leave my island and take nothing."

"I don't need your oil. As to warriors—"

Achilles slammed his wine cup onto the table at his side. "You aren't going to leave without me. That much is clear. My mother tried to keep me from this war, but I do not share her desire to shelter in boredom. I am a warrior, and that is the life I choose."

Was the shadow that fell over her husband's eyes her imagination or the mark of accepting his predicted, early death? Her heart felt as if these warrior kings pounded it into a bloody lump.

Achilles rose and paced, reminding her once more of a lion. He ran one of his huge hands through his red-gold hair and turned to face Odysseus. "King Lycomedes is right that he has no warriors to contribute under his leadership. There are a handful of young men who will go with me, better than leaving them to cause trouble here now that they have a taste of being true warriors. And Patroclus, of course. But before these brother kings, Agamemnon and Menelaus, hear of our dealings on Skyros, you will sail with me to my father's kingdom. You will make a proper request of him for his warriors, the Myrmidons. My father's dignity as king demands that. He will send them under my leadership if I ask him to, but do not insult him by going around an old man."

So it was settled. Mia fought the tears that would show a weakness she could not tolerate at this moment. Achilles, her beloved Pyrrhus, would abandon her and their son. She would never see him alive again, unless fate had hidden twists that even a goddess could not see.

"We are agreed," Odysseus said. He turned to the silent Diomedes. "We need to retrieve our men and be sure they are not causing any fighting." He shifted to Achilles. "Tomorrow? As the winds pick up mid-morning? We will have both ships and all our men at the harbor waiting for you."

So soon? She felt a tightening around her chest like a leather strap yanked hard. One night, only one night together?

She sought her husband's gaze. The fierceness of a warrior softened when she looked into his eyes. He stepped toward her, leaned down, whispered, "I have not forgotten you, but I cannot avoid this fate."

The two unwelcome kings departed with bows to her father and empty words. Silence fell on the room.

Achilles knelt by Mia's chair and took her hand. "You'll have Pyraki to love. A prince for the island. Our marriage meant something." Mia noticed he did not say "means something."

Her father rose, perhaps to leave them in peace for their short time. "Calchas only pronounced your husband was needed for this war's success. Whatever early death the goddess foresaw may not be this at all. Pyr— Achilles will return, satisfied with this chance to show his prowess and gain his fair measure of glory as young men yearn for. Goodnight." He left the throne room. At his signal, the servants followed him out.

Dione, her vigilant friend at her side, gave her shoulder a squeeze. "I'll check on the small prince. These goings on have riled him over much."

And she also slipped away.

The oil lamps on brackets along the walls flickered, and the coals in the central hearth sent their glow through the dimness of the big room.

Mia rose, drawing her husband up with her. His fluid grace caused a sudden lump in her throat. She swallowed that down and leaned against his chest.

His arms reached around her, pulling her into an embrace so strong it sparked a small glimmer of hope that he could not bring himself to leave her.

"We should go to our bed," he said, but before he could release her, a dreadful brightness filled the room.

Mia's heart stuttered, and she buried herself against Achilles's chest as if she were Pyraki. She'd known this must come, but Thetis's delay had caused her alarm to wane.

"What have you done?" The question crashed over the room. The air seared and sparked. Lightning crackled through it.

Shaking rattled Mia's body, even with her husband's arms locked around her, even with his whispered, "I won't let go" in her ear. She pictured Thetis prying away those strong arms like the small inconvenience they were to a goddess.

"Mother," came Achilles's deep voice, "you cannot interfere with fate any longer. You tried. Out of love, you tried."

"I made an agreement with these mortals. You would be hidden, safe. Foolish of me to trust any such crawling worms, but now—"

"No, Mother. Stop. You are immortal and thus unaccustomed to failure, but fate is stronger than you, and you must accept that."

Thetis emitted a shriek of fury that shook the palace walls. Achilles's arms tightened around Mia, but she couldn't stop trembling.

Achilles drew in a long breath. "Mother, for your love of me, listen. My wife and every mortal on this island concealed me in every way possible. It is not their fault that I was discovered."

"Not entirely," Thetis said. "Some of the blame lies with that interfering seer Calchas. He also must die. He gives his foretelling skill far too readily to greedy kings. I'll shut him up for setting these swinish kings on your scent."

"Stop!" Achilles spoke with such command that Mia feared his mother would strike at him. "If *you* cannot overcome fate, why should any mortal be able to? Do not take out your devastation about my looming fate on either this vexing seer or Mia and her family. Especially not Mia. My wife's sorrow will not last forever as yours will, but it will run as deep for its brief time."

Another immortal cry answered him and filled the throne room, but this one was heavy and human with grief. "You would have me do nothing, my child, when the pain of loss is unbearable, even now while it yet lies in the future?"

"Will causing the suffering of others lighten your loss?" the goddess's son asked. "Without mercy, the fates cut each thread of time and place, the measure of a man's life. You should never have known how short my life will be. Better for both of us if you had not, but that is the past. Let us begin anew. I will be who I must be. You will savor a mother's love for as long as the fates grant."

There was silence. Achilles's arms did not loosen, so Mia kept herself buried, but she wondered if a goddess could learn and change.

Thetis let out a keening wail. The sound harrowed Mia's heart with her own baby son's imagined loss, her arms suddenly unbearably bereft of his warm, wriggling body.

"Mother, there is comfort for you here," Achilles said. "Comfort in my son. My son who will live after me. My son who needs his mother so that he can thrive. You love me, but you forgot to love your grandson."

33

The morning had come too soon. Mia and Achilles had joined their bodies in all the ways they'd discovered together, although they'd both been exhausted from the raid, the decisions, the divine visitation. Mia had slept tucked against her husband so that she was surrounded by his body. Dragging herself from that shelter was the hardest thing she had ever done. As she dressed and turned her mind to what he should take with him and to his good-bye with his son, each movement cut her with loneliness like walking on shards of broken pottery.

Not much later, a quiet procession of people trudged down the royal mountain track and along the wider trail that followed the coast to the harbor. At the front went several servants and donkeys carrying loads, and her father, the guards Achilles had mentioned would accompany him along with people who must be those men's families, and to one side, Patroclus, who kept his distance. *He* wasn't being parted forever after. She tried not to picture her husband's arms around his companion, their bodies as close as hers and Achilles's had been last night.

She fought down anger and hurt that Achilles was leaving her. Now wasn't the time to let it out. But he was a warrior, and he hadn't fought to stay with her. She needed to scream and strike out, not walk calmly toward the end of her marriage. Thetis's flailing threats against the seer Calchas echoed in her mind. As safe and right a target as any. She turned her own futile fury on that faceless man and cursed him for bringing on her loss. His words drove the determination to seek out Achilles at any cost. She imagined Thetis striking him forever silent or driving a lethal ray of light like a spear through his heart.

But still, she walked along the track to the harbor. On one side, the wind stirred up ripples across the sea so that the sun glistened blindingly off the water. On the other, the steep, rocky cliff-face rose. There was only one path forward, and she hated it.

She and Achilles went side by side at the back of those going to say farewell. Pyraki perched on his father's shoulders, one giant warrior hand holding him steady. The little boy crowed in delight, unable to understand that he would never again sit this way. Tears ran freely down Achilles's face. He held Mia's hand and softly spoke to her about his hopes for their son, advice he deemed necessary in these final moments. Some of it made Mia almost smile at its inappropriateness for so small a child, but she'd remember and pass his father's words on to a grown Pyraki when he could understand these essentials for a true warrior. Even as a toddler, the little boy reflected his immortal parentage, not only in his red-gold hair, but in his unusually large frame, strength, and agility for a child of his age. She supposed she'd feel obliged to pass on his father's warlike advice far sooner than she'd want to.

Achilles tugged at her hand, and she looked up into his face. "Your father is king," he said in a low voice, "but you are the better ruler. Trust yourself. Outsmart your father when you must."

This advice surprised her. Achilles and her father did not get along, but this was more direct than he usually dared allow himself. Parting words now when there'd be no more difficult harmony with her father to maintain. Sadness mingled with warmth at this praise for her skills with her people.

He squeezed her fingers. "Raise Pyraki to rule as you would, not how your father does."

"Pyraki may have something to say about how he'll rule. As himself, neither as me or his grandfather."

"A warrior and a king."

Her rule, which he praised, had no warrior to it, but she smiled at her husband, who for a moment slid up the hand steadying his high-up son so that it caressed the soft tufts of Pyraki's copper hair. The little boy took that loving gesture as an invitation to arch his back and let go of his hold. If Achilles's hands were not so large and strong, their son might have had a bad spill. Instead, he received a laughing commendation for his bravery from his father. Mia frowned, but this wasn't the time to object.

Achilles turned to her. "The hardest thing is balance." She thought he referred to Pyraki on his shoulders, but it was far more than that. "Part of me is immortal. Part human. Every day I struggle to keep them in balance, to feel human enough and yet glory in my divine strength. Pyraki will face the same. I'd hoped to teach him how to be both, but that will be up to you."

To her? How could she understand how to be a god and a man? She studied her husband's face but saw no hint.

Then he added one more piece of advice. "I know my mother's visits feel terrifying and dangerous to you. But there may come a time when you need to bring her to your aid or Pyraki's. To plead for her, stand on the shore of her watery kingdom where the sand meets the curling waves. Call to her at that liminal place between land and sea, and she will hear you." He hesitated. "She is likely to come without harming you."

Mia hoped she would never need to use that counsel.

The sea lay to their left. The foothills of the royal mountain rose on the right, leaving a narrow coastal plain. That overly perceptive king, Odysseus, had mentioned mid-morning winds, and a breeze caught Mia's veil and pulled it out toward the sea. She should take comfort that the man stealing her husband knew the details of sailing and might get them quickly and safely to Phthia and old King Peleus, Achilles's father. She was glad the son had honored his father in this way. The poor man must have suffered his divine wife's scathing distain far too often.

And then the road curved to the right, the point of land shielding one side of the harbor clear to view. They walked farther, and Pyraki gave a childish shriek of excitement at the sight of the two ships, their bows drawn up a short way onto the sandy beach. These were warships, swift and shallow in the water, with room for men and their gear, a minimum of food stores and water, and not much else beyond the rows of oars that could substitute for wind for short periods of time. The proud warriors would serve as oarsmen and keep their grumbling quiet. Her husband had told her about these things when they'd sailed together. It had explained his skill and speed at rowing. The fat ships of traders that her island depended on were moored further around the harbor, in the deeper, more protected bay.

Odysseus crossed the sandy beach toward them. "We've restocked what we needed," he said. "Paying well for the food," he added with a toss of his chin toward Mia. "All of my men are on board except a few to push us off. Get whatever you want loaded on quickly. We'll go while this wind favors us. I feel a storm coming, but we'll sail in front of it."

Mia looked at the blue sky, but then noticed behind them at a distance, a faint pile of gray. The air on her skin felt moist, not parched as it had for so long. This wily sailor might be right about rain coming. She tried to feel happy for the island's farms.

Achilles lifted Pyraki down and put him into her arms. He gestured to the guards going with him and gave them instructions. They hurried to follow his orders. Their faces were eager. No dark circles underlay their eyes as she'd seen under her husband's. She glanced to the mothers and fathers who had come to say good-bye to these young men. That's where the dark smudges showed—and streaks of tears. These families would not think kindly of Achilles when these ships disappeared on the horizon.

Pyraki wriggled and squawked at being held by his mother. "Wawus. Go wawus."

She let him slip to the ground and knelt beside him to speak at his level so he'd listen and perhaps understand. "I know you want to go with the warriors. Your father would love nothing more than to take you with him, but for now you must stay with your mama. You will be a brave little boy and help your mother take care of our kingdom. You can do that, can't you? Hold my hand, and we'll watch the men load the armor and swords onto the ships."

Pyraki pulled on her arm. She humored him, walking closer to the ships and warriors. The servants and donkeys gave up their loads. The young Skyros men climbed the gangplank onto one of the ships. A handful of warriors stood ready at each ship to push them into the water.

Achilles walked to her. He swung Pyraki up and pressed him close. "Do what your mother tells you, little warrior. Do you promise?"

Pyraki looked confused, his eyes moving between his father and mother.

Achilles laughed and kissed his son. "Do the best you can, little warrior."

To her he said, "I don't know what to say. Good-bye seems cruel but it's all there is."

"I love you," she said. "I'll do *my* best with Pyraki."

He set Pyraki on the ground and turned to her. "I love you." He wrapped her in a long hug and a lingering kiss, then broke away. "Good-bye."

He turned and loped to the ship, flying into a leap and swinging himself aboard. No climbing the loading ramp for him.

Pyraki ran toward the ship. Mia grabbed him and picked him up. "Wave good-bye to your father. Wish him fair sailing." She struggled to get out the words. Her tears had broken loose, running down her face.

She turned. The clouds on the opposite horizon had grown almost black and piled higher even in this short time, promising at least a temporary end to the drought. It would be enough, combined with the adjustments they'd made to drier farming. Her villagers would survive. She turned back to the ship. *Keep him safe from the storm.* Surely his sea goddess mother could do that.

For a bitter moment, she considered whether the wrongness of her husband's life on Skyros had somehow caused the drought, his immortal misery disrupting the balance of the seasons. His love for her and their son should have been enough for happiness. It should have been, but he was sailing away. Her tears felt cold on her cheeks.

Pyraki looked at her crying and started wailing.

"Hush, my son. You don't want to miss the men pushing the ships off the beach. Then they'll swing on board as your father did. Watch how warriors set sail."

The mighty pushing by the half-naked warriors caught Pyraki's attention and their leaps on board. Both ships floated free of the beach. Oarsmen navigated into more open water, then slowly past the protective point, and into the unencumbered sea.

Mia told Pyraki to watch for the sails to go up, the men pulling on great ropes. Mother and son watched as the black hulls and splashes of white sails glided out of sight.

PART II

Ten years later

34

"Don't call me Pyraki, Mother. My name is Pyrrhus. I'm a man now." The sun flashed with blinding power off his red-gold hair—more light than mortal strands of hair could spark.

Mia squinted at the brightness coming from her towering son. "You're twelve years old. Closer to being a grown man, but not yet there." She exchanged an amused look over her shoulder with Dione who walked a couple of steps behind.

The three of them walked on their way to the royal harbor, Mia and Dione struggling to keep up with Pyraki's long strides. They passed under the shade of the olive trees along the trail by the practice field, and Mia glanced up at the sharp angles of her son's face and the piercing green eyes so different from his father's. She used to look inside her husband's changing moods through the shifting shades of his eyes. Pyrrhus had no such variations, a quality Mia had long noticed he shared with his grandmother Thetis. Achilles had said immortality would be strong in his son, but she suspected he had not imagined it this dominant. Her remarkable son filled her heart, but sometimes she wished he was less remarkable.

"You are very tall." She smiled at him, rubbing his back with her hand. "Tall and handsome."

"I can beat every one of grandfather's warriors. I'm bigger and stronger than any man on this stupid island." He braced his hand on the pommel of his sword and walked even faster.

"Which will make you a commanding king of this island." Mia took hold of his arm to remind him to slow down. "But only if you show respect for your kingdom. You know that being grown up is not only about size and strength. But I will call you Pyrrhus and tell your grandfather to as well. You're old enough to leave behind your childhood nickname."

It felt strange to call her son by the name she'd used for Achilles. The intimacy of her brief time with her husband still clung to that name. Achilles was the man who'd left her. Pyrrhus had been the lover with whom she'd explored the ways two people can give each other pleasure and deepen their bonds with the entwining of their bodies. Ten years had not softened the desolation of loneliness that faced her each night when she lay down in an empty bed, that haunted her every time she opened her eyes to daylight and knew she would face each decision, each joy, and each difficulty without that one person to whom she was inwardly bound and could trust to share candid understanding.

She shook off the familiar weight of loneliness and looked up at her son with a welling of visceral motherly love. She had her son's company, quite enough challenge to keep her occupied.

Feeling restless that morning, she had greeted the news of an approaching ship with interest, using it as an excuse to leave the palace and get outside. News of the war at Troy and her husband came to her only via ships, sometimes by messages directly from Achilles, sometimes by vague gossip and rumor of the war that had drawn almost every warrior from around the islands and mainland and yet dragged on and on.

At one point news had come to her that there was another prediction from the seer Calchas she hated so much, the one who'd foretold that only with Achilles could the Greeks take Troy. This time Calchas had pronounced that the war's end would not come until ten years had passed. That couldn't have pleased the brother kings who paid him for this prophecy. When she'd said that to the trader who'd brought her the gossip, he'd muttered something about how they should pay the seer for predictions that better suited them. A long war might mean a longer life for Achilles, so she'd been glad when Calchas's divination seemed to be coming true.

She had given up trying to imagine what the city of Troy must look like to be so invincible. Those two cursed warrior kings who'd stolen away Achilles, Odysseus and Diomedes, had thought they only needed to bring the great demi-god Achilles to Troy to knock it down like a child's tower of blocks. He probably could do that if the circumstances were right, but even she knew wars had layers and human complexities that would impose limits. And they hadn't understood her husband's true nature, his struggle to balance his immortal half with his human one. But he was lost to her forever. Only their son filled the void Achilles had left in her heart.

Unfortunately, that morning Pyrrhus had overheard and had jumped at the chance to hear news of his father. He always did. Anything about his heroic warrior father was Pyrrhus's great passion. She understood what it felt like to be abandoned by a parent, to wonder why a parent cared for something else more than their child. Now she knew that wasn't a true understanding of how her mother had acted, nor of Achilles's choice, but explaining that to Pyrrhus hadn't softened the wound he carried but strenuously denied.

Because the harbor was the source of connection to his father, Pyrrhus spent more time among the traders and sailors than she thought good for him, but it was one of the arguments she let be. Today she was enjoying his company, even if he had overblown ideas of his readiness to take on manhood.

The ship her watch had spotted was a trading ship, not a warship straight from Troy, and it rested deep on the sea, full with a load, as far as her sharp-eyed watchman could tell. She'd initiate discussion with the captain about his goods, whether he had Troy news or not. Her father continued to be a savvy negotiator, but she had her own style and different notions of what the island needed most. It helped to be first at the discussion some of the time. Once she initiated a negotiation, her father usually had the good grace to admit she had useful approaches, even if they differed from his.

The trail widened as they left the steep mountain slope and turned toward the harbor along the coast path. Dione stepped up beside her, and Mia looped her arm through her maid's. They both carried the scars and joys of motherhood, although Dione's little girl made the job of mothering simpler than Pyraki did. She corrected herself, *Pyrrhus*. She should remember that simple way to please him. Dione and Galene had waited five years for their baby. Galene adored his daughter with no hint of disappointment at not having a son. Mia had grown to respect Galene.

Fast footfalls behind them made Mia turn to see who came. One of the king's messengers. He ran with a hand raised to signal to her. She stopped and tapped Pyrrhus so he would also.

The panting messenger bowed. "Princess, Prince. The king wishes you to wait for him. He set out shortly after you did and will be here shortly."

Mia fought a flare of annoyance and dismissed the servant with a wave of her hand. There was nothing to be done about this change of plan but accede to it. Dione drew a cloth from the sack she carried and spread it on a boulder that would serve as a seat. Mia sat, leaving room for Dione despite her maid's small shake of the head. Her father liked to criticize their closeness and trust.

Pyrrhus looked up the trail, but she'd already done that. No sight of her father yet. Waiting as commanded wasn't suiting her active son. "I'll go ahead," he said. "I've got business at the harbor anyway." Off he ran, so fast it was pointless to try to hold him back.

Mia caught Dione's eyes. "What business?"

Dione shrugged. "Gods help us if he thinks he can take on traders on his own now."

"My father would probably think that was a fine idea."

"It might teach the prince something other than the fighting he loves."

"It would if he had one of us near to keep him from foolishness.

Or rather *me* nearby because my father has yet to learn to control his grandson's urges."

"He adores the young prince. Grandparents are always softer."

Mia drew Dione down to sit beside her. Dione was far more than a servant to her, and she didn't care what her father thought about that. A firmer hand from her father raising Pyraki would have been welcome, but she doubted it would have counted for much.

Eventually her father stumped down the trail with an escort of four guards. She would have been similarly escorted with a guard or two if she hadn't had Pyraki at her side—*Pyrrhus*. Her son did have a point about his prowess as a warrior. If that were all it took to grow up, he'd be a man.

"Where's my grandson?" Lycomedes called out.

Mia rose. "He ran ahead. Restless as usual. We'll catch up to him at the harbor."

They walked the rest of the way in silence. She'd expected her father to own up to this intrusion or at least apologize for making her wait, but he only gave her a nod and fell into step beside her. Dione slipped to the back. The guards were split, two going in front and two behind. A noticeable procession as her father enjoyed—and she disliked.

By the time she and her father arrived at the harbor, Pyrrhus stood on the shore talking with the captain of the newly arrived ship. Her son's face was flushed, but whether from excitement or anger, she couldn't judge as she approached one step behind the king.

Pyrrhus turned to his grandfather. "This captain was at Troy, supplying the army. He saw Father, even watched one of the daily battles."

"From a safe distance," the captain said with laughter in his voice. "I'm no fighter unless someone unwelcome tries to board my ship."

Mia left this conversation to her father. She didn't have use for a man who thought deadly battles were humorous entertainment. Somewhere in one of those battles her husband would die. That was Thetis's unshakable belief.

"Father almost breached the walls of Troy," Pyrrhus burst out. His voice vibrated with zeal. "There's a place where the walls have a barely perceptible weakness. No one else could exploit such a small flaw with success, but father nearly did it, would have overcome the defenders and surmounted the wall, but daylight gave way to darkness, and he had to fall back. If only I'd been there to fight with him. I wouldn't even let darkness stop me."

Dismay like a stone weighed heavy in the pit of Mia's belly. This was the sort of tale Pyrrhus most loved, driving his determination to match his father. Her husband had gone to Troy because life on Skyros constricted the person he believed he was. Somehow these mountains and plains, the surrounding broad expanse of sea and sky had not held room enough for a warrior like him. Stories like this captain's fed a similar belief in Pyrrhus. She would not lose her son.

Lycomedes put his arm around his grandson's shoulder, rising on his toes to reach. "Achilles is a fine warrior. It's good to hear he's almost brought this long war to an end. He'll be home soon enough, and then he'll tell you even better tales. Run back to the palace. Leave me to discuss the boring details of what this captain wants for his shipload of goods." Her father pulled at Pyrrhus's arm, encouraging him to go.

She was glad her father took on the job today of distracting Pyrrhus from his dreams of Troy. It was the king's fault that it had gotten so out of control. Her father happily fed Pyrrhus's eagerness to be a warrior. The boy's fighting prowess looked to him like kingliness.

Her father and she agreed on the necessity of quelling Pyrrhus's ideas of fighting at his father's side. Pyrrhus was only twelve, but even now, what had been an idea ridiculous enough to dismiss as sweet but childish, was becoming harder to dissuade him from as he outgrew everyone else on the island. There was the danger of death in battle, especially with such an inexperienced warrior as her son, however invulnerably immortal. Neither her father nor she would trust the boy to war. But there was another, perhaps greater danger. Once connected at Troy to his father's men, the Myrmidon warriors of Phthia, he would choose the far more powerful throne and kingdom of Phthia to return to, not Skyros.

Mia watched her son's exhilaration turn to anger. He yanked his arm from his grandfather. "I will hear everything this captain has to say about my father." His voice lifted to a shout, deepened like a man's, but with too much of the defiance of a spoiled child to carry authority.

The captain stepped away. "Your majesty, later when it suits you best." The captain withdrew, meaning, Mia guessed, to remove the source of trouble and wait for a more advantageous time for deal-making.

But he did not know her son.

With the sickening slither of his sword drawn from its sheath, Pyrrhus leapt after the captain. "Stay!"

Pyrrhus looked ready to kill the man—or his grandfather. The four royal guards stood frozen.

"Pyrrhus." Mia stepped between her son and the alarmed men. She pitched her voice soft and soothing. "We can invite this captain to the palace to accept a cup of wine and share his tales, if you like. That would be seemly and appropriate. First you must put away your sword and calm yourself." She added in a voice that could not hide the exasperation boiling inside her, "No true warrior throws such fits."

Her son stomped away from her, swinging his sword in angry slashes like a child's tantrum. Mia longed for her husband's help.

35

Mia slipped in to take her seat on the dais below her father. The throne room was cluttered with groups of men wishing to speak with the king—or her. Mia recognized some nobles and village leaders who shared her sense of how the kingdom would thrive. There was always some tugging between her father and her, but this morning was unlikely to present major disagreements.

She'd gradually put to rest the latest worries about her son's warrior dreams. It had taken days for him to settle after that captain's tales had fired him like a bonfire that spreads to surrounding grasslands, out of control and purely destructive. But nearly a moon's cycle later, peace seemed restored. He was occupied with the guard and other princely duties. She could give her full attention to what mattered, the daily concerns of her people.

The room echoed with the noise of conversations competing over each other. They'd fall silent when the herald banged his staff on the ground, but for now the shadowy space with its red and mustard walls hummed like a hive in action.

Noise of frantic, heavy footsteps drew her eyes to the throne room door as it was thrown open. One of the scouts raced in. Everyone turned to look at the winded man. Mia sat up. This was one of her most trusted scouts.

Achilles had initiated the scouts ten years earlier, and she had extended and improved their reach. Her father had always relied on the tower guards to keep watch, and they did report the important sightings of ships. But Odysseus's use of the sheltered harbor on the western side, now referred to as Raiders' Haven, had confirmed the value of Achilles's scouts even to Lycomedes.

The scout gasped out, "Ship sighted at Raiders' unloading forty men." He leaned down, his straight arms braced against his thighs, trying to catch his breath. "I shouted warning at the gates for citadel alarm."

"Good work." The king rose. His chief advisors hurried close. "Send out word of this raid. I'll go now and take command in the citadel."

Mia watched the advisors scattering outward. The citadel was still inadequate, but she'd made sure they had a much better plan for alerting the island, protecting the people, flocks, and harvests. She left the throne dais to follow her father.

In the open throne room doorway, Pyrrhus appeared.

Her alarm rose. Her son would demand to fight, to lead. He was too young by far.

"Stop!" Pyrrhus shouted. "Some rat of a scout came bawling to the citadel about a raid. There's no raid. The soldiers are mine."

His soldiers? She shot a look at her father. His face had gone white.

She moved fast toward her son, as did the king. "Explain yourself and be quick," her father said when they were close enough for dropped voices.

"I sent for mercenary soldiers to strengthen our defenses. Mother and you are always complaining that this stupid island doesn't have enough men. I solved that problem. Call off the alarm."

"Mercenaries? You encouraged mercenaries to take over my kingdom?" Lycomedes's eyes went wide.

Pyrrhus made a dismissive gesture with his hand. "*I* command them. They'll do what I tell them to."

Mia grabbed her son's arm, glaring when he moved to shake her off. "What have you done? You are twelve years old and no hardened mercenaries are going to listen to you. What have you promised them? Now they're here, they'll strip our island if you don't satisfy their demands."

"I've watched Grandfather negotiate. He has a treasury from which to pay. And I'll bring back far more from the raids I'll lead them on."

"Raids?" Her voice rose in a shriek. She glanced around her. Too many people had overheard this shameful conversation. Worshiping his father to an extreme degree was understandable. But how could her son be so foolish about mercenaries? "How did you hire them?" She took a guess, picturing his time spent at the harbor talking to every sailor who would listen to him.

"It wasn't easy. You should be proud of me. Raiding is how warrior kings get wealth. I've heard the bard's tales. My father and Odysseus —all true kings go raiding."

Lycomedes took his grandson by the chin. His fingers dug into the young man's flesh. Unwise to provoke Pyrrhus, but Mia stood back. "True kings choose the best course for their kingdoms," her father said in a fury that lost none of its force for being barely above a whisper. "Raid your neighbors, and soon they will join forces against you. A kingdom must be able to fight off the enemies bred by its greed. Skyros survives because it holds little to steal, and it does nothing to provoke surrounding kingdoms. Now you have invited ravenous mercenaries to eat it alive. I was leery of your father's excessive power, but it was my own grandson I should have feared."

Her father released the boy's chin. It surprised her that Pyrrhus had not struck his grandfather in reaction to that grip. But Pyrrhus's shoulders sagged. He was accustomed to his grandfather indulging his whims. She saw he truly had not expected this reaction. He knew too little of the world to deploy his strength and size sensibly.

She reached for Pyrrhus's hand. "Why didn't you talk with us first?"

"I'm the greatest warrior. I need men to fight at my side like my father."

"That does not answer your mother's question, Pyraki," her father said. "But now I must contain these invaders. Why did you land them at Raiders' Haven?"

"So I could train with them first before I brought them to the citadel. I wanted to prove to them I am a great warrior whom they must obey."

Her father shook his head. "At least you understood that they would take some persuading. Come with me now. I will use your size and prowess as I negotiate their departure."

"No!" Pyrrhus yelled. His hand went to his sword as if he would treat his grandfather as his enemy.

"Stop it," Mia said in the voice she always used to break through his wrong-headedness. Constraining him by force had never been possible. "Do you want to destroy your kingdom? Reduce it to rubble like the ruins at the northern tip?"

"That's not—"

"You are an impressive fighter," Mia said, with no softening of her voice, "but you are a child in your thinking. A warrior uses his sword under the command of his king. You will do exactly what the king needs you to. You have brought disaster on your own kingdom. Now undo that harm."

36

The mercenaries used burning and destruction as their bargaining tool. They'd go when they were paid sufficiently. Pyrrhus had drawn them with promises Skyros could not match, his imagined raiding wealth. Her father and his guardsmen, Pyrrhus among them, had driven them by fierce fighting to the shore along one of the isolated coves. The mercenaries could have killed their way through the king's line, but he'd shown them he could take them on, cost them some of their lives. He bought them off and ordered their ship brought around. She and her father could only hope the mercenaries would stay away. What they'd gained was small enough not to encourage a return, although it had been all that Lycomedes's treasury could pay.

After seeing the raiders' ship disappear on the horizon, her father put Pyrrhus to cutting timbers, plowing, and other labor in the villages and farms where the raiders had burned and destroyed. He told his grandson, with Mia's full agreement, that he must do everything he could to repair the harm he'd caused. Nothing would bring back the lives of guardsmen who had fought well. Pyrrhus seethed in humiliation, unlike Achilles, who'd understood how much goodwill his men could create with such work.

Mia required Pyrrhus to oversee the pyres of each of the lost guardsmen. But even so, she didn't see in her son an awareness of the tragedy he'd brought on them. His mood darkened. His violent reactions grew more frequent. His desire to fight beside his father had not dimmed.

She spoke to her father. The idea she had was risky. They might lose Pyrrhus. But it might save the boy from himself.

MIA CHOSE the isolated cove where the standoff against the mercenaries took place. The losses here would remind her to hold firm no matter what she faced in her beseeching.

She left her escorting guards well back from the shore, out of sight or hearing. She had not brought Dione with her. Clouds scudded across the sky, piling up on the horizon and growing grayer.

Alone, to bring Thetis to her aid, she stood where Achilles had instructed, in the narrow space between land and sea. She had not used this advice before today. Drawing the goddess against her will would be a different matter than the scattered, surprise visits with her grandson Thetis had chosen over the years—always in places like this, isolated from the palace and villages. Mia hoped today's desperate appeal would not fatally infuriate the goddess.

Thetis's willingness to visit her grandson had surprised Mia. Thetis's love seemed hard and sharp to Mia, but the goddess wanted to see her grandson, and surprisingly, Mia. It wasn't that Thetis *liked* Mia, but they had come to a grudging relationship of shared responsibility for Pyrrhus. Pyrrhus's immortal side needed guidance of a sort Mia could not fathom. Achilles had offered Thetis that role, and when his goddess mother took it on, Mia won a smidgen of respect from the goddess. Apparently, Pyrrhus challenged even his divine grandmother. Nonetheless, Thetis doted on her big, strong warrior grandson, not always usefully.

Would that hint of respect protect Mia? The risk didn't matter. She had to act. The moments large and small piled up in her heart, moments when her son needed guidance to become a better man, moments that passed without change.

This morning yet another.

In the women's quarters before she set out, Pyrrhus sat in his chair, polishing his sword as it lay across his lap. Dione carried in the breakfast tray. She lifted a plate of bread and cheese to the table beside Pyrrhus. It must have passed over his beloved sword, or perhaps Pyrrhus only feared it had. He yanked aside the sword and struck Dione with a blow to the chest of his powerful fist, slamming her to the ground. Mia feared he might have killed Dione.

He stood over her shouting, "You stupid bitch. You dripped brine on my sword. You've damaged the bronze." He rubbed at the blade as if that justified his violence.

She'd flown to Dione's side, helping her sit up, relief drenching her insides when Dione insisted she'd taken no serious hurt. Of course Dione would say that when it was the prince who'd hit her, but Mia had held her maid's hand and looked into her eyes, talked in the silent language they used between themselves about Pyrrhus, and seen Dione was hurt but would be alright. This time.

She'd reprimanded her son. Asked him how he could react so savagely.

He'd looked puzzled. "She deserved my fist for her carelessness. She's a servant. Who cares?"

Dione, who'd been as much a mother to him as she was. "No one deserves your fist outside a battlefield. How can you not understand that?"

He'd stormed out, saying she was as stupid as her servant. What punishment could she devise when he was stronger than anyone else and ignored anything she said that did not suit his wishes?

So here she was. Mortal guidance had failed.

Mia took a deep breath. As long as Pyrrhus lived and needed his mother, Thetis seemed likely to tolerate her worm of a daughter-in-law, but there was an unpredictable streak of fury in Thetis that Mia could not trust. A streak her son shared.

Raising her arms in prayer, Mia called out, "Thetis, primordial goddess of the sea, foremost among the Nereids, sovereign of sea nymphs, and mother of my beloved Achilles, hear me calling to you. If it is not too great an intrusion, I beseech you to come to me. Your grandson needs you."

Mia waited, watching the sea for signs of divine disturbance.

A shadow, cast by a cloud, moved across the rippling water of the cove. The pine trees on the nearby slopes surrounded her with their resinous spice, and the sea air filled her chest with fresh saltiness. The wind, driving toward the shore, caught her veil and cloak, waving them behind her as if adding their beckoning to her prayer. The early spring day was warm enough that she did not gather the bulky folds around her but let them fly.

Briefly, she gave in to the notion that her clothes were urging her to flee inland, away from the coming goddess, but obeying that silent warning would get her nowhere. Her son's imbalance between divine body and mortal sense was beyond her power to repair.

"My grandson?" The divine voice sounded like beach rocks rolling against each other when a wave recedes. "He was only proving his mettle."

Mia whipped around to see the goddess stationed on an outcrop of boulder and bristling shrubs. Against that solid backdrop, the woman's form she'd taken was translucent and wavering, as if she had not yet committed to being present. The outline of trees seen through the goddess's hovering shape caused Mia a wave of dizziness. Blinking that away, she stepped to the sand beneath the goddess's perch.

Mia bowed and then looked upward, an awkward angle that she suspected was intentional. "Goddess, thank you for answering my prayer."

"You claim my grandson needs me. Explain. I have felt no such necessity calling me as I have in the past."

"You say he was only proving his mettle—so you know of the crisis he caused by hiring mercenaries?"

The goddess's face and hands had turned opaque, but her clothes and body remained as ill-defined as a wisp of mist. One hand gestured upwards. "Helios on his daily ride across the sky observed some fighting on Skyros. He can never resist delivering gossip to whomever it will most disturb." Mia was glad she had not been the cause of the scowl that accompanied this explanation. "I commanded Zephyr to gather me news on his blustery wings. Besides the yearnings of my grandson and the acts of mercenary soldiers, he whispered news of my grandson laboring like a common farmer. That displeases me, but I did not interfere. Do you wish to make me regret that restraint?"

"You and I do not perceive my son's deeds or yearnings in the same way. It is precisely because he needs some immortal understanding and guidance that I called on you. There is one among the immortals who has mentored many semi-divine young heroes. My son needs his teachings as much as Achilles did at this age."

"Chiron?"

Mia nodded, adding another bow of respect. "Yes, the centaur. Your wisdom is far greater than my weak understanding. Would a stay with Chiron be good for Pyrrhus? On Skyros, without a sufficient teacher, he struggles to be fully himself. The actions that his strength makes possible are destructive and lack the wisdom age would bring, if only he could wait to acquire it. But for one of his physical prowess, patience and waiting appear impossible."

"You are willing to let him leave you?"

Mia closed her eyes for a moment. That was the sorrow. The broken shard tearing at her heart. "To be happy, he needs Chiron. I would not be parted forever." *Not like I was from your son Achilles.*

"Mount Pelion where Chiron makes his home is a considerable journey from here." There was a testing quality to Thetis's statement. Could Mia bear a long separation from her son?

Mia braved a direct look into the goddess's eyes, showing her she would endure what she had to and choosing silence as her answer.

Her silence was also a test for the goddess. Would Thetis admit that the extended journey, at least, wasn't necessary, that she could bring Pyrrhus to Chiron in a single moment? And carry him back home to his mother in the same otherworldly way? But such a use of divine power wasn't for a worm like Mia to suggest out loud.

Once, while Mia lay in Achilles's arms, he'd described with a shudder how Thetis had brought him to Skyros in an instant, a disorienting, terrifying instant. He'd hated the lack of control inflicted on him, the arrogance that was willing to lift him away from where he wanted to be and put him in an unknown place.

Instead of an experience like that, Pyrrhus would no doubt prefer an adventuresome journey by ship and on foot where he could prove himself as a hero, exactly the kind of trouble Mia wished to prevent. She would admit that much to Thetis if need be, but what she'd hide was her father's and her desire to avoid a journey that could tempt her son with the allure of visiting nearby Phthia, the more powerful mainland kingdom where his other grandfather, Peleus, ruled and might wish to keep him.

But Mia's silence had prompted no response from the goddess. Thetis grew fainter before Mia's eyes. The green of the trees came more sharply through Thetis's sea mist shape.

Panic flared in Mia's chest. Mortals must beg for favors from gods, not test them. "Please grant us your help."

The mist tendrils shaped like a woman grew so faint Mia thought the goddess was gone. But then she heard, like the distant sound of waves, "You fear losing him, but you don't fear enough. Beware the risk you are willing to take."

"For Pyrrhus, I have to."

Seared onto her heart was the image of Achilles's ship sailing away—forever. She would fight to bring Pyrrhus home again after this necessary journey, even if she had to grapple with a goddess.

37

Mia and Dione, with Dione's five-year old-daughter Phoebe skipping at her mother's side, journeyed from the palace toward the village called Rivervalley. The walk climbed along the river, pleasantly shady and accompanied by the sounds of cascading water and birdsong. The settlement nestled among pine trees, its olive and fruit orchards fed by the river that meandered down through the mountains before reaching the plain at the foot of the royal mountain.

They reached the outskirts of the village. Eight timber and mud-brick huts clustered close in a circle, creating a protected open space at the center for preparing food and other work. Mia directed her two guards to stay at the edge of the village and then led on toward the cooking fires where some women gathered.

Mia enjoyed Phoebe's happy play. She had suggested that morning that Dione bring her with them. Neither said aloud that it felt more comfortable to bring Dione's little one now that the volatile, unpredictable prince was away. Before, Mia had made a habit of bringing her son on such trips, striving to develop his understanding of his people. Unfortunately, a day lost to military training inevitably vexed him, and sometimes he lashed out in frightening fits that Mia controlled with difficulty.

She appreciated Phoebe's sweetness, but she missed her son and felt his absence as if someone had reached into her chest and torn out some vital part of her. But he would return, and that deep-seated need for her child would drive her less sharply. Meanwhile, there was also relief. Chiron would lighten her burden of loving a child so . . . singular. The centaur would instill what she could not.

Pyrrhus had whooped with delight when his divine grandmother appeared to him and told him she would whisk him off to Chiron's cave on Mount Pelion. He knew the tales of heroes trained by Chiron, and most of all, he wanted to do everything his father had done.

Whether Thetis had intuited Mia's wishes, or she followed her own divine inclination, Pyrrhus had disappeared in a shocking momentary flash of light that left Mia aching in worry afterward, however much avoiding an ordinary journey had been what she wanted. Eventually she chided herself enough times that Thetis would not harm Pyrrhus, that his father had survived a similar experience, but in that case, even against his will. Pyrrhus must be safe and happy.

As they passed through the encircling huts and came near the cooking fires in the center of Rivervalley, Dione caught Phoebe up in her arms and sat her on her hip. Mia lifted an arm in greeting. A familiar face responded, a woman named Anthe. She rose and bowed to Mia. Over many visits, Mia had grown to respect this woman with gray-streaked hair and a jawline softened by sagging pouches. She was the wife of Rivervalley's informal leader. Unlike a king or princess, the leaders that arose in each village came with the assent of the rest of the residents, an occasionally shifting process. Sometimes the men so chosen seemed savvier than the others, sometimes more gracious, but often fuller of bluster. Occasionally, it seemed the man had bullied his way to leadership. She suspected that of this village's leader, but she valued Anthe's advice.

"Princess, we're honored," the woman said. The others tucked their heads without saying anything. Mia was accustomed to their shyness around her. It would fade if she stayed awhile. To find out what was on their minds, what troubles they faced or joys, she had to be patient, friendly, and quiet.

A young woman approached the cooking area, bracing with one hand a basket on her head. Her graceful movement, high cheekbones, and strikingly large brown eyes drew Mia's attention. The pretty little girl she remembered, Anthe's daughter Meli, had crossed into womanhood. After lifting down her basket, Meli knelt at a grinding stone near the cooking fires, scooping some grain from the basket onto the stone and bending into the labor of crushing the hard barley against the flat surface with a stone.

"Meli's help must be welcome now that she's grown," Mia said to Anthe.

"Meli's a good girl," the woman said. "I'll miss her. She'll be helping her husband's ma soon."

"I'm sorry for that," Mia said. "Letting a child go out in the world, no matter how much they need to, cuts deep in a mother."

"I would have chose one of our village boys. Held Meli near. But not her father. He had other plans. But I'll find plenty of reasons to visit her."

"Which village?"

"Grainrich." The woman pointed north.

Mia nodded in understanding. Grainrich lay next to the northernmost plain, the island's largest flat growing area, fertile fields of barley and wheat, even broader than the river plain below the royal mountain. Grainrich was not far from the ruined city where no islanders would go. She pictured a young man she'd talked with there, son of that village's leader. "Leaders joining their families together?"

The woman nodded. "Their grain to our olives. He's a good boy, and Meli likes him well enough. I made sure of that."

Mia smiled. "I'm glad." Mia indicated an empty stool with a question in her eyes. "May I sit by your fire and rest a bit? We had a pleasant walk, but I'm winded."

"Of course, Princess." The woman signaled to another to bring a cup of beer. It was the routine. Dione would have something also, but not through this formal back and forth. Mia welcomed a cool drink, but she wanted to listen to their conversation and let drop some questions.

The woman pointed toward Dione's Phoebe. "That one isn't winded." She smiled at Phoebe, wriggling her way out of her mother's arms and setting off.

"No," Dione said. "Never winded. Princess? I'll—"

"Go, chase Phoebe. I'll call you if I need you." Her maid would collect her own observations and conversations.

The afternoon wound on, women coming and going with their tasks, but also talking about this and that in passing. They knew from Mia's past visits that she was listening and would consider problems that they aired. She was relieved not to hear anything new. The familiar challenges of her island kingdom were enough.

Mia also paid a visit to the village leader, walking to the orchard where he worked that day, Anthe accompanying her, along with Dione and Phoebe. He was proud of the news of his daughter's betrothal, going on about it as a proud father. Mia liked him better than she had in the past. Maybe she'd been unfair, or he'd mellowed. She complimented him on his orchards, having learned enough about olive pruning to make her flattery meaningful.

Her father would call her day a waste. A king spoke *to* peasants. He did not converse and listen. In his view, there was little of use to be learned from these farming families. Mia had found otherwise and showed him what she gained enough that he did not quarrel with her about these visits. She'd told him once that if they were to rule so small a kingdom, they could at least enjoy the advantages. Being able to travel around and know her people in each part of the island was one of them.

She didn't like to admit it to herself, but she savored the simple day so much partly because she did not have to keep watch on Pyrrhus. Chasing Phoebe was nothing compared to holding back her son. Her father viewed his peasants with a royal disdain that she didn't like but accepted. It limited his rule but not overly so. But that was nothing compared to the innate contempt her son had toward all mortals, even, if he could face it, himself. There was too much Thetis in him, too much to live contently as a mortal, yet too little to be a god.

On the walk back from the orchards, with Phoebe's high, chirping voice singing a skipping song, Mia tipped her face to the sun's warmth. Over the ten years without Achilles—so much more than the time she'd had with him—she had concentrated on small pleasures. His foretold short life at war had stretched for what felt like many years, long enough that sometimes she believed he'd return to her. He would once again lift her into waves of such intensity that she'd wondered at the time if his immortal side caused those feelings.

But in the meantime, she sustained herself with small delights, and the gentle spring sunshine was one of them.

A deep male voice roared, carrying on the air, her son's voice. She glanced at the women on either side of her, thinking she'd heard her far-away son through some immortal trick that they'd be excluded from. But they'd both stopped with alarmed expressions.

Mia turned at the sound of footsteps crashing down the wooded slope edging the path. Pyrrhus swung his sword at tree branches and bushes as he stomped and slid down the steep hill. "Mother! He won't teach me. He refuses. How dare he!"

He? Was that Chiron? "My son," she called out, "it's good to see you. What brings you home so soon?"

Pyrrhus came toward them, his eyes bulging with fury. Holding his sword with both hands, he swung at the trees as if cutting down enemies. The village woman and Dione, with Phoebe in her arms, backed away. Mia stepped in front to protect them.

Better trees than people, but he'd damaged his sword with this flailing, his beloved sword, a bad sign at how far he had lost himself in rage. No good warrior mistreated his weapon like that.

She glanced ahead on the path. The village huts stood close by. Pyrrhus's voice had drawn three children, running to see what created the uproar. She tried to wave the children away.

"Pyrrhus," Mia called, "Come tell me. Put up your sword. You'll break it against the trees." She darted a look at the children. They'd slowed in the face of a giant with a sword, slowed but not stopped. Behind them appeared Meli, the newly betrothed daughter.

Her son fought a mastic shrub, sending slashed branches and leaves flying. His eyes were glazed in madness, his teeth bared, his neck taut bands of flesh contorted with anger.

She climbed toward him. "Pyrrhus, stop! Slow down, and you can tell me your grief."

He charged down the hill, carried by his forward motion, his sword still out, seemingly blind to her or anything in his way. She jumped out of the blade's way, tripped, and landed on her seat. Scrambling to stand, she heard screams and saw with a shock of panic that Pyrrhus raced toward the children as if to run them through.

She ran and yelled, "No! Pyrrhus, they're children. Look where you're going."

Faster than Mia could catch up, Meli threw herself in front of the children and raised her arm, still clutching in her hand the grinder stone.

The prince barreled toward her, sword ready. High pitched screams filled the air.

Mia shrieked, "Stop! Pyrrhus, stop!"

Meli hurled the heavy stone at the prince. It slammed into his chest, knocking him back enough that Mia reached him and grabbed his sword arm. In a moment that seemed to stretch out, she saw his eyes wide with surprise and his lips drawing back in a snarl. In that moment of his shock, she stopped him and knocked his sword to the ground.

Her brief control over him vanished. He howled in fury, flung off her hold, and then struck her across the face with a blow that sent her flying back. She stumbled and caught herself. Her cheek burned. Her anger even more.

She stepped between her son and his fallen sword.

"Take the children," she said softly to Meli, who, along with the three children, seemed turned to stone.

Her words broke the spell holding the girl, and she backed away with the children, like a shepherd coming upon a boar, careful in retreat not to provoke a charge.

Mia's two guards came running from the other side of the village. Their faces registered that they'd seen enough to be horrified.

"That peasant girl threw a stone at me," Pyrrhus said. "She'll pay for—" His gaze moved in the direction of the two approaching guards, and he stopped.

Mia stepped back and put her weight on top of his sword to prevent her agile son from sweeping it up into his hand. He'd have to confront her first. "Tell me what happened with Chiron. I'm sorry he angered you, but you cannot attack your people because a god offends you."

The two guards sidled up beside her. They gave Pyrrhus deep bows and addressed him as their commander.

"Let's return to the palace," Mia said. "You can tell me what happened on the way." She handed Pyrrhus's damaged sword to one of the guards. "The prince will need this repaired." Then she headed toward the trail through the river valley, and thankfully, Pyrrhus walked with her.

His chest heaved with ragged breaths, not from exertion, she knew, but from the inner fire that fury often seemed to light inside her son. These fits whipped and scorched him long after the event that sparked them.

The villagers had disappeared inside their huts or into the orchards. Mia saw a glimpse of Anthe in a doorway, and she tipped her head in a gesture of respect toward the woman and put her hand on her heart, the best she could do for now as apology. No one had been hurt, but the terror the prince had inflicted would leave lasting marks, and she doubted this village would ever trust him.

Dione fell into step well behind, Phoebe in her arms, the child wide-eyed and silent.

As they picked their way beside the river, Pyrrhus ranted about Chiron, as much to himself as to her. She let him rage. Gradually she realized what had happened.

After three days spent with Pyrrhus, Chiron had summoned Thetis. He pronounced Pyrrhus irredeemable and told her to remove the boy. Chiron refused to waste his time on this one. Pyrrhus had witnessed this shame.

He had not drawn the right lesson from it. Pyrrhus shrieked that Chiron was a fool, weak, and too concerned with music and healing to be a worthy mentor for a true warrior.

Mia repeated what Achilles had said about Chiron. How much his father admired the centaur, the variety of things he'd usefully learned, including fighting with every suitable weapon, but also how to heal war's wounds and spread the fame of heroes through song. It was as though she spoke to a wall. The only response he gave was a muttering she only partially caught. Something about a peasant bitch that chilled her heart.

She looked meaningfully at the guards, "You'll watch over the prince with care?"

The guards nodded. They seemed to understand that she meant keep the prince from harming anyone. She'd be more open about that later out of Pyrrhus's hearing, but his anger would die down, and he'd be glad to ignore that he'd been here.

They climbed up toward the palace and citadel. She said to her son, "Go to the barracks. You'd prefer living there to the women's quarters, wouldn't you?" His face brightened. She sighed. Perhaps with time, the shame he couldn't yet face would bring him around. By then, her cheek might no longer be bruised purple and green.

38

The black-hulled, sleek warship shot over the water, its white sail billowing. The guard on watch at the citadel had run to Mia with news of the sighting. Such warships came with messages sent by Achilles. There was always the chance that *this* warship was instead full of raiders, so guardsmen marched from the citadel, ready to form up wherever the ship beached. Pyrrhus marched with them under the command of the captain of the guard, a position Pyrrhus thought he should hold. His grandfather put him at the head of one cohort and told him to show some level-headed leadership and then he would be given more responsibility. Pyrrhus's duties would keep him occupied, whether there was a battle against raiders or not. That would leave Mia time to receive the message without her easily inflamed son.

Mia accompanied her father down the mountain. They stood where they could watch the ship's approach on a promontory jutting out into the sea between the base of the palace mountain and the royal harbor.

As the ship drew closer, Mia glimpsed the bright turquoise banner with a dolphin on it, her husband's sign to her. For the briefest moment, she imagined Achilles on board, but she dismissed that idea. He wouldn't arrive with a single ship. But it would bring his messages.

"Not raiders," she said to her father, pointing. She watched its course as the rectangular sail lowered and twenty oars slid out on each side of the shallow hull like the legs of a giant water bug. "It's headed to the royal harbor as it should. Let's go meet it."

With her father, she took the track toward the harbor, the sea stretching out on one side of the path, the citadel and palace looming high above on the other.

She used to dread each ship's arrival, fearing news of Achilles's death, but ten years had passed, and she'd worn that panic threadbare. She'd begun allowing herself to imagine Achilles's eventual return. Now more than ever, she needed him. Their son could only be helped by his father. Pyrrhus insisted on being like his father in every way, but he did not know him. Instead, he imagined a fierce, inhuman warrior that suited his own inclinations, and the boy copied that illusion.

How to guide Pyrrhus so he grew into a good future king was a question that skittered and thrashed around her thoughts. There seemed only one answer, and it was out of her control—Achilles. She needed her husband to come home.

From a rocky hillock above the beach, Mia watched the ship. The oarsmen maneuvered the narrow ship so that it pointed its bow at the shore within the protective harbor bay. Men jumped into the water and their strong arms hauled its front end onto the shore.

A gangplank dropped to the shore of pebbly sand, and two men disembarked, one old, one young. The younger man looked, from his noble dress and deferential air, like squire to the older. They both wore tunics edged with woven multi-colored bands, but the old one also bore signs of kingship, a gold-embossed sword belt, armbands studded with gems, and a circlet of gold holding down thin strands of gray hair. These men differed from past messengers Mia had received. They were not lowly sailors assigned the task of delivering news and racing back to war. Unease settled over her heart like frost blanketing newly sprouted wheat.

Proper hospitality to guests must be offered before she or her father could question this kingly delegation. Even asking their names was ritually forbidden until hospitality sealed both guest and host under the law of Zeus to do no violence against each other. Such rules made travel safe, but in this moment Mia's impatience rose intolerably. Each required stage felt agonizingly slow to her apprehensive heart: the long walk up the mountain, the servants pouring cups of wine and laying out bread, skewers of lamb, figs, and cheese, the eating and drinking. If the two men had fallen into cheerful pleasantries with her father as they sat around the throne room hearth, she could have calmed the rising thrum of her heart. But they wore solemn faces and avoided her eyes.

Her father waited until they'd finished the meal. Then he asked who they were and the reason for their visit. "You came under my son-in-law's banner, so I assume you bring us news from him." Her father spoke in this hopeful way, but there was no conviction to his voice. His glance toward her carried sympathy that she wanted to shout away.

"Not *from* him, no." The old man leaned forward in his chair, shaking his head in a sorrowful way and gusting out a deep sigh. "As to our names. This youngster, Eudorus, came to assist me. He's a strong captain among the Myrmidon warriors." The old man patted the other's arm. "I am Phoinix. Achilles's father, Peleus, made me king of the Dolopians when I had to leave my own home, driven by my father's unjust rage. In return, I helped raise Achilles as if he were my own son. He missed a mother's touch, and I often served as nursemaid before I started him on the warrior skills he craved. Of course, he soon far exceeded what I could teach and turned to Chiron for immortal polishing. But when he set off for Troy from his father's court ten years ago, with his army of Myrmidons, fierce fighters his father gave him command over, I went with him, as counselor and fatherly friend."

Mia pressed her fingers into the arms of her chair to hold in her need to speed along this dithering, long-winded old man. His manner showed what must be coming, but she refused to believe such terrible news as long as he postponed a direct telling. She ignored the chill that seeped through her limbs.

The old man finished a long drink of wine. "That fatherly role is why this sad duty fell to me. No mortal hero could strike down Achilles, best of the Greeks, but even he could not withstand an arrow shot by the god Apollo."

Her hands quivered, spilling the wine she held onto. There it was. She would never see Achilles again. Her beloved husband killed by an arrow. Dead. Her heart rebelled, but she pounded it with the word, *dead, dead, dead*. Killed *dead* by a god.

Down the old man's wrinkled cheek ran a tear. "The Trojan prince Paris claims the deed, but no one believes such a bloated boast. You only have to take one look at Paris to know he's no warrior to fight Achilles." The elderly king covered his eyes with his hand. "Even now, I cannot believe he is gone, even after laying his dear body on the pyre. I warrant, he lost heart after Patroclus's death. But we mounded a memorial over his ashes, his and Patroclus's joined forever as he commanded. Any ship sailing past Troy's shore can see the great hill piled up so men in future times will remember the warrior who was the best of us."

Mia felt the tears welling in her eyes and batted them away with her lashes, except they refused to stop and drenched her cheeks in their outpouring. She didn't want a great memorial hill. She wanted the warm skin and muscles of her husband. She wanted to search the depths of his sea-layered eyes. Hear the rich tones of his voice, singing and laughing. She wanted to run her fingers over the contours of his chest, twine them in his red-gold curls. She wanted him alive.

He was *never* coming home to her. She'd lied to herself in the end. Tricked herself into hope, and now she had to fill her memories with a mound of dirt, a pile of honor, as if honor would warm her heart.

The old man wept. Even the young one wiped away tears. Her father looked ill at ease with this outpouring of love he'd never shared for Achilles.

What had the old man said? Something about Achilles lying with

Patroclus forever. She drew her handkerchief from her belt and dabbed at her cheeks. At least that meant Patroclus was dead. She drew in a shuttering sigh. She didn't mean that. Not really. Patroclus had been a good man. His diplomatic words had kept her father and Achilles from coming to blows. He'd tried to soften the hurt of his presence. The love between Patroclus and Achilles had come before hers. And it seemed Achilles could not live without Patroclus, lost heart without him. Unlike her. Achilles had *chosen* to live without her. Admitting that didn't lighten her sorrow, but it gave her room to breathe. She had known from the beginning that Achilles would die, and she would live on. *Live, Mia, live. That's your duty. You know how to live alone. You have done it for ten years.*

Sunk in her grief, she'd missed a piece of the conversation, but now the old king, Phoinix, said something that brought her back. "Achilles was not only the best warrior, he was the best leader of men. The Myrmidon fighters feel his absence. There's no one to take his place. Peleus is older than me. He cannot come to Troy and take command of his army. Yet none of the men want to abandon the siege, now after so long, and lose out on the riches. Troy cannot hold out much longer. We can all taste the city's fall, grasp the loot in our hands. Young captains like Eudorus will have to do the best they can."

"We need an Achilles," the younger one said, surprising everyone when he spoke up for the first time. "A leader we can rally behind. He was extraordinary, and no one ordinary can take his place."

It was lucky Pyrrhus was not hearing these words. He would imagine this young captain described him. Mia glanced at her father. He had grown increasingly uneasy, shifting in his chair and taking gulps of wine.

Lycomedes lifted his wine cup. "There will never be a warrior like Achilles. We drink to his memory."

Her father's clever response aimed to discourage any similarity these men might see between Pyrrhus and their lost commander. Clever. Luckily, an inexperienced twelve-year-old wouldn't be seen as a suitable leader. Not just by his cautious mother, but these seasoned fighters. Surely that was true, no matter Pyrrhus's size and prowess.

At that moment, the throne room doors swung open, and Pyrrhus entered. He'd removed his armor, fortunately. Still, he towered over any man in the room and did not look like the boy he was.

"My son," Mia said. "Come take your seat. You must be hungry. These two men come from Troy." She glanced at her father and saw him narrow his eyes and grimace in pain. What could they do otherwise? Lie to Pyrrhus about his father's death?

Phoinix sat up in his chair. He beamed in wonder at her son. "What a fine, big boy you've become." Pyrrhus gave the older man a respectful bow and sat, eyes locked on this newcomer. Phoinix said, "Your father was also much bigger than any of us by a young age. How old are you?"

"Twelve, sir. You knew my father when he was young?"

Phoinix repeated his nursemaid tale with an added detail of baby Achilles spitting up on him many a time. Pyrrhus frowned. This was not what he longed to hear. When Phoinix mentioned Chiron, Pyrrhus's face flushed.

Pyrrhus interrupted the rambling story. "What news do you bring from my father?"

With a sad shaking of his head, Phoinix leaned nearer to Pyrrhus and patted his hand. "I'm sorry to say, your father is gone."

"What do you mean, gone?" The red flush intensified across Pyrrhus's face.

"He was struck down on the battlefield. His companion warriors raised a—"

"No one can kill my father." Pyrrhus leapt up from his seat. "Not on the battlefield. He's the best fighter of all." Pyrrhus was shouting, his denials echoing around the large room. "He's going to train me to fight like a true warrior. He's coming home. To me." He backed away. "You're lying." Pyrrhus ran out of the throne room.

Mia rose to follow him, but perhaps he needed to be left alone.

Lycomedes spoke softly, "It's hard for a child to accept a parent's death. He looks grown, but he's still so much a child."

Phoinix nodded. "Immortality does not sit comfortably in mortal flesh. His father was often like this, struggling to contain his anger. Such sad news will take time. Target practice with a spear might help."

"He's young enough he might simply need his mother," Mia said and started to the door.

"Princess!" She turned and paused at Phoinix's call. He added, "He's fortunate to have a loving mother to get him through the difficulties of a half-immortal childhood. Achilles led the Myrmidons to Troy at seventeen. He seemed so very young to everyone, but he inspired respect and love from his men. Your son will grow into manhood soon enough."

At seventeen Achilles hadn't been the skilled leader Phoinix claimed. He'd dealt poorly with her father and needed Patroclus's advice to keep from fatal blows.

"Twelve is a long way from seventeen," Mia said, "essential years at that age, but with time, I'm sure he'll be as brilliant as his father."

Her father frowned, but she would not diminish her son's reputation as a warrior—what he excelled at and the only thing that brought him happiness. He shone as brilliantly as Achilles, even if that light arose from a different nature.

"My son needs me." She bowed and left the throne room. Her son might need her, but she doubted she could help him.

39

Mia had found her son in the citadel. Pyrrhus refused to give his mother a chance to help him, shouting at her to leave him alone. She'd stayed quietly by the postern tunnel for a long time watching him. It intrigued Mia that after practice sword fights with various guardsmen who couldn't hold up under the prince's onslaught, he'd turned to spear throwing. As Phoinix had suggested. Like father, like son? Pyrrhus threw at the targets with such force that they fell to pieces and frightened guards set up fresh ones. No one came near him if they could avoid it. Eventually, she decided her presence was feeding his fury, not offering him solace, and she'd gone to her sleeping chamber to grieve alone.

During a long sleepless night, the heaviness of her grief for Achilles overwhelmed her. It couldn't be that she'd never hold him again. She'd been warned from the beginning, and yet, faced with the final words, her body refused to accept the pyre, the still corpse, the selfishness of the god who struck down her husband. For what? A stifling blanket of cold sorrow settled over her, forcing her to feel its weight, to accept it as part of who she must be from now on.

Her bed felt cold and hostile. She left it as soon as gray hints of dawn showed through her open window, taking a seat in the dim, silent women's hall. Gradually the light around her turned golden with the sun's rays. She'd have to go act as hostess to Phoinix and his squire. Getting out of her chair seemed impossible enough.

It would have been better if Pyrrhus had accepted the sad news enough that he could talk with the old man, hear more about his father. There'd be no one else who could describe Achilles's childhood. The idea of hearing such tidbits drew her out of her chair. She'd savor them even if Pyrrhus couldn't.

Footsteps sounded in the corridor. She glanced toward the doorway.

"Oh good," her father said when he saw her. "You're up. I was afraid you'd be laid low by your grief. I'm so sorry for the loneliness you must be feeling."

"I'm used to being alone. As are you."

He nodded and shrugged. "It's worse for you. I'll try to help you through. I found Pyrrhus last night. The guards warned me of his spear practice—that it seemed like it might never stop. I made up a story to distract him and let him absorb the news. Perhaps he'll accept it slowly. I told him we'd received reports of a rampaging boar near one of the northern villages and that we should protect the villagers by hunting it. There is really a boar in the forest there. I'd planned on a hunt, but only for the pleasure of it. The beast hasn't strayed near the village. But Pyrrhus took me very seriously. On his own, he arose before dawn this morning and led a contingent of the guard to hunt it down."

"That was good of him. He does love to lie late in bed, not rise at dawn." She had a brief vision of boars running wild on the island and providing useful work for her son each day, and almost smiled at such an absurdity.

"I must admit I'm glad to keep him away from our visitors. He doesn't need to hear how greatly they want a new leader."

She rested her hand on her father's arm. "Thank you for giving him something to do that he loves. I'd thought he might benefit from hearing about his father from someone who knew Achilles so well, but I think you're right. He'd get ideas that they didn't intend."

"I should go find Pyrrhus and make sure he comes upon the boar's den. If you're willing to see off our visitors. Do you mind?"

"Go. Be with your grandson. That's best." She headed to the room in the men's guest quarters where Phoinix and Eudorus would have been brought breakfast.

Mia feared Phoinix would expect to stay longer. But the old man was eager to set out, noting he'd sent out Eudorus earlier to check, and the winds were just right to bring him back to Troy quickly. "Those young men need guidance. I can't fight as they do anymore, but I know war strategy."

She smiled at him. "Let's set out for the harbor. As you've seen, it's a bit of a walk."

He tucked his head in agreement. "Better going down than up, although old bones like mine don't favor the plodding down much, either."

She signaled two guards to accompany her, and they fell in behind.

She led the old man and Eudorus through the palace and out the gates to the trail down the mountain. She let Phoinix take her arm, a polite gesture that she suspected would steady him more than her. "You knew my husband far longer than I did. As I struggle raising Pyrrhus, I wonder how you managed."

Phoinix's gaze took on a faraway look. "His great strength and speed got us into trouble at times, but he always regretted the worry he caused. He was only happy when he had big enough challenges before him. When there was no longer anyone fit to fight Achilles, Chiron took over. Achilles gloried in the battles at Troy. He came into his full prowess. If there'd been victory sooner, not the long dragging out without progress, the war would have been good for him."

Mia pressed her lips together. Good for him? The war had killed him. It wasn't her fault that Skyros felt like a boring cage to Achilles and he hadn't been happy. He had loved her no less for that. Phoinix carried on describing his favorite battles at Troy and the routines of life in the camp. It sounded miserable to her, but filling in the emptiness of the years with these tales helped her.

Nonetheless, she was glad to leave Phoinix and Eudorus at the shore. She made sure the harbor attendants had refreshed the supplies of food and water on board his ship. Phoinix, like the other men around her, valued fighting prowess over all else. Her son would have liked Phoinix if Pyrrhus had stopped hating him for bringing the news of his father's death. But Pyrrhus had lost his chance to get to know the old king. They wouldn't meet again.

40

Pyrrhus had returned from a successful boar hunt, according to his grandfather, but he now lived in the barracks, and Mia saw little of him. He did not talk about his father's death with anyone as far as she knew. She dreaded bringing it up, but she'd have to at some point.

Then one day early in the afternoon, a grim-faced messenger came to the palace from Rivervalley, the village where Pyrrhus had threatened the children with his sword. With a contingent of guards, she and her father hurried along the river to the circle of huts.

The village men stood outside their huts, not off in the orchards or other work, sullen anger showing in their faces and posture. The women were nowhere to be seen.

One of the men spoke up, "He's gone. Don't know where. But look in there. See what the prince did." The man pointed to a dark doorway in the largest of the huts.

Lycomedes stepped inside and paused. Mia came to the open doorway. Her father bent over and groaned. When her eyes adjusted to the dim light, she saw a body and blood, splattered across the man and the floor, pooled underneath a gaping wound across his neck and throat. She forced herself to look long enough to realize she gazed upon the village leader's corpse. The copper tang of blood gagged her, coating her insides with each breath.

She backed out of the hut.

Her father followed. He turned to the man who'd spoken. "Explain what happened and why you lay this at the prince's hand. Mind yourself. He's a boy. This is hardly something a twelve-year-old would do."

A woman's keening rose from one of the huts, Anthe's voice, the widow. Mia left her father to the men and went toward the grieving sound.

She waited inside the doorway. "May I come in?"

Four women crouched on the hut's dirt floor. One woman was bandaging Anthe's arm. The dead man's wife did not seem to notice this care, but Mia's presence interrupted her keening so that the dim room fell silent. Another woman had her arm around the daughter, Meli. Dark stains that looked like blood covered both the mother's and daughter's clothes. Meli's dress was torn. With one hand she held it closed over her legs and chest. Her eyes had a hollow stare. Her face had been beaten. Mia's hand touched her own cheek and the faded bruises there.

She wanted to leave these women and their sorrow. This wasn't her son. It couldn't be. He had a temper, but not this. He was only twelve. But caught in her mind was the look on Pyrrhus's face after the grinding stone struck him, the threatened *she'll pay*, the muttered *bitch* she couldn't forget.

Mia stepped into the hut and knelt near Meli and the woman comforting her. Meli's torn skirt didn't completely cover her legs. A smear of blood ran along the inside of a thigh. Mia forced herself not to look away.

When she lifted her gaze, the older woman stared at her. A challenge.

Looking into Meli's vacant eyes, Mia's throat closed, but she fought out the words that had to be said. "Meli's been beaten. Was she...taken?"

A hint of surprise flitted across the woman's face. She chewed her lip and then nodded.

The words scratching over a raw throat, Mia whispered, "My . . . son did this?"

The woman's eyes grew wide. She looked away from Mia's gaze, but she nodded.

The corpse she'd seen. The doting father she remembered from her visit. "Meli's father? How did he . . ."

To Mia's surprise, Anthe answered. "He must 'a snuck upon her. Your prince. She were back at the hut. We were off by the pressing ground. One cry she got off sometime. Went through my heart—and her father's. We ran. The rutting was . . . He'd forced her on the ground, his hand crushing her mouth. My man grabbed him, tried to pull him off, but that sword was near to hand. I tried, but . . ." She fell silent.

Mia found it hard to draw in air. The baby she'd held, the growing boy, the beautiful young man. She couldn't match this hut of women and the heavy sorrow of their words with her child. She pressed up from her knees and stood. "I will tell the king."

She hadn't done enough to prevent this. She'd warned the guards, but they couldn't keep watch over the prince every moment. She had not imagined this, not at all. But she should have. A mother cannot look away from her child.

Harm comes to unattended children. She'd braced herself for that and kept him safe. But to look at him and see this. How could she bear it?

Before she went out and faced her father and the men of the village, she laid her hand lightly on Meli's tangled hair.

Meli, that's what her mother and father had named this girl with eyes now emptied of life, as if she too had been slaughtered like her father. Meli, the simple word "honey," a pretty name for a girl raised among orchards filled with beehives. By giving her that name, her parents must have wanted her to be sweet as honey. But their daughter had turned out brave enough to defend others, fierce enough to humiliate a prince. It had come to this.

41

The wind brushed against Mia's face, cool and fresh. She sat in the bow of the royal sailing boat. Not the small servants' boat she and Achilles had sailed together. This boat and its crew carried members of the royal family around the island. Her mother had used it to escape the palace, and she'd always brought her daughters with her. Did her mother's heart still ache with longing to hold her children? What advice would she offer her oldest daughter?

Mia looked down into the clear, turquoise water and tried to imagine what Achilles would have done for his son at this crisis. How could Mia protect her son from himself? How could she protect her people from her son? He would be their king someday. If he'd been struck with remorse, she would have hoped such a horror had jolted him out of his immortal scorn, reminded him of his human side, begun to change him into a future king she did not dread. But Pyrrhus went about his life on Skyros with no change of heart.

Achilles's voice refused to echo in her memories. The remembrance of his touch was elusive. Her grief for him and her anguish for their son intermingled. She could not endure the one for the inseparable, pressing weight of the other.

For their son, she had done what she could, but her efforts felt like stopping a colossal, god-sent sea-wave with one hand. Guards, appropriate for a prince and thus acceptable, accompanied Pyrrhus everywhere, keeping watch, and reporting to the princess. Her father paid blood guilt to the dead man's family. For his crime, Pyrrhus should have been banished from Skyros for a year to seek purification from another land's king. Her father refused to consider this step. His grandson was prince and needed on Skyros too much. She kept silent because she knew she couldn't change her father's mind, but time away from Pyrrhus's homeland no longer seemed like a fearful danger to be avoided at all costs.

As for the harm Pyrrhus had done the village girl, Mia had delicately navigated conversations with the family of the young man Meli was betrothed to. Sometime in the upcoming seasons, the marriage would go ahead. Meli wanted that, so Mia did.

Her father and the menfolk of the village believed a prince could take what he wanted. The villagers hated him for what he'd done, but they didn't cry out against him for it. To them, the prince had not cast shame on Meli as some other man would have. This was good for Meli, and Mia wanted to mend the harm her son had done as best she could.

To her father, the "trouble," as he referred to it, was over. He promised to guide the prince, but he took no new actions.

With his own inner division between human and god, Achilles would have understood, better than anyone else, the conflict inside his son. If she could put herself in her slain husband's heart once more, perhaps she'd see the way forward. So she'd called for the royal boat to be prepared for her, and the crew sailed her toward the bay beside the ruined city at the northern tip of the island. If there was a place she could feel Achilles's presence entirely separate from the tangles of her son's failings, it was among those crumbled walls with their silent, haunted dead. Away from the frustrations of Achilles's life on Skyros, her husband had found peace here. On the shore below the ruins, they'd been closer together, hearts and bodies, than any other place.

The wide bay lay ahead. She told the servants who sailed the boat to land on the end of the bay farthest from the ruined city. They were happy to do so. Their shuttered looks showed how little they liked coming here. After the necessary maneuvering, they drew the bow onto the sand beach.

"Stay with the boat. I wish to be alone." She spoke to the one serving woman who'd accompanied her as well as the crew. She hadn't brought Dione, who would have felt compelled to stay with her and try to soften her grief and anguish. It was only in the pain that she would find an answer. If she found one at all.

Two servants dropped a gangplank onto the beach. She tucked a basket of food and wine on her arm and disembarked, heading across the wide arc of pebbles and sand edged with brilliant blue. Strewn around her were branches turned gray from exposure to the sea and bits of white shells as empty of life as the fallen walls she headed toward. Her sandals slid backwards with each step in the loose sand.

She reached the rise of land near the point and made her way up on a track barely big enough for rabbits. Walking with Achilles's arm at the ready had been easier. When she reached the first of the collapsed walls, she clambered over it and entered what was left of homes, streets, and temples. No distinct road or path lay open without navigating piles of fallen stone and mud bricks. She felt like an animal burrowing into the ground as she worked her way into the heart of it.

On one side of the obstructed path she followed, stood a doorway, still standing with fragmentary walls on either side of it. When she pushed on the door, the planks of wood came apart, falling to the ground. She stepped through, although she couldn't go far because pieces of collapsed walls and roof blocked her way. Most of the space was open to the sky.

She turned to leave this pile of debris, but a dark, curved piece of wood poking out in one corner caught her eye. She put down her basket, picked her way to the wood, and cleared away the dirt and stone burying it.

She gasped when she recognized what it was, an ebony cradle. Such a precious, hard wood for a child's bed. It was tipped upside down so that its arched rockers stuck up. She took hold of it and gently flipped it over, placing it on the floor after clearing a spot with her foot. The thickness of the rockers, base, and end pieces had held up, although the slats along both sides showed only as upright fragments of some other wood and empty holes in the wood base where they'd been joined. She crouched down by what was left of the cradle and pinched a tuft of fabric clinging to a splintered edge, examining it. Wool, still faintly red-purple, the color of dye made from sea snails, so costly only kings and queens wore it. What child had slept in this?

Achilles would have marveled at this discovered cradle. He'd been so disappointed the day they came here to find so few objects left behind. She found herself laughing at the realization he would have ordered an ebony cradle like this made for their son and a blanket of royal purple. She felt the closeness of those years when there had been the three of them. Their son's infancy had bound them together, when Pyrrhus had preferred his father's chest to any other cradle, and she had held him close as he nursed. Often Achilles had lain beside her on their bed as she fed their baby, one of his long fingers stroking his son's cheek and red-gold hair.

This place was a good one to listen for the remembered voice and counsel of her lost husband. She brushed off a stone for a seat. Sunshine shone down on her from the blue midday sky. She let her questions and worries about Pyrrhus jumble in her mind, her gaze focused on the empty cradle.

Where are you, my husband? Come help me. I need you.

She sat until the hardness of the stone dug into her thighs. The sun had shifted and cast the shadow of the broken wall across the cradle. She wiped away a tear that rolled down her cheek. She'd been foolish to think coming here would help.

She glanced again at the rocker and smiled. She *had* found Achilles for a moment, remembered their life and his love for her and for Pyrrhus. She'd had a moment of pure grief unburdened by the troubled Pyrrhus she now mothered. She stood. That would be enough.

Her basket of food rested by the doorway. She picked it up and climbed through the fallen city toward the outer edge where what remained of the fortification wall stood, away from the sea where she knew if she looked down, she'd see the little cove where they'd picnicked and made love. She no longer wanted to return to that place. She'd leave that memory untouched.

Instead, she found one of the crescent-shaped portions that scalloped the fortification wall, the feature Achilles had so admired. Her warrior son would also. It was more appropriate for the guidance she sought, although now she didn't expect to find any.

Much of the fortification had tumbled down, but what still stood rose to her shoulder, and she used the many holes in the wall for footholds up. The inside had filled with broken stone and dirt, making an uneven surface to stand on. She found a small hollow where grasses had grown in the dirt and spread her cloak as a blanket.

Mia took some bread and cheese from her basket, although she had no appetite. She felt embarrassed that she'd thought she could find guidance for her son by coming here. She'd blame it on her need for a brief time to put aside the burdens of her life and grieve.

A strange rushing sound drew her eyes upward to something in the distant sky she couldn't understand. It surged toward her. She cried out and crouched low to the ground. Enormous snakes curled and writhed across the sky, pulling a golden chariot. The snakes had wings like dark sails that swept up and down with such force that the wind gusted against Mia. Their scales gleamed and sparked like flames. As if they'd cast a spell, Mia couldn't drag her gaze from them, couldn't move her limbs, couldn't jump down into the protection of the broken walls of the haunted, dead city.

In the chariot stood a woman with black hair whipping around her face, her gown and cloak flowing back from her tall body, reins held with both her hands.

For the briefest moment Mia thought she must be Thetis in a furious form after her son's death—but no. She remembered. Medea's tale. From her great crimes, flying serpents had drawn the sorceress away in a golden chariot.

Medea had come to exact revenge. Why now after all this time? For what? The unwise use of her story to inspire fear?

The snakes soared directly above Mia and then made a wide curve until they hovered over the wide plain inland of the dead city, the chariot floating behind, still close to Mia but with enough distance now that she could breathe.

Shouts and screams sounded from the beach along the bay. Small figures ran toward her across the sand. The servants she'd left behind at the boat had seen this threat and braved facing it for her.

A booming voice rang out, "Stay away. Any closer, fools, and I will slay all of you *and* your princess."

Mia stood up, stretching her arms to wave them off. They could see her. She saw them turn toward her, hesitating. "Go back. Go back." Her voice couldn't carry to them, but this godly sorceress had filled the whole plain and bay with her warning. They fell back.

Mia faced the sorceress. She shouted, "Why do you come now? I never meant to offend you."

"Meant or not, what do I care?" Medea laughed, a sound like a raven's screech. "Did you think I would not feel outraged?"

42

Medea leapt down from her chariot, her feet skimming goddess-like above the ground as she moved toward Mia. The winged serpents remained in place, hovering and writhing over the land, their fiery scales flashing, and black tongues, the length of Mia's arm, flicking like whips in the air.

Mia braced her arms against her sides and drew herself up to her full height. She had won the respect of Thetis, a far greater immortal than this terrifying menace.

Medea wore a glistening diadem in her dark hair. Golden embroidery encrusted her loose gown of shimmering black.

The sorceress stepped from the air onto the rough ground of the fallen tower where Mia waited. She threw Mia a challenging look. "I want to see the woman who dared use my life for her own ends."

Mia resisted the urge to step back. "Thetis, my husband's goddess mother, says you laughed when she told you what I'd done. Were you hiding your true feelings from your cousin, afraid of her greater power? She visits Skyros to dote on her grandson."

"You don't wish to anger me with empty threats."

"No, I would not." *Ah, so Thetis could be a threat to this puzzling being.* "But I welcome you as guest. This is a humble offering." She indicated her spread-out cloak, the simple foods she'd laid out, and the wineskin she'd drawn from her basket. "Let me pour you a cup of wine. I apologize that I did not bring a feast suitable for a queenly sorceress, but I did not know I would have such company, although the last time I came here, Thetis chose this place to visit."

"Poor, powerless mortal princess." Medea's lips turned up, part smile, part snarl. "Frightened by her visitors. Don't come to this place if you don't like to see us. It's this place. So many humans died here in a single day when Poseidon roared over the city with his deluge and shook its foundations with a pound of his fist. Those of us who dislike pathetic humans find the rich shadow of mortal loss intoxicating. And we can sense your living presence amid the dead and find you when otherwise you would be lost in the muddle of humanity. So, I have come at last to meet the storyteller."

"I didn't expect you'd ever hear my telling of your story."

"I did. Thetis enjoyed reporting the details." Medea stepped forward and sank gracefully onto the cloak.

Mia undid the wineskin's wooden plug and poured into the small ceramic cup she'd brought. She passed the cup with a bow of her head. She rummaged in the basket and pulled out a bowl's lid that would serve as cup for her and poured.

The princess lifted her cup to the sorceress. They both drank. Now they were bound as guest-friends who could not harm each other without offending Zeus, king of the gods. Medea gave her a knowing look that hinted she did not care whether she offended the king of gods or not.

Medea put down the cup. "My cousin told me of your plan. The way you stopped up your people's mouths with fear of my revenge, like the wooden plug in that wineskin." She pointed a long, elegant finger at the wineskin lying by Mia's thigh. "Clever. I liked it."

Mia let go a breath she did not realize she'd been holding.

A tip of the sorceress's head showed she noticed that release. "Although I gather it failed."

"My people did not give away Achilles's secret." Mia heard the quavering in her voice and tried to quell it. "His prowess revealed him in the end."

"Yes, in the end, but only after a mother's ache for her daughters had put the hound on the trail. Then of course, there's fate. That governs even the most primeval of goddesses."

"You are well informed."

"I don't think Thetis knows of your mother's role. I can keep that to myself if I wish."

A jolt of fear shook Mia. She countered, "You must understand that ache for children irretrievably lost." These unwise words came out before Mia knew she'd thought them. But she had to know. "Is that part of the bards' tales true?"

"That I slew my own children? Drew the dagger across their small, soft throats?"

A gagging horror filled her at Medea's words. Mia mutely nodded, weighing the pain in Medea's voice. Did it hold any of that horror? Or only anger at Mia for her brazen question?

"Yes, I took their lives. I had to."

Mia shuddered. An unimaginable act. No mother could ever *have* to do such a thing, could she? Nothing in Mia's experience could excuse it or explain the emptiness that must lie in this woman to turn her so monstrous.

Medea's eyes held Mia in a gaze, hard and cold. "Worse by far than the crime you attributed to me, but that was gruesome enough. You have a bloody imagination."

"I . . ." She couldn't summon words, couldn't converse in this way as if they chatted about ordinary choices.

Medea raised an eyebrow. "How dare you be so shocked, when in your version of my story you made me tear my brother into pieces with my own hands, a *baby* brother no less? You must have known when you made it up that the lying betrayer Jason cut down my brother. And my dear brother was a capable warrior at the time, well able to defend himself—if I hadn't disarmed him with a sisterly beseeching first."

Wresting accustomed words from a flood of emotion, Mia muttered, "I didn't mean to offend you."

"You didn't. It made for a good story and served your purpose. I like a storyteller who can change her listeners forever—especially with gruesome fear."

"I wasn't the one who sang the tale."

Medea laughed that cawing sound again. "Men never let us sing the tales, but you outsmarted them. You made the bard into a doll you breathed life and knowledge into. That is why I came. I wanted to meet that woman."

"Thank you." Mia supposed the sorceress meant these things as compliments, but to her they rang as grim and uncomfortable.

"You should know, little princess, that I have suffered every moment since I murdered my sons, three innocent little ones. I would give anything to have them alive and with me, but I do not regret what I did."

"I cannot make sense of that." Mia looked down at her hands resting in her lap. She'd never turn them to such madness. She wanted this killer away.

"No? It had to be done, no matter the price of sorrow I had to pay. Listen."

Mia shook her head, but she would have to. She thought she understood what had driven Medea to seek her out. The sorceress needed to convince someone of the rightness of her deed—but that someone was Medea herself.

Mia looked into Medea's eyes and made herself a receptacle, whether for healing or horror, she didn't know.

"There was no other way," Medea said, her voice not faltering. "I had to stop the arrogance of men—not just my husband Jason, but all men like him who put on wives like clothes and toss them aside with no mind to their hearts or the bonds that grow between two people through joining in love, through the daily gestures of care. Jason could ignore what we felt for each other, and even think he could banish his own children in exchange for his rise in power that this new wife would bring him. But I knew he would suffer as much as I if I broke that arrogant illusion."

Mia watched the smooth lines of Medea's face, looking for some sign that the sorceress listened to her own words, words that carried such conviction within Medea's voice but revolted Mia's heart.

"I could only destroy his grasping delusion by killing his children. Like a dam that holds the rising waters year after year without any hint of weakness, but when a raiding force chops into its timbers, it lets loose a destructive torrent across the land, so I breached Jason's confidence in the rightness of his choices by chopping down our children."

Medea touched Mia's arm.

Mia jerked her arm away. She couldn't bear such a polluted touch. "Wouldn't it have been better to take your children somewhere safe where you could be happy together? Leave your arrogant husband to rule badly with his new royal bride?"

"I didn't care how he ruled or with whom. I cared how he lived. I broke through his grand view of himself, crushed it under the sorrow and reality of his children's dead bodies—bodies I stole away after he saw them so he could not even mourn them properly. I destroyed him and through him I put all men on warning."

Mia could not control her disgust. "You killed your sons for some formless warning to men?"

"You are mistaken. My bloody deed gave unforgettable form to my warning. It will linger in all men's hearts across the ages, a curb against their selfish grasp for power at the expense of womankind. It is my undying glory."

Mia said, "Men talk of winning undying glory through their deeds in battle. My husband chose that life over raising his son and ruling his realm. Men often pay for glory with their own lives. You offered a different payment, your sons' lives. That was no fair bargain for this 'great' purpose you saw, this lasting change in men you hoped to bring about. Accomplish what you must solely with your own fated portion of life—whatever that might be. Besides, for the unbearable price you paid, I do not see any alteration in the ways of men."

Mia pushed herself to stand. She glanced across at the flying serpents yoked to the golden chariot. They seemed to her now suspended in some other world or time, visible here but not actually present. "I do not understand who or what you are, nor how you are not undone by regret and grief. Perhaps when you look across the world, you find some comfort in the choice you made." Mia braced herself for vengeful fury. Rash to have been so blunt, but she had to say something.

"You wouldn't choose as I did," Medea answered, her voice sizzling with insult. "But don't be so smug. I have heard about your son. You face unbearable choices. See what you do about him."

MEDEA TURNED in scorn away from Mia and stalked back to the winged serpents yoked to her chariot. With flashes of flame and billows of smoke, the great winged creatures with their writhing, scaled bodies launched into the sky, lifting the sorceress ever higher until she disappeared. Mia let out the breath she'd held and waited for her heart to slow enough to begin the journey over the destroyed city to her boat.

She'd angered Medea, and she doubted she had given Medea whatever the sorceress sought in coming to Skyros, but then, Thetis never seemed satisfied either with what Mia could offer. Goddesses, or whatever Medea was, disliked interactions with mortals too much to take enjoyment or comfort from them.

She glanced across to the far side of the bay where her boat and servants waited for her, warned off but not reassured. They must be terrified for themselves and their princess.

Mia shivered when she thought of Medea's sacrifice of her children. She didn't want Medea's voice echoing in her mind. The sorceress had set her children's lives as the price of vengeance on her traitorous husband. Unthinkable and unbearable.

However Mia had disappointed Medea, the sorceress had fired her parting words as revenge. The sorceress was viciously good at vengeance. Her taunt hit true. "You face unbearable choices. See what you do about him." Pyrrhus.

Unbearable sacrifice and children. Unbearable sacrifice and her small kingdom. An unbearable sacrifice that would be hers, not his.

Had fate sent Medea to prod another mother into hateful action?

43

Dione looked horrified when Mia told her what she planned to do. "You can't," Dione said and wrapped her arms around Mia. "You'll break your heart."

"It's an unbearable sacrifice for a mother, but I must."

"You think that now, but you won't when he's gone." Her maid's voice was full of the anguish Mia shared. "Wait a bit. He'll grow and change."

"Grow and change? He needs to, doesn't he?"

"He's the prince, I —"

"I know, you can't criticize him, not even to me. But you know it's true. You and I tried to shape him. When he was still a toddler, you and I could both remind him to mind his strength, so he didn't hurt others."

"Then there was tantrums," Dione said, her practical honesty winning out over meekness.

"Yes, loud and long. And he didn't pay any attention to us. Now any warning, even from me, might bring a fatal outburst. I turned to my father to help guide my unruly boy. That went nowhere. At least you *saw* the problems, even if you can't say anything."

Mia held up her hand to stop Dione. "And don't say grandfathers are always that way. He wanted a prince so much he made himself blind to everything."

"You can't take away his prince."

"No, but others can. I only need to make them think my son is all that stands between them and their victory over that cursed city. What Achilles could not do, Pyrrhus will. Or so I'll be sure they are told."

"Don't do this. Your father—"

"My father will never know my role. Only you and I. How would I have gotten through without your sympathetic ear all these years?"

Dione shook her head. "I'd stop you if a maid could do such."

"I often listen to you, but not this time." Mia squeezed Dione's shoulder. "Achilles told me I should teach Pyrrhus how to balance his human and immortal sides. How was I supposed to do that? I cannot turn away from the truth. Not anymore. He has grown too dangerous."

Dione frowned, and her eyes shaded over with sadness.

HIDDEN IN A LINEN SACK, Mia carried the jewelry her mother had secretly sent her. It would be enough for the bribe, and her father did not know she had it. He could not follow it back to her. The one link that could connect her to this fateful act would be the trader she'd use as go-between.

To seal his mouth, she'd take a similar strategy to the one Pyrrha had suggested long ago she take with her steward to gain his confidence and win his allegiance. Mia had gotten a muddled result then, but the tactic was sound.

The trader she chose went often to Troy, as so many did these days to supply the huge Greek army. But he also came regularly to Skyros, and he was young. He would hope for a long, profitable relationship with the rulers of Skyros. She had only to convince him that she would ensure his ongoing benefits. Her father was growing old and left more to her, and there'd be no notoriously volatile prince to interfere if the trader followed through with her plan in complete secrecy.

She'd developed strong negotiating relations with several traders in recent years, purposely independent of her father. Her father occasionally objected, but her success silenced him. She hadn't had this use in mind, by all the gods, but now her quiet work would serve her well. Unlike some of the others, this young trader didn't think he was taking advantage of her each time they made an agreement. She'd realized some of the others did and used that error of understanding to turn deals even more to her favor. But this trader saw her for who she was. He didn't underestimate her. She'd seen that he trusted her far more than her father, for good reason. They made fair bargains which both she and he followed through on. Now she would make one unusual bargain with him and pay him well for it when it came to fruition.

On the outside, meeting with him was nothing unusual. It would draw no attention. As usual, her guards took up their position out of hearing. Dione stood at her side. She thought she was prepared, determined. The trader climbed from a small rowboat he'd used to get to shore. His loaded ship lay heavy in the water of the bay. He walked toward her across the pebbles and sand that lined the shore, and Mia's throat closed tighter with each of his steps. Once she said the words, sent him off, there'd be no going back.

She'd faced an empty bed for ten years, but not an empty life. She'd had her son. She loved Pyrrhus from deep in her womb. He challenged her, but he was so beautiful and commanding. Her whole body ached with the thought of losing him. Dione was right. She should listen to her maid, her friend. Somehow Pyrrhus would be a better king than she feared.

The trader came closer. Only a few more strides, and he'd reach her. He frowned. Her panic must show on her face.

She didn't have to choose this suffering for herself, nor did she have to betray her father. But could it even be a betrayal, when she knew in the end it would be easier for her father, not harder? Ruling with Pyrrhus would be hard. And the need for a prince, the obsession that drove her father's leniency toward Pyrrhus, had waned as everyone grew accustomed to a princess assisting the king. She was helpful and respected. Pyrrhus was not. These were painful truths.

She imagined Pyrrhus once her father died. Once the small restraint of "king" had vanished. That would be the end of her influence. It would be the end of her kingdom's modest well-being.

Could she choose the unbearable pain of losing her child?

The trader's face looked puzzled, the lines deepening on his brow.

"Good morning," she said, using all her strength to draw her lips into a welcoming smile.

44

Mia stayed behind in the palace when word came of a warship sighting, and her father and son went down to greet the visitors. The watch had spotted the turquoise dolphin banner flying from its mast. It would be news from Troy.

A twinge of guilt crept through her at her father's flash of panic when the watch reported Achilles's banner. He'd be worried about the lure to his grandson of that bigger kingdom, that other throne Peleus could offer, and worse, the army of men Pyrrhus's father had commanded at Troy. An army without a leader. Pyrrhus talked incessantly about needing more warriors. He'd even brought up hiring mercenaries again, how this time he'd control them, and the raids he'd take them on. Her son was famished for men to lead into battle, and no fighters were better than Achilles's Myrmidons.

She'd spoken to her father, "Whoever it is, we'll need a proper feast to welcome them. It's my job to organize that. My husband is gone, no longer part of the army at Troy. This ship will doubtless bring news for men, not for a widow."

It was cowardly of her to put off facing these visitors. She feared seeing their intent and feeling the finality of it as they studied her son and saw a warrior. She feared they'd see her heart breaking before they told her their purpose, before she should know it—that they were taking away her son.

Her plan might have gone awry, and this ship came for something else. The waiting might break her.

Then two kings, Odysseus and Phoinix, entered the throne room beside her father, and she knew. Here were the clever strategist and Achilles's old nursemaid. A brilliant pairing for this purpose, no doubt Odysseus's design.

Like a bird in a snare, her son would be caught. She'd built the trap, and now she'd have to live with the snapping cord pulled tight around her only child.

Pyrrhus marched in with the others, by far the tallest and biggest, a warrior through and through. He was excited and happy with their well-known visitors.

But then she glanced at her father and saw determination in his face. He sensed the danger that was coming, even though he did not know her role in it, her betrayal. She saw unusual strength in the way he pulled back his shoulders, set wide his stance, and placed an unconscious hand on the pommel of his sword. Her father marshaled for battle. Odysseus might be outmaneuvered.

She tried not to want her father to succeed.

The long formalities of welcoming and feeding guests came to a close. She'd arranged the men's chairs in an arc, her father, Pyrrhus, Odysseus, and Phoinix filling them, and Mia separated, opposite and to one side. She'd used her womanhood to place herself out of this scene.

"What brings you to our small island?" her father asked the two kings. "Achilles's death sundered our connection with the affairs at Troy. I cannot imagine why you think it worth coming here, although my dear daughter will appreciate if you have brought tokens from her husband's possessions for her to grieve over and memorialize."

Mia wondered if he'd seen something being unloaded from the ship that brought this lie to his lips. It was an artful misdirection, but as futile as an opening spear throw that lodges in a foe's shield, not his chest.

Odysseus answered, "You leave out this fine young warrior, Achilles's son. He binds you to Troy." The wily king reached over and laid a fatherly hand on Pyrrhus's arm. Odysseus was as powerfully broad-chested as she remembered from his participation in the "raid" that had snared her husband, but next to her son, he seemed unimpressive until he deployed his resonant voice, like a spell cast over the room. "Pyrrhus looks in every way like his father's son, ready to lead men into battle. His father was still young when he took command of King Peleus's Myrmidons." Odysseus turned to old Phoinix. "The boy looks even taller and stronger than his father, doesn't he?"

"A powerful warrior, certainly." The old man had aged since his visit bringing the news of Achilles's death. There was a slight tremor to his hands and a frail tentativeness in his movements.

She flicked her gaze to her son. He sat tall, his chest thrust out, an eager light in his eyes, filling up on these warriors' words.

Lycomedes nodded as if in agreement. "Skyros's prince has uncanny strength. How could it be otherwise with such a father? You older warriors know that the youngest warriors are often the strongest and fastest, but they lack what wins the battles. Their lives are often wasted in the press of battle for which they are not prepared. He will grow up and train on Skyros. When he is a man, he will be a great bulwark for Skyros, a warrior king. His mother and I have long treasured how fine a prince we have to take my place on the throne."

Odysseus's lips twitched up as he listened to her father. "I would never waste a man's life. Each goes into battle with his own hopes." Dark curls framed the king's face around rich brown eyes that she was sure missed nothing. She had never seen eyes that seemed to take in so much while exuding a calm stillness.

"We come," old Phoinix said, "driven by the gods, not by the will of men."

"The gods?" Alarm sounded in Lycomedes's voice. Cold filled Mia's chest. She heard the snap of the trap she'd readied.

"The implacable will of the gods," Odysseus echoed. "The war at Troy has reached a stalemate. While we had on our side Achilles, the greatest warrior of the Greeks, we had hope of taking the city, but after his death, the war stays mired in blood and deaths, but no progress. King Agamemnon called upon the great seer Calchas to learn the gods' will and tell us what we needed to take the city. He studied the flights of birds and found an undeniable portent in them. He pronounced that only with the leadership of Achilles's powerful son could we ever bring down Troy. There is no other way. Agamemnon sent us to bring young Pyrrhus to Troy. He will take command of the Myrmidon warriors."

Pyrrhus leapt from his chair. "Leader of the Myrmidons! I'm ready to leave right now."

Odysseus laughed. "We'll wait for daylight and the winds."

"No!" Her father rose and braced a hand on his grandson's shoulder as if to hold him there. "Pyrrhus stays on Skyros."

Mia saw Odysseus signal one of the men he'd left positioned by the door. Four of his soldiers left the throne room. Those men must have concerned her father, but these Greek kings were friends, in name at least, whose men could come or go. To treat them otherwise would be to turn them into enemies.

Lycomedes stood protectively by his grandson. "Before you came to take Achilles, the goddess Thetis foretold that small men would take her son and use him for their greedy purposes, then cast him aside to an early death. *She* saw the future all too well. I will not let you do the same to my grandson. He is the finest of Skyros, and he will stay here to rule as king."

Downward lines of confusion deepened on Pyrrhus's face. He looked from his grandfather to Odysseus. Lycomedes had thrown a sharp spear. An early death, cast aside to an early death like his invincible father, Achilles. Instead, stay, rule as king.

Phoinix tottered up from his chair and stood by Pyrrhus, edging out Lycomedes despite his seeming frailty. "The goddess knew of her son's death, warned him of it, and yet my dear Achilles chose to fight as a warrior must at the forefront of his men. Thetis is a mother as well as a goddess. Her loss, even before it happened, gave her a bitterness that she put unfairly into her words. We did not cast our beloved

Achilles aside. We laid his ashes in a memorial for all time. And not for greedy purposes. Not at all. He fought in defense of his men from the slaughtering blows of Prince Hector, an invincible hero of Troy. Invincible until your father killed him. These are not motives of greed or smallness. These are the lofty deeds of men in war."

"You are lying," Lycomedes bellowed. "Making up heroic tales, when the truth is death and blood and unstoppable slaughter. Pyrrhus cannot yet understand the magnitude of what you drag him off to. I will not let you deceive him."

"I do understand fighting," Pyrrhus yelled. "You are afraid of it, but I'm not."

The double doors of the throne room swung wide open. The brilliance of what they revealed was so great that Mia assumed a divine visitation. Did Thetis concur with her father? Did she come to stop her grandson's departure?

Her eyes adjusted. Odysseus's soldiers carried in armor, but not armor like any she'd seen before. It gave off an otherworldly glare that could only come from divine workmanship. To face a warrior encased in that terrifying light would drive off every foe.

The soldiers approached Pyrrhus. One spread a purple cloak on the mosaic floor, and they laid upon it the huge breastplate and other chest pieces, sword, helmet, greaves, and most extraordinary, the shield. The work was a marvel. On top of the layered bronze, an immortal craftsman had laid gold, silver, and precious stones of a multitude of colors into a design of detail so precise that the people shown upon the surfaces appeared to move and interact. Women danced. Men fought and died. Workers brought in a harvest of grapes and another of wheat. Nature intermingled with men. Leaves fluttered on trees. Waves curled and fell. The sun's chariot flew across the sky. A half-moon rose, casting silver light upon the other side of the world.

The beauty of it froze Mia.

She heard her son's gasp.

"The armor of Achilles," Odysseus's deep voice announced. "It is yours, Pyrrhus, to wear into battle at Troy. I received it as a gift upon your father's death, but I gladly give it to you if you will take your rightful place over the Myrmidon warriors. I think we must give you a suitable name. No longer Pyrrhus, redheaded boy, but Neoptolemus, young warrior."

Pyrrhus grabbed the shining helmet and placed it on his own head. He lifted the breastplate, and Odysseus and Phoinix fell into position around him as squires to tie on the armor, adding each piece in order.

Mia dragged her eyes from her son and turned to her father. He stood, stooped over, one arm wrapped around his middle as if in pain, the other hanging limply at his side. She went to him and wrapped her arm around his shoulders and held him up.

"We can't stop him, can we?" her father asked.

"No. Not after that." She pointed at the blinding armor.

"He's never coming back, is he?" her father said. "Even if he takes Troy and lives, he won't come here."

"No. If he did, it would be to add Skyros as an afterthought to a larger kingdom. Send him off with your love. It is all we can do. Unbearable, but the only choice we have."

45

Mia stood on a rise above the harbor beach. She'd wept while she set out everything her son should take with him. Then drenched her pillow during the long, dark night. She'd hoped the winds would have fallen and forced a delay, given her a few more days to look upon her son and love him.

But curse the gods, the winds were favorable and steady. The sleek warship was restocked with food and water. Her son's possessions stowed on board. The great pile of armor glistened in a space between the rows of oars. Everything was set.

The grandfather had embraced his grandchild, and then with a shake of his head, he'd left, muttering he could not watch the departure. So, she stood alone on the rocky scruff of land.

Her son had consented to a motherly hug, for a moment, then leapt aboard the ship the way she remembered his father had. Sailors pushed the hull into the water, pulling themselves aboard when the water lifted the ship.

She watched the warrior-sailors hauling up the big sail, muscled backs leaning into the work. The white rectangle flapped for a moment and then filled, billowing forward, causing the ship to leap across the water toward the mouth of the bay. Soon it would leave the harbor's shelter. Leave Skyros behind.

People talked about heartbreak as if a heart were a ceramic cup that cracked when dropped. She'd never thought much about the idea. But now she knew—as if she had dropped her heart from a height like the top of the royal mountain, smashing it far, far below against the hard-packed dirt.

Her knees buckled. She sank toward the ground. Then a strong arm slid around her waist and held her up.

Dione had slipped up beside her. "You didn't think I'd leave you alone, did you? I saw your father leave." Her daughter Phoebe stood quietly at her side.

Mia brushed a tear from her cheek. "Thank you."

The little girl gave her a smile, a balm to Mia's sorrow, reminding her of the people and kingdom she'd chosen over a life with her son.

Breaching the harbor's limit, the warship found the open sea beyond.

Its dark hull and swelling cloud of sail showed against the lapis lazuli sea. She captured the beauty in her mind, stored it away for a tapestry, a remembrance to soften the pain.

Phoebe let out a cry. "Dolphins are leaping in the harbor. They're following the ship."

With the graceful arcs Mia remembered, the sleek dolphins chased her son's ship. Tears ran down her face. They were a gift to her, a confirmation.

One dolphin took the lead, its curving jumps higher than the others, its rounded snout pointing at the warship. For a moment it stopped and turned its open mouth back toward her, and the breeze seemed to carry its chattering message to her. *You have not abandoned your son. I am with him. A friend and helper when he is afloat and needs one.*

A mother must protect her child. That is her undeniable duty, but protection is complicated. She watched the dolphin's joyful leaps. She had not failed her son. She had done what he needed and what she had to, no matter the pain. She pictured the beautiful, free creatures her mother had chosen for the walls surrounding her children, leaving them behind, a daily presence of love.

In one harmonized movement, the whole group of dolphins vaulted into the air and plunged back to the sparkling sea. *We are here with you. We share your broken heart.* Achilles's protective companions. A good sign.

"Thank you, my love."

ALSO BY JUDITH STARKSTON

Hand of Fire (also in the Trojan Threads series)

Tesha Series:

Priestess of Ishana

Sorcery in Alpara

Of Kings and Griffins

Flights of Treason

The Scent of Slaughter and Love: A Bolthar the Griffin Novella

If you enjoyed *Achilles's Wife*, please leave a review on Amazon or your favorite book site.

AUTHOR NOTES

Achilles's Wife reinterprets a myth about Achilles's early life before the Trojan War. In this myth, Thetis, Achilles's goddess mother, hides Achilles among the women of King Lycomedes's court on the island of Skyros. She does this to prevent him from going to Troy and fighting in a war she knows will cause his death. Achilles and the princess, Deidamia (sometimes spelled Deidameia), have a relationship, and eventually, she gives birth to his son Pyrrhus/Neoptolemus.

The Greek kings believe from one of Calchas's oracles that they can only win the war if Achilles fights with them. So, Odysseus uncovers the young warrior's hiding place by one of various tricks, depending on the version, sometimes by laying out jewels and other womanly baubles for the royal women and also a sword or some other manly weapon, and, of course, Achilles reaches for the weapon despite his female garb and blows the clever disguise. No one would recognize him without Odysseus's brilliant trick, now would they?

This myth pretends that the biggest, greatest warrior of the age, even at this young teenage stage, could be effectively hidden by dressing him in woman's dress (a disguise that is supposed to fool even those living daily around him). It strains credulity, and indeed, in the modern period this myth has often been done up as a humorous tale of a young man in drag getting the beautiful princess pregnant and fooling no one for long.

That funny version, while good for comic opera, for example, wasn't the story I wanted to tell, and mine would center on Deidamia not Achilles. Deidamia gets little mention in any of the fragmentary versions we have, but she's the person I was interested in. I took seriously Achilles and Deidamia's experiences together and had to find a way to tell a heartfelt story with respect, rather than the slapstick that can arise in the traditional versions. Before I had figured out how to do that, I began an exploratory draft, and a novel solution (pun intended) to the inherent silliness of the extant versions arose under my fingertips. You'll find that reinterpretation of the myth in this novel's prologue (in a prologue not a chapter because it is the only part told from Achilles's point of view).

My approach involves an act of extreme maternal cruelty by a goddess who doesn't understand or care what being human feels like, a "magical" divine transformation that pushes Achilles into crisis. Achilles's need for support from a friend while suffering dysphoria (to use an anachronistic term I couldn't use in the novel's ancient setting) became integral to the overall story of Deidamia, her interactions with Achilles, and her growth and positive transformation as a human being. I hope I did sufficient reading and other research to represent Achilles's temporary inner discord with believability and sympathy. What happened to Achilles in this telling is a myth outside of reality, but it needs to be woven through with threads of real human experience, and I have tried to do that with respect and understanding.

You may be interested in the classical sources of this lesser-known "side" myth about the most famous Greek warrior. The ancient references to this myth are scanty until the Roman period, and even then, thinly developed.

Jenny March in *Cassell's Dictionary of Classical Mythology* (p. 467) says, "The earliest evidence for the tale of Achilles among the women of Scyros is a (fifth-century) painting by Polygnotus (Pausanias 1.22.6)." Euripides wrote a now lost tragedy about it called *The Scyr-*

ians. In his *Library of Greek Mythology,* Apollodorus has scattered information about the relationships between Achilles, Deidamia, Lycomedes, and Pyrrhus/Neoptolemus.

The longest extant version of this myth is found in the Latin writer Statius, who wrote near the end of the classical period, c. 45 – c. 96. He covers the episode of Achilles and Deidamia in the first book of his unfinished epic the *Achilleid*. In the modern translation by Stanley Lombardo the whole tale takes about 30 pages.

At the start of his telling, we see that Statius's Thetis must beg other gods to help her. She can do little on her own. Thetis first attempts to persuade Neptune to drown the Trojans to protect her son from dying in a war at Troy, and then, when that fails, she decides to conceal Achilles in "shameful feminine attire." She retrieves her son from Chiron without letting the centaur in on her true plan, which Chiron would prevent as disgraceful.

Having carried off her sleeping son via a chariot drawn by dolphins, Thetis tries without success to get Achilles to agree to hide out dressed as a girl. Achilles balks at womanly clothes until he sees Deidamia and falls in teenage lust with her beauty. Thetis exploits this turn of events, getting him to cooperate with the disguise now that he sees it will let him hang out near the princess.

Eventually, Statius's Achilles rapes Deidamia amid some Bacchic revels. Deidamia is timid and passive in this relationship, which, out of shame, she conceals from her father, even after she gives birth to a son. Other than her maidenly modesty and quivering fearfulness at any disturbance, Statius gives us little sense of Deidamia. She's a prop, and Achilles, while impressive looking with weapons in his hands, is reduced to a randy teenager easily manipulated by his lust for sex and violence. In a sentence or so, Statius dismisses the problems that would surely arise from the concealment of their romance, the pregnancy, and Achilles's maleness by saying Deidamia's trusty childhood nurse took care of all that.

Deidamia has one active moment when Odysseus and Diomedes arrive looking for Achilles. The still-disguised Achilles grows excited at Odysseus's description of the coming war, and his behavior is giving him away, so Deidamia drags him out of the feast. Unfortunately for her, the next morning Odysseus springs his trap by tucking a shield and spear among some feminine trinkets and Bacchic drums that are offered as presents for the women. Statius didn't limit himself to only one version of Odysseus's ploys. After Achilles has revealed himself by grabbing the weapons, one of Odysseus's men blows a war trumpet to trick Achilles into positioning himself to fight off a non-existent attack, thus revealing himself twice over.

Then the remaining issues are wrapped up in a hurry, with Lycomedes agreeing to a marriage that was consummated so long before that there's a surprise baby grandson in the bargain. Achilles sails away the next day after telling Deidamia he will maintain fidelity to her and return with lots of strong Trojan handmaidens for her.

We wouldn't have any complete ancient version of this myth without Statius's *Achilleid*, so his telling is important, even if limited in its emotional depth, and for this modern reader, frequently unintentionally humorous.

While discussing my sources, I should also explain why I treated two goddesses the way I did, Thetis and Medea.

I portray Thetis not as a minor sea-divinity, one of many Nereids, but as a goddess of great power. She is, by implication, a goddess whose origin precedes the Olympians or whose power is somehow outside of the usual Olympian pecking order.

There are various indications of this view of Thetis in the mythic record, particularly the story of her assistance to Zeus when the other gods tried to overthrow him. She is the one who can call upon the hundred-handed giant Briareos, and with the giant, she releases Zeus from his chains. She is also the goddess who can give birth to a child capable of overthrowing his father—whoever his father might be, even Zeus. Zeus forces her into an unwelcome marriage to a mortal to avoid another generational overthrow such as Chronos and Ouranos suffered. She can thus both prevent and cause cataclysmic change in the divine power structure. She's not a lowly sea nymph.

This makes her intimidating and downright terrifying, which I liked for my novel.

Thetis's uncanny power also gives Achilles cosmic significance and cosmic problems. His divine portion is too much to contain in a human body without consequences both in his lineage and in his psyche. My portrayal of Thetis relies in part on Laura Slatkin's book *The Power of Thetis*.

Medea is not usually present in the myth of Deidamia. My involving this sorceress came about as I worked on the plot. I was looking for (or Mia was looking for) a handy "monster" sufficiently well-known to scare everyone into silence. I narrowed down which parts of this complicated mythical woman I included and relied mostly on Euripides's *Medea*. I chose to emphasize her more-than-human goddess stature, although she seems more like a mortal woman in some classical portrayals. I also gained a great deal from reading *Medea: Essays on Medea in Myth, Literature, Philosophy, and Art*, edited by James J. Clauss and Sarah Iles Johnston.

As to the question of "historical accuracy," this is a myth retelling so none of the events are likely to have happened as I have described. If you are interested in the question of whether the Trojan War ever happened, go to my website (JudithStarkston.com) where I have several posts on that and related subjects. Some version of conflict happened on the western coast of what is now Turkey in the Late Bronze Age at a site of a great city called Troy (among other names) that we now know from its many layers was inhabited for centuries.

This myth about Deidamia and Achilles, however told, always takes place on the small island of Skyros in the Greek Sporades. I stayed on the island for three weeks so that I could portray this world in a vivid, lived way. The sea, the beaches, the pine forests, the plant life, the steep mountain that formed the eagle-aerie location of my imagined Mycenaean palace—all these details stay with me from my time there, and I have tried to make them real to my reader.

I explored the island's archaeological remains. The traces of Mycenaean layers on top of the mountain are buried under later, mostly Medieval structures such that nothing beyond a general location can be surmised. I had to depend on my knowledge of other exemplar sites and my imagination to build Lycomedes's palace and citadel.

The "haunted ruins" described in this book are based on the actual ruins called Palamari on the north tip of the island, which would have been destroyed centuries before the mythic/legendary "Trojan War" time of this story. It is only a hypothesis that this fortified city of the "horseshoe" type might have been partially destroyed by a tidal wave and then abandoned at the time of the eruption of Thera around 1600 BCE. These ruins are an evocative and dramatic feature of Skyros.

The world I've portrayed is based on what I've learned about the culture of the Aegean islands in roughly the Mycenaean period and somewhat earlier. I've occasionally pulled details of daily life, such as clothes, from later Greek life, creeping forward into the Archaic period which followed the Mycenaean. I did that to create a world that will "feel" fully Greek to most readers—something which Mycenaean life might not always accomplish. This is a myth retelling, not a history book.

My frescoes and architecture are based on archaeological evidence, although mostly not from Skyros. I've been "building" Late Bronze Age palaces, fortifications, and temples for many years over the course of six novels, drawing on many sources read over decades. For this book, my new deep-dive came from a lovely book called *Keos XI Wallpaintings and Social Context, The Northeast Bastion at Ayia Irini* written by Lyvia Morgan. The book studies the fragmentary frescoes of the island of Kea, which give impressive glimpses into the realities of daily life in the ancient Aegean world. But Morgan has done far more than portray one piece of architecture and art on one island because she compares frescoes from other islands such as Santorini and places them into a social context hard grounded in the evidence. Her way of thinking and literally piecing this world together sparked my imagination and lit up new ideas for Mia's home and life.

ACKNOWLEDGMENTS

This book received essential suggestions and inspiration throughout its composition both from my local face-to-face critique partner Tim Schooley and from my on-going Phoenix based group who have stayed on Zoom post pandemic so I can meet with them from California. Many thanks to the insights of Christine, Bob, Julie, and Diana.

I also owe huge thanks to my developmental editor, Eileen Rendahl. Both her big view and her line-edit suggestions were incredibly perceptive and led to a much better book. I also want to thank my walking buddy, Linda, for being willing and eager to listen and respond as I talk out plot problems and ideas in my writing. Lucky for me, she's such a widely read friend and offers good advice.

My research trip to Skyros was greatly enriched by two people whom I'd like to thank for their time and attention.

Christina Romanou, an archaeologist based in Athens, who excavated at the Palamari site on Skyros (the "haunted" city in the novel) shared her knowledge of the island's Mycenaean locations and other key information that I did not find in publications. Without her expert steering of my focus in advance of our trip, I would have made some unfortunate mistakes about key locations on the island. *Achilles's Wife* is a novel grounded in myth, but also in a real place, and, as much as possible, I want to base the story in Skyros's history and archaeology.

The other person who helped make the trip my husband and I took to Skyros both delightful and informative was Maria Panagiotopoulou, the manager of the house we rented. Besides providing the perfect house for us, old and historic but freshly done, she helped orient us on the island and connected us with what we needed, which was especially helpful because things like car rentals are somewhat nonstandard on Skyros. We had a lovely time on this small, less-traveled-to island with gorgeous beaches, sea, and mountains, along with layers of history and archaeology. The picturesque capital, a village spilling along a steep mountainside, is accessed mostly by footpaths. It was a trip away from the usual infrastructure of tourism and crowds.

Many thanks to my family and especially my husband who supports my writing in countless ways and is always up for some travel to peek back into the ancient world.

ABOUT THE AUTHOR

Judith Starkston writes historical fantasy and mythic retellings set in the Bronze Age of the Greeks and Hittites. Her six novels bring women to the fore—whether Deidamia or Briseis from the Trojan War cycle of myths or a remarkable Hittite queen whom history forgot, even though she ruled over one of the greatest empires of the ancient world. Judith has degrees in classics from the University of California, Santa Cruz and Cornell and lives in Davis, California. Find her newsletter sign-up (and a free novella), book reviews, and posts about archaeology and history on her website JudithStarkston.com

www.ingramcontent.com/pod-product-compliance
Lightning Source LLC
LaVergne TN
LVHW091705070526
838199LV00050B/2284